THE
SILVER
STATE

THE
SILVER
STATE

A NOVEL

GABRIEL URZA

ALGONQUIN BOOKS OF CHAPEL HILL 2025

LITTLE, BROWN AND COMPANY

Copyright © 2025 by Gabriel Urza

Hachette Book Group supports the right to free expression and the value of copyright. The purpose of copyright is to encourage writers and artists to produce the creative works that enrich our culture.

The scanning, uploading, and distribution of this book without permission is a theft of the author's intellectual property. If you would like permission to use material from the book (other than for review purposes), please contact permissions@hbgusa.com. Thank you for your support of the author's rights.

Algonquin Books of Chapel Hill / Little, Brown and Company
Hachette Book Group
1290 Avenue of the Americas, New York, NY 10104
algonquin.com

First Edition: July 2025

Algonquin Books of Chapel Hill is an imprint of Little, Brown and Company, a division of Hachette Book Group, Inc. The Algonquin Books of Chapel Hill name and logo are trademarks of Hachette Book Group, Inc.

The publisher is not responsible for websites (or their content) that are not owned by the publisher.

Little, Brown and Company books may be purchased in bulk for business, educational, or promotional use. For information, please contact your local bookseller or the Hachette Book Group Special Markets Department at special.markets@hbgusa.com.

Design by Steve Godwin

Library of Congress Control Number: 2025931687

ISBN 978-1-64375-667-7 (hardcover); ISBN 978-1-64375-669-1 (ebook)

Printing 1, 2025

LSC-C

Printed in the United States of America

For Raija

Dumbfounded, I stood before the court, trying to figure out
if there was a state of being between "guilty" and "innocent."
Why were those my only alternatives? I thought.
Why couldn't I be "neither" or "both"?

—PAUL BEATTY, *The Sellout*

My accusations against the law are also my confession.

—VANESSA PLACE, *The Guilt Project*

THE
SILVER
STATE

PART I

JURY SELECTION

AS A PUBLIC defender I learned early on that jury selection is often the most critical moment of an entire trial. It's here that you, juror—the final arbiter of truth, the ultimate adjudicator of life and death—are chosen, along with all of your bias and compassion, your weakness and strength, your ignorance and wisdom. And it's here, as well, that you meet me for the first time. That you begin to form your judgments.

But even before we first meet in the courtroom, I've convinced myself that I know you. A week earlier the court will mail a questionnaire to a list of sixty-five prospective jurors pulled from DMV and voter registration records.

Who are you? this questionnaire asks, in so many words. *What is your age, your profession? How far did you get in school? Are you related to a member of law enforcement? Have you ever been arrested? Have you or someone you know ever been the victim of a crime?*

By the time we come together for jury selection a week later, my investigator has checked your social media accounts, has run your record, has reviewed your employment history. I know what music you like, who you are married to, what part of town you live in. I tell myself that I know you.

But there's always that rush when you're brought into the courtroom that first morning of the trial, your names drawn at random from an old-fashioned raffle tumbler by the court clerk, the prospective jurors stepping forward from the courtroom gallery when your names are read aloud. You are sunburned, or hungover, or happy to be here—to not be at work, or at school, or at home. You come in your Sunday best, or with a quiver of excuses why you shouldn't be asked to serve on this jury. Illness. Children. All of this I make note of on my little cards, the grimace when your name is called, your attention to the judge's instructions. I put pluses or minuses next to your names, amend the score on your stat card. It's pseudo-science, something barely more than assumption and stereotype. But I make these notes because I need to feel like there's a logic to it all, like there's a process. If there is process, there is control.

After the judge has welcomed you to the courtroom and asked a few stock questions, it's the prosecutor's turn. She'll go into her usual speech about reasonable doubt and following the law and indirect evidence. She's boring because it's her job to be boring. *We're all here to make sure this defendant has a fair trial,* she'll say, which is a lie, of course. She may ask if you understand that circumstantial evidence is admissible to prove a defendant's guilt, a clear indication that she was unable to find a single direct witness to the crime. To illustrate the concept of circumstantial evidence, she will invariably present the following scenario: *One night, you go to sleep and there's no snow on the ground. And when you wake up, the driveway is covered in snow. Is it reasonable to assume,* she will ask, *that it snowed the night before?* And you nod, of course. This is what she's saying: that my client's guilt is as obvious as a snowy driveway.

Finally, when the prosecutor's done with her questions, it's the defense attorney's turn. We get—at last—to speak.

I stand at the edge of the gallery, a low wooden rail the only thing separating me from the sixty prospective jurors who bothered to show up today. Somewhere hidden in this group are twelve people who will be asked to stand in judgment of my client, to decide guilt or innocence.

I consult my little score cards, but the words on them are suddenly just words, the future seemingly unknown, unpredictable. *Who are you?* I wonder. I try to peer into your mind, but you've become illegible. *Are you really willing to listen to my version of events, to give my client the benefit of the doubt?*

ONE

THE LETTER ARRIVES in my office mail on a frigid afternoon in April, layered between a new case file and a Violation Report from the Division of Parole and Probation. The envelope is bent at the corners, slightly off-color, as if it was in circulation for a while before being mailed. My name is written in smudged graphite above the address of the Washoe County Public Defender's Office in downtown Reno. In the top left corner are the sender's name and inmate number, care of the Northern Nevada Correctional Center.

The letter is from a man whose name I am afraid to say out loud, even after all this time. He had a name once, of course: Michael Keith Atwood, aka My Former Client. But he became a ghost a long time ago—through all the years of post-conviction hearings and petitions for habeas corpus. Now, when Michael Atwood surfaces in infrequent news articles or notices of appeal, my mind reflexively redacts the name.

I remember him now as words on a criminal complaint read by a court clerk on the first day of a trial that began eight years ago. He is Murder in the First Degree, and he is Sexual Assault. He is Battery Causing Substantial Bodily Harm, and he is Kidnapping in the First Degree. Or I remember him as a series of autopsy photographs, as a ripped T-shirt sealed shut in an evidence locker, as the smell of old blood fused into cotton and polyester. He is nameless and faceless, because to consider his name or to remember his face would mean to remember that an innocent man is in prison.

"If he dies in there, it's not because of anything *he* did," C.J. said once, a few weeks before Michael's trial was to begin. We had been working late on a Friday, the office quiet and empty, the conference table strewn with police reports, investigative memos, and forensic photos marked to be entered into evidence. I had begun to pack up my things for the night, but C.J. had insisted on staying. "You know the facts as well as I do. If he dies in there, it's because of what we didn't do."

I thumb the letter, unable to bring myself to open it. I place it on the corner of my desk, next to a reading lamp. On a bookshelf across the room sits the yellowing plaster bust of a man's head—an old trial exhibit that I inherited with the office. The eyes of the bust are fixed upon the letter. The cracking plaster lips seem almost to move, to demand that I remember Michael Atwood and everything that comes with him: The dead woman. Judge Bartos. C.J., wherever she is now.

The Nevada desert is said to be filled with old ghosts, the dry basins overflowing with the dead, stacked like layers of sediment on the valley floors. Past lives ended unjustly or prematurely, in anguish or in panic or in rage. But what are we supposed to call the living ghosts—the ones like Michael Keith Atwood—entombed in prison walls, capable of reaching out to us through telephone lines and pencil-addressed envelopes?

Because anything sounds better than opening Michael's letter, I turn my attention to my unending, forever-growing caseload.

There's the usual bustle of noise and activity in the halls of the public defender's office this afternoon—secretaries and paralegals answering phones and sorting files, attorneys and investigators walking clients or witnesses into offices or conference rooms. I close my office door before queuing up the latest bit of evidence to be uploaded to a new Major Violators case, a low-resolution video from the Reno Police Department with the file name "Gregory Lake Interview." On Center Street five stories below, the streetlamps are just flickering on along the Truckee River, mixing with the blues and pinks and purples of the downtown casino lights.

The video begins in a familiar windowless room with a metal table and two chairs, a bald man in a grey suit leaning against the corner of the table. This time it's Detective Turner waiting in the interview room, but if it's not Turner, then it's Villanueva or Jones with his shitty cop's goatee and his "just one of the guys" baseball hat on.

Turner is in his casual mode—casual for Rob, anyway. His suit jacket is folded over the back of one of the chairs in the interview room, and he's even got his sleeves rolled up. On the video, I watch him loosen his tie a bit, wipe the sweat from his bald head with the back of a hand.

As soon as my client comes into view, I know the interview is not going to go well. Greg Lake is a motel lifer I've represented on and off for the past eleven years, since the time he was certified up to be tried as an adult for a burglary when he was seventeen. He tracks a little slowly even when he's sober, as if he's never matured past early adolescence. In the video, though, he's clearly fucked up, that tweaky bounce to his step, so I know where this is going. Not with a cop like Turner who—despite the general disagreeability of his character and the annoying primness of his suit and tie—is not a complete fucking idiot.

I remind myself that when things "don't go well" for my client in these meetings, *my* life usually gets a lot easier. I look at the running time at the bottom of the screen—an hour and forty-four minutes, which is just about how long it takes a cop like Turner to elicit an unassailable, bulletproof confession. "Nothing to defend" means none of the work of conducting a preliminary hearing, of hunting down witnesses, or filing pretrial motions and arguing with the DA over admissibility of evidence. Instead, it will be a fifteen-minute discussion with the district attorney while we get the plea bargain hammered out, a half-hearted squabble over the sentence range, and then on to the next case.

On the screen, Turner shakes Greg Lake's hand, and I see Greg laugh a little when Turner calls him Gregory. Nobody calls him Gregory. Turner laughs too, like he's in on the joke. Like he's just another one of the guys Greg rolls with down by the Gold Dust Inn or at the nickel slots in the Cal Neva, his sleeves folded up, just casual fucking Turner.

I haven't seen Greg Lake since our last court date a year ago—sentencing for a simple possession charge where my five-minute argument to Judge Bartos landed him sixty days county time at Parr Boulevard. Greg had already done a month in jail, which meant he'd be out in another few days with good time. Nothing.

"Don't fuck this up," I told him as he was being led out of the courtroom. He shook his head and smiled in that way that said he was already thinking about all the ways he was going to fuck this up.

As if to prove me right: Greg's twenty pounds thinner in the video now, which makes his big ears stick out from his shaved head even more than usual. He moves in that amphetamine cadence, herky-jerky and bird-eyed in his dingy winter parka, and I know he's been up for a couple of days at least. He wipes a forearm across his lips, over and over. It's a gesture that borders on obscene.

I've seen hundreds of these interrogations, and the script never changes. Regardless of what he's accused of—it could be shoplifting or it could be murder—at *some* point early on in the interview the detective buys my guy a soda or offers to take him outside for a smoke. It's like they realized they didn't need the whole "good cop, bad cop" bit. All you need is the good cop. People were furious a few years back when a white supremacist killed nine people at a church and the cops bought him lunch at Burger King during the interview. But these people don't realize that this kid signed his own death sentence for a Whopper, fries, and a Dr Pepper. From the cops' standpoint, eight dollars is a fair price for a recorded confession to nine premeditated murders.

Sure enough, as soon as Greg sits down across the table from Turner in the interview room, he starts to fidget. His knee jogs nervously below the table. He cricks his head to one side and then the other. Turner leans back in his chair, looks at his watch as if he's gauging to see if the time is right, then sets his predictable little trap.

It's a simple formula: coffee for the drunks, a trip to the vending machine for the stoners. When in doubt, cigarettes. For Greg Lake today, it's soda or a smoke, because that's what tweakers want—a Mountain Dew is kryptonite, a Marlboro is a werewolf's silver bullet.

"Here it comes," I say out loud to my empty office. Perched atop a file cabinet on the other side of the room, the smudged and chipped plaster bust of the dead man stares back at me, tight-lipped in disapproval. The dead man knows by now that I should be beyond frustration. That I should not be upset by something that I know to be true: that Greg Lake is about to speak.

I push away from the desk, swivel my chair so that I'm facing the office window, away from the dead man's bust. In the casino parking garage across the street from my office, a middle-aged woman blows smoke out the cracked window of her station wagon. She pinches the bridge of her nose, as if trying to remember something. I watch her staring past me, out into the dimming light of the desert hills to the east. She smokes the cigarette down to its filter, then slips the butt out of the crack in the window before starting the car and rolling the window shut. She rubs her hands as if waiting to leave; behind her, a small sedan wheels around the corner of the parking garage. I wonder, briefly, about the woman. Did she just finish her shift at the casino? Is she a blackjack dealer or a bartender? A tourist who spent the day playing dollar hands at the Cal Neva?

On the video, Turner leans in toward Greg, who flinches like someone just popped a balloon.

"You OK, Gregory?" Turner asks, his voice thin and tinny in the computer speakers. He takes a pack of Chesterfields out of his pocket, knocks one out, and puts it, unlit, between his lips. Greg sucks his cheeks in, wipes his mouth again in that obscene way. "You need anything?" Turner continues. "Soda, maybe? A smoke?"

For all the predictability of this routine, there's no getting around its effectiveness. Each time I find my clients in Greg's position here in these interrogation rooms, nervous-eyed and cornered, I think, *No, this will never work. It's too obvious.*

But in the video Greg is already standing up. He follows Turner out the door and off-screen, and I'm left watching an empty room. I push "fast-forward" as Greg and Turner go outside for their smoke, hoping against what I know will be true. *Greg's high out of his mind*, I tell myself, *but he's not* that *stupid or desperate*. He knows better.

At his sentencing the year before, Greg had looked as close to normal as I'd ever seen him. A little color in his face, and he wasn't sweating under his eyes like he normally did. He'd come to court with a sign-in sheet and a thirty-day chip from Narcotics Anonymous meetings at the Washoe County Jail that he showed Judge Bartos, and even *I* half believed it. I'd gone over the rules with him before the hearing, like I do with all my clients. Look the judge in the eye.

Don't try to talk like a lawyer. Don't argue with the judge. But above all, keep your mouth shut until I say so. It was Rule Number One, something C.J. hardwired into me during my first year as a public defender.

"Got it," he'd said. "Mouth shut. Got it."

And yet now, when I resume the video, Turner is leading Greg Lake back into the interview room and I can see that Greg is laughing. He sits back down and Turner pats him on the shoulder, glances quickly at the glassy eye of the video camera in the ceiling corner like he's saying, *Here's your confession, you piece of shit defense attorney.* They sit across from each other, my client sipping at a straw coming out of a green soda can.

"Don't do it, Greg," I say to the computer screen. "Keep your fucking mouth shut."

But he talks. Of course he does.

Turner smiles and nods. Greg keeps going, building steam. He starts to talk about his family, about how he was in foster care for two years and it wasn't a good situation. Turner nods again. *Of course. Of course.*

"Sounds like you've had a rough life," Turner says, all sympathy.

"Man, you don't even know." Greg leans in, sips from the crooked straw. "You don't even know," he says again.

They talk for an hour, and as they do, the sun goes down over the western Sierras outside my office window, beyond the casino towers downtown. A few Jeffrey pines are silhouetted on a ridgetop, backgrounded by clouds torched copper and vermilion. Soon the only lights remaining are the gaudy neons of the Eldorado Casino.

While Greg finishes his first soda, Turner knocks on the door of the interview room. A uniformed officer sticks his head in, then reappears a minute later with an unopened can like it's room service, Greg talking the whole time. As Turner slides the soda across the table, he asks casually about the shooting that took place that evening, at a biker bar off east Fourth Street. Greg is eyeing the second can of soda when he says *sure*, like it's no big deal. Turner pries open the tab, takes the straw from the first can and puts it in the second, then slides it back across the table. The entire time, Greg is talking, confessing. Between sips of Mountain Dew Greg transforms, unwittingly, from "subject" to "defendant."

You might expect that Greg—oblivious to this new title—will feel betrayed or angry when, at the conclusion of the conversation, Turner says, "You understand, Gregory, that I'm going to have to place you under arrest while we get this figured out." You might think that as the uniformed guards come in to place the handcuffs on his wrists, Greg will finally realize his mistake, that he will try to take it all back. You would be wrong.

I TURN OFF the video, knowing what will come next: A forensic technician will collect the soda cans and the cigarette butt, which they will use to obtain DNA samples without having to go through the hassle of securing a warrant. They'll have him stand up, and they'll take photographs of his head and his body, of his fingernails and of his clothes. Because the case involves a firearm, a lab technician will put brown paper bags over Greg's hands, will secure the bags with painter's tape around the wrists to preserve any gunshot residue. Greg will be booked and processed, strip-searched and deloused. And just like that, Greg Lake and I will be back on a collision course with each other.

He'll have a video arraignment within seventy-two hours, where a judge will read him charges that he won't understand and set bail that he won't be able to post. He will be appointed a public defender—me—and given a court date. In a week we will have our first in-person meeting, where I will explain exactly how fucked he is. I'll tell him that the man he shot in the blur of a methamphetamine-induced psychosis ten days earlier died at the scene, on the floor of a dive bar in downtown Reno. I will also inform him that a second man—an innocent bystander hit with a stray bullet—is still in the hospital, that a fragment of bullet perforated the man's intestine, and that he may yet die of sepsis, in which case the district attorney will amend the criminal complaint to include a second count of Murder.

TWO

WHEN I GET home, it's after eight; Rosa is already in bed and Sarah is drowsing off in front of the television. Spread across the living room floor are stacks of articles strewn with yellow highlights and Sarah's blue-ink marginalia; she's presenting at an academic conference on western expansion next month and has procrastinated in completing a paper titled "Plunder in the Silver State: Mining and the Erasure of Indigenous Lands in Early Nevada." She rouses at the sound of the electronic beeping as I start the microwave.

"No problem, Santi," she says, getting up from the couch. "She only cried for a half hour before she fell asleep."

Before I can apologize, she gives a sleepy wave and shuffles off toward the bedroom.

On nights like this one—in the down days after the holidays, watching Greg Lake's confession—I'm often visited by the dead woman. I feel the ghost of her reaching out from eight years earlier, even as I warm my dinner. Even as I uncinch my tie and hang up my suit jacket among the half dozen in the bedroom closet. I wait for the sensation to pass, but when Sarah is asleep and the late-night news is over, the dead woman is still with me.

I slip out of bed and creep downstairs, stopping at the hall closet next to Rosa's bedroom to retrieve a pair of old jeans and hiking boots. I linger for a moment outside my daughter's doorway, listening to the hum of the electric aerator in her fish tank. In the dim glow of the night-light I can just make out the small form of her body in the covers, surrounded by stuffed pandas and unicorns and koalas. I breathe the sour smell of her clothes in a clump atop the dresser, hear the in-and-out of her breath.

On the windowsill next to her bed I find one of her small altars—a series of tiny plastic figurines arranged with religious precision. It stirs up something in me, an old ritual, and I touch my forehead, and then my sternum, and then once on each side of my chest. It's a vestige from Sunday school that I've never been able to shake, though I stopped taking Communion when I was thirteen. I listen to my daughter's breath through the dark, and it seems that even this most basic, most instinctual of functions is beating out my prayer: *one two three four, one two three four.* I close the bedroom door, retreating downstairs to the garage door, the old empty prayer in my grandmother's Spanish trailing behind me. *Padre.* Breath. *Hijo.* Breath. *Espíritu Santo.* Breath. *Amén.*

The garage is heavy with the scent of damp cardboard and engine oil, and when I lift the garage door, crisp night air floods in along with the yellow glow from a string of streetlamps. I engage the clutch and release the emergency brake, rolling silently down the driveway and into the street. I crank the wheel hard to straighten the truck out, and then, safely away from the house, I turn the key.

I FOLLOW THE highway fifteen minutes out into the Nevada desert, the glitter of streetlights and downtown casinos disappearing in the rearview mirror behind the dark masses of the rangeland. I steer past the trailer parks and desert homesteaders, through a small new subdivision of stucco homes and prefabricated fencing encroaching up the mountains. It's been a few years since I've been here, and I lose my way for a minute on the new roads. Soon, however, the uncracked asphalt gives way to gravel, and I recognize the looming dark shape of a water tower. I continue past, the wheels of the truck skidding for purchase as I climb a washed-out mining road.

The road flattens, smooths. Gravel kicks up against the undercarriage of the truck, and the headlights illuminate oversized excavators and backhoes looming like prehistoric creatures in the dark. Flat building pads are carved out from the hillside, their boundaries marked with small fluorescent flags. I slow the pickup to a stop at the far end of the development, the headlights settling on a hillside populated by rabbitbrush and cheatgrass, yellow stalks of wild rye and dark fingers of greasewood. Stepping out, I breathe in the heavy smells of the high desert, feel the cut of the winter air. I search among the scent of dust and brush for something else, something elusive and dark.

I feel the familiar impulses rousing again, the calls to prayer. But instead of indulging them, I hunt out a stale cigarette from an old pack stashed in the back of the glove box. I lean against the door of the truck, the window down. I hear the ticking of the engine cooling, the sound of metal contracting. The topography slowly comes into focus as my eyes adjust to the desert dark: the mountain's heavy shoulders, black stands of juniper in the higher reaches. I smoke the cigarette down to the filter before stubbing it out against the heel of my boot.

I hike up a small ravine to a basalt ledge protruding from the hillside, then flick off the flashlight. Squatting down, I rub the dirt between my thumb and forefinger. Rhyolite and siltstone, sandstone and granite and slate.

I can feel the dead woman here. The entire container of her life—her childhood home in Southwest Reno, her years on the varsity volleyball team at Reno High School, her daily commute to the work she loved as a physician's assistant. Her wedding at Bartley Ranch when it snowed unexpectedly, the difficult birth of her only son at Saint Mary's Hospital on the night of a presidential election—spilled out on the dirt around me.

Eventually, I speak to the dead woman. Anna Weston.

"Hello?" I say into the night air. "Are you still here?"

I stumble over the first words, the head rush of the stale cigarette still pumping along the circuits of my brain. And then they come, building on one another, until I am telling her what I don't allow even myself to consider: Thoughts. Acts. Omissions.

There is a wall that I have been constructing since my first days as a public defender, and the wall is this: Keep your mouth shut. *Cierra la maldita boca*, as my grandmother used to whisper to me in church. It's C.J.'s First Principle and the Golden Rule and the First Commandment all wrapped up in one.

And yet, tonight, I ignore it. I tell the dead woman about the unopened letter waiting back at my office. I tell her about Greg Lake, and about his interview with Turner, and then I feel the need to explain *why* I am confessing to her. I admit that there was something else that I saw, just for a moment, in Greg Lake's confession, and in the recordings I've seen from all the hundreds of other interrogation rooms. The detective's small comforts—a soda, indulging a nervous habit—they allow something to happen. He's trapping his suspect, of course. But he is also ministering to them, in a way. These little kindnesses open up something in them like a vein of silver in a mountainside, and from out of that vein spills their most basic instincts: denial, and anger, and the simple want to survive, to preserve their own life. But at the same time, for just that moment—despite the lifetime in prison that his confession has all but guaranteed—the suspect is consumed with something else. Lightness. Grace, maybe, or some small bit of atonement.

There is a legal term that comes to mind: *corpus delicti.*

It's a principle I learned in law school, a Latin phrase that translates roughly to "the body of the crime." Here's what it means: A defendant cannot be convicted based on his confession alone—there must be some external evidence that a crime has been committed. In the most literal sense, there must be a body.

And so maybe this explains why I decide to make my confession to the dead woman tonight: the lack of a body, the lack of corroborating evidence. The knowledge that my words alone won't endanger me, that I can be both guilty and immune from prosecution. No one wants to believe that Michael Atwood is in prison only because C.J. and I failed him. No one wants to believe the words of a convicted killer.

The dark and cold settle back in. I take the pack from my jacket pocket, shake out the last cigarette. I strike a match, and the warmth and light that fill my cupped hands create, for a moment, a world within a world. I flick the spent match into the dirt and drag on the cigarette. I strike another match, and then another.

Somewhere in the city beyond the mountains my daughter is breathing her unconscious rhythms, her bed strewn with stuffed animals and children's books. I reach down again to feel the earth in my hands, dried and cold and wicked between my fingers. I speak to the dead woman, fumbling to explain about Michael Atwood, the man in prison for her death, and about his letter waiting in my office.

"Are you there?" I say out loud. "Can you hear me?"

PART II

OPENING STATEMENTS

WHEN JURY SELECTION is completed and the clerk has read your name aloud—after you have lodged your objections, after you have called your spouse or childcare provider or boss to inform them that you have been selected for jury duty—you are guided up a set of three steps and seated alongside eleven strangers in the worn pine chairs of the jury box.

From here you begin to take in the scene as the players assume their places: The judge at the bench, the faint outline of a coffee stain on the chest of his black polyester robe. The prosecutor at her desk, leafing through a banker's box of evidentiary motions, witness profiles, and questioning lines, copies of documentary evidence. At the defense table, I am taking one last look at the notes for my opening statements. And there—hidden behind me at the defense table, nearly lost in the bustle, the only person who seems to not have a job—sits the defendant. They're glancing anxiously about the room, trying to remember where they've been instructed to look and where not to look, what to do and what not to do with their hands, what their posture or their smile or their lack of smile might indicate to you, juror, about their relative guilt or innocence.

After the court clerk has completed a formal reading of the charges, the prosecutor stands from her desk, a tabbed binder in her hands. She takes her time, fastens the top button of her suit jacket, lifts the podium from the center of the courtroom and moves it in front of the jury box to establish a sense of comfort and propriety, as if rearranging the furniture in her living room. She opens her trial notebook, pauses for dramatic effect that always serves its purpose; the jury involuntarily leans in, the gallery hushes. And then the prosecutor begins her opening statement.

An opening statement is, quite simply, a promise. A promise to you, juror, of the evidence that each side will present during this trial, of what testimony will be provided, and how the logical conclusion of this evidence will prove or disprove the defendant's guilt.

The prosecutor offers her promises. She displays photographs and timelines and statutes on the courtroom video screen. You are introduced to a cast of characters who will soon become intimately familiar to you: the defendants, the witnesses, the victims.

"The evidence will show . . ." she says, flipping through slides of her PowerPoint presentation. "The evidence will show."

When she is done, she takes her time, gathering her notes, deliberately closing her binder, before returning to her table. And then it is my turn.

When I begin, I aim for a tone of somber familiarity; we have spoken already during jury selection, after all. The images that I begin to project are nearly identical to those of the prosecutor, but my promises somehow contradict those that the prosecutor has just made.

"The evidence will show," I say. "The evidence will show."

Be wary, juror. Even now, what is presented as unequivocal fact is most often pure conjecture. You are already being told whom to believe, being asked to ignore the mandates of the law in favor of something inarticulable—fears and prejudices and desires. The question already being presented is not *Who do you believe?* but rather *Who do you* want *to believe?*

THREE

I WAS ALL of twenty-five years old when I landed my first job out of law school: a first-year attorney at the Washoe County Public Defender's Office. After seven years away at school I had been back in Reno for three months—just long enough to study for and pass the Nevada bar exam. Long enough to start to realize that the place I thought I was returning to had changed in my absence. The year before, my parents had moved across the country to be closer to my mother's family. Most of my high school friends had left for work, or married, or otherwise disappeared. Even the city itself had changed, large tracts of the desert around town now scarred by housing developments abandoned during the market collapse, old casinos hastily converted to downtown condos.

When I reported to the lobby of the public defender's office for my first day, the large receptionist sitting behind an inch of bulletproof glass hardly bothered to acknowledge my existence. At my cheerful "hello," she glanced up briefly from her screen, then reached a thick thumb to a button on her desk. The doorway buzzed loudly, followed by a loud mechanical clack. I stared dumbly at the door until the buzzing stopped and the lock clacked shut again. She exhaled audibly, then tapped a ballpoint pen against the glass window between us.

"I'm Santi," I said. Her name was Joanne—we had met briefly the week before, when I'd interviewed with the chief public defender, Pat Russo. "I'm supposed to start today."

"I know who you are," she said, her voice full of annoyance. "Open the dang door when I buzz you in."

She pushed the button again, and this time I pulled the door open. On the other side of the safety glass her radio blared an advertisement for gold bullion, the spokesman noting the historical rise in value of precious metals, its ease of use in a post-apocalyptic economy.

"C'mon, then," she said. She stood from the desk and began to make her way down an aisle of cubicles. As I trailed behind, a few of the paralegals caught my eye as if to say that we were in on the same joke, offering a quick wink before returning to their computer screens and open folders.

"You're taking over Melissa's caseload," Joanne said, pausing at one of the closed doors that surrounded the grid of cubicles. I nodded as if this meant something to me, as if I'd been told who Melissa was or what her caseload might entail. What Joanne wasn't saying, what Pat Russo failed to mention in my interview the week before, was *why* I was taking over Melissa's caseload—that after twelve years of working as a public defender she'd lost her law license. That there had been a series of client complaints, first to Pat, and then—when nothing happened—to the state bar association. No one told me that she had recently divorced or that she had lost custody of her two children. All of these things I would piece together later, through bits of gossip that slipped out in elevators or after staff meetings, through clues I discovered in case files or from court staff.

Joanne riffled through a ring of keys before plucking one out and unlocking the door. "Pat said to apologize for the mess," she said unapologetically. "We have a request for someone to come clean the place out, but who knows."

She swung the door open onto a cramped office that barely fit a small veneered desk and two plastic office chairs. A single bookcase sagged under rows of books: a bound copy of the Nevada Revised Statutes, *Strategies for Legal Defense of DUI Cases, Basic Perspectives on Criminal Investigations, 101 Mistakes in Forensic Evidence Collection, The Case Against Criminal Defense.* Like a haiku on the bottom shelf sat three hardback children's books.

On the wall, a large corkboard was papered with business cards for inpatient drug treatment programs, psychiatric hospitals, and forensic experts along-side take-out menus for a pizza chain and a nearby Thai restaurant. I stepped over to the single narrow window that looked six stories down onto a sliver of downtown Reno. Across Center Street a rough-looking group of a half dozen people clustered around the front of the city library, waiting for the doors to open a half hour later. On a bus bench, a teenaged girl sat on a man's lap smoking a cigarette.

"You have a view of the courthouse, at least," Joanne said.

In the bottom corner of the window, between a casino parking garage and the balcony of a weekly motel, a single column of the courthouse's yellowed limestone peeked out.

"You don't have anything scheduled until Thursday," she said, dropping a printout of a weekly calendar on the desk. She pointed to a squat file cabinet wedged into the far corner of the office. "All your files are in there, if you want to start getting caught up." And before I could ask any of the thousand follow-up questions I had—*What's in a file? What's scheduled for Thursday? Who's supposed to tell me how to be an attorney?*—she shuffled out into the hallway, closing the door behind her.

I sat at the desk, staring at the calendar Joanne had left—a series of dates and times, courtrooms and case numbers, types of hearings and last names. In the hall outside the door I could hear phones ringing, muffled conversations, the hum and click of a copy machine. Under the calendar for Thursday, I found my name, S. Elcano, next to the words "Department Nine," followed by four last names: Hernandez, Jacobi, Isner, Walton.

I felt the sudden impulse to make lists, to take inventory of all the things that I didn't know and promised to look up later. When I slid open the top drawer of the desk to look for a pen, I found a tangle of silver paper clips, several throat lozenges, two empty bottles of ibuprofen, and a bent pad of Post-its. A note written on the top of the pad read *Pick up Eliza at practice, 6:30.*

I closed the drawer, then found myself searching the room for further evidence of its prior occupant. My gaze landed on a light grey sphere the size of a volleyball, hidden behind a stack of old American Bar Association journals on top of the bookshelf. I squinted across the room, trying to make sense of the shape. Finally, I dragged a chair over to the shelf and reached up to turn the ball around. It was only then that I realized what I was holding.

The plaster cheeks sagged just a bit with age, or perhaps with baby fat. The corners of the bust's eyes creased imperceptibly, as if squinting or perhaps even smiling. The lips were full and pouty, the neck as thick as a leg of lamb. On the back of the skull were three round stickers the size of dimes, multicolored and numbered, where each of the bullets must have entered.

Who was he? I wondered, though I wasn't sure the head was even a "he." The features were smooth and sexless, and I tried to imagine the plaster face with long hair, with plucked eyebrows or makeup. I reached up and palmed the face, carrying it over to the desk—its curves and divots oddly familiar in my hand, the sensation at once intimate and impersonal.

I wondered what series of events had led the head's owner to this moment, the frozen instant in which three pieces of metal made their way through his brain. And then I wondered who might have taken the man's life, before coming to the slow realization why *this* head had been left in *this* office—that my predecessor had been his killer's attorney.

Who are you? I wanted to ask the head. *How did this come to be?*

I turned the bust over in my hands, looking for something to tell me the dead man's identity. No case number, no date, no exhibit number. At the base of the neck a single word—*Washington*—carved into the plaster in a sloping cursive. It could have meant anything—the name of the artist who had created the dead man's bust, or the place where it was made. It might have been the name of the dead man himself, or perhaps the name of the person accused of killing him.

"I ask everyone for one year," Pat had said the week before, after he had offered me the job. "You don't need to promise to stay here for thirty years, and you're not going to get disbarred if you quit tomorrow. But if you take this job, I want you to commit to a year."

At the time, there had been nothing to think about. In addition to a paycheck, the position seemed infinitely more interesting than writing briefs and billing in six-minute increments at a civil litigation firm. The only thing to do was to nod, to say "Yes, of course." But now I felt that a timer set to "one year" had already clicked back to "three hundred sixty-four days, seven hours, nineteen minutes."

I rolled open a drawer of the file cabinet. Inside were dozens of the manila folders that I'd seen on the secretaries' desks outside. They varied in size from the width of a pencil to as wide as a Bible, spilling over with documents.

I removed one of the larger files at random. The typed label read "Collins, Steven. BATTERY/SUBSTANTIAL BODILY HARM, POSS. STOLEN PROPERTY x 3." On the first page of the file was a typed, half-page memo addressed from "Attorney of Record" to "New Attorney," and signed "Melissa Tardiff." In a short paragraph, the memo set out the pertinent facts of the case—two bottles of Canadian Club whisky, one pocketknife, one ex-boyfriend, three independent eyewitnesses, one psychiatric evaluation—as well as a summary of past court hearings. The letter was dated two weeks earlier but felt like a message delivered from beyond the grave. After her signature, the memo ended with two ominous words: *good luck.*

In a packet of medical records attached to the file the emergency room surgeon's clinical notes cataloged a series of stab wounds to a man's left side and back, resulting in a collapsed lung, substantial internal bleeding, and nearly eighty sutures.

A separate envelope attached to the file contained a collection of a dozen glossy photographs. In the first photo the man's jacket had been cut open with a medic's shears, wads of gauze and spent hypodermic needles visible on two stainless-steel tables next to the emergency room bed. Where the jacket had been cut away, the faded blue tattoo of a woman's name ran across the man's shoulder blade, bisected by a ragged wound as long as my index finger. In the next photograph the surgeon's blue-gloved hand was spreading open the wound, revealing a canyon of muscle and fat two inches deep.

I closed the file and slid it to the corner of the desk. Out in the hallway beyond the door I heard a group of men laughing. The file cabinet loomed in the corner, filled with dozens more cases like the one I'd just opened. I began paging through the files in the top drawer, read the litany of charges:

ARSON 1st

POSSESSION/INTENT TO SELL

BURGLARY

POSSESSION CONTROLLED SUBSTANCE x 2
DRAWING AND PASSING
BURGLARY
BURGLARY x 2
BURGLARY
POSSESSION/INTENT TO SELL

The set of drawers seemed to be growing, to be taking on a human presence in the room. To possess an internal heat, to respire.

I looked to my only companion in a room brimming with dark forces. The plaster head's blank gaze stared down from the top of the bookcase, its ambiguous grin at once amused and alarmed.

FOUR

I'D BEEN AT Melissa Tardiff's desk for five straight hours, making my way through the top drawer of the file cabinet, when I was distracted by the sound of a man yelling from the street below.

I stretched my shoulders as I walked to the sliver of window to investigate. Thursday was already looming large, and as I watched the street six stories down, I tried to remember my single semester of Moot Court, to recall the archaic formal language that I'd been taught the courtroom required.

"May it please the court," I said to the window. "May I beg the court's indulgence."

Below, on the corner of Center Street, a shirtless man with wild white hair approached two kids sitting on the bus bench. One of the boys had a skateboard that he rolled idly underfoot, and the two were passing a cigarette back and forth, not noticing the man until he was standing on the sidewalk in front of them. The man was dragging a large black garbage bag and seemed to be having a one-way argument with the empty air, turning away dramatically before pointing excitedly at the uninhabited sidewalk. The kid with the skateboard said something to his friend, then flicked the lit cigarette in the direction of the ranting homeless man. The man brushed wildly where the cigarette had struck his pant leg, then continued on with his tirade as the boys stood, laughing, and walked down Center Street toward the river.

Across the street, I noticed a bald man in a suit and a woman in black slacks and a blouse. They were also watching the shirtless man, who by now had turned his attention to a nearby stop sign. I was momentarily struck by a strange sense of triangulation—me watching them as they watched the man. Behind him, the bald man in the suit leaned over to say something to the woman. The two crossed the street toward the public defender's office, the bald man heading to the entryway while the woman turned off toward the stop sign.

I felt excitement rising as the woman approached the shirtless man from behind. When she was close enough, she put a hand on the man's shoulder. He jerked, wheeling wild-eyed against his assailant. The woman was now speaking to the man, trying to calm him down. I watched her reach into her handbag to retrieve something, and then I realized that she was shaking two cigarettes out of a pack. She put both in her mouth and lit them, then handed one to the man. He eyed her suspiciously, then reached out to take the cigarette.

They stood there like that, both smoking, until the man leaned over and said something to her. She laughed, then said something back. *What could she possibly be telling him?* I wondered. Suddenly the woman was pointing up at the county building, the insane man following her index finger up to my office window.

FIVE MINUTES LATER a red light flashed on my office phone. When I answered, I recognized Joanne's nasal voice at the other end of the line.

"A Mr. Milan is here to see you," she said. Her voice seemed to barely hide a gleeful excitement. "He seems *very* eager to talk to you."

I looked at the calendar the receptionist had given me that morning; while other attorneys' names were listed next to "client meeting" times, the space next to my last name was blank.

"Does he have an appointment?" I asked. I heard Joanne guffaw.

"I'm pretty sure he does *not* have an appointment," she said. In the background I heard another female voice laugh, and then I heard my name being repeated by a ragged male voice. I stood and walked around the desk, stretching the phone cord to reach the window. The sidewalk where the shirtless man had stood a moment ago was now empty.

"Is Mr. Milan . . ." I began, not knowing exactly how to put it. "Does Mr. Milan have a shirt on?"

Joanne snorted into the receiver, obviously delighted by the question.

"He does *not*," she said.

"He does not," I repeated.

"Shall I tell him to wait for you in the conference room?" she asked.

"That'd be fine," I said. I hung up the phone and stared dumbly at the closed door that led out to the conference room where Mr. Milan would be waiting.

I went to the file cabinet and pulled out a file that read "Milan, Joseph M." on the index tab. Flipping open the folder, I found a five-page psychiatric evaluation dated two weeks earlier, diagnosing Milan with acute schizophrenia but concluding that "despite endorsing several classical delusions (government surveillance, a tendency to create his own words or grammatical constructions, etc.)," Mr. Milan understood the nature of the proceedings against him and was able to assist his attorney in his defense, and was therefore competent to stand trial. *How could a man who spoke his own language be competent to stand trial?*

I heard Mr. Milan bellow my name from the lobby. I picked up the receiver and again dialed Joanne.

"You know, I don't think I'll have time to see Mr. Milan this afternoon after all," I said. "Would you mind asking him to reschedule?"

"Hold, please," she said. I heard her dampened voice as she spoke to someone nearby, the receiver muffled by her palm, and then laughed. "Sure," she said when she came back on the line. "I'll have him call you."

I had a hard time believing that Mr. Milan would ever call me back, but all I wanted was to avoid a public spectacle on my first day.

What if he doesn't leave? I wondered. *Can I call the police on my own client?*

As Milan continued to protest from the waiting room, I tried to remember the Legal Ethics class I'd taken in spring—duties of candor, conflicts of interest, avoiding the comingling of client funds. We had never discussed Mr. Milan, I was sure of that.

FIVE

IT WAS NEARLY seven in the evening when I finished reading through the last cases in Melissa Tardiff's filing cabinet. The sound of the janitor's vacuum crept in under the door, and I stood and stretched behind the desk.

I couldn't stop doing the math. I had been assigned eighty-three clients in total. They'd been charged with an array of misdeeds running the gamut from the mundane (driving without a license, possession of marijuana, shoplifting) to the absurd (battery with a deadly weapon—glass dildo) to the blood-chilling (kidnapping with intent to commit murder). When I tallied up the total years that all eighty-three of my clients might serve in prison, I learned that 1,411 years of human life resided in the cabinet.

The day's worth of caffeine and stress that had accumulated in my vital organs now seemed to be making its way outward; my fingertips vibrated unnaturally, my heart rate skipped like a quarter being tossed in a dryer. I dropped down onto the office's industrial carpeting and forced out a set of twenty push-ups. I was halfway through a second set when I heard a knock at the office door. I assumed it was a janitor investigating the light still on in my office, but when I opened the door, I found the woman I'd seen talking to Mr. Milan on the sidewalk earlier.

"Don't tell me you're working late already," she said. I was flushed, still breathing hard from the push-ups, and had the sudden irrational fear that she might think I'd been masturbating. She leaned past me into the doorway, maybe trying to get a glimpse at whatever erotica I might have left out on the desk. She seemed disappointed to find only the eighty-three files spread in no particular order across every available horizontal surface in the office: desk, filing cabinet, chairs, floor, bookshelf.

"Trying to get a sense of my cases," I said. I waved an arm into the office grandly, the way you might welcome a Kansan to Oz.

She nodded, as if still considering whether she wanted to engage me in further conversation. Up close, I could see that her hair was a copper brown streaked grey, pulled back into a tidy bun. She was thin-faced, and her green eyes squinted in a way that made it difficult to guess her age. Forty? Fifty?

"C.J.," she said, extending a hand. "They told you about me yet?"

I vaguely remembered Pat's comment at the end of my interview the week before, when he'd mentioned that I'd be paired up with someone named C.J.— and Joanne's chortle in response.

"Not yet," I said. She nodded again, skeptically. With other people it might have been considered an awkward silence, but there was an unhurried quality to C.J. that put me at ease.

"I'm your partner in Department Nine," she said. "Judge Bartos. Know anything about him?"

"I've only been an attorney for a week," I confessed.

"Well shit," she said. "You don't know much of anything, do you?"

She laughed, not in an unfriendly way, then pushed past me into the office. Through the window behind her a lamp turned on in one of the weekly motels across the street, and I saw a man drinking from a water glass in the silhouette. C.J. lifted a stack of files from one of the chairs on the visitor's side of the desk and dropped it casually on the floor. She rolled the cuffs of her starched white blouse back to her elbows before sitting down.

"You have a real sense for design," she said, leaning back to take in the chaos of the office. I followed her into the office and sat down at Melissa Tardiff's desk. Yellow sticky notes curled from the tops of police reports and out of the pages of the statute book. Her gaze paused momentarily on the fifty-page *All You Need to Know About Criminal Law* that I'd recently ordered online, before landing on the opaque sphere of the bust's head looking down from the bookshelf.

"A lot of this is left over from the last attorney," I explained.

"Melissa," she said.

"Right," I said. "Melissa. Did you know her?"

She looked past me out into the lights of downtown in a way that could have been either wistful or bored.

"Sure," she said. "She was assigned to Department Nine with me, same as you. We worked together for seven years."

I began to put together why she was here now, in my office. She was feeling out her new partner, trying to get an idea of who she'd be stuck with for the next year, assuming I kept my commitment to Pat.

"Listen," she said. "You've been in this room for what—twelve hours now? How about we hang it up, grab a drink on the way out?"

I'd been thinking about a beer for eleven of the last twelve hours, but I also wondered if this might be some sort of test, either of my sobriety or of my work ethic.

"I would," I said. "But I have four cases set for—"

"Hernandez, Isner, et cetera. Yeah, I know," C.J. said. "I'm taking them. We'll get you in court next week. Besides," she said, nodding at the yellow-flagged statute book I'd spent the entire day in consultation with. "You know that book's four years out of date, right?"

WE WALKED FIVE blocks from the office to the Over Under, a small bar with a pool table and dartboard crammed in between a twenty-four-hour bodega and a dilapidated CPA's office. The bar's walls were papered with peeling concert flyers, the ceiling beams exposed in a way that might have been fashionable except for the bits of pink insulation still clinging to staples in the wood. C.J. greeted the bartender by name, a tattooed woman in her early fifties with a pack of menthol cigarettes tucked into the middle of her sports bra. I felt absurdly conspicuous—we were the only two people in the bar in business clothes, or even with shirts that had sleeves—but C.J. seemed oblivious, nodding to a table of bikers across the room.

"Bars around here are filled with either lawyers or clients," C.J. said, as if guessing at my line of thought. "Personally, I prefer the clients."

I watched the bartender spit on the ground as she walked back toward the taps, pouring two pint glasses without taking our order.

"So what about you?" she said. "What're you doing here, anyway?"

"Here?" I asked.

"Yeah. *Here*," she said.

"I'm not really sure," I confessed. "Reno, because I grew up here. I still have a couple friends in town. The PD's office, because—I don't know. I want to—you know—*help* people."

C.J. raised an eyebrow. Even as I said it, I realized how cliché it sounded.

"And it at least seems interesting," I added.

She laughed, then quickly wiped away her smile the same way Pat had when I'd interviewed with him the week before. I wondered if this might be a learned behavior, some technique that I myself might one day adopt.

"*Interesting*," she said. She glanced at an incoming text message on her phone. "Yeah. It's interesting, all right."

The bartender set the pints in front of us on the bar, and we settled onto bar stools.

"So?" I asked.

"So?"

"So, what are *you* doing here?" I said.

"I didn't realize there was going to be a cross-examination," she said. She took a sip of her beer, as if buying time, before starting.

She had failed out of two universities and a community college, C.J. told me, before completing a general education degree from a state school in Wyoming. After graduating she tended bar for five years in San Diego before applying to law school. She'd landed in Reno on a whim—a family friend offering her a free place to stay while she studied for the bar.

"It was Pat's first year as the chief public defender," she said, shaking her head. "Four PDs put in their two weeks when the county commissioners made him chief—good old boys that wouldn't work for a fag. Got me a job, though, and a couple other attorneys that aren't here anymore."

I winced involuntarily at the slur.

"Not my words," C.J. said. "But you need to get used to that. If you stay in this job, you're going to hear it all, and from just about everyone."

"How long ago was that?" I asked.

"Sixteen years in July," she said. She shrugged, as if answering a question I hadn't asked. "That's what they say around here. Stay for three or stay for thirty."

AN HOUR LATER I was happily buzzed, half-heartedly arguing with C.J. about the cases set for Thursday. I was trying to explain that I could be ready to handle the four court appearances on my calendar. There was no part of me that actually *wanted* to take the cases, or even believed that I was capable of doing the job, but I still thought this might be a test, a chance to jump into the deep end early. C.J. brushed me off with a carelessness that suggested she saw through to the insincerity of my offer.

"Don't worry," she said, motioning for the check from the bartender. "In a month you'll be begging me to take cases for you."

The bartender waved C.J. off, instead retrieving the pack of cigarettes from her bra and tapping one out. C.J. peeled a twenty from a silver money clip and slid it under one of the empty pint glasses.

"I told you," she said. "Client bar."

Outside, the autumn air was cold and sobering, a breeze blowing through my thin slacks.

"I saw you talking to that guy on the street earlier," I said. "One of my clients—Milan. You know him?"

"For probably ten years now," she said. We started walking back toward the neon lights of downtown Reno. "He's a frequent flier, comes in for a tune-up every few months when he goes off his meds. Nothing violent, usually."

She seemed unsurprised when I confessed that Milan had been in the lobby that afternoon, and that I'd asked the receptionist to send him away. We walked past the blinking lights of a strip club, the fluorescent glow of a mini-mart.

"That was my idea," she said. "Joanne and I had money on whether you'd talk to him or not."

We walked in silence for a moment.

"So?" I asked finally.

"So what?" she said.

"Did you win?"

C.J. smiled in that way of hers that I would become so accustomed to—that smile that betrayed nothing, conveyed neither information nor emotion. She gave a quick wave goodbye and turned off down a side street, the orange lights of her car flashing as she unlocked the doors.

"See you in court Thursday," she said over her shoulder. "Calendar starts at nine."

SIX

I ARRIVED AT the courthouse at eight fifteen that Thursday morning, wearing the same two-button suit I'd worn all week. The collar of a new dress shirt cut into my neck, the cuffs tight around my wrists, sweat already pooling in the small of my back.

"PD?" one of the bailiffs asked, stopping me at the courthouse security checkpoint. Behind me was a line of courthouse employees, defendants, police officers, witnesses, and prospective jurors, all waiting for the morning calendars to begin in the courthouse's dozen district courts.

I nodded, holding out a new county ID badge dangling from a lanyard around my neck. For the first time since my summer as a lifeguard I felt the sense of authority and of status that came with a title. The bailiff shrugged, nodded me through the metal detector. In the leather attaché my parents had given me for graduation were the four files that I'd pulled from my file cabinet. Even though C.J. would be handling the cases, I still felt a weight to the bag, as if it carried not only the files but the people themselves.

I made my way up a creaky set of wooden stairs worn smooth from a hundred years of lawyers, past a hallway lined on each side by black-and-white photographs of judges who had presided in the courthouse: fifty unsmiling white men in black robes.

Two empty benches ran along the walls on either side of a pair of locked doors. Affixed to one door was a placard that read "Department Nine, Hon. David Bartos." I glanced down at my watch—it was eight thirty—and tried the door again. Finally, I sat on one of the benches in the empty hallway and waited.

I studied a mural of Nevada's state seal on the wall across from me, a dozen feet tall: granite mountains backgrounding a small homestead, a hatted farmer cutting wheat with a scythe, telegraph wires strung from a pair of poles. It captured nothing of the Nevada I knew.

Ten minutes later, a metallic clank sounded at the door and a sheriff's deputy's head emerged from the courtroom. She scanned the empty waiting area before noticing me.

"Defendant, victim, or family," she said.

"I'm sorry?" I asked. I looked around to see if she might be addressing someone else in the empty hallway.

"Are you a defendant, a victim of a crime, or the family member of a defendant?" she said. She seemed irritated to have to ask the same question a second time. Her demeanor didn't improve when I explained that I was a new attorney in the public defender's office, or that I was waiting for C.J.

"Wait inside if you want," she said. "In-custodies will be up in five minutes."

I had imagined that the courtroom itself would bear some resemblance to the courtrooms of movies and television: marble, ornately carved banisters and benches, gilded eagles, and bronze Lady Justices. But instead, I followed the bailiff into a windowless room walled in cheap wooden paneling. The counsel desks looked like repurposed kitchen tables, and the fold-down gallery seats might have been purchased secondhand from an old high school auditorium. I took a seat in the front row, behind a wooden rail separating the gallery from the tables marked "prosecutor" and "defendant." A few minutes later, a man in a chocolate-brown suit entered through the lobby doors carrying a banker's box filled with paperwork. He seemed not to notice me as he passed, nodding to the deputy.

"Morning, Cherise," he said.

"Hey, Neil," the deputy said, looking up from a clipboard. A sharp knock came from a door marked "Jury Room" to the left of the judge's bench, a six-foot-tall monolith with all the ornamentation of a two-by-four. The deputy went to the doorway, selecting a key from a jingling cluster at her belt. She unlocked the door to a tall, mustached officer trailed by a dozen men in faded blue jumpsuits, their wrists shackled to their waists with steel cuffs and chains. Three female inmates followed in bright orange prison clothes, with the procession being brought up by a paunchy young deputy who looked bored, if not hungover.

It was an eclectic bunch—a silver-haired white man who was missing several front teeth, two older Black women who seemed to walk in tandem, a brown-skinned man in his forties whose arms were tattooed with Bible verses in Spanish, a lanky, sickly-looking man with skin the color of butter. The last inmate was a young woman who looked barely old enough to drive, her black hair close-cropped and skin the color of an old penny.

I thumbed through the stack of files on my lap, trying to match names to faces, faces to crimes and victims. The line of prisoners followed the paunchy deputy into a jury box that ran along the side of the courtroom to the left of the judge's bench. In a quick monotone, the deputy read out the rules of the courtroom—stay quiet, don't attempt to communicate with friends or family members in the audience, come down when your case is called—before instructing the group to sit.

Behind me, the gallery had begun to fill with people entering from the lobby. I remembered the bailiff's question earlier: *Defendant, victim, or family?* The district attorney began to unload manila files from his banker's box, casually taking notes on a yellow legal pad. I eyed my watch—court was set to begin in ten minutes and C.J. still hadn't arrived. The sickly-looking inmate caught my eye, then motioned me over to his seat, his eyes bulging with nervous urgency. I opened a file at random from the attaché and began flipping through it, taking notes that weren't notes, pretending not to have seen him.

Just as court was about to begin, I saw C.J. enter through the courtroom doors talking to a white-bearded man in a flannel shirt and wraparound sunglasses. She carried a stack of files a foot wide in the crook of her suit jacket. Spotting me in the gallery, she motioned for me to follow her through the swinging gate to the defendant's table.

"You got your files?" she said. I didn't like the way she said "your files." It implied an ownership that I hoped I didn't have. I nodded, reaching into my pocket to finger the small piece of tinfoil that contained a one-milligram Xanax tablet. "Give me Arrieta."

I flipped through the four files in the leather attaché, pulled the one labeled "Arrieta, Bernard," and slid it across the defense counsel desk to C.J. I noticed that only the prosecutor's table had chairs behind it—the defense table stood awkward and alone, attorneys and defendants left to stand. Neil—the district attorney who had come into the courtroom earlier—was leaning back in a leather-backed chair reading a red file as if he were skimming the Sunday newspaper.

C.J. took up the Arrieta file and flipped through it, skipping over dozens of pages of charging documents and witness statements at a time, before pausing momentarily on a sentencing report prepared by the Division of Parole and Probation. She closed the file and scribbled three illegible bullet points on the manila cover, then pushed the file aside.

"Next," she said. "Lucas."

After we had repeated the process for the three other files in my attaché, she stacked the folders on top of hers and handed the entire weighty pile to me.

"OK," she said, starting for the jury box. "Let's go talk to these guys."

In the jury box the group of prisoners sat sullenly, waiting to talk to their attorneys. One man was twisting a pinkie meditatively through his ear canal, while another tried to silently mouth something to a woman in the gallery before being admonished by the bailiff. I followed C.J. to the young woman I'd noticed when the bailiff led the prisoners into the courtroom. Up close, I could see the high angle of her cheekbones, the dark peach fuzz on her forearms as they lay across the lap of the orange county-issued jumpsuit. She was, I realized, Ruth Walton—one of the cases that I'd read and reread in preparation for her hearing today. The details from the police report were still fresh in my memory: Driving Under the Influence, alongside a felony for Eluding a Police Officer. She'd been stopped just outside the town of Nixon on the Paiute reservation at Pyramid Lake, an hour north of Reno. She ran the only two stop signs in town, trying to ditch the tribal police before wrecking her mother's Ford Aerostar into the high school's chain link fence, all in broad daylight. The toxicology reports in her file said she was at a .16 percent blood alcohol level—twice the legal limit.

"This is Ruth," C.J. said, sitting in the empty seat next to her in the jury box.

I leaned against the wooden rail that separated the jury box from the rest of the courtroom, trying for a posture that suggested competence. "Ruth, this is Santi. He's taking over Melissa's cases."

"Hey C.J.," a voice hissed from the row behind us. I turned to see the sickly inmate who had tried to catch my attention earlier. "We get to go home today or what?"

C.J. took a second to turn around and scowl, which the man answered with an oblivious smile. She leaned back in toward Ruth, the three of us huddled together around the railing.

"It looks like Melissa has a good deal set up for you, yeah?" C.J. said. She pushed over four stapled pages that she'd removed from the file so that Ruth could see them. "We're going to plead guilty to the felony today, but you get to go to inpatient treatment for the alcohol. You finish the treatment, and this all goes away."

C.J. picked up the guilty plea, shook it by a corner as if to demonstrate its transience. The young woman nodded, her eyes wide and unblinking. I could see her arms trembling, the steel links clicking against each other around her waist.

"Do I get to go home today?" Ruth said. Her voice was soft and trembled in the same way her hands did. C.J. shook her head, jabbed her finger at the paperwork.

"This guilty plea says that you go to *inpatient* treatment today," she said.

"Hey C.J.," the man interrupted again from the second row. C.J.'s head snapped up, a momentary violence flashing in her eyes.

"Keep your damned mouth shut for a minute, Greg," C.J. said sharply. "I'll get to you when I get to you."

Greg Lake stopped fidgeting in his chair, his sudden stillness more unsettling than his squirming. He said something under his breath that might have been an apology or might have been a curse, but C.J. ignored it. She flipped back to the third page of Ruth's guilty plea, pointing to a paragraph at the top of the page.

"This says 'inpatient today,'" she said. "You finish your inpatient treatment in twenty-eight days, they let you out. You go home, you stay sober, you take some classes. In six months, you come back here to court. Your new lawyer here says some nice things about you, the judge says, 'Great job, Ruth,' and the felony goes away."

"I thought I was going home," Ruth said quietly. Behind us, the bailiff instructed the courtroom to stand as the judge—a small man with wiry silver hair and oversized glasses—entered from a door to the right of the bench.

"I have ten more clients to talk to, Ruth," C.J. said. There was an edge to her voice now, a hint of the anger that I'd seen when she'd quieted Greg Lake a moment before. "This is the deal that you and Melissa agreed to, right?"

Ruth nodded.

"Your new lawyer here is going to read this guilty plea to you," C.J. said. She slid the paperwork down to me. "When he's done, sign the paper."

C.J. pointed over toward the defense table, chairless and alone in the courtroom. The judge had taken his seat on the bench. He said something to the court clerk, who laughed over-effusively.

"When that old man in the black robe calls your name," C.J. continued, "you and I stand up there together. You say 'yes' to everything the judge asks you, and we get you out of jail and into treatment. Got it?"

Ruth nodded again.

"No surprises today, right, Ruth?" C.J. said.

She shook her head. The shackles clinked against her thin wrists.

"Good answer," C.J. said, her tone suddenly turning warm. She patted her on the arm and offered her a motherly smile. "Just do what you need to do and this all goes away, OK?"

And then C.J. was gone, off to deal with Greg Lake in the second row, leaving me alone with Ruth. We both watched C.J. for a moment, the way she seemed to be in continuous movement. Her face flashing at angles like a knife, one second soft and sympathetic, the next stern and cold. Her hand darting out to open a file or produce a pen or brush a fold of hair from her face.

In the jury box next to us a few other attorneys were reviewing paperwork with their clients. I smiled weakly at Ruth, then slid into the empty juror's seat next to her. The bailiff called a name and the gallery went quiet, though the attorneys continued to lean over their clients' shoulders, whispering into their ears, pointing at paperwork.

"Hi," I whispered apologetically. "I'm Santi."

I held out my hand before remembering that her arms were bound to her sides by the steel shackles. She leaned over so that her right hand was angled up awkwardly, and I reached down toward her waist in a way that caught the bailiff's attention from her podium at the end of the jury box. I felt the warmth of Ruth's fingertips, her skin dewy and pliable like some amphibious creature.

"Sorry," I confessed. "I'm new at this."

"It's OK," she said. "Me too."

She glanced toward the back of the courtroom to where a middle-aged couple sat, both dressed in tidy flannel shirts. The man held a baseball hat folded in his lap and was grimacing in our direction.

"Your parents?" I asked.

She nodded.

"Well," I said. "Let's get this over with and get you home."

I had only made it through the first page of the guilty plea when I noticed C.J. waving a manila file at the end of the jury box, trying to get my attention. She had already finished with the man in the second row and was now on to the next client. She pointed at her watch, then pantomimed a signature.

"You don't have to read it," Ruth said. "I know you all are busy."

I shook my head. We were close enough that I could smell the faint odor of sweat from her county jumpsuit. For that moment we might have been just two people chatting at a bar or a bus stop.

I started in on the second page of the guilty plea, my finger following along as I read quickly and quietly. In front of us, a second inmate had been called down to the counsel table, where a tanned, slick-haired private attorney waited for him. I recognized the lawyer from somewhere, a billboard or a TV ad. He straightened his lapels in a rehearsed, cocksure sort of way, and I thought I caught the district attorney rolling his eyes at C.J. as the attorney began his presentation.

When the bailiff called Ruth's case five minutes later, I'd only finished reading through three pages of the four-page plea. I shot a panicked look down the jury box, in time to see C.J. mouth the words *What the fuck*. She pantomimed the scribbling motion again, making her way toward us in the jury box as she simultaneously acknowledged Ruth's presence in court to the judge.

"C.J. Howard, deputy public defender, Your Honor," she said, almost to us now, motioning for Ruth to stand. "On behalf of Ruth Walton, who is present in court and in custody."

I flipped to the last page of the plea and pointed at the blank line above the word *defendant*, then held out a cheap ballpoint pen. Ruth tipped herself over awkwardly, taking the pen up in her fingertips. She wrote the first letters of her name, followed by a scribble that trailed off into the word *defendant* on the line below.

"Ms. Howard," the judge said. There was irritation in his voice, something tired and parental in the way he said it. "Do you need more time with your client?"

"No, Your Honor," she said. Ruth Walton was being beckoned out of the jury box by the bailiff, shuffling across the courtroom to where C.J. stood, her chains singing softly as they dragged behind her.

I watched from the jury box as Ruth told the judge she agreed to all the terms set out in the guilty plea that she had not read, then affirmed she was satisfied with the services of her attorney, to whom she'd talked for less than five minutes.

"OK, Ms. Walton," Judge Bartos said at the end of her plea, already reaching over for the next file on the docket. "You're going to be released from jail today into an inpatient program. Do what you need to do, come back here in six months, and all this goes away. Got it?"

C.J. gave her a small pat on the back, as if to say *I told you so*, and then turned to the next file as Ruth shuffled back to the jury box.

FOR THE NEXT three hours I watched as C.J. skipped effortlessly between a dozen clients. She joked with Judge Bartos between sentencings, argued passionately to get probation for a single mother, leaned in to confer with the district attorney before the two stipulated to a rehabilitation program for a young man caught with meth.

When the court calendar finished just before noon, I gathered up the morning's files and we began to make our way out of the courthouse. C.J. had entered three guilty pleas, set one case for trial, and done another four sentencing hearings, but she didn't look the worse for wear. Outside the courthouse, I squinted into the midday sun. C.J. took off her suit jacket and folded it over an arm.

"Two prelims set for this afternoon and then we get to go home," she said. "Easy day, honey."

We were standing at the Virginia Street crosswalk, and she pantomimed a cast across an imaginary river.

"Finish up my memos, read tomorrow's cases." She jerked the imaginary rod back, as if she'd just hooked into a trout. "I'll have a line in the river by six."

"Hey," I said. "What's the story with that young woman—Ruth Walton?"

C.J. stopped short, as if she'd just now realized I was there, that I wasn't just some figment of her imagination she'd been talking to.

"Why're you asking?" she said. "Don't tell me you like the little brown ones—the reservation girls? That your type?"

"No," I said, feeling myself flush. "I mean, not like that. Just, you know, she seemed . . . normal."

She shrugged, as if disappointed in my answer.

"You read the file," she said. She seemed already bored with the conversation. "Young kid from the reservation. Plenty of free booze around the casinos here in town, but it's a forty-five-minute drive back home. The tribe has jurisdiction, actually, but they always leave it to us to prosecute. Trust me. You'll see plenty of Ruths."

SEVEN

THAT AFTERNOON, AS I walked back to the studio apartment I'd rented that summer, I felt a happy sense of accountability. I had a place to be the next morning, a paycheck on the horizon. I hadn't specifically sought out—or prepared for—a career in criminal defense, but it seemed to check many of the same aspirational boxes that had brought me to law school in the first place. A flood of legendary defense attorneys ran through my mind: Clarence Darrow. Barry Scheck. Atticus Finch. Johnnie Cochran. Matlock.

I cruised aimlessly through downtown, over the old Virginia Street bridge and past the shallow trickle of the Truckee River, through towers of grimy casinos with aspirational names like the Gold Dust or the Riverboat, the Silver Legacy and the Atlantis and the King's Inn.

My friend Jasper and I had spent all of high school plotting our escape from Reno—but when it came time, I was the only one who had left, first for college in California and then for law school in the Midwest. And I had been surprised to miss Nevada as soon as I'd gone—the desert basins and churning mountain ranges, the seediness of a small gambling town, the unpredictability of the early morning hours with Jasper when Reno buzzed with nervous energy. But I'd only seen Jasper a handful of times since I'd been back; instead, I'd spent the summer locked in my studio apartment with stacks of study guides and practice bar exams.

I parked back at my apartment building and walked the five blocks downtown to the Saint Lawrence, still in the suit I'd worn to court that morning—a charcoal two-button with a white shirt, my tie folded in the breast pocket of my jacket.

Jasper was behind the bar when I arrived, taking an order from a heavy-set, bearded man. The restaurant was in a renovated old building, the planked floors pleasingly worn, large beams running the length of the ceiling. Young professionals a few years older than me gathered around bistro tables and in booths, picking at farm-to-table appetizers and nursing expensive cocktails.

I watched for a moment as Jasper poured gin into a shaker, chatting casually with the customer. He was wearing the same uniform he'd had since we were kids—a white T-shirt and jeans. He had filled out from his gangly teenaged body, his face darkened with stubble. But there was also a sameness to him; it wasn't so much that I could still see the child version of him, but instead that the adult version of him had always been there even when we were kids.

When Jasper finished making the drink, he took the man's credit card over to the register behind him. Waiting at the end of the bar in my suit, I began to feel like a child playing dress-up in his father's clothes. The sameness of Jasper's shirt and jeans reminded me of my own changeability, how in the years we'd known each other I'd passed from the button-ups of middle school to the Nike athleticwear of freshman year to the silk-screened band shirts and baggy pants of senior year to the khakis of law school—a sad evolution of characters, while he had always remained the same. As if there had never been any doubt for him—who he was and who he would always be.

"Hey bartender," I said, stepping up to an open seat at the bar. "What's it take to get some fucking service over here?"

Jasper looked up at me over the top of a pair of heavy-rimmed glasses, his familiar smile flashing in the dim of the bar. He stood, brushed his jeans with his palms, and then abruptly walked around the bar and embraced me.

"Well, goddamn," he said, taking in my clothes. "You look . . ."

"Yeah," I said. "I know."

"You're supposed to be—what? A mortician now?"

"Close," I said. "First day of court."

He seemed to consider the implications of this information. I'd hoped the politics of the job—fighting the government to preserve the inalienable rights of the common man—might outweigh the general sense of selling out by having gone to law school in the first place.

"So?" he said. "You survive?"

He slid a beer across the bar and we chatted for a few minutes, me catching him up about C.J., and Ruth Walton, and Greg Lake's constant interruptions. Finally, a woman motioned to him at the end of the bar, pointing at her empty martini glass.

"Listen," he said. "I'm done at seven. River?"

"Sure," I said.

"Plenty of time for you to go home and change clothes," he said.

AFTER I'D CHANGED into jeans and a T-shirt, I walked the two blocks of California Avenue toward Virginia Street. Even in the plain light of afternoon, the familiar seediness of downtown was on full display: weekly motor lodges teeming with foot traffic, kids playing in empty, weed-choked swimming pools. For the first time, I felt like I was back in the Reno I had grown up in.

I took my time, wandered the backstreets of the city. This was the Nevada I knew: slick-haired and shifty. I remembered middle school afternoons with Jasper, staring through the front window of the porno store I now walked past, sneaking into the buffet lines at the Circus Circus to eat shrimp cocktail and German chocolate cake until we were sick. Dashes from mini-marts with blocks of beer hidden under our jackets. High school bonfires in the hills, first kisses on desert lakeshores, awkward hand jobs from first girlfriends in the sagebrush.

While my family subscribed to a more optimistic, maybe naive version of the American Dream, Jasper's dad had instilled in him a belief in personal sovereignty and the right to self-defense. This presented itself in Jasper in irregular, dramatic ways—there were the occasional fights, blood and hair and teeth. But there were also larger evils that seemed to swirl around us just out of sight, that Jasper seemed to have an innate knowledge of: That a classmate's father had been killed tending bar during a robbery gone bad. That a boy at another elementary school had gone missing, only to be found in California several days later.

I found Jasper at our old spot, a deep eddy in the riverbank just at the edge of downtown. A six-pack of cheap beer sat next to him, one ring already empty.

"Help yourself," he said, nudging the beers in my direction.

I pulled a can out, then squatted down on a tree stump at the river's edge. Upstream, a woman was casting a fishing line out into the haze of an afternoon mayfly hatch; the water unspooled around her waders in looping rivulets, the line drifting lazily in the current.

"I drove by the old neighborhood last weekend," I said. "You been up there recently?"

Jasper shook his head. "Not in years."

We had both grown up on the north side of Reno, in an area that once-upon-a-time hadn't even been part of town, just a handful of one-acre tracts run scattershot through the foothills. It was a place where the paranoid anti-government set had moved to get away from zoning laws that frowned upon the backyard practice of Second Amendment rights, or where people like my parents were simply sold on large parcels of cheap land. Paved roads trailed off into the desert; property lines were delineated by broken-down automobiles and snake-infested lumber piles rather than fences or hedges.

But over the years Reno had slowly crept outward to envelop the unincorporated properties of the Sierra Highlands, as a developer eventually rechristened the area. Houses were built and bought and mortgaged and remortgaged until the market fell out, and now half the subdivided homes sat vacant, their sodded lawns as dry and brown as straw, paint curling off fences in the summer heat. I'd followed our road down to Jasper's house, wondering if the museum of automotive parts that had littered the yard had similarly been replaced or if his family might somehow still be there. I drove the road three times before I realized that the house had been razed entirely, the lot now choked with cheatgrass and sage.

Jasper took a drag from his cigarette, blew a bit of ash absently from the tip. There was something in the action that reminded me of his father, who'd had a cigarette hanging off his bottom lip regardless of whatever else he was doing—cooking dinner, or with his head inside a car engine, or reading on the front porch.

"Your parents' place is just . . . *gone*," I said. "Like, *wiped from the face of the earth* gone."

"Oh, they lost that place ages ago," he said.

His family had gone through a "ration of shit" several years earlier, he told me, which might have involved mortgage debt or might have involved a plot to overthrow the government but, regardless, had resulted in his parents' move to an apartment complex in a gloomy east Reno suburb. I got the sense that he was constantly editing, that he was never quite revealing the whole truth.

"Go out for a bit?" I asked when we had finished the last beers. My empty studio loomed heavy.

"Can't tonight," he said, scrolling through the screen on his phone. "But soon, yeah?"

"Sure," I said.

We made vague plans to meet up in the next week, then gave each other an awkward hug before Jasper left in the direction of downtown. When he was a few steps away, he stopped, turning on his heels as if he'd just remembered something.

"It makes sense," he said, shaking his head. "The public defender thing."

"Yeah?" I said doubtfully.

"Seriously. You'll be great."

"Thanks," I began to say. But he had already started off again, the familiar shape of his lean shoulders receding into the afternoon light. I stood alone at the edge of the Truckee River, swaying with an evening buzz, the sky dimming, the shrieks of children in the park behind me mixing with the warble of water over river rock.

Upstream, the fisher jerked the tip of her rod skyward, and I heard the high sing of the reel. I followed the line, glowing yellow in the last of the evening light. The small arc of a fish's body hovered momentarily, weightless, suspended between one world and the next, before crashing back down into the river.

EIGHT

IF MY MORNING with Ruth Walton in Bartos' courtroom was C.J.'s way of letting me dip a toe in the waters, then my first day of preliminary hearings was baptism by fire. The next Tuesday afternoon I followed C.J. past a line of people thirty deep at the security checkpoint of Reno Justice Court and through the employees' entrance. She set her stack of files on the conveyor belt of the metal detector, then nodded to the sheriff's deputy who stood waiting on the other side.

"New guy," C.J. said to the guard. I tapped the plastic badge that hung from a lanyard over my suit jacket, as if to confirm this fact.

"He going to last?" the guard said.

"Oh, who knows, Dale," C.J. said. "Don't bother learning his name just yet."

I waited for my two thin files to emerge from the conveyor belt—these were the first cases that I would be handling myself. At a preliminary hearing, C.J. had explained, the prosecutor is required to call witnesses to establish probable cause—some minimal proof—that a crime has been committed and that the defendant is responsible. It's a low bar for the prosecutor, but an important opportunity for the defense to cross-examine witnesses at the justice court level and begin to test the evidence.

I had prepared myself for the fact that I might actually be forced to appear in court for the first time. The Xanax I had swallowed before we left the office was now arriving, and as I followed C.J. up a flight of stairs into the lobby of Reno Justice Court, a pleasant dullness began to settle in.

We stepped into a lobby churning with people: prosecutors and defense attorneys, police officers and witnesses and confidential informants, victims of crimes and social workers, family members hoping just to get a glimpse of their husbands or girlfriends or sons who had been transported to court for preliminary hearings or misdemeanor trials.

A bank of windows was manned by a half dozen court clerks—mostly women—all wearing lanyards with county IDs identical to mine. Above the windows a monitor listed the afternoon's cases by last name, as well as the prosecutor assigned to each case. As C.J. had instructed, I took my place in line behind two attorneys—the first a tall man with thick grey hair, a TV extra in the part of "seasoned attorney," while the other was squat and perspiring, shoving along a worn briefcase with his foot.

"Thought it was a goddamn *venereal disease*," the taller man was saying when the clerk called them forward, the other attorney laughing as he stooped to collect his briefcase. "Itched like a sonofabitch."

When they had checked in, I stepped up to the open counter, sliding my files toward the court clerk, a strawberry-haired woman in her twenties.

"I'm here on Mendez and Alder." Even this was a line I'd rehearsed over the previous days, speaking the words out loud to the plaster bust on my office bookshelf. The clerk glanced at the names and case numbers printed on the tab of my files, then back at a computer monitor.

"You the new PD?" she asked, still looking at the screen. "New Melissa?"

"That's me."

She pushed the two files back across the counter.

"Mendez is a no-show," she said. "DA is Neil Hadley. You guys can have Courtroom E for the failure to appear. Drew Alder is over there with his mom in the corner." She pointed across the lobby to where a pasty kid in a collared shirt sat next to an older woman. "Hadley's on that one, too."

I tried to square this kid with the Drew Alder I'd read about in a series of police reports detailing a nearly fatal car accident that had occurred the month before. The blood test that had come back positive for both alcohol and a prescription opiate, and two witness statements identifying Alder as the driver of a vehicle that had blown through a stop sign and into the passenger side of a Subaru.

"OK, you're up on Mendez," the clerk said.

"I thought he wasn't here," I said.

She looked at me blankly for a moment.

"You still have to go on the record for the failure to appear," she said. "Oscar will take you to Courtroom E."

A large sheriff's deputy holding a clipboard nodded for me to follow him through a tall wooden set of double doors. Inside, the gallery of the small courtroom was empty. Neil Hadley, the prosecutor who had been in Judge Bartos' courtroom for Ruth Walton's guilty plea the week before, sat alone at the counsel table poking at his phone.

I followed the bailiff through the swinging gate and toward the counsel table, not sure what I was supposed to do without a client. I'd spoken to Mendez by phone two days earlier, when he'd told me he wanted to contest the charges if the DA wouldn't reduce the felony offense to a misdemeanor. Hadley nodded briefly in my direction before returning to his phone. There was a loud buzzing sound from behind the judge's bench, and then the mechanical clang of a door being unlocked.

"All rise," the bailiff said in a voice devoid of gravitas. A white-haired justice of the peace entered through a door behind the bench and unceremoniously took her seat. Hadley made a motion approximating standing before sitting back down at the prosecutor's table, taking one last glance at his phone before pocketing it and opening the file on the desk before him.

"OK, looks like we're here for a preliminary hearing," the judge said, glancing at a computer screen next to her on the bench. For the first time, she looked up into the nearly empty courtroom. "And it looks like we're missing a defendant. Is that right, Counsel?"

My chest tightened as all four sets of eyes in the courtroom turned in my direction. The facts of the case were straightforward: Mendez had been caught on video selling marijuana to an undercover police officer. I'd spent the entirety of my Saturday afternoon memorizing the case file, highlighting statutes and pulling case law. I had been prepared to negotiate with the prosecutor, to confer with my client, to conduct a preliminary hearing if a favorable plea couldn't be negotiated. I'd found a bit of obscure case law from 1908 relevant to the issue of search and seizure. I'd prepared to question the arresting officer about how the marijuana had been tested, how protocol for chain of custody had been violated. I'd written up questions for cross-examination and outlined an opening statement that—I hadn't yet realized—wasn't even allowed in a preliminary examination. But C.J. hadn't told me what to do if my client didn't *show up*. I looked to my left, where David Mendez should have been standing, and made a motion that seemed to feign surprise.

"Your Honor, may it please the court," I began. It was an old bit of legalese with roots in British common law, and by the looks that Hadley and the judge both gave me, it was a term that hadn't been used in a Nevada courtroom in the last century. The judge grinned widely. I heard Hadley cough into the elbow of his suit jacket.

"Go ahead, Counsel," she said, leaning forward on her elbows, seemingly delighted by my statement. "Please the court."

I turned again toward the place where Mendez should have been standing.

"It appears, Your Honor," I said. I paused, noticing for the first time the stenographer typing each word I said. I envisioned the record I was now building, each word solemnized in Courier New. How this transcript would read when it was typed up later in a petition for ineffective assistance of counsel. Was I incriminating him, just by stating the obvious? But what other choice did I have?

"Yes, Your Honor. It appears that Mr. Mendez is not present in court this afternoon."

"Well, that *does* please the court," the judge said, still delighted. "Anything else to add, Counsel?"

On the table next to me was a legal pad filled with notes for the preliminary hearing that was not going to happen. I flipped through a few pages, as if Mendez might be hiding somewhere in the margins.

"No, Your Honor," I said. "Nothing further."

"State?" the judge said, turning her attention to Hadley.

"State would request a warrant be issued for the arrest of the defendant and a bond of ten thousand dollars," Hadley recited in a bored monotone.

"Sounds reasonable," the judge said. "So ordered."

She turned to me again, in a way that wasn't unfriendly.

"What that means, Counsel, is that if Mr. Mendez is found, he'll be arrested. His bail will be ten grand, and we'll come back here and do it all over again. Sound good?"

I nodded.

"And hold on to all those notes, Counselor," she said, smiling broadly. "If your client ever shows up, I'm sure it will be one hell of a preliminary hearing."

"Yes, Your Honor," I said. The bailiff put a hand to his mouth.

"OK then!" the judge said, standing to leave.

I followed Hadley and the bailiff back out into the lobby, where the crowd had thinned. Across the room, Drew Alder was still waiting near the corner, thin and pitiful. His cheeks were blotchy with late-adolescent acne, pale and flaky from some acidic cleanser, above an Adam's apple that stuck out like a knot on a tree. He was dressed in a collared shirt, ill-fitting brown slacks, and a pair of old running sneakers. On the bench next to him a woman in a department store print rummaged through a black purse.

When I'd read through the entire cabinet of case files my first day on the job, the case had stood out not only for Andrew Alder's clear culpability, but also for the injuries it had inflicted: a two-year-old child left with a collapsed lung and broken arm, his mother with compound fractures in both legs. The photographs had been horrific, and the medical reports made clear that the accident could have easily resulted in death, that the injuries would likely haunt the victims for life.

"This is a real dog-shit case," C.J. had said while glancing through the file a few days earlier. "But then, you probably knew that."

There might be some procedural issues, I'd suggested—it was unclear whether the police had read Drew his *Miranda* warnings before he confessed. The toxicology reports had shown a combination of alcohol and opioid metabolites in Drew's system, which we might be able to use for an involuntary intoxication defense. C.J. just shook her head.

"You know he should be looking at a DUI Causing Death, right?" she said. She held up the evidentiary photos from the file. "Look at this kid. A jury would send him away for life if they could."

"But—"

"The best you can do is beg Neil for something short of the maximum. Something that gets him out of prison before he's thirty."

Now, in the courthouse lobby, I tried to imagine Drew Alder walking out of prison as a thirty-year-old. I wondered if he had any idea of the turn his life had already taken. Across the room, Neil emerged from Courtroom E still scrolling through his phone. He glanced up just long enough to spot me, then started over in my direction.

"You talk to your client yet?"

"Not yet," I said. "I've been talking with C.J., and I think there's a *Miranda* issue here . . ."

Neil raised an eyebrow suspiciously.

"A *Miranda* issue? On a case with three eyewitnesses? Where his toxicology was off the charts, and with *those* two victims?"

I started to fumble through my notes before he held up a hand.

"Anyway, the cop on scene isn't here, so we can't do the prelim. I can make a motion to continue, or you can just stipulate—your guy is out of custody anyway. Come to my office sometime in the next few weeks and we can talk the case over, maybe come to a resolution. Good?"

I nodded noncommittally. I thought back to a lecture from my first week of law school about the merits of the American adversarial system of justice. Wasn't Neil my adversary, after all? Should I be agreeing to *anything* he suggested?

"Great," he said. "I'll tell the clerk. Go let your guy know. He should be glad to have an extra couple months outside, anyway."

WHEN I RETURNED to my office, I found a voice message from an inpatient substance abuse program called New Horizons in the town of Fallon, forty minutes east of Reno. A small female voice came on after the program's pre-recorded message.

"You probably don't remember me," the voice said. "This is Ruth. Ruth Walton."

The voice paused awkwardly. In the background I heard a television playing, the sharp bark of another voice.

"You're my attorney, and so I wanted to tell you that they got me into that program today." Her voice had a faraway feeling to it, as if she'd forgotten who she was talking to. As if she were talking to herself. "I have three months sober, if you count the time in jail."

I wrote her name on a Post-it, planning to call her back at the program, but over the next few days the note was lost in a blur of new cases and clients, new hearings and research. The next week, however, I found another message waiting on my phone when I got back from court.

"This is Ruth again. Anyway, just wanted to say that I'm doing good here." There was a lightness to the voice, as if it had regained its youth. "They told me to call you. To give you an update. Three more weeks, my counselor says, and they're sending me home."

"Don't get your hopes up," C.J. said when I mentioned the messages. "It just makes it harder when they disappoint you."

NINE

C.J. WAS RIGHT: There were plenty of women like Ruth and plenty of young men like Drew Alder. In the next months a rhythm began to emerge from the daily chaos of the court calendar.

I shadowed C.J. in the courtroom and on visits to see clients at the jail. I followed her to preliminary hearings and bail hearings, and after court I'd tag along with her to Starbucks for coffee or to the Over Under for a beer. In the rare times I had caught up on my work by the weekend, I would meet with Jasper and his girlfriend, Natalie, for drinks or a late-night dinner after their shifts had ended.

I took notes on the scripts that C.J., Judge Bartos, and the district attorney all seemed to follow: who says what, who stands where, the cues to stand up or sit down or read your bullet points or shut the fuck up. I studied this script, rehearsed it out loud to the plaster bust of the dead man on the bookshelf after the office emptied out for the night. When my time to stand up in front of Judge Bartos in district court came, I forgot the name of my first client, misplaced the guilty plea of another. A third defendant refused to go forward with a plea that had been set up six months earlier by Melissa Tardiff, my predecessor.

"How am I going to plead guilty to a felony with a lawyer I never met?" the man asked Bartos. The question seemed eminently reasonable, and I could do nothing but stand at the defense table like a spotlighted jackrabbit until C.J. stood from the front row of the jury box to ask for a brief continuance. As I handled the next case on the docket—the scheduling of a motion hearing—I could hear C.J. leaning next to the client in the jury box, berating him in a barely contained whisper.

"He's ready," C.J. said to me when I had finished with the last case. "Ask to go up next, before he changes his mind."

IN THESE FIRST months Bartos would huff with annoyance at each slipup, and I felt the eyes of not only the court staff but also the other defendants waiting in the jury box, of the family members packed into the gallery behind me. But after court each day C.J. would wave off my missteps, happy for a reason to place the blame on the judge or an unreasonable client or an unethical argument by the DA.

"The victim's a piece of shit," I soon found myself arguing to Neil in the hallways of Reno Justice Court, pointing to a line in a police report, trying to negotiate a lesser charge to a domestic violence case. "She admitted to the cops that she'd been shooting up all night. How's that testimony going to play at trial?"

If Neil believed me, or if he just didn't want the hassle of fighting a motion to suppress evidence, he would offer a lesser offense, or stipulate to probation, or occasionally even dismiss the case outright. And because Neil, most of the time, *was* reasonable, when he disagreed, it became my job to deliver the bad news to the client.

"We *could* go to trial," I'd tell my clients, the unsigned guilty plea already in my hand. "Absolutely. But they're probably going to get you for a weapon enhancement. That will add five years, and you know Bartos is going to hammer you at sentencing."

I'd learned to phrase our conversations like that, as if they were the ones making the choice even though the choices as I presented them offered no alternative.

"We have no issues for trial," I'd say. "We have no issues."

"I feel like I'm not doing my job," I told C.J. one day after court. "I feel like I should be getting in there more, should be going to trial."

"I hate to break it to you, but this *is* your job," she said. "Haven't you figured out that the real work takes place out here? If you're going to trial, usually it's because someone's fucking up."

***

BETWEEN HEARINGS, C.J. would often hang out in the courtroom lobby chatting with a group of bailiffs and district attorneys about baseball or football or their most recent fishing trips. They would pass their phones around, showing off photographs of a recent catch, discussing with obsessive detail the places and times they fished, the rods they used and flies they selected.

"You ever fish?" C.J. asked one afternoon as we loaded our bags into our cars in the parking lot of the public defender's office. The trunk of her SUV was strewn with waders and fly boxes and rod cases.

"Not really," I said. "A couple times when I was a kid."

"Well, not trying to tell you how to live your life or anything, but you really should," she said. "It's a vital but untaught part of criminal defense, in my opinion."

That's how I began to join C.J. after work and on weekends, at Pyramid Lake an hour north or along the Truckee River that ran through town. At her suggestion I purchased a nine-foot graphite trout rod that broke down into four pieces, which all fit pleasingly into an aluminum tube. The handle was soft cork, the rod light and lively in my hand; a flick, and the fly was out twenty-five feet over the water, the gauzy feathered wings of the lure alighting on the surface as delicately as a mayfly.

I practiced my cast in my apartment parking lot after work, mimicking the motion of the old men on the instructional videos C.J. sent me, the steady rhythm of the rod like a metronome, until I could hit a No Parking sign from forty feet away. I learned to identify the louvered wings of an elk hair caddis, the stubby emerald of a soft hackle bead head, the scraggly beard of a crystal leech, the punky spikes of a parachute midge.

That spring I spent hours on end in frigid river water untangling birds' nests of monofilament, lines snagged by driftwood and willow stands. C.J. taught me when fish weren't biting because of the light, or because I was using the wrong fly, or because the water was too silty or too clear.

And a few months later I was gathering around the bailiff's station with Neil and the rest of them before court, showing off pictures of my first rainbows and browns, laughing at some story of a missed mammoth cutthroat trout, before we returned to the work of bartering lives.

TEN

IT MUST HAVE been late that spring when I first heard the name Anna Weston. A brief mention on the local news broadcast:

In other news, Reno police are investigating a missing person report, the newscasters told us. *Thirty-year-old Anna Weston . . .*

She was only five years older than me, close enough in age that we might have gone to school together once, I thought. A graphic with identifying information flashed onto the screen, and then a photograph. She was young and beautiful, chestnut hair and perfect straight teeth, blue eyes. Her cheeks ruddy above a pink hooded sweatshirt.

A brief description, the number of a witness hotline, and then the next story about the year's snowpack and the corresponding reservoir levels, about the continued decline in home prices or the junior college transfer expected to start at quarterback that weekend.

In other news, it's been three days since local woman Anna Weston was last seen leaving a South Reno gas station . . .

In other news . . .

In other news . . .

ELEVEN

"**HEARD YOU'RE MEETING** with Hadley this afternoon," C.J. said one morning, sipping at a Starbucks cup. I was reading over my files on the other side of her desk; I'd found it was easier than walking over from my office every time I had a question.

"Where'd you hear that?" I asked, a bit annoyed. It was May now, and I'd been at the job for seven months—long enough to feel like I didn't need someone constantly looking over my shoulder. She shrugged, then returned to her computer screen where she was shopping for new fishing waders.

"We're supposed to talk about Alder," I said. "DUI Causing Substantial Bodily Harm."

Drew Alder's case had been delayed several times—I'd requested a continuance so that an investigator could be assigned to interview witnesses, hoping for any sort of defense. I'd scoured the police reports and case law, but the case seemed hopeless.

"So?" she asked. "What's your play?"

I had prepared to argue the few tenuous legal issues that I'd researched when I met with Neil that afternoon, but thought better of telling C.J.

"Thought I'd take your advice and beg for something less than the maximum," I said.

"Good strategy," she said, still staring at her monitor. She began cleaning her teeth with a fingernail, then stopped abruptly.

"Just as a heads-up, you should be prepared for some . . . bullshit," she said.

"Bullshit?"

"You know," she said ambivalently, scraping at a lower incisor. "You're still the new guy, so he's going to fuck with you a little. Let you know who's boss. Standard alpha male bullshit."

"So he's going to, what—try to kick my ass? Insult my manhood?" I'd picked up on C.J.'s way of talking around things, of speaking in vague terms that highlighted my ignorance.

"Well, Neil likes to do this thing with the new guys—he did it with Melissa when she started up, and he did it with Lance, too," she said. "He has this little basketball hoop in his office."

"OK?" I said, picturing the toy basket I'd had in my undergraduate dorm room. "So what?"

"So what," C.J. said. "So, he's going to give you a shot, and if you make it, you get what you want. Maybe dismiss a count, or stipulate to minimums. If you miss, he maxes your guy."

"I'm supposed to make a jump shot to save ten years of a kid's life?" I said.

"Yeah," she said, and laughed. "Fucked up, right?"

"It's malpractice," I said, turning toward the door. "I'll file a bar complaint if he tries that shit."

C.J.'s mouse abruptly stopped its clicking. When she looked around the screen at me, her eyes were narrowed in the way I'd seen once or twice in court by then, when a district attorney strayed from an agreed-upon plea negotiation or when a witness went sideways on the stand. She stood, then walked across her office to close the door.

"Listen," she said, returning to her chair. "I'm *trying* to help you out. But you don't seem to understand that."

I began to protest, but C.J. held up her hand.

"There's a lot to *this*," she said, waving her hand over her office, seemingly encircling what resided not only inside but outside—the courthouse across the street six stories below, the downtown casinos and weekly motels, even the desert range stretching out to the east. "It doesn't come naturally to anyone, as far as I can tell. But it isn't easy to say out loud, sometimes. Does that make any sense?"

In the months I'd been a public defender, I'd found it hard to articulate what I'd seen and learned to other people, to Jasper and Natalie when we met up on weekends or to my parents when I talked to them on the phone. I'd felt myself editing out the most difficult details from these conversations—the burgundy bruises across a child's back, the cry from the courthouse gallery when someone's son was sentenced to twenty years in prison.

"Yeah," I said. "It makes sense."

"You file a complaint against Neil, and two things are going to happen," she said. "The first thing is that the Nevada bar will dismiss the complaint, because it's not provable. Even if it *was* provable, he'd get a written reprimand and we'd be right back where we started. The second thing that would happen is that you'd get blackballed, not just by Neil but by every DA in that office. That means no plea deals. And not just for this guy," she said, pointing to the Alder file open in my lap. "But for everyone on your caseload. That means every case gets set for trial, and all the rest of your guys go to prison for a lot longer than they would have if you hadn't made that complaint."

She exhaled. A weariness seemed to settle over her. She reached across her desk for the Alder file. When I handed it to her, she began skimming the few pages of memos that I'd written, summarizing the weak legal arguments I'd been preparing for my meeting with Neil.

"He's bringing you in to fuck with you," she said. "He's just making a point. He doesn't care about this case, but he knows you do."

"What's the point he's trying to make?" I asked.

C.J. shrugged.

"The same point they're always trying to make. That they hold all the cards."

"I'M SORRY," THE receptionist said when I arrived at the district attorney's office that afternoon. "Mr. Hadley is in a meeting with Mr. Waldren. He'll be just a few minutes."

I took a seat in the waiting room, having already been warned by C.J. to expect a fifteen-minute wait. The DA's office was in a new county building attached to the courthouse. The vacant lobby was devoid of the old-milk and antiseptic smell that haunted the entry of the public defender's office; the wood molding was unchipped, the carpets were unscuffed and unstained. As

I waited, the black glass eyes of a taxidermied mule deer stared at me from the wall across the room.

When Neil opened the security door into the lobby twenty minutes later, he was already shaking his head in feigned apology.

"Sorry," he said, leading me down a hallway of office doors emblazoned with the names of prosecutors that I recognized from courtroom dockets and office gossip. Taveres. McConnelly. Johnson. Goodwin. "Got stuck in a meeting with the boss."

He ushered me into an office that was—like Neil himself—a carefully curated presentation of an image. I noticed a framed photograph of Neil holding an iridescent rainbow trout up to the camera; another of Neil leaning against a split-rail post next to a blond woman and two young children, everyone in matching blue jeans and crisp white collared shirts. His suit jacket was hung neatly from a wooden hanger against the wall, and his desktop was empty except for a single red file labeled "*State v. Alder, Andrew.*" It was as if the office were a set designed to capture the idea of a prosecutor's office. Across the room, I spotted the miniature basketball hoop mounted over a garbage can.

"So," he said, leaning back into his chair. "You want to talk about Alder."

"Actually," I said, pulling a file from my bag, "before we get to Alder, I was hoping to talk to you about Keiferson."

"Keiferson," Neil said.

"Set for prelim next week."

Adam Keiferson was a two-time felon charged with Possession of a Controlled Substance. It was as unnoteworthy as they came—C.J. had already assured me that Bartos would send him to prison for the standard sixteen-month maximum, no matter what the defense attorney or the prosecutor argued. Neil seemed momentarily caught off guard, but recovered quickly.

"Sure," he said, swiveling to the oak file cabinet behind his desk. He began flipping through files. "Give me just one second."

He pulled Keiferson's file and skimmed the charging documents and case notes. When he finished, he looked at me over the top of his glasses.

"So?" he said, waving the file at me. "What's there to talk about here?"

"Well," I said slowly. "I think there's a stop issue."

"A *stop* issue," Neil said incredulously.

To pull over a car or stop a suspect on the street, the police need to establish probable cause that a crime has occurred. In Keiferson's case, he'd rolled a stop sign on Virginia Street in front of a cop car—the only stop issue was whether the arresting officer had lied about Keiferson rolling through the intersection. And even if he was lying, C.J. had pointed out that there wasn't a court in Nevada that wouldn't believe the police officer over a two-time felon with three grams of methamphetamine in his ashtray. I could see Neil gearing up to tell me everything that was wrong with my argument, before catching himself.

"Tell you what," he said. A smile crept into the corners of his mouth. "See that hoop over there?"

I looked across the room toward the toy basketball hoop over the garbage can. Neil slid open the top drawer of his desk and removed a yellow foam ball the size of an orange.

"One shot," Neil said. "You make it, I'll drop Keiferson to a gross misdemeanor. You miss, and he pleads to the felony."

Neil eased back into his chair with a contented smile as I feigned first surprise and then internal conflict.

"This is fucked up," I said. I forced a laugh.

Neil shrugged, then rolled the yellow ball across the desk to me.

"He's guilty anyway," he said. For the first time he seemed genuinely friendly, like we were in on something together. "What do you have to lose?"

I held the ball in my hands, thinking about what it meant. Sixteen months. I bounced it once or twice in my palm, trying to get the feel of its weight.

"For a gross?" I said.

"Yep."

Then, without saying anything more, I aimed the ball at the hoop and threw.

The ball seemed to hang in the air, and for a moment I was afraid it might actually go in. When the ball bounced off the backboard, grazing the rim, Neil and I both exhaled loudly.

"Sorry, buddy," Neil said. "Thought it had a chance for a second there."

I slumped in my chair, assuming a posture of defeat. Neil rolled his shoulders contentedly in his chair.

"So," he said. "We done here?"

I picked up the leather attaché and began to leave, then stopped.

"We forgot Alder," I said.

"Right," Neil said distractedly, still bloated with the victory of the missed shot. "What about him?"

"Well," I started slowly, as C.J. had instructed. This is what I had come for, but being impatient now could waste it all. "He's a good kid. No priors, has a job . . ."

"What're you looking for?" he asked, still looking in the direction of the toy basketball hoop.

"Drop one count, no objection to probation?" I said, leaning in.

Neil glanced briefly at the red file on his desk, then flipped a hand in my direction as if he were tossing a coin to a peasant.

"Yeah," he said. "I'll do that."

As he walked me back to the lobby, Neil clapped me on the shoulder amiably.

"Word of professional advice," he said. "Work on that jump shot."

TWELVE

THE NEXT DAY I convinced Drew Alder to plead guilty to the single felony charge of Driving Under the Influence of a Controlled Substance Causing Substantial Bodily Harm—an easy job, considering the alternative: irrefutable evidence of guilt, sympathetic victims in the form of a mother and child with serious injuries, Neil arguing for massive jail time at sentencing.

"Does this mean he's going to prison?" Drew's mother, Carla, had asked while he signed the guilty plea in my office.

"It's always a possibility," I'd told her. "Though I think we have a *very* strong case for probation."

By the time Alder's sentencing hearing arrived two months later, I'd already handled dozens of sentencing hearings in front of Bartos. Most of these cases had been negotiated by Melissa Tardiff, so I'd felt little ownership over them. C.J. had taught me how to collect mitigating information before sentencing hearings, to submit therapist's reports and Alcoholics Anonymous sign-in sheets and employment verification letters. Or, in the absence of these, in the language of the court that I'd begun to speak, to simply ask Bartos to give a guy a break, because life was hard.

Now, I was finalizing my notes for Alder's sentencing hearing, one of the first pleas I had negotiated myself and by far the most serious. I wrote out a series of bullet points to support my argument for probation: Age. Intoxication. Lack of criminal history. Contrition. Likelihood of success under the supervision of a probation officer.

Despite the soundness of these arguments, I had a nagging sense of foreboding. My heart tensed as I pictured myself at the defense counsel table next to Drew. My breathing felt irregular. The edges of my vision began to blur and constrict.

I stood abruptly from my desk and walked across the office. If a panic attack like this hit while I was in court, I would need something more than a few bullet points to save me—it could be the difference between probation and prison for Drew.

I printed my notes and walked down to the office bathroom. Looking into the mirror, I cinched my tie and straightened my suit jacket. I imagined Judge Bartos at his bench, the injured mother and child in the gallery behind me. I closed my eyes and tried to conjure Drew's pimply face in the mirror next to me, his sad thrift store formals, but nothing came. I left the script on the lid of the bathroom garbage can and jogged down the hall to my office. When I returned a minute later, I had Washington's head tucked under my arm like a football, his white plaster flaking off onto my suit jacket.

I placed the head on the counter next to me. It wasn't much of a stand-in for Drew—thicker in the face, bald, inanimate. But I could imagine Drew sitting at the counsel table next to me now, the physicality of him, the effects of his proximity.

"Better, right?" I asked the head.

The bathroom smelled of industrial cleaner, and the fluorescent lights cast unflattering shadows over my face, making my nose look longer than it was, highlighting the dark circles under my eyes. I removed my watch and set it on the edge of the sink, taking note of the time. Eight twenty.

"Good afternoon, Your Honor," I read from the first line of the script. "Santi Elcano from the Washoe County Public Defender's Office on behalf of my client, Andrew Alder." It was the stock introduction that I had used at the beginning of literally every hearing I'd done, but I suddenly didn't trust myself to even remember my own client's name.

"Good afternoon, Your Honor," I repeated. Washington's chalky face stared back at me. "Good afternoon, Your Honor. Good afternoon."

***

I WAS STILL tweaking the script the next morning—just a few hours before Alder's hearing—when I heard a knock on my office door. C.J. stuck her head through the doorframe and looked curiously at Washington's head, which was still facing me on the desk. She pinched her brow, wincing a bit, as if she was just realizing something.

"You have that sentencing this afternoon, Gato?" C.J. said. It was a nickname that she had begun calling me recently, after one court defeat or another. *You remind me of this cat I had when I was a kid*, she'd said. *A little black kitten—cute little fucker, but he used to keep walking headfirst into the sliding glass door.*

She stepped into the office and looked out my sliver of window down at the street corner below, and I remembered the first time that I'd seen C.J. in person seven months ago, talking to my psychotic client Joseph Milan. "The kid who ran over that woman and her kid."

"Alder," I said. I pushed Washington's head over to the corner of the desk.

C.J. turned away from the window and sat heavily in one of the two chairs across from me. She looked to where I had moved Washington, and seemed to be about to say something before stopping herself. Instead, she shifted her attention to me. I was trying to be polite, but I still had to read through the final version of my sentencing argument.

"Anything I can do for you?" I said, setting my notes down. I started to flip through a blue three-ring binder of documents that I'd submitted to the court in support of our argument for probation. Clean drug tests since the day Drew's mother had posted bail. Letters from high school teachers. Pay stubs from his job at a distribution center where he'd been working since high school. Attendance sheets to Narcotics Anonymous meetings.

"You shouldn't wear that suit today," C.J. said.

"What?" I asked. I was wearing one of the two suits I'd bought a few weeks before—a navy-blue two-button that I'd spent half a paycheck on but fit perfectly.

"Don't wear that suit today," she said again.

"What the hell are you talking about?" I said, abruptly closing the binder.

It had begun to annoy me, how C.J. would get suddenly cryptic like this. These non sequiturs that made sense only to her, little games she played for her own amusement. "What's wrong with this suit?"

"Nothing's *wrong* with the suit," she said. She reached over and palmed Washington by the top of the head, swiveling the bust so that it faced her.

"Can you not touch that?" I said. "It's an exhibit."

She took her hand off Washington's white dome, holding up her hands defensively.

"Look," she said. "You like that suit, right? I can tell. You've worn it a few times lately. You always seem—I don't know—a little happier when you wear that suit."

I started to shake my head in protest. I was self-conscious about having to continually cycle through the few professional clothes that I owned, and it irritated me to realize that she'd been keeping tabs.

"It's a nice suit," she said. "You look good in it. Just don't wear it this afternoon, OK?"

"Why shouldn't I?" I asked. "You just said it was a nice suit."

She didn't say anything for a moment; instead, she pinched her brow again in a way that suggested she resented having to say what she was about to say.

"I used to have this suit, OK?" she said. "Grey wool, cut like a diamond. Loved that suit. It was like, every time I put it on, I was bulletproof. I'd run through an afternoon calendar, then meet up for a date after work."

It was the first time she'd ever mentioned a romantic life, and we both shared a look, as if she'd broken some unspoken rule. When she finally smiled, it was a sad, tired expression.

"OK," I said. "So, what happened to it?"

"I wore it to this sentencing," she said. "Child abuse case, bad facts. My client got consecutive maximum sentences from Bartos. That was the last time I ever wore that suit."

We sat there in the morning light of my office, C.J. slumped in her chair across the desk from me. I looked down at my highlighted pages of notes, the handwritten annotations that lined the margins.

"It's not going to be a good day today," she said. "He fucked that woman up.

And her kid, too, for Christ's sake. Bartos is going to max him. You know that, right?"

I didn't say anything back. Somewhere now, Drew was at his mother's house getting ready for court. Shaving his pimply cheeks, slicking his hair back in the way he had for each of our office meetings. Buttoning the new shirt that I'd instructed him to buy.

"And the thing is, Gato," C.J. continued. "There's always a part of you that'll think of this bad day, about that kid sitting in prison, each time you put on that suit. Trust me. You'll hate it just a little bit, and it'll take you off your game when you need it most. It'll just have a little bit of that stink from today on it, forever."

C.J. looked at me apologetically. She knew she was watching me realize, for the first time, that Drew was going to prison that afternoon.

"You've got another suit here, right?" she asked. She looked around the room hopefully.

"Back of the door," I said.

"It's a nice suit," C.J. said, standing to leave. "Don't waste it on this."

She closed the door to my office behind her, and I was again left alone with Washington. The stacks of papers, the blue binder filled with copies of mitigation documents already filed with the court, suddenly felt like props, like a plastic knife used in the high school production of a Tennessee Williams play. They were merely background in a script whose outcome had been determined long before.

I locked the door, kicked my dress shoes off against the wall, and began changing.

As I did, I thought about Drew Alder and his mother at home. When I'd convinced Drew to sign his guilty plea, I'd told him we had a good shot at probation. It was the answer he'd wanted to hear, and it was the answer I'd wanted to be able to supply. I'd convinced myself of the fact so thoroughly, and been so encouraged by the spark of hope I'd seen in his mother's face, that I had somehow managed to overlook the fundamental facts of the case.

In Drew's file was a series of photographs that a police officer had taken on scene as the paramedics and firefighters worked to extricate the woman and her son from the crumpled car. The folded door that had pinned the woman's legs to the steering column. The child's car seat knocked askew in the back seat, the footwell littered with broken glass and stale Cheerios.

I flipped through the pictures now, the force of the accident suddenly brought back to life in glossy photographs. The woman's shirt stained to the hem with blood, the narrow blue ribbing of the paramedic's plastic intubation tube. The terrified eyes of the woman, the whites of the sclera streaked through with burst blood vessels. These were the images the judge would see before he sentenced Drew. And I also knew that the woman from the photographs, the one with the terrified eyes, would be in the courtroom as well.

Katelyn Dyer.

She had a name, I reminded myself. Katelyn Dyer would be in the courtroom, and she would speak to Bartos, because even if Neil wasn't objecting to probation, a victim is always allowed to address the court at sentencing. She would tell Bartos that she had been sure she would die there in that car that night, or worse—that her son would die—and the photograph projected in the courtroom, the glint of terror visible in her eyes, would prove the point. It would be so simple for Bartos to weigh these against the script in my pathetic blue notebook.

I picked up the telephone and dialed the number for Drew's mother, not sure exactly what I was about to do. I couldn't tell him to skip the court hearing. But I was also duty-bound to give my client an honest assessment of their case, and I hadn't done that. I'd told Drew that he would likely be sentenced to probation—that life as he knew it would remain the same, more or less. But that had never been true.

The phone rang on the other end of the line. I would just tell Drew I had made a mistake, I thought. I reminded myself that it wasn't *my* fault that he was in this position. I hadn't gotten in the car, hadn't driven drunk, hadn't run the stop sign. Hadn't confessed. For the first time, I began to hate him.

The phone continued to ring. I wasn't telling him *not* to show up, but if he left town . . . well, that would be his choice. And as a bonus, I thought guiltily, I'd be spared having to make the argument, having to see him handcuffed and led away to prison while his mother watched.

The phone rang twice more before his mother's recorded voice came on the message greeting. I nearly hung up, but brought the receiver back to my mouth. Whatever I was about to say would be easier to leave on a voicemail.

"This is Santi," I said. "I'm calling about Drew's sentencing this afternoon." And then, in so many words, I told her that if Drew came to court today, it would be the last time she would see her son outside of a prison visiting room for the next decade.

AT ONE FIFTEEN I was pacing the lobby in front of Bartos' courtroom. The room was filled with the usual families in their best clothes huddled up next to the person there for court. I saw Neil sitting on a bench next to a banker's box filled with the afternoon's case files, laughing with two undercover detectives. They were always easy to spot—the clothing was just a little too on the nose, a little too uncomplicated. Beards that were conspicuously unkempt, T-shirts with logos for mixed martial arts brands or motorcycle companies. Neil, on the other hand, always dressed well, and now he was in a royal-blue suit with light chalk lines and a pressed white pocket square. He caught my eye, then made a motion like he was taking a jump shot. I wanted to walk across the lobby and aim a fist through his Adam's apple.

When the bailiff emerged from the courtroom ten minutes later to call the afternoon's calendar, Drew still hadn't arrived.

"Hey, Counselor," I heard a voice say. Neil was leaning back against the wall, waving a red file at me. "Your boy Alder going to make it today?"

I made a show of looking around the lobby, then shrugged.

"Should," I said.

I noticed C.J. farther down the bench, talking with one of her clients—an old man with a wild white beard. They were both looking at a stack of papers on the man's lap—a guilty plea, I guessed—and C.J. was pointing to a place on the lower half of the page. The man was shaking his head agitatedly, and C.J. briefly put a hand on his knee, patting him reassuringly, before pointing back to the page.

When the bailiff called the afternoon's first case five minutes later, Drew was still nowhere to be found. From the back of the gallery a young woman about my age walked unsteadily down the aisle followed by Bill Owens, one of the private lawyers I recognized from a billboard near the airport. The bailiff held open the low swinging door that separated the gallery, and the two shuffled over to the defense table. From the bench, Bartos was leaning back in his chair staring out the window, as if already contemplating the great balances of justice.

"Can you believe this horseshit?" C.J. whispered as I took a seat next to her in the front row of the gallery. "Owens has three cases, and he gets called first. I've got one plea and I'll be here until the end of the calendar, I guarantee you."

This was one of C.J.'s great peeves—the fact that private defense attorneys were treated better than public defenders. At the counsel table Owens was making his pitch to Bartos, who was still staring vacantly out the window. The attorney's arm was around the shoulder of the young woman, who was now sobbing uncontrollably. She was slim and pretty and had flat brown hair, and she had nice clothes on. A blouse and skirt and high heels. Something she might have worn to a job interview.

"Drew's not here," I whispered to C.J. She looked at me blankly. "Andrew Alder. The kid that . . . the DUI that almost killed that woman and her kid."

She reached over to give me a congratulatory pat on the knee.

"Good deal," she said. "Makes life easy for you, right?"

Neil was making a short statement to Bartos, confirming that the State was agreeing with probation for Bill Owens' client. The judge swiveled away from the window and regarded the woman for the first time.

"You tell him?" C.J. asked.

"Tell him what?" I said. I felt my face flush, thinking of the phone message I'd left a few hours earlier. I heard Bartos address the young woman, crotchety and indignant; I could tell by the tone that he was just going through the motions, scaring her a bit before giving her probation. He flipped through the sentencing recommendation from Parole and Probation, shaking his head.

"Not to show," C.J. said. "That's what I would have done."

"No," I said. I eyed the attorneys around us in the gallery seats. "Keep your voice down."

Owens and his client were on their way back from the counsel table, the woman still crying, but less now, Owens patting her on the shoulders, winking at her parents, who were waiting by the door leading out to the freedom of the lobby. I scanned the faces in the gallery again. Still no Drew.

A HALF HOUR later the clerk called Drew's case. I stepped into the gallery, alone, and took my place at the defense table.

"Well, Counselor?" Bartos said, stroking his grey goatee. He seemed to take in the scene, my blue binder with my script and my copies of the exhibits I'd submitted to the court. "Any idea where your client is?"

"No, Your Honor," I said. At the prosecutor's table next to me, Neil scribbled something in his red file.

"State?" Bartos said.

"State would move to have the defendant's bail forfeited and request that a bench warrant be issued for Mr. Alder's arrest," Neil said without looking up from his file.

"So ordered," Bartos said.

"Nice job up there, Counselor," C.J. whispered as I took my seat next to her. "Three years of law school for that?"

"She put up the house," I said, almost to myself. "For his bail."

"Not your problem," she said. She tapped a finger impatiently on her legal pad. Her client, the man with the white beard, looked equally impatient in the row behind us.

"So what happens now?" I asked. "She just loses the house?"

"Of course. But she knew that," C.J. said. "If he's smart, he'll get out of town. You told him to get out of Nevada, right?"

I shook my head.

"Well, if he has any brains, he'll get out of town anyway," she said. "They'll pick him up and bring him back for sentencing eventually, but it could be a couple years. And by then, with any luck, you'll be out of here and someone else will have to deal with this shit."

I thought now about the message I'd left on Alder's phone, wondered whether it might be used against me one day. I remembered what C.J. had said once about leaving as few fingerprints as possible in a file, and at the same time

I was disgusted with myself for worrying about this instead of about Drew and his mother.

"Finally," C.J. said when the clerk called the next case.

She and the white-haired defendant were making their way to the counsel table as I exited the courtroom. I pushed through the crowd of people at the entrance to the courthouse and started back toward the office. The afternoon sun baked against the boxy black suit, sweat running between my shoulder blades before pooling at the top of my underwear. Five minutes later I was back in my air-conditioned office, the lights off and the door closed, the blinds drawn over the skinny window. I tried to ignore the red light flashing on my office line, indicating a voice message was waiting. It would be Drew, or it would be his mother. There had been a mix-up, or car trouble. I would only have to make a call to the courthouse, to have the clerk stop the forfeit of his bail and quash the warrant, and we would be back in court for his sentencing in a week, the same catastrophic sentence waiting like the great guillotine of his life, the moment that would divide all else into "before" and "after."

I wanted only for the day to be done, for Drew to disappear forever or, as C.J. had said, at least long enough to be someone else's problem.

When I summoned the nerve to press "play," what I heard was not the sound of Drew Alder's voice, or his mother's. Rather, I heard a woman's voice, light and youthful, as if beamed in from another life.

"It's Ruth Walton again," the voice said. As she spoke, I remembered, guiltily, that I had never responded to her earlier calls. "Just wanted to tell you that I'm back home at my parents'. I have my certificate and everything. I know you're busy, so if I don't hear from you, then I'll see you at my sentencing hearing next month."

THIRTEEN

ABOVE ALL OF this, like an unsettling background noise, hung Anna Weston's disappearance.

She had been gone for nearly two months now, and still the police seemed to be no closer to finding her, or to telling us what had happened to her. We followed along as the newscasters grasped at possibilities, eager for anything to report. News reports were filled with interviews with friends and neighbors, with pleas from her family. We eyed her husband with suspicion as he stood alongside Detective Turner in the press conferences.

The husband was almost too perfect in his grief—his handsome face clean-shaven, his golden hair swept back, his hands folded at the waist of his perfectly ironed shirt. Wasn't this who we'd always been told to suspect?

Perfect families are always the most dysfunctional.

There was a comfort in that thought, wasn't there? If the perfect husband had been responsible for Anna Weston's disappearance, weren't all of us imperfect people somehow safer?

FOURTEEN

"**WHO YOU HERE** for?" asked a burly, tattooed orderly at the front desk of Lake's Crossing, the county-run psychiatric hospital. It was my first time visiting Lake's Crossing, and the facility had a dated, 1960s air: linoleum floors, safety glass, and mechanically locking steel doors.

"Joseph Milan," I said, pointing to the county ID hanging from a lanyard around my neck. "I'm his attorney."

I hadn't seen Milan since he'd been escorted screaming out of the office my first day on the job. He'd failed to appear for the misdemeanor case he'd had pending that fall, and had recently been arrested for impersonating a police officer. But instead of being detained at the jail while they awaited court, clients like Milan—people who suffer from meth-induced psychosis or just plain old psychosis—are shipped off to Lake's Crossing, where they're medicated to a state of catatonia that allows them to be legally prosecuted.

The orderly took my ID and placed it in a drawer in his desk, then provided me with a plastic tag that read "visitor." Inside, I heard a voice screaming unintelligibly, something full-throated and animalistic. I said a little prayer to my Xanax god, but already I could feel my pulse quickening.

The orderly pushed a button behind his desk, and I heard the now-familiar buzzer that accompanies the unlocking of institutional doors. Another orderly in nursing scrubs led me into a dining hall, where a dozen people milled around a series of metal cafeteria tables. They were all men, dressed in street clothes, and the room had a disturbingly normal feel to it.

"Milan!" the guard called over. A head popped up from a cluster of patients gathered around a chess board. "Attorney visit."

A lanky white man with buzzed silver hair stood from the table and started in my direction, carrying a small notepad.

"You my attorney?" he said. "New Melissa?"

"That's me," I said. He looked nearly unrecognizable from the person I'd seen ranting on Center Street almost eight months earlier, and I marveled at what a month of involuntarily administered psychotropic medication could do.

We shook hands, and he guided me to a vacant table near a window that looked out onto a concrete courtyard. The window was laced with chicken wire, but otherwise we might have been two friends at a restaurant table. Milan smiled benignly before rubbing his hands together.

"Well, then," Milan said. "Where to begin."

"Generally, I like to start by reviewing the charges against you," I said, diving into my usual spiel. I had expected to find Milan still in the throes of his delusions, based on the police reports that I'd read in which he had attempted to arrest several residents of the weekly motel where he was living; it seemed that the psychiatrists had had some success in medicating him back to reality. I unfolded his file and began to flip to the police report I had highlighted earlier. Milan blinked at me for a moment, seemingly astounded. Finally, the benign smile returned.

"I'm sorry," Milan said. He jotted a note on his notepad, then returned his attention to me. "But I think there's been a misunderstanding. You see, *I'm* here as *your* court-appointed attorney."

Now I was staring, perplexed. I looked around for the orderly who'd brought me over, as if he might provide some sort of external verification, but he was already back at the nurses' station, paging through a magazine.

"No, Mr. Milan," I tried. I could hear the uncertainty in my own voice, and I had the sudden, irrational sensation that I was lying. "I'm here to interview *you*. I'm your public defender—we have court next—"

He held up a hand, twisted his face into a distorted grin. His head corkscrewed to an angle that oddly projected sympathy, as if he suddenly felt sorry for me.

"I'm sorry to interrupt, Mr. Albin," Milan said. "But I just have to correct this delusion of yours before we move forward."

He adjusted the collar of his shirt, a worn blue oxford that I now realized bore a striking resemblance to the shirt I myself was wearing. Behind him, I noticed another man speaking to himself in a corner.

"My name," I said. "My name isn't *Albin*—"

"I need to be clear about this," Milan said. He began taking notes on the stenographer's pad that he'd brought to the table. "You're at a locked psychiatric facility..."

"I *know* I'm at a locked psychiatric facility," I said. "I'm here because I'm your public defender and we have court in—"

"I have to stop you again, Mr. Albin," he said patiently.

"I'm *not* Mr. Albin," I snapped. "My name is Santi, and I'm your public defender."

I gripped the yellow legal pad in my lap, covered in notes uncannily similar to the notes Milan was now taking on *his* pad. The noises of the room had grown suddenly louder. Intolerably loud. I touched the plastic visitor's badge that I'd been given at the front desk, as if it were my last tether to an old and dissipating reality.

"Fine," Milan continued, scribbling rapidly. "Well, whoever you are, you need to understand that you've been committed to a locked psychiatric facility. You were found ten days ago, in a state of what is known as methamphetamine-induced psychosis."

I glanced down at my notepad, saw the words *methamphetamine-induced psychosis* that I had written at my office that morning. I eyed the locked steel door next to the nurse's station. I suddenly had the sensation that the longer I stayed at this table talking to Mr. Milan, the less chance I'd have of being allowed to leave, and the more his reality would become true. That it would be Milan who would walk out that door, and into the parking lot, back to his life as a public defender. I stood abruptly, felt the eyes of two orderlies swivel in my direction.

"I'm sorry, Mr. Milan, but I'm going to have to cut our meeting short." Milan looked up from his notes.

"Mr. Albin," he said calmly. "We have court next week. As your attorney, I need to discuss the state of your case. Trial strategy."

His voice disappeared into the clatter of the dining room behind me. A beefy orderly watched me cautiously as I approached the door, my heart at full gallop, willing myself not to break out in a dead sprint for freedom. *They're going to let you leave*, I repeated to myself. *They're going to let you leave.*

I was about to push on the handle of the door when I heard the orderly's voice behind me.

"Sir," he said sharply.

Here it was, I thought. The moment I realized I had been living in a psychotic reality. *How many times have I already done this?* I wondered. *How many times am I condemned to repeat this delusion?*

I swiveled, trying to steady myself. Across the room, I saw Milan already deep in conversation with another inmate. I heard the familiar buzz, felt the mechanical clank of the door unlocking beneath my palm.

"Sir," the orderly said again, holding my county ID in his hand. "I need your visitor's badge before you leave."

FIFTEEN

"**WELL, FIRST YEAR** down," I said. The plaster bust stared mutely from its perch on top of Melissa Tardiff's bookshelf. "What are we doing to celebrate?"

I'd taken to speaking to the dead man on evenings like these, when the other attorneys and office staff had gone home for the night, when C.J. went off to who-knows-where, and the building was left quiet and abandoned.

"Fine," I said. "If you're in for the night, I'll see what everyone else is up to."

It was a stupid little joke, but as soon as I'd said it, I was set upon by an acute sense of loneliness. I'd been back for a year, and still felt as adrift as I had after law school. Was this really what I was destined to do forever? Did I really want to end up like C.J., sixteen years later?

Drink? I texted Jasper, before I had the chance to continue on that circuit of disastrous thought.

I sat alone in the empty room with the bust of the dead man, waiting for Jasper's reply, hoping to head off a series of intrusive thoughts by sheer will-power alone: A misdemeanor trial set to begin the next week. Neil Hadley, happy at home with the catalog family from the framed photo on his desktop. A year's worth of evidentiary photographs, blood and bone, torn clothing, bruises and ballistic tests.

Finally, the screen of my phone lit up.

Nine p.m.?

An hour later I was waiting for Jasper at a bar that served overpriced cocktails in half-pint mason jars at tables made from upcycled barn wood. People wore dressed-down business clothes, slacks paired with bespoke sneakers and expensive-looking T-shirts. We usually met up at dive bars like the Oasis and the Over Under, old Reno standards that had happily accepted our fake driver's licenses in high school, and I was surprised that Jasper had recommended something so trendy. But when he crossed the street toward the restaurant, he was in his same old jeans and white T-shirt, and I had the passing realization that he'd chosen this place not for himself, but for me.

I waved Jasper over to where I was nursing a happy-hour-priced beer, but he was intercepted by the restaurant hostess, an attractive woman with tattooed arms who kissed Jasper on the cheek in a way that seemed more like Midtown Manhattan than midtown Reno.

"Well, look at this," he said, spotting me at the bar. I held up my beer glass awkwardly. Jasper reached over the bar to shake hands with the bartender, a guy around our age with a perfect three-day stubble. Over Jasper's shoulder, I saw the hostess sneak another look in his direction before sliding a phone from her back pocket and poking at the glowing screen.

We stayed at the bar as it first filled and then emptied with the after-dinner crowd—bald men with sunburned scalps emptying pints of beer while women in business suits gathered around glasses of white wine and cocktails verdant with muddled herbs. After our third round I admitted to Jasper how over my head I was at the public defender's office. I told him about the millennium of prison time that the file cabinet in my office currently contained, and how all I wanted was to quit before I was forced to go into the courtroom again, to disappear into the ether like Melissa Tardiff.

"You're not going to quit," he said.

"Sorry, but I am," I said. In my year at the PD's office I hadn't really entertained the thought of quitting, but as soon as I'd said it out loud, it felt suddenly true, a solution perfect in its simplicity. "I could . . . I don't know. There's lots of other jobs. I could—"

"Fine," he said. "So you're quitting. What are you going to *do*—I mean, seriously? Be a corporate lawyer? A fucking ambulance chaser?"

I felt my face flush, and turned my phone over to check the time. It was nearly one in the morning.

"You're going to be fine." He said it with the confident matter-of-factness with which he had always said all things, the way that could convince you of something you knew to be false. "Just trust me."

"You think so?" I asked.

"Of course," he said. "Besides, you love it. It's all you talk about."

I wanted to argue that it was all I talked about because it was all I *had* to talk about. I'd been working so much that I'd hardly had time to go out on weekends or do much more than squeeze in a quick run in the hills before the workweek started again. But I also knew that Jasper was always eager to hear about my cases, to hear about the drugs and the sex and the criminal stupidity.

"That kid with the prescription bottles last week—you saved his ass. You know you did."

He was talking about James Gilly, whose drug trafficking case I'd managed to get dismissed after one of the prosecutor's witnesses went sideways during the preliminary hearing. Jasper was right: I'd never felt so low as in the worst moments of the past year, but I'd also never felt so much gratification as I did in the best.

I drained the last of my beer, then motioned to the bartender for the bill.

When the bartender arrived with the check, Jasper waved me off, leaving a neat stack of twenties on the bar before standing to leave.

"What are *you* doing these days, anyway?" I said, changing the subject. He'd quit his job at the bar a month earlier, and as far as I knew, he hadn't found another.

He waved a hand, shooing the question away like cigarette smoke.

"I'm doing my own thing," he said vaguely. "It's working out all right."

This was in the days before cannabis legalization, when anyone willing to accept the risk could make the two-hour drive over the Sierras to buy straight from the old hippies growing on the San Juan ridge. Jasper had started making these runs back in high school, a side project selling eighths to jocks and heshers in the locker room bathrooms, and I knew this was what he meant by "doing his own thing."

He glanced over a shoulder; the hostess with the tattooed arms had disappeared from her podium by the entrance, and a busboy was clearing tables while the last group of diners lingered over empty wineglasses.

"Everything OK?" I asked.

"Yeah. Sorry," he said. "Why don't you come over to my place? They're closing down here anyway."

JASPER DROVE US to his house, an unremarkable two-story in one of the many new neighborhoods built on speculation just before the economy fell apart. The rest of the houses on the block were large and dark, their driveways empty, their curtainless windows opening to abandoned living rooms and kitchens.

"I know what you're thinking," Jasper had said the first time I'd visited, unlocking a wrought-iron security door. "It's a friend of mine's—she's hardly ever here, so Natalie and I just kind of look after the place."

I followed him into a living area that was lit a dim yellow from a floor lamp that hung over the shoulder of a reading chair. The room felt claustrophobic despite its expansive size; it smelled like must and raw cannabis. The shutters on the windows were closed, the doorways leading out of the room black and uninviting. On a chipped coffee table, a suitcase-sized guitar amplifier sat with its back panel undone, a soldering iron and small metal clamps, kinks of colored wires running off small spools. Rewiring amps, soundboards, and other electronic equipment had been another of his father's "skills for the apocalypse" that Jasper had turned into a side business.

"Smoke?" he said, already crumbling a bit of weed into a cigarette roller.

"Why not."

I watched him pinch a filter into one end of the roller, then clamp it shut, feeding cigarette paper into the roller like paper into a typewriter. I'd come to look forward to these evenings with Jasper, a couple of idle hours before I returned to my apartment. There was something so enjoyably banal in those moments, a peaceful silence between us, a sense of unspoken comfort that I'd been missing ever since I left Reno for college.

He lit the joint and handed it to me. A pleasant heavy-headedness arrived with the first drag, a numbness spreading out into my fingertips. My mind drifted to Ruth Walton, who had failed to appear for her sentencing hearing that week. She had done everything the court had asked—had completed the inpatient substance abuse program, had found a job and been compliant with her pretrial services officer. She would have had her felony dismissed if she had only shown up, but instead she had a warrant out for her arrest. I wondered if she might still be at her parents' house, out on the Paiute reservation, if there had been some miscommunication, car trouble, or some other intervening event that had prevented her from showing up. I could send an investigator out to find her the next day, I thought. And then I found myself thinking back to my own trips out to the Pyramid Lake Paiute Tribe Reservation in high school, camping on the shores of the desert lake, great bonfires of pallet wood burning until the late hours of the night.

In the spring of my senior year a group of us had driven to the lake for a last camping trip before graduation, cars circled along the shoreline, a dozen of us drinking and screaming as a fire raged and then dwindled. Only a few of us were still awake when a football player named Reid Wilson staggered away from the orange circle of firelight, stripped, and waded into the lake. I heard the splash of his broad shoulders breaking the surface of the water—a sound identical to that of the half dozen others of us who left the bonfire to swim that night—and then he was gone.

A tribal police boat found Reid's body the next afternoon, nearly two miles from our camp. When we gathered at his memorial in the high school gym a few days later, we embraced and wept in the bleachers, trying to make sense of what had happened.

The memory was broken, suddenly, by the sound of the doorbell ringing. I checked the time on my phone, saw that it was nearly two in the morning. Jasper had already stood and was starting toward the door.

"Hold up," I told Jasper, alarm flooding in. I could already see the police officer at the door, was already imagining the list of offenses visible in plain sight from the doorway. I began to scoop the cigarette roller and its contents into the drawer of the coffee table, my mind working the calculations: the penalty for simple possession of marijuana (misdemeanor), the penalty for being under the influence of marijuana (a felony). I could be disbarred, could lose my job.

"Don't worry," Jasper said. He was already opening the door, ushering in a young white woman with dreadlocks. "This is Leah. Leah—"

"Good to meet you," I interrupted before Jasper could say my name. Jasper looked at me over the top of his glasses, then pointed Leah to a seat on the couch. I sat frozen with the cigarette roller in my hand, hyperaware of the fact that I was still wearing my suit from court that afternoon.

"Sure, man," Leah said. "Good to meet you, too?"

Jasper disappeared into the kitchen, then returned a few seconds later with a large plastic container lined with a dozen baggies filled with "a leafy green substance that, through my training and experience, I identified as marijuana," I imagined the police report would say. It's what the reports always said. The baggies and small electronic scale would be considered "indicia of sales," another felony. I wondered what else Jasper might have in the house, what other felonies might be looming over my head.

"I've got to head out," I said, standing to leave.

"Sorry," Jasper said. The woman looked up from a baggie that she was smelling intently, and shrugged apologetically. "You need a lift?"

"All good," I said. "Think I'm going to walk. It's nice out anyway."

I picked up my suit jacket from the back of Jasper's couch and started toward the door.

"Next weekend?" Jasper said.

"Sure," I said.

"Let's do it again, man!" the young woman called from the couch.

Jasper smiled, then abruptly stepped over and embraced me, the smell of tobacco heavy in the canvas of his jacket.

I heard the metal rattle of the security door clanging behind me, and then I was out in a suit and tie at two in the morning, the perfect buzz going, the lights of downtown Reno glittering like flakes in a gold pan before me.

SIXTEEN

ANNA WESTON HAD been missing for six months and there hadn't been a single significant development in the case. Rather than fade away, however, her story only seemed to gather energy, to build like a desert thunderstorm. She was a regular installment on the nightly news, a segment as reliable as the weather or sports, her image projected in the corner of the screen as the anchor spoke.

Still no updates in the case of Anna Weston, the Reno mother who went missing...

Coming up next, a plea from the family of Anna Weston for any information...

Nearly six months after the disappearance of Anna Weston, and still...

THE MEDIA HAD settled on a photograph, as if by some unspoken consensus. The collage of images that had accompanied the earliest news stories—a formal portrait from her wedding, a snapshot from a backyard barbecue, another on a waterfront dock in which she held a glass of white wine—had been edited down. Now each newspaper, each television station, each Reno Police Department flyer, used only a single image.

In it, she was backgrounded by the yellow angle of a doorframe, a glint of light from somewhere in the kitchen behind her. Her hair was straightened and parted carefully, the waviness in previous photos ironed away. A thin gold necklace hung over a black sweater. Her smile was still just a bit off-kilter, a detail we recognized from the other pictures, the ones that weren't used any longer. She might have been leaving to an office party or a wedding rehearsal.

That was the image that haunted us from posters and billboards and social media posts. In the candlelight vigils held at local high schools, and in the green ribbons that had begun to appear around town.

"Think they'll ever find her?" I asked C.J. as we drove to the jail one afternoon for client visits. We'd just passed another of the billboards, Anna Weston's face beaming down at us before it was replaced with an advertisement for a fast-food restaurant.

"Her?" she asked, nodding toward where the sign had been. "Alive? Is that what you're asking?"

I'd never thought of Anna Weston as anything *but* alive, I realized. She'd become a fixture in my small life, as constant and alive as C.J. or Jasper or Judge Bartos.

"Yeah," I said. "I guess so."

"Not a fucking chance," C.J. said.

THE LONGER ANNA Weston was gone, the more we came to know her. Through special news reports we learned that she had been in the honors society in high school, that she had met her husband at a sorority event at the university. Friends and family told us she was a patient mother, a well-liked physician's assistant at a local clinic, a generous friend, and supportive sister.

But people also began to whisper—that there had been trouble in the marriage. That there had been another woman, or another man. That there had been financial difficulties. That she had been erratic at times, or prone to depression. She could have run off with a lover, or wandered off into the desert and ended her own life.

We began to parse the subtext of the weekly pleas issued by Anna's mother. We noticed that she no longer addressed her daughter directly, no longer asked for her safe return. Instead, she asked only for information. *Any* information.

We could feel the police grasping at straws, the desperation that had settled over their search for Anna Weston. They pleaded with us, nearly begged. They offered cash rewards, first one hundred thousand dollars, and then a quarter of a million dollars, for "any information on the whereabouts of Anna Weston or leading to the arrest of her abductor."

Rob Turner—the detective I'd cross-examined in several preliminary hearings over the past year—had been tasked with talking to reporters, updating them with the information that there was no new information. He was never identified as a homicide detective, as if to deny the unspoken probability that, as C.J. pointed out, Anna Weston was almost certainly dead. That she had almost certainly died terribly. We all knew this, though we clung to the other improbable option: that she was alive, that she needed only to be found. As if she had merely been misplaced, as if we might discover her, alive and unharmed, in a place we'd simply forgotten to look.

We latched on to the small bits of information we did have. In the security footage from the gas station where Anna Weston had last been seen, the shadowy image of a pickup pausing momentarily in the background, the brake lights flaring grey in the black-and-white security video, before vanishing into the night. Was there some meaning to be found in the flash of a brake light?

Time continued to pass, and still she remained a ghost.

SEVENTEEN

MY SECOND YEAR, distilled: the legal representation of another couple hundred defendants of all ages and races and genders; the consumption of an array of alcoholic beverages with C.J. to celebrate or commiserate in a week's work; clients dragged from a courtroom in handcuffs or crying with relief; the regular refilling of my Xanax prescription; afternoon runs in the Reno foothills; more cocktails, or cannabis, or just a bit of a Schedule 1 narcotic from the end of Jasper's car key; the occasional weekend fling after the bartender announced last call.

I learned which cases were winners and which were losers. When to take a case to trial because you could beat the DA based on the facts and the law, and when to take one to trial just because the prosecutor needed to know you were willing to make them do the work. I learned which DAs would dismiss a case because my client had been profiled, and which ones would add a gang enhancement any time three Black men were in the same car together.

I came to look forward to hearings like Drew Alder's, when clients simply never showed up. They failed to appear because they forgot they had court, or because they were high and didn't want to get drug tested by the judge, or because they and everybody else knew that if they showed up, they'd be sent to prison. Once a client failed to appear because he had died, I later learned—two days before, he'd driven his car into the side of a Mediterranean restaurant and been ejected through the front windshield onto a table of baba ghanoush and dolmades. No matter what the reason was, I loved these cases the most because

I simply wrote the letters *FTA* in the hearing memo and the case was closed and removed from my file cabinet.

Things were happening that I was aware of only in the most hazy and imprecise sense. During the days I swam in a morass of violence, illegality, and vice. During the nights I did everything I could to forget that the day had existed. It was from this duality that a new marker began to emerge—the person I had been before the public defender's office, and the person I would now always be.

I was twenty-six years old.

I BEGAN TO look for what C.J. called *good losers*: defendants with long criminal records and defenseless cases. Clients like Dwight Martin, a sad old meth addict who'd been caught on camera throwing a cinder block through a pawnshop window at four in the morning to steal a purple electric guitar. These were the cases that made for good courtroom experience, where a loss at trial would result in roughly the same outcome as a plea negotiation.

"You're looking at a felony burglary," I told Dwight over the videophone the first day we met. "But to be honest, with your history the DA isn't going to offer you anything on this."

"Nothing?" he said. He scratched anxiously at his close-cropped grey hair. "I'll plead to a gross misdemeanor right now. Stip to the max. You can tell him that."

I could tell that Dwight had been around long enough that he spoke the language, so I spoke the language back.

"I already tried," I told him. "She's offering to plead straight up, free to argue. Same thing we get if we take it to the box."

"Really?" he said. Behind him on the screen a bailiff escorted another inmate back to the holding cell. "She really ain't going to offer *anything*?"

I shook my head apologetically. It was true, of course. But C.J. had pointed out early on that it was a great case to get trial experience with—a full felony jury trial with no real stakes. I also knew that I hadn't tried as hard as I could have for a better deal, something that might at least shave a month off his inevitable sentence.

"You need to get in there, Gato," she'd said. "It's like losing your virginity.

You don't want your first time in front of a jury to be with a client who might actually be innocent, do you?"

"I don't say this often," I told Dwight. "But we don't have much to lose by going to trial."

He sat there for a second on the other side of the screen, just a few stories below me in the courthouse holding cell, as if considering his options before realizing that he had none. The oversized prison jumpsuit drooped off his shoulders, the phone held limply in a hand shackled to his waist. Behind him, I heard a guard shout the name of another in-custody defendant. I looked down at my next case file, one of five set for that afternoon, and scribbled a few notes on the cover.

"All right, then," he said, shrugging. "Let's take it to the box, then. Fuck it."

IT WAS A short trial. The next morning we met Dwight in the holding cell behind Judge Bartos' courtroom, where he changed into the thrift store suit and shirt that C.J. had selected for him from the public defender's office client wardrobe.

"So, what do you think?" he said as we started toward the empty courtroom. His limp grey hair had been freshly trimmed at the jail the night before, as C.J. had instructed. His usual white stubble was gone, and his cheeks were boyish. "Do I look like an innocent man?"

C.J. looked him over, then nodded approvingly.

"Well, Dwight," she said. "If they convict you, it's not because you don't look good."

We picked a jury and finished opening statements before the lunch recess. Bartos seemed bored to the point of near-unconsciousness, stirring every once in a while to check his email on the monitor at his bench or whisper something to the court clerk.

I stumbled through a short opening statement that stressed the State's high burden of proof and Mr. Martin's right not to testify in his own defense. Neil called only two witnesses—an RPD detective and the owner of the store Dwight had broken into. He showed the surveillance video of Dwight throwing the cinder block through the store window, grabbing the guitar, and fleeing.

Immediately after, he played a video of Martin confessing to the crime during an interview with the detective. By three that afternoon I had cross-examined the State's witnesses, made a few objections, and given a closing argument that began with the line "What *is* reasonable doubt?"

As Neil began to replay the video of Dwight breaking the store window during his closing argument, juror number five—a woman in her midsixties wearing a San Francisco 49ers' T-shirt—nodded off in the second row. The jury was no longer taking notes; they just looked ready to be handed a verdict form.

"Nice job, Gato," C.J. whispered to me during Neil's rebuttal argument. "I think a couple might still be awake."

She was kidding, but I'd gone for broke in my closing argument, and at least *one* juror might be wondering whether they could be *sure* it was Dwight in that video. At least one juror would consider the heavy burden the State had to prove their case beyond a reasonable doubt. What had once seemed like a sure loser could very well result in a hung jury, maybe even an acquittal. There *had* been doubt, hadn't there?

After Neil's rebuttal Bartos read the jury their instructions and sent them to the deliberation room. The attorneys were told to stay near the courthouse in the event the jury had any questions, and just like that, Dwight was again handcuffed and led back to his holding cell in the basement of the courthouse, and C.J. and I were back out in the afternoon sun.

We hadn't even walked the four blocks back to the office before I felt my phone buzzing in my pocket. It was Marcia, the court clerk.

"Jury's back," Marcia said.

"What's the question?" I asked.

"No question," she said. "They have a verdict."

I stopped abruptly in the middle of a crosswalk, stunned. A car honked its horn.

"Ah well," C.J. said. I didn't even have to tell her. "You kept them out for . . ." She checked her watch. "Fifteen minutes, at least."

She pointed up to the cobalt sky above us, grinning.

"Somewhere up there, Clarence Earl Gideon is smiling."

EIGHTEEN

I WAS OVER AT Jasper's house one afternoon during that spring of my second year when he introduced me to Caroline, an ER nurse at Saint Mary's Hospital. I had been off work long enough to finish a second beer, which meant just long enough to forget the day behind me but not long enough to begin worrying about the next morning. When Caroline followed Natalie into Jasper's backyard, she was still wearing a green set of scrubs, her blond hair pulled back into a loose ponytail, sipping at a beer that Jasper had handed her.

"Natalie says you're a lawyer," she said, after Natalie had abandoned us on the patio. It was May, the afternoon air still cool, Caroline slouched down in the faded plastic patio chair as if melting under the last bit of afternoon sun.

"Public defender," I corrected her. Ordinarily, it was the other way around—me correcting a client when they said, *This sounds serious. Think I should hire a lawyer?* But now I felt the need to distinguish myself from just another stuffy suit out of law school doing document review and billing three hundred dollars an hour.

"Public defender," she said, trying out the words. She stretched her arms above her head, kicked her shoes off.

I shrugged, then tipped my beer back. I shook a cigarette from a pack on the patio table, the lighter spitting sparks before catching. I'd come directly from Bartos' courtroom, where my seventeen-year-old client had been sentenced to prison for four years. Caroline seemed just as distracted as I was; she kept checking her phone, then turning it off, checking it, then turning it off, the blue light of the screen flashing like a slow beacon.

"So?" she said. "Like, *Law and Order* stuff?"

"Yeah," I said. "I guess."

"You got that missing woman case?" she asked hopefully. "Anna something?"

"They've got to catch someone first," I said.

"Oh. Right."

The screen of her phone lit up, and I watched her type something quickly into the blue bubble of a text box before switching off the screen. I guessed she was texting Natalie inside the house, pleading to be rescued.

"Anyway," I said, trying to save the conversation. "If they ever catch the guy who did it, yeah, it could come to our office. But there's an attorney, Dan, who handles all the murders."

I took another drag from the cigarette, another pull from my beer bottle. She looked pretty, I thought, sitting there slumped into the patio chair that was nearly the same faded green as her scrubs, squinting a bit with the exhaustion of the workday.

"OK," she said. "So I have to ask. Have you ever had a client that you thought might actually be guilty, but you had to represent them anyway?"

I laughed involuntarily, nearly coughing beer onto my lap. Caroline straightened in her chair. "What?" she asked coolly. "What's so funny about that?"

"I'm sorry," I said. "It's just, I've been doing this job for almost two years, and I don't think I've had six clients who were actually *innocent*."

I felt bad for laughing—we both knew Natalie had been trying to set us up, and Caroline had been good-natured about it. And it was nice just to be talking to someone who wasn't a lawyer, or a client. Someone who wasn't looking for an angle, that I didn't have to jockey around.

"I didn't mean to laugh," I tried again.

"So what exactly is it that you do?" she asked finally. "I mean, if they're all guilty anyway . . ."

The easy answer lingered in my mind—the answer that I would have given when I was a law student, or the answer that I gave my parents each time we spoke on the phone. That public defenders keep the system honest. That the system is set up so that some guilty people might get away, but at least innocent people won't get sent to prison. All the old Atticus Finch bullshit.

"I don't know," I said instead. "I'm still trying to figure that out."

We were both quiet for a moment. Caroline picked absently at the label of her beer bottle, then reached over to my pack of cigarettes on the table between us.

"Who even smokes anymore, anyway?" she said, and smiled.

She tipped out a cigarette, then leaned in over the lighter. Her face glowed momentarily in the lighter's flame, long shadows casting off her nose and lips. She had a small mole on her left cheek and a barely perceptible scar at the corner of her eye, and I thought how well these little imperfections complemented her.

"What?" she said, looking at me suspiciously.

"Nothing," I said. "It's just, you probably think I'm an idiot. I don't even know what my job is."

She dragged deeply from the cigarette, holding the smoke momentarily before blowing it slowly out into the evening sky. She brushed her palms over the faded green of her hospital scrubs, then sat with her hands at her sides in a way that reminded me of the defendants in their jumpsuits sitting in Judge Bartos' jury box each morning.

"Nah," she said. "I get it. We get those cases a couple times a week in the ER. Car crashes, usually. Or suicides. Or just old people. You know, people that everyone knows aren't going to make it. But you still have to do the thing. You hook them up—CPR, defibrillator, the works. Everyone knows they're going to die, and you do all the work anyway, and then they die."

"That's grim," I said.

"It is," she said. She smiled sadly. "But you still have to do it. You still have to do the work."

We were both silent for a moment.

"You like it?" I said. "I mean, other than the times when you're trying to bring people back from the dead?"

She snorted a laugh. "Today my first patient was an eighty-six-year-old with severe vaginal discharge. The next guy was a diabetic with a necrotic abscess that I spent an hour picking dead tissue out of."

"Fuck."

"So yeah, I like it."

When they came out to the yard to find us both laughing, I saw Natalie give Jasper a look as if to say *I told you so.*

"We're thinking about heading to the restaurant for a couple drinks," Jasper said. "You in?"

Caroline looked down at her dirty scrubs, then shrugged.

"You up for it, Counselor?"

I DROVE ALL of us to La Vecchia, the Italian restaurant where Natalie worked. We took up an abandoned table in the corner of the bar where we stayed until long after the restaurant had closed, Natalie dipping occasionally behind the bar to mix another round of drinks while Caroline and I traded ER and courtroom stories. We spilled out into the street, the four of us along with a skinny waitress named Laura who had been drinking with us for the last hour. Jasper started in the direction of his house, his arm slung over Natalie's shoulder.

"Where's everybody going?" I called.

They turned back to find me standing next to Caroline, dangling a set of car keys in the air. Jasper's expression slid from surprise into recognition, as if he was intuiting what I was thinking.

"This a good idea?" he said.

"A great idea," I answered. By then the night had achieved a sort of velocity, and I wanted only for it to keep going.

Fifteen minutes later we were loaded back into my car, Caroline in the passenger seat next to me, and Laura, Jasper, and Natalie crammed into the back. Natalie passed around a bottle of wine she'd taken from the restaurant as we climbed the winding highway up the Sierras, until we crested the Mount Rose summit and began to descend into the blue-black valley of Lake Tahoe, the lights of Incline Village sparking at the water's edge.

I parked at a turnoff just south of town, and the five of us stumbled through the cool night air down a dirt path to the water's edge. Laura and I set to gathering a bit of wood, while the rest stood near the inky water passing what was left of the wine.

Soon we had a small fire going. The entire world beyond the firelight evaporated, and we were only there, Jasper childlike and familiar in the moonlight.

I watched him attempt a drunken handstand, Natalie bursting into laughter as he crumpled headfirst into the grey sand, the tinny sound of music warbling from the speaker of someone's phone.

I caught Caroline's eye across the fire. She smiled at me, and I knew then that we would end up together that night, just as she seemed to know it, too. It was all set in stone, agreed upon in that look. She slipped around the fire so that we were suddenly next to each other, the flames warming our faces while a chill gathered in the darkness at our backs.

"I can see why Jasper talks so much about you," Caroline said. Next to me, I felt a shiver run down her back, and she rubbed her hands together in front of the fire. She tipped the bottle of wine up, then flopped back onto the beach, her dirty-blond hair spilling across the cold sand. Across from us, Natalie and Laura were chasing Jasper down the shore, the sound of their laughter disappearing into the night beyond us.

"Because we get drunk together?" I said. I lay back next to her, both of us staring into the glittering starlight. I could hear her breathing, feel the small warmth radiating from her. "Because I drag you guys up to this freezing beach in the middle of the night?"

"Nah," she said. I felt her hand slide into mine, our fingers twining loosely. "I don't know. You both just seem . . . I don't know. Like kids again."

"That's it?" I said. From the darkness we listened to our friends' whoops bouncing through the granite boulders of the beach. She leaned in, and when we kissed, her lips were cold against mine.

"That's it," she said.

NINETEEN

THEY FOUND ANNA Weston's body in late June, a little more than a year after she'd gone missing. Two men four-wheeling through the tailings of the played-out gold and silver mines in the Virginia City highlands, stopping so one of them could piss. It was so close to Reno—five miles as the crow flies from where Anna Weston had last been seen—and yet it was remote country, a barren tangle of ravines and old mining roads climbing the west side of the range. They'd noticed a shred of clothing, a torn stretch of denim streaked through with rusty red that had blown down a drainage, one of a hundred they'd passed that afternoon, climbing steep inclines and making their way through a case of Coors. The men had only to walk to the edge of the dirt road to spot her, a leg twisting grotesquely out of an overhang a couple hundred feet up the hillside. They waited an hour to sober up, then called out to the Washoe County sheriff.

The story made its way to the courthouse before it hit the media, one of the on-scene deputies texting the news to a DA waiting for his afternoon calendar in the lobby of Reno Justice Court. No one should have been surprised, and yet everyone seemed to be. The news crackled through the lobby, from DA to public defender to bailiff. Even the judges appeared unsettled by this new unspoken thing coursing through the courthouse; during arraignments and sentencings they seemed distracted, preoccupied, at times nearly unaware of the men and women before them waiting for their fate to be handed down.

In the sky east of town, sheriff's and news helicopters jockeyed over the desert canyon. Police dogs from three counties combed the hills. Investigators took photographs of tire tracks, bagged crumpled water bottles and other bits of trash found nearby, zipped them into plastic bags and booked them into evidence. Already, the terrible artifacts had begun accruing.

By eleven that night all the local news channels were reporting from the scene, young field reporters in logoed station vests shivering in the cold night air a thousand feet above Reno. Behind them, police tape stretched awkwardly between service vehicles and juniper branches while sirened pickups wheeled in the desert night.

The next evening, the story of Anna Weston's murder made the Las Vegas news, and had even been picked up by several stations in Sacramento. For a second night newscasters broadcast from the crumbly desert road, the lights of the casinos downtown shimmering like stardust behind them in the last light of evening.

What was it that we felt that night, as our photograph of Anna Weston was transmitted across the West, as news anchors spoke her name? Was it pride, or something like it?

PART III

THE PROSECUTION'S CASE

AFTER OPENING STATEMENTS the prosecution begins their case. You're interested now, juror. Enough has been hinted at, promised, that you're intrigued to see what comes next, to see who can fulfill their promises.

Because they are first in order, the prosecutor is charged with establishing the setting, the characters, the basic reality that underlies all of the events.

But the prosecutor can't simply stand up and tell you, the jury, her version of the story.

The physical evidence—a toxicology report, a supermarket surveillance video, the murder weapon, a victim's bloody clothes—may be admitted only through witnesses, people who will testify to the evidence's source and its authenticity.

The prosecutor will have a strategy in calling her witnesses and admitting her evidence. As you listen to the witnesses' testimonies, as you see each new exhibit brought into the courtroom and carried through its mechanical process of admission into evidence, the prosecutor's argument might begin to feel scattershot; in your mind, these disparate parts might not yet feel like a cohesive story. But the prosecutor is crossing items off a checklist—each witness or piece of evidence satisfying an element of the crime she has alleged. She is setting her trap, laying her groundwork.

Here's how we know what the defendant did, the prosecutor is showing you. *This is where the crime occurred. These are the instruments he used. Here are the people he spoke to. Here are the things that he touched. This is how we know his guilt.*

TWENTY

"YOU DON'T KNOW how lucky you are to work in a building like this," Sarah says. She has come to meet me at the county courthouse for lunch, something we do once or twice a year. I smile, trying to stay in the moment, to not think about Michael Atwood's letter or about Greg Lake's case. She cranes her head back, admiring the courthouse's neoclassical flairs, the intricate marble detailing, oblivious to the bench of clients waiting to piss in a cup before their drug court hearings. "It feels like these walls hold so much . . . I don't know . . . *time.*"

"You get used to it," I say. She rolls her eyes at my cynicism.

"You know it's a beautiful building. When are you going to let me see you in trial sometime?" she says. "You've seen me lecture before."

"Maybe someday when I finally get a good case," I say.

When we first began dating, she invited me to sit in on one of her graduate seminars. During her lecture she was smart, articulate, and funny—a polished, heightened version of the person I went to bed with each night, but it was always still her. Still Sarah.

It's never been like that for me. Instead, when I walk into the courtroom, the person she married—the bumbling father, the caring husband—recedes into the distance. He is replaced by something ironclad, honed and impermeable. I know she would never recognize the person I have to be in here, in the courthouse, and she would realize she's always known only half of me.

We walk down a creaky wooden staircase to the first floor, the balustrades wobbly with age, the wainscoting scarred with a hundred years of damage.

"If these walls could talk …" she says, running her fingers across the chipped plaster.

"If these walls could talk, they'd probably scream," I say.

"Why would you say that?" she asks. "It's history."

She once enjoyed my sarcasm, but lately these types of comments seem to grate on her, as if they indicate a continuing slide from skepticism into bitterness.

"Sorry," I say. "Jesus. Just a joke."

She's defensive of the courthouse, perhaps, because of a recent initiative to tear the old building down. It's too outdated, the bureaucrats argue, the cost to renovate greater than just razing it and starting over. They're right, of course; it's one of the oldest buildings in Reno, a city that reconstitutes itself every few decades, whose very identity is its transience. The original courthouse facade is a Classical Revival, silvery limestone and Corinthian columns topped with a zinc dome, though the old building is now saddled by a hideous municipal wing added in the fifties to accommodate cheap new courtrooms as the city grew.

We have our own history here; Sarah and I filed our marriage certificate five years ago, the month before our daughter was born. It's also the same courthouse that made Reno famous in the thirties and forties for quick divorces, attracting the who's who of broken marriages. The writers Sherwood Anderson and Pearl S. Buck, the boxer Jack Dempsey. In 1956 Arthur Miller and Saul Bellow both stayed at the nearby Pyramid Lake Guest Ranch to meet the Nevada residency requirement for their divorces. Rita Hayworth came to Reno to get divorced *twice*. Surreally, General Douglas MacArthur, Dracula (Bela Lugosi), and Bugsy Siegel were all divorced in Reno, as was the surrealist André Breton.

More recently, it's the courthouse where a local pawnshop owner shot the judge presiding over his divorce case, and where Steve McCray, a prosecutor I worked with for eight years, shot himself on the front steps last Christmas. He's the second DA to kill himself during my time in office; I know four defense attorneys who've tried—explicitly tried, too, not the low-level drinking to death that's commonplace on both sides. Prosecutors just seem to be better at it.

This isn't the history that Sarah thinks of as she gazes up at the domed room of the rotunda, but it's my history. Now, the old courthouse is in disrepair, and like all things in Nevada the bulldozer has it in its sights. The zinc dome leaks, and you have to steer through a series of five-gallon paint buckets set out in the lobby to catch water during one of the infrequent rainstorms. A hodgepodge of architectural additions creates not just aesthetic but logistical and safety issues: Judges ride in the same elevators as the shackled defendants they are about to sentence; defendants walk past witnesses waiting to testify against them. Old court files are stored in a basement that has flooded several times over the decades, destroying evidence and paperwork, guilty pleas and murder weapons. Even the disused holding cells in the basement are carpeted in accumulations of pigeon shit.

As we make our way outside, down the limestone stairs, Sarah takes my hand in hers. She gives a little squeeze, and I manage to return the gesture.

If only you could know what I know, juror. That this is our judicial system incarnate: the stately veneer, the authority granted by history. Within the walls, rot. In the basement, excrement. *This* is the place where you are called to render justice.

TWENTY-ONE

LUNCH GOES ABOUT as well as most things between us these days—pleasant, courteous. We share a sandwich and ask about each other's days, carefully circling the subjects we fight about at home. The long work hours around a recent trial, Sarah's upcoming conference in Santa Fe, whether to visit her family in Indiana over Rosa's spring break. When I return to the office, it's with a sense of relief.

Today is one of the rare afternoons where the week's files have already been memo'ed, the perpetual list of client voicemails responded to. I still have a couple of hours before I need to pick Rosa up from kindergarten, so I consider how best to use the county's time.

The obvious answer would be to open Michael Atwood's letter waiting on the corner of my desk. I should get it over with, spend the afternoon dealing with whatever procedural or personal demands the letter might entail—a request for copies of his evidentiary file, a final plea for help or "fuck you" for having failed him. But this task feels too large, too daunting, so instead I collect the discovery I've received on Greg Lake's murder case—only a few police reports, witness statements, and autopsy photographs at this point—and drive fifteen minutes north to the Washoe County Jail.

The jail is built into the foothills north of Reno, in dry scrubland that had once been considered remote until the slow tide of stucco homes continued its creep outward. Now, the jail is practically in a neighborhood; across the street is a strip mall with bondsmen's offices, a car wash and an auto parts store, and then a string of cul-de-sacs and apartment complexes. I park in front of the jail lobby, a two-story building that might have been a corporate office but for the fact that it is surrounded by twelve-foot-tall fencing topped with razor wire.

The lobby is a current of movement—families and girlfriends arriving for afternoon visiting hours, green-clad deputies in their bulky Kevlar vests, social workers with county ID badges hanging on lanyards, a father at a video monitor holding a phone to his daughter's ear so that she can talk to a woman in an orange jumpsuit. I check in at the front desk, handing the clerk Greg Lake's file. He types Greg's name, scanning a finger across his computer screen, before jotting a housing unit number onto a blue Post-it note.

"You're on the Hill," he says. "Housing Unit Twelve."

I pass through the metal detector and the alarm sounds, but the clerk waves me through anyway. I stand in front of a large metal door with shatter-proof glass until I hear a loud clack; from a control station surrounded by protective glass a sheriff's deputy motions for me to enter, and suddenly I am inside the jail. I am in custody.

Before me stretches seventy-five feet of white industrial linoleum flooring and white cinder-block walls. The mechanical door closes behind me, and I get the same irrational surge of panic that I always feel at the jail. There is an implicit sense of trust in these people, that the deputies will let me out when I ask to leave. But I know it is only this—a trust in the system and in my place in it.

More doors, more clangs.

I arrive at a control room filled with black-and-white monitors and computer screens manned by yet another deputy in a green uniform and Kevlar vest, a black baseball hat pulled low over her eyes, a brown ponytail sticking out the back. The control room is surrounded on all sides by the same protective glass, which gives the deputy the appearance of a goldfish in a bowl, a cage within a cage. When she notices me, she clicks a button on one of the computers and points to a sliding door, and I hear the familiar clang.

In this next hallway are three inmates, dressed in dingy orange prison scrubs and plastic slippers. I quickly take in the men's faded blue tattoos, the gleam of the jail's fluorescent lights on their shaved scalps. The room smells of cold hamburgers and antiseptic spray, and I feel a compulsive desire to wash my hands, to scrub anything that makes contact with this place.

"Wall!" a deputy shouts from down the hall. The three men, in unison, halt their conversation and turn away from me, standing with their noses against the concrete wall. After I have followed the orange dashes past them, the men start again down the corridor, picking up their conversation where they'd left off. It is an almost religious hierarchy imposed by the guards—*you shall not look at the civilians*. I approach another inmate—an old man with a black-and-grey beard who might have been my grandfather—and he, too, turns to face the wall until I pass.

The orange path leads me to yet another hallway, this one long and winding, unbroken by security doors. This is the long walk to the Hill, a newer series of housing units set apart from the rest of the jail. Attorneys dread the long hike out to the Hill; the corridors are freezing in the winter and scorching in the summer, and if you're unlucky, the guard in the Area Control won't realize you're in there and you'll be forced to wait at a locked door for a half hour.

As I make my way through the concrete corridor toward the Hill, I hear footsteps approaching, and then suddenly I am in the long hallway with a half dozen inmates. There is usually a deputy with groups like this, but this time there isn't.

We all stop, a pregnant moment of recognition, the unspoken understanding of actual power, of my powerlessness in the moment, the inversion of the courtroom power structure. The difference between us, between our teams, couldn't be more obvious—the six of them in their county-issued oranges, me in my slacks and blue button-up. I glance up at the blinking security camera, assuring myself that they are watching, that help will arrive in time if I need it.

"Wall!" the inmate at the front of the line—a young kid with Sureño tattoos stretching across his biceps—suddenly calls out. The group shuffles out of the center of the hallway and against the concrete wall.

"Thanks," I say to the young man.

"Fuck you, bitch," he says under his breath as he passes. The inmate behind him, a bald, middle-aged white guy, laughs.

I try to commit the young man's face to memory. I may, after all, soon be appointed as his attorney. He may have power here, in this hallway, but not out there. Not in the courtroom.

WHEN I ARRIVE at Housing Unit Twelve, a guard points me to a small room filled with cleaning supplies. It is, I realize, the same room where C.J. and I spent so many hours with Michael Atwood.

I am reminded, briefly, of Michael's unopened letter locked away in my briefcase in the car. As I walk toward the meeting room, I half expect C.J. or Michael to be waiting for me, as they were so many times that year of the trial, but instead it is Greg Lake, smiling his dopey smile.

"Bet you didn't expect to see me again," he says sheepishly.

"Not for this," I say, holding up the file.

Greg shakes his head in an aw-shucks kind of way, as if to say, "Gosh darn it!" As if that file doesn't contain a man's life in it, and in this moment I hate him for his stupidity.

"You see the interview?" he says.

I nod.

"Kind of ran my fucking mouth again, didn't I?" he says.

"You sure did."

"Well, *fuck*," he says, staring at the wall. And then, as if remembering something, he unfolds a ratty piece of paper, smoothing it on his lap.

"I've been going to meetings again," he says hopefully. He slides over the paper, and I glance at the half dozen signatures on a Narcotics Anonymous sign-in sheet from the jail.

"That's great, Greg," I say. "But I'm not sure this is going to help us much this time."

He sighs, and for a moment we both sit there in the antiseptic light, staring blankly at the stacks of toilet paper and folded orange jumpsuits on the shelves of the cleaning room.

"I'm fucked on this one, ain't I?" Greg says.

I'm about to start my usual speech, about process and evidence and burdens of proof, but I stop myself. I realize that he's not asking me this question as his attorney, but that, somewhere along the line, we've become friends in our own sort of way.

"Yeah," I say. I put the legal pad down on a rack of paper towels in the cleaning closet. "We're probably pretty fucked."

He sits there for a moment, taking this information in.

"Well, if I have to do this," he says finally, "I'm glad it's gonna be you."

TWENTY-TWO

ON THE WAY back from the jail I stop at a convenience store before driving to Rosa's kindergarten. There is a six-pack in the back seat and I have twenty minutes to kill before I *have* to go in to pick up Rosa—before the school calls Sarah to tell her that I've once again neglected to pick up our daughter at the appointed time—and so I pop a can and pour it into an insulated coffee mug in the cupholder. The playground outside the school is empty, the swings whipping in the afternoon wind; on the radio station they're playing "Folsom Prison Blues," and when Johnny Cash sings *I shot a man in Reno, just to watch him die,* I can't help but laugh, thinking of Greg Lake in his bunk up at the jail. Another parent pulls in next to me, waving as she heads toward the front door, and I hold up the coffee cup in greeting.

The sky goes dim outside, parents arriving and leaving in the parking lot around me. When I finish the beer, I riffle through the leather briefcase, looking for a piece of gum or a breath mint before I go into the school. Instead, I find the envelope with Michael Atwood's name on it.

The woman who had parked next to me earlier returns to her car, her arms overflowing with a blanket and an insulated lunch box and various art projects that the kids have completed during the day. Behind her trails a toddler, barrel-chested and swaybacked, his round belly leading the way. The boy is crying, his dirty face red with anger. As she loads the boy into his car seat, the woman offers me a pained smile, the look of solidarity that all parents know. She leans closer toward my window, squinting into the glass, and it's only then that we recognize each other.

"Is that you?" Caroline says, brushing a swath of blond hair out of her face.

I roll down the window and smile. We both take quick stock of the other; she somehow looks the same age that she did a decade ago, despite the child crying at her side. There's a calm about her, the ugliness of our breakup evaporated with time, and I have a flashing memory of her naked body treading in a mountain river that first summer. At the same time I am acutely aware of what she must be seeing in me now, the softness that has settled in around my neck, the dark moons under my eyes.

"You're still working there?" she asks, as if reading my thoughts.

"Yeah," I say. "Still there. You still in the ER?"

"Oh, God no," she says. "That job almost killed me. I'm a school nurse now—scraped knees and stomach bugs."

I smile. She glances at the coffee cup in the center console of the car, as if she knows its true contents.

"How old?" I say, nodding to the boy.

"He'll be three in August," she says. "Yours?"

"Five."

Can she really be five years old? I think, even as I say it. It feels like only yesterday that Caroline and I last shared a bed, since we last made love in the fusty old downtown studio. *Can time really move in such large jumps?*

Behind her, the boy continues to wail at the car door.

"Gotta run," she says apologetically. "Meltdown. You know how it is."

She rests her hand for a moment on the door of my car, and something passes between us. Some shared understanding or memory.

"Glad we ran into each other," she says.

WHEN CAROLINE IS gone, I return to Michael's letter, which is waiting for me on the dash. I slide a car key into the fold of the envelope, a tear jogging down the crease, and before I can think better of it, I begin to read.

The letter is short, written in tidy block letters on a ruled piece of paper, as if Michael had been trying to approximate the formality of a typewriter:

> Dear Santi,
>
> It has been a long time since you have received a letter from me, I think. I hope that you remember me and my case. I was represented by

you and by Ms. C.J. Howard and Mr. Daniel Osterman in CR09-1857. I was found guilty of Murder in the first degree and sentenced to Death.

I know that you are a busy man and that you are no longer my attorney. I hope that you will be able to visit me at your earliest convenience at the Nevada State Prison when you are able to.

Thank you for your time.

[signed]

Michael Keith Atwood

When I get to the end, I read the letter again, this time staring into the words, trying to glean their subtexts. In a strange way, I have been expecting Michael's letter for a while now. He's been on my mind ever since his name surfaced in the paper earlier this month. The headline had said it all: "Anna Weston's Killer Withdraws Appeals, Asks to Be Executed." Under the headline was Michael's familiar face, blurred with age, the boyishness of his narrow face and ruddy cheeks hidden now by a week-old stubble, wrinkles at the edges of his mouth, his skin a ghostly white.

The last time I saw Michael in person was at his post-conviction appeal hearing seven years ago. That time it had been me on the witness stand for a change, being examined by his appellate attorney. I can remember looking across the courtroom at Michael from the witness stand, his attorney next to him holding up a stack of papers.

"Is it *common* for you, in your work as a defense attorney, to contract with an expert on false confessions in preparation for trial?" the attorney said, a stink on the word *common*, the implied disdain of the question familiar to me. He waved his copy of a report written by an expert witness with whom C.J. and I had consulted before Michael's trial but who ultimately had never been called to testify.

"No," I answered from the witness stand. "It's not common."

I offered no more than the absolute minimum necessary to answer the attorney's question. By then I had seen a hundred witnesses trying to argue their way out of a question; I knew the only thing that mattered were the words the court stenographer was typing on her keyboard below me.

"And did you and Ms. Howard think that this witness would have been *crucial* to mounting an affirmative defense of actual innocence for Mr. Atwood?"

"Yes," I answered.

When I had finished testifying, I walked past the defense table on the way out of the courtroom.

"Hi," Michael whispered as I passed.

"What the hell do you think you're doing?" Michael's attorney hissed. "Do *not* talk to him."

Michael gave me a resigned smile, squirming in the oversized orange jumpsuit. He seemed adrift, as if he were a child dragged to court by a parent, caught up in the great tide of predestination.

And now, after so many years without hearing from him, after announcing the withdrawal of all his rights to appeal, Michael is reaching out to me again, whispering through the bars of death row.

What does he want? I wonder. *Why doesn't he just say in the letter?*

But this is what makes a ghost, isn't it? The unfinished business, the thing left unsaid. Their inability to communicate with the living.

TWENTY-THREE

MY DAUGHTER HAS turned morbid in her fifth year. She is obsessed with death, and every night before bed this week we have been reading a book titled *Deadly Animals*, where we learn about a venomous octopus in Australia and man-eating pythons in Sulawesi. I sense her thrill at each turn of the page, each new mechanism of death. Her small body goes rigid under the sheets, her viny fingers curling against the book's glossy hardback.

Today, however, her class has started a unit on the pyramids of Egypt. She arrives home simmering with new facts that she delivers, transposed and convoluted, so that Sarah and I are left to translate her spoken hieroglyphics.

"Do you even know about *mummies*?" Rosa asks, a suggestive intonation to her voice that, had we been in court, I'd have objected to as a leading question.

"There's a river called the River Styx," she says, the words imbued with a didactic authority, though I know that in her mind she is thinking of *the River Sticks* and not *the River Styx*. "There's a boat that takes the mummies from the live part to the dead part."

"Well," Sarah says. The historian in her can't help but correct the girl. "I think in Egypt it was maybe the Nile."

"Teacher says that everyone goes to the dead part," Rosa says, ignoring the correction.

"What else did you learn about today?" I ask. "Did you work on your letters?"

Sarah catches my eye, amused at my attempt to change the subject; she thinks I worry too much about the girl, about her nascent obsession with mortality. It's as if Rosa can sense my aversion to death, knows about my inability to watch movies with gore, or kidnapping, or sadistic killers.

"And they make mummy *cats*, even," Rosa says, undeterred. "So the owners can stay with their pets forever."

She pauses, as if suddenly remembering something. She even puts a hand to her chin, a pantomime of thinking that she's adopted from the cartoons she's allowed to watch on weekends.

"When am *I* going to go to the dead part?" she says. She asks the question with an implied entitlement, the way she'd ask *When do* I *get to drive a car?* or *When do* I *get to drink coffee?* Sarah and I share another look, and I try to telepathize the words *I told you so* across the expanse of the living room.

"Not for a long time, I think," Sarah says. The girl mulls this response over, leaning her head against the blue back of the sofa. I wonder if she's noticed the qualifier *I think* in her mother's answer, the implied uncertainty of this addendum.

"That's right," Rosa says, as if settling the issue. "And when do you go to the dead part, Daddy?"

"I don't know," I say. I think of the dead man in the Lake file, now waiting on our kitchen counter. "Not for a long time, I hope. Not until I'm very old."

"How old are you now?" she asks.

"Thirty-six," I tell her, the number feeling surprisingly young when I say it out loud. Michael Atwood's letter and my run-in with Caroline have brought back a time that precedes all of this—the house, Sarah, the girl. It feels like a life that belongs to someone else entirely. I read once that the human body replaces all of its cells every ten years. Is this what my clients feel, I wonder, after a month or a year or a decade in prison? How absurd must it feel to be incarcerated, to live an existence constrained by acts committed by another person entirely?

The girl looks to her mother, her mouth open in shocked delight.

"What?" she shrieks. "You're as old as a mummy!"

TWENTY-FOUR

IN THE DAYS since receiving Michael Atwood's letter I keep waking in the middle of the night with an inexplicable impulse to look in on Rosa. I have been checking, I realize, to see not just that she is all right but that she still exists. That she has not somehow disappeared, fallen into some fold of space or time from which I will never recover her.

Michael's letter has jarred something loose; Rosa has transformed from someone I love into something that must not be lost. I find myself dwelling on the many ways I have seen people disappear, the hidden dangers that most people seem oblivious to. The black of the girl's window swims with silent hunters.

WHEN I STEP into the elevator this morning, I find Pat waiting, his suit neatly pressed, his grey hair slicked back in a sharp part. It is his last year as chief public defender, and he looks none the worse for his thirty years on the job, his eyes lively, his smile sympathetic.

"Saw you got Lake's homicide," he says. I shake my head, thinking of the year of headache that the case will surely provide. "You good for it?"

"Sure," I say. "Danielle is going to second-chair. It'll be good experience for her."

We are quiet for a moment, and there is only the low hum of the elevator rising through the building. The elevator stops on the third floor, and when the doors part, there is no one waiting.

"You see in the paper about Atwood?" Pat asks.

"I saw it," I say. "Just got a letter from him, actually. Wants me to come see him."

"Yeah?" Pat asks, raising an eyebrow. "You going to go?"

"Can't really say no," I say. He nods.

"You know, you gave him a hell of a defense," he says.

"No," I say, remembering Michael's face, flat with shock, the moment the verdict was read. The rapid-fire sound of the photographers' cameras on us. "I don't think we did."

The elevator doors open onto the reception room, where several clients are already waiting. Pat sighs, then reaches up to put a hand on my shoulder, as he has done so many times over the years.

"You sure you're OK?" he asks.

"Sure," I answer. "I'll be fine."

WHEN I CHECK on Rosa tonight, I find her facedown, her arms clutched around her small pillow. She is splay-legged, her back rising and falling in the dimness. She is, I think absently, the same age that Anna Weston's son was on the night she disappeared, which means that now he would be nearly fifteen. I think back to my own childhood, my memory only stretching back to around five or six—early birthday parties, a visit to the sheep ranch in eastern Nevada where my grandfather had once been the foreman.

Would Anna Weston's son remember her now? I wonder. Does he still have some fleeting memory, some quicksilver image of her face or faint echo of her laugh? Or has that, too, disappeared entirely into that hole in the mountain?

TWENTY-FIVE

THE NEXT AFTERNOON I return to Greg Lake's file to prepare for the preliminary hearing set for next week. I have been putting it off; I have no appetite for his case, or for all I know it contains.

But I've returned all my calls, prepped all my cases for the week. The only thing left to do is open the folder that Joanne left on the corner of my desk three days ago. As I do, I feel the old walls go up: The muting of all sensation, the coldness of a car crash. A full-body flinch, muscles tightening as they wait for impact.

The paperwork at the front of Greg Lake's file is all charging documents, inventory sheets, and witness statements. I skim them with a detached interest, possible legal defenses and mitigating circumstances eliminated with every page.

I arrive at the stack of photographs taken on scene by the police department's forensic investigator. The photographs are printed on glossy photo stock, each image framed in a white border. The series begins with wide-framed shots of an old biker bar on east Fourth Street called the Dilligas Lounge, which is an acronym for "Do I Look Like I Give a Shit." Outside the Dilligas the familiar faces of homicide detectives, patrol cops, and investigators linger in the foreground or lean against the building, as if they've just stepped out of the bar for a cigarette or a phone call. The next two dozen pictures are taken inside the bar, dimly lit and dingy. Half-empty beer glasses and oily melted cocktails are scattered over the bar, jackets and purses wadded in the corners of booths as if the patrons had suddenly vanished.

I arrive at the first image of the victim—a man in his early twenties, killed by three rounds from a .22 revolver in this stupid honky-tonk. The body is splayed out in the left third of the photo, head thrown back at an awkward angle, mouth agape, dark hair spilling onto the carpet. He is wearing black jeans torn at one knee, a blue flannel shirt; a brass casing glints on the floor next to him. On the right side of the photo, a pool table is strewn with beer bottles and billiard balls. A single beam of early morning sun casts from the front door of the bar across the table and over the body; the victim's arm and chin are bisected in a warm yellow light. It could be a Renaissance still life: the discarded excesses of the scene's inhabitants, rich in its detail and vivid in color.

I'm accustomed to the intimacy of evidence like this. Photos of our clients' houses, laying out the secrets of their bedrooms and basements and glove boxes. We tear apart their closets, examine the spilled contents of their dresser drawers. We see their socks and sweatshirts and sex toys, the tubes and bottles of their bathroom cabinets. We scroll through text messages and photographs on their cell phones, read their emails, and study the pictures on their social media pages. We learn their affairs, their habits, their sexual predilections.

I continue my way through the Lake photographs, which are interesting only in these sorts of unexpected details. The clean hole that a stray round leaves in the wall of the bar, sunlight piercing through like a skewer. A bent-edged copy of a novel titled *The Dying Grass* wedged under the broken foot of a pool table. A military dog tag attached to a set of keys left forgotten on the floor.

Next, I open an email with an attachment labeled "*State v. Gregory Lake*, Autopsy Photos." I feel Washington glaring down at me from the bookshelf, and I wonder if he sees himself in these photographs and police reports. The screen flickers with thumbnails of three hundred more images, all in the familiar grey tones of the medical examiner's lab, and I begin my slow trudge through them.

There is a predictability to these photographs, a rote reliability to their order. In the first photos the bodies are stretched out on an examination table in the clothes they died in, illuminated by the examiner's severe fluorescent lighting. Their mouths are open, most often, their fingers spread wide. If they have died violently—a car accident, or a beating or gunshot—they will be patinaed in dried blood, their clothes torn and stained an oily black. The photos read like an old film, the images capturing something that resembles a story if flipped through quickly enough. We see the medical examiner's disembodied hands disrobe their subject, using crimped scissors to cut away the bloody clothing, placing each item into evidence collection bags. When the body is undressed, the examiner cleans away the blood, exposing the body's most intimate features: their breasts, their genitals, the folds of skin and fat, hair and scars and blemishes that were hidden away for a lifetime suddenly on full display. We see the violent intrusions—a bullet wound entering the thigh, a knife through a breast or into the buttock or shoulder blade, a rib cage crushed under a steering column—and these, too, feel like intimacies we have no business seeing.

The coroner's intrusion continues now, and as I scroll through the photographs of this dead man—I haven't been with the file long enough to even remember his name—I begin to take notes on a legal pad. The examiner's gloved hands reappear next to a new incision running the length of the sternum, this time holding a scalpel familiarly between thumb and forefinger. In the next photo the examiner is holding back the skin of the entire upper torso like a magician's reveal. The viscera gleams, the organs naked in the examination room's spotlight. I can feel the filter settle into place, the one that allows me to look at this photograph, and the next one, transforming bodies into objects.

I FINISH SKIMMING the coroner's report at home tonight while Rosa reads a book about a forgetful alligator and Sarah cooks dinner, the smell of garlic and onions hanging over the photographs.

Sarah walks past me, and I catch her looking over my shoulder at the screen of my laptop, where I have left one of the autopsy photos up. In it, the boy from the bar is dead on the coroner's table, one eye cracked open, his rib cage exposed and awful. She flinches, and I snap the computer screen shut.

"I'm sorry," I say. "You weren't supposed to see that."

"It's OK," she says.

But there's a part of me that thinks I've intended this, for her to have just a glimpse into the world I leave behind each afternoon. It's the only way I seem to know to communicate with her these days, this JPEG of a murder victim on the coroner's table, his cranium sawed open like a summer squash.

As we get Rosa ready for bed an hour later, I can tell that Sarah is still thinking about the image on the computer. She shows me little kindnesses, squeezes a shoulder as she walks by, asks if she can get me a beer while I read Rosa her bedtime story.

"Take a shower with me?" she asks later, after the girl has gone to bed.

It's a signal she's adopted over the years, midwestern code to tell me that she's in the mood to make love. But the filter is still in place, the one that removes humanity from human bodies. I hold up the Lake file in answer, even though there's nothing to really do. I've read the file, made my notes.

I can already see what will happen at his preliminary hearing next week, and at his arraignment in district court a month from now, and even after that, a hundred years into the future.

TWENTY-SIX

I AM WOKEN in the middle of the night by Rosa's scream. The girl's voice calling for Sarah, who remains in the bed next to me, asleep or feigning sleep. Rosa is upright in bed when I arrive, her covers thrown back, the dark room illuminated by a small night-light that casts green stars across the ceiling. Her small legs are curled to her chest, her face flushed with sleep, wild-eyed.

"Nightmare?" I ask.

She nods.

I sit next to her on the bed, rub her back through the soft cotton of her pajamas.

"Want to tell me what it was about?"

She points to the book on her nightstand, next to a small pyramid made of sugar cubes that she constructed in school for Ancient Egyptians Week. The book is titled *Mummies*, and on the cover is the plaster image of a body wrapped in grimy linen strips, lying cross-armed in a gilded sarcophagus.

"You had a bad dream about this guy?" I ask, picking up the book. "The mummy?"

She nods again.

"She had a bony face," she says. Her eyes are fixed on the bedroom wall, replaying the scene. "And she was evil, and she had bloodless eyes."

Bloodless. I love these misused words she's begun attempting, lifted from some chapter book or movie; I can feel her reaching out, trying to define the edges of her life.

"You're OK, Pokey," I say. As I rub her back, I feel her tiny shoulders slacken, sleep starting to settle back in. She points at the book.

"Can you take it out?" she whispers.

"Of course." I pick the book back up, its glossy cover cool against my fingers. "How about this—tomorrow, we can write our own story about the mummy. One that isn't so scary."

It's something Sarah's begun doing, a little ritual to scare away nightmares that she read about in a parenting blog. Rosa had another nightmare last week, this time about a sea witch from an old Disney movie. The next morning Sarah sat down with a pad of drawing paper and the two wrote a new story about the witch, but this time it was a story where Rosa could make the witch do what she wanted, eat ice cream or fart or go to swim lessons.

"See?" Sarah said, Rosa laughing with delight. "There's nothing to be afraid of."

The girl nods at this idea, then curls down into her blankets. I lie next to her, and we both stare at the green stars projected onto the ceiling, her breath small and singular in the silence.

When she is back asleep a few minutes later, I slip out of the room, taking the book with me. I slump down onto the couch and flip absently through the pages. The book is written for children a few years older than her, I realize. The pencil drawings of the mummification process spare no details: Organs are cut from the body and placed into terra-cotta urns. A cadaver's brains are extracted through the nostrils with long metal hooks. *Jesus*, I think. *It's no wonder she's having nightmares.*

Outside, to the east, the night sky is just beginning to grey. I think about the day ahead of me, about Greg Lake asleep in his cell at the county jail, Michael Atwood waiting a mountain range away at the Nevada State Prison, and I am overcome by a preemptive exhaustion.

As I slide back into bed, I feel Sarah stir under the covers. I slip a hand over her waist, letting her nestle into the hollow of my body. The window blinds turn opaque with morning light as I hold tight against her, clinging to the safety of this miniature world.

TWENTY-SEVEN

IT HAS BECOME a compulsion this week, ever since the arrival of Michael's letter. I should be preparing for tomorrow's cases, or updating my files from court last week, or taking Rosa to play in the park. But instead I am at my computer, pulling up news reports from the year Anna Weston went missing.

The first video begins to play, and for the first time in many years I see Anna Weston's face.

It is only the briefest mention on a local news broadcast—a missing person report filed by a husband, a series of photographs of her familiar face—what I know now to be the foreshocks of all that was about to follow. I scroll through the archives, clicking on one link and then another, a penitent's pleasure each time a new video loads. The screen fills with lost television reports and old newspaper articles, and though it's the last thing I want to do, I keep clicking, hurtling through time toward the current moment. Toward today.

It's like waiting for a train wreck to happen, the early signs of danger invisible to the passengers aboard. I notice that at some point the television anchors begin referring to her by her first name only, *Anna*, as if she'd been an old acquaintance, a niece, or a friend's daughter.

"They act like they know her," I tell Washington irrationally.

She disappeared on the night of April fourth, somewhere between the Gold Rush mini-mart and her home on Green Meadow Circle. I come across one of the first bits of evidence to make it to the news, four days after she disappeared: the lurching surveillance recording of Anna pulling into the gas station in her maroon sedan. In the video her grey, pixelated form emerges from the car to pump gas; she checks her hair absently in the side mirror as she waits for the tank to fill. Already she feels spectral, disappearing between each footstep in the series of still frames.

I click through one video after the other, reliving the week of her disappearance. In the background of each video, of course, lurks the other ghost: Michael Atwood, and his living death in the Nevada State Prison thirty miles south in Carson City. I can see his life, too, in there. In the need for an answer to Anna's disappearance, even if that answer is the wrong one.

Outside my office door, I hear Terry Larsen berating his client over the phone for not showing up to court. Another video begins playing, and I recognize Anna Weston's mother speaking at one of the first news conferences, from the front steps of the Washoe County Sheriff's Office. Her face is drawn and her eyes are ringed with exhaustion, but still I can see Anna in her, the unmistakable jawline, the dark waviness of her hair.

"Anna is a bright, beautiful young woman," her mother tells us. She is flanked by a deputy in a khaki uniform staring grimly out from behind a pair of aviator sunglasses, and a balding young detective in a dark suit whom I recognize as Rob Turner. "We want her to know that her family loves her, and that we just want her back home."

This wasn't just a mother's bias, a tendency toward exaggeration; Anna Weston was, undeniably, beautiful. Not just back-of-homeroom, girl-down-the-street cute, but beautiful in a cosmopolitan, New York City sort of way, in a way that seemed almost not real. Chestnut hair with reddish highlights, a tan that suggested to us that she might have once been a lifeguard during the summers. When the *Reno Gazette* ran a front-page article a week after Anna Weston's disappearance, the reporter noted, "A graduate of the University of Nevada who had majored in psychology, the attractive thirty-year-old went missing in the early morning hours of April fourth." That one word, *attractive*, caught our ears like a dog whistle. This was something understood, never spoken aloud—the loathsome sentiment that perhaps we were so concerned *because* she was so attractive.

Would Anna Weston's case have captured us, we secretly wondered, if it weren't for these looks? If it weren't for her smile that bespoke innocence, American values, sexual longing? Would there have even *been* a headline if the story had been "Homely Fast-Food Employee Missing Since Tuesday"?

Would we even care?

TWENTY-EIGHT

THERE'S AN ADDICT'S urge to keep watching, but I force myself to turn off the videos. I have yet to prepare for tomorrow's hearings, and a new batch of discovery in the Greg Lake case sits unread on my desk, but a text message from Sarah reminds me that dinner reservations have been made, that any dereliction of this spousal duty will be considered a capital offense.

Date nights like these have become rare events, often symptomatic of accumulating marital tensions—tensions that I am unaware of until Sarah demands that I set aside a night from work. It's unlike her, small extravagances like these dates. A halibut collar with yuzu butter entrée, a fifty-dollar bottle of wine, several options for water. It's against her midwestern sensibilities, this type of frivolous spending, when there are college savings accounts to be tended, orthodontia costs to be considered. When I question her occasional insistence on a nice dinner, or on something she likes to call a "staycation" in one of the downtown casinos, she tells me that an expensive dinner is cheaper than a divorce. Even this relative lavishness, she admits, is an overall economic gain, a sound investment in the long run, the marital equivalent of buying bonds.

"I put our names in for seven o'clock," she reminds me now, through the cracked bathroom door. The floor of the shower is littered with plastic toys in bright primary colors, the enamel iron-streaked near the fixtures. I soap the back of my neck, the soft layer that seems to have appeared nearly overnight across my midriff. "Steven and Bea will be over at six thirty."

Steven and Beatrix are the younger couple who moved into the house next door last fall, arriving in a dusty white U-Haul with Utah plates towing an older-model Subaru. The previous owners were foreclosed upon two years earlier, and I'd grown used to the quiet of the abandoned house. The front lawn had gone fallow, the planter boxes leaking potting soil at the joints, colorful annuals and herbs replaced by opportunistic foxtails and nettle, the curtainless windows opaque with dust. But Sarah had brightened at the arrival of the couple, at "new blood" in the neighborhood; she had knocked on their front door with a bottle of shiraz from the closet that first afternoon, had later delivered a cardboard box of Tupperwared meals when news arrived of some family tragedy—a parent's death, I think.

Lately, Sarah has nurtured the relationship with the new, younger neighbors into something more regular, something that seems to border on codependence, though she would never admit as much. I'll often return from work to find that Steven and Beatrix have been beckoned in on the way back from a walk to the dog park, three green-tinted cocktails sweating in the afternoon heat, our daughter trying in vain to retrieve a mushroom-colored tennis ball from Steven's panting retriever. Or I'll come home to find the house empty, Sarah's familiar laugh trickling over our shared fence as she chats with Beatrix, now pregnant with their first child.

A few minutes after I emerge from the shower, I hear the doorbell over the noise of Rosa's movie. I find Steven waiting on the front step, an open bottle of beer in one hand, a paperback in the other. He's in his late twenties, handsome in a wholesome, boring way. His hair is cut short, his face sun-flushed from a recent camping trip that Sarah recounted to me over dinner the night before. He pushes a pair of sunglasses up onto his forehead with the hand holding the beer, smiling easily.

"Ready for the big date night?" he asks, in a way that could easily carry an element of sarcasm or condescension, but doesn't. "Bea and I are going to expect you guys to return the favor after the baby comes. You know that, right?"

I'm used to Steven's easygoing confidence. I *like* him, even. He doesn't bore me with a play-by-play deconstruction of the 49ers' loss to Green Bay on Sunday, or tell me about how *insane* it's been at work this week, or roll his eyes at something the wives say in that approximation of sitcom life that other husbands do. He rides his mountain bike regularly on the yellow singletracks that switchback up Peavine Peak just north of our houses, but he never feels the need to advertise it. In his living room, the bookcases suggest a reader with many interests, entire shelves dedicated to North American geology or to Faulkner or Mesoamerican civilizations. But again, these things go unmentioned. Instead, he is content to pour a round of drinks, to ask about a trial that he saw my name attached to in last week's paper. He brings over good beer—good bourbon, even—and yet I've never seen him drunk, no hint even at tipsiness. So it's no surprise to find him in my doorway now, beer and book in hand.

He follows my eyes behind him, where I had expected Beatrix to be waiting.

"Bea's staying home," he says, as if intuiting my thoughts. "Morning sickness. But in the afternoon. You know how it is."

"Sure," I say as Steven follows me into the house. I hear Sarah from the living room, coaxing my daughter away from the animated movie playing on the television and into her pajamas. "Of course. Sorry to hear it."

OUR TABLE ISN'T ready when we arrive, so we order cocktails at the bar while the waitstaff wend their way through the busy restaurant. By the time our appetizer arrives, we are well past the green neck of a middle-of-the-road California red, and I can see Sarah begin to relax. Her shoulders slump attractively. She laughs a little too loudly at something I say. She lets her hair fall into her face, the new streak of grey at her temples nearly touching a vibrant green asparagus puree bisecting her plate.

"This is nice, isn't it?" she asks.

"It is," I say, because it's what she wants to hear, but also because it *is* nice. She begins to tell me about the most recent bit of department gossip—a colleague who's leaving her wife for a younger woman—and I settle happily into the normalcy of the moment.

As she talks, I find myself wondering if she misses the version of me that she first fell in love with, if she thinks back fondly on the man she met at Judge Beatty's cocktail fundraiser eight years ago. The person who taught her to fly-fish, who took her backpacking in the Sierras for the first time. What happened to that man? How had this more serious, more changeable husband come to replace him?

When we first met, the nightmare of Michael Atwood's case was barely in the rearview mirror. But by then I had figured out how to package the anxiety that my job had infected me with, how to hide it away for weeks or even months at a time. I could wear a jacket and slacks to a cocktail party, could have just two glasses of wine at a museum reception and then head home. I had learned by then to make small talk, to introduce myself as a lawyer and not as a public defender, to smile and change the subject when people said, "I bet you get some pretty wild cases!"

We had been introduced at the judge's reception by a mutual friend, and had later found ourselves alone on a balcony overlooking the garden. She was a newcomer to Reno, she'd explained, an assistant professor at the university just finishing her first semester.

"What do you teach?" I asked.

"I specialize in the history of Indigenous land and resource disputes," she said. "Sounds boring, I know. But it's actually fascinating."

"It doesn't sound boring at all," I said.

She eyed me suspiciously, then began to describe a book she was writing on land ownership in the northern Great Basin during western expansion.

"It's been all archival research so far, but I'm just about to begin my fieldwork," she said.

"Have you been out to the Lagomarsino petroglyphs?" I asked.

My father had taken Jasper and me there once, a rusted face of basalt in the eastern foothills etched over in elaborate drawings of snakes and deer and sheep, of strange spirals and abstract patterns. I found myself telling Sarah about the six-foot rattlesnake that had emerged from beneath a warm boulder, the grotesque thickness of the animal's body, the evil flatness of its pendant-shaped head after my father had cut it off with a shovel.

"That's horrible!" Sarah said, tensing her body comically. "You *have* to take me there!"

Eight years later, she's looking at me across the table of the restaurant now, her face flushed with wine.

"We should do something this weekend," I tell her. "Go camping, maybe. Get out of town like we used to."

The look of surprise on her face reminds me how long it's been since we've done something as a family, something as time-consuming and frivolous as a weekend camping trip.

"Really?" she says. "You don't have too much work?"

I reach across the table, as if reaching through the past eight years of our lives, and take her hand in mine.

"No," I say. "Of course not."

IT'S NOT UNTIL halfway through dinner that the thought begins to surface. I lose track of our conversation, involuntarily returning to the image of Steven standing alone in our front doorway, the sound of a hollow coconut dropping in the movie Rosa was watching. My mind begins to sort through a decade's worth of files, narrowing the number of cases to fit the scenario, before finally landing on its horror reel: Kenny Varos, aged eight, pulled off a bicycle on the way to a friend's house, found beaten and sexually assaulted two days later. Andy Valenti, a client who was arrested at seventy-two years old for possession of child pornography—a charge that came as a surprise to every friend and family member my investigator interviewed. Sarai and Savannah Mason, molested by an uncle for three years before the younger girl was caught with her hands in a classmate's underwear by her first-grade teacher. All the ghosts, out wandering through the summer night.

"You still there?" she asks.

I lurch back into the present tense to find Sarah quiet now across from me, watching me carefully.

I smile weakly. When I reach for the wine, her hand catches mine, briefly, as if to verify that I am, in fact, still there.

"Sorry," I say. I begin to recite an excuse, almost rote by now. Work. Busy. Trial next month. She waits out this recital, and when I'm done, she doesn't say anything back, and there is a silence between us that is filled with the racket of the busy restaurant.

Suddenly, acutely, I want to be away from this place. I rub my hands across the tablecloth trying to distract myself, but I am dragged back to the doorway, to Steven standing alone. The bottle of beer in his hand now seems perverse, lascivious. *How well do you know him?* I ask myself. I think of Rosa, her animal-printed pajamas and Disney-brand bedclothes now evidence, her small body already a crime scene. There is a tightening in my chest, the restaurant growing smaller, the noise suffocating. It's a ridiculous thought, a betrayal of someone I've only known to be good, to be kind and responsible and unperverse. It's the worst accusation you can make, and so I promise myself that I won't articulate it.

"Do you want to go?" Sarah asks.

I shake my head. I pour my wineglass three-quarters full. The food on the plates suddenly looks cold, pools of animal fat coagulating between the bones and the flatware. *How well can you know anyone?*

"It's fine," I say. "Really."

She waits, as she has learned to do in these moments. She offers her smile that says, *Go ahead, whatever it is.* I feel a kick at my shin, as if she's physically prodding me forward, out of myself.

"This is going to sound ridiculous," I say, and already I feel the relief of articulating my paranoia, of releasing it into the open.

"I *know* this is going to sound ridiculous," I say again. "But you're not worried about Steven at home alone with her, are you?"

The idea becomes more absurd as I say it, more improbable and more offensive. I can see Sarah's revulsion already beginning to register, and I am flooded with shame, with weakness, with humiliation. But also, there is something else: relief. Suddenly, the burden of responsibility is no longer mine alone. If something happens, it'll be Sarah's fault, too.

"What?" she asks. She is incredulous, in a way that precludes even the possibility of concern. "Of course I'm not *worried.* What are you saying, exactly?"

"I'm not *saying* anything," I say. "I just started to worry . . ."

And then Sarah's revulsion subsides almost as quickly as it arrived, replaced by a deep, familiar sorrow. She reaches across the table again, this time as if to hold me here, in this reality of hers, free of victims and perpetrators, of demons and witches waiting hidden in the forest for a child to skip into their grasp. It's what I first fell in love with, her midwestern sensibility, this implicit inclination toward good in the world, her economy of possibility.

"There's *nothing* to worry about," she says. She's emphasizing the important words now, as if speaking through a sputtering radio connection, hopeful that at least these words will make it through. "Steve is a *good guy*. He's our *friend*, and he's doing us a *favor*."

"I know," I say. "I'm sorry."

The thought begins to recede, as do the images—the evidentiary photographs and medical records and girls the same age as my daughter alone on the witness stand, small and fearful. I catch a waiter's attention as he passes, and force myself to ask for coffee and the dessert menu.

THE RESTAURANT IS on a promenade next to the river, a newly renovated strip that's part of the recent downtown revitalization, and after Sarah pays the check, we walk slowly back toward our car. In the new amphitheater across the river, a band brought in by the city for the summer arts festival plays calypso, the sound of a steel drum clanging across the noise of water and traffic. A few dozen people sit on blankets and folding camp chairs on the lawn in front of the stage, clad in broad-brimmed straw hats and sunglasses. They pour chardonnay into plastic wineglasses sold at an upper-middle-class camping store. They swab cubes of ciabatta through various dips.

Behind them, a half dozen men loiter almost out of sight at the edge of the river, drinking from a bag that they pass between them. Nearby, a young woman sits against a garbage can brimming with trash, her legs folded against her chest, dragging pensively from the butt of a cigarette. A man from the group notices her, and breaks away from the circle. He is short and hunched, and I recognize him as Matthew Block. Or rather, first I remember him as Burglary reduced to Shoplifting a couple of months earlier, three weeks' credit for time served and four days of community service, and *then* I recall his name.

It's the first time I've seen him in anything other than the jail's orange jumpsuits or the shimmering belts and bracelets of steel shackles. He gives the woman a playful tap with the toe of his shoe, and she laughs, and I am surprised at how happy he seems. How unburdened.

We drive away from downtown, north up Keystone Avenue toward our house where our daughter waits, alone with Steven. The black outline of Peavine Peak looms in front of us, rising from the desert floor.

"I'll text Steve to let him know we're on our way," Sarah says.

And there it is again. That pinprick.

"Don't," I say. "We're almost home anyway."

It's only after I've said it that I realize my motivation: to catch him unaware, to perhaps uncover some clue, some small detail that confirms my darkest fears.

"What are you doing?" Sarah asks, and I know that she understands my rationale, or at least some version of it. There's an edge to her voice this time, as if we've reached a place that is new to both of us. "Where is this going?"

I steer the car through the dimming night, toward the shadowed mountain at the edge of the city. The sun is below the mountains to the west when we arrive home. I thank Steven for babysitting, forcing an approximation of gratitude, of lightness, into my voice. I can feel Sarah's eyes on me, the unspoken words hovering thickly above us. When he is gone, I go to Rosa's room to find her happily asleep, the bedroom smelling pleasantly of the cedar shavings in her gerbil cage. Sarah flops onto the couch and wearily begins to watch a crime procedural, while I retreat to the bedroom. It's there, as I am changing out of my work clothes, that my phone screen lights up with a text message.

Glad I ran into you the other day, the message reads. When I realize the message is from Caroline, my heart skips with an unfounded guilt.

You too, I write back. *You seemed really happy. Really good.*

Thanks, her next message reads. *I hope you're taking care of yourself.*

I erase her message, but a minute later the screen lights up again. This time, there is no message, only an attached photograph that I haven't seen in a decade. In it, she looks exactly as I remember her: blond hair pulled back, an old T-shirt and cutoff jeans, her neck flushed with summer sun. She is posing at the edge of a crystalline pool set amid an amphitheater of polished granite. I am standing next to her, an arm slung over her shoulder, my chest bare and thin and tanned. I can remember the day perfectly, every moment of that lost afternoon.

I am just beginning to compose a response when I hear Sarah opening a drawer in the other room. She probably wouldn't care about the photo ordinarily, but the night has gone badly already. And besides—there is something about the photograph that I want to keep not just from her but also from myself.

I take a final look at these two people, these two strangers who seem so happy, so unaware of all that's to come, and then I delete the message.

TWENTY-NINE

IT IS IN that frenetic morning hour of the next day—between bites of a toasted English muffin and swallows of coffee, the slapdash ironing of a shirt for court today, Rosa dawdling at the door, refusing to follow Sarah to the car—that the call arrives. I recognize the prefix of the incoming number as a state phone line; in all likelihood it will be an inmate calling from prison with some post-conviction gripe, or perhaps an officer from the Division of Parole and Probation with bad news about a client under supervision. But when I answer, the female voice at the other end instead identifies herself as Jessie, a social worker from the Nevada State Prison.

"Are you familiar with an inmate by the name of Michael Keith Atwood?" she asks.

At the front door Rosa tugs at her mother's pant leg. The mug of coffee in Sarah's hand lurches, splashing a brown stain across her white blouse.

"Goddammit," Sarah snaps.

"Yes," I say into the phone. "I was his court-appointed lawyer. But that was a long time ago."

Rosa's face crumples; her breath starts to hiccup, and I know that in a moment she'll be crying. Sarah glares at me from the sink, dabbing with a paper towel at the spreading coffee stain. I point to the phone, pantomiming an apology, and retreat into the relative quiet of our bedroom.

"I'm sorry," I say into the receiver. "This isn't a great time. Is there something I can help you with?"

"I'm afraid I have some bad news concerning Mr. Atwood," she says. There's a manicured empathy to her voice, as if she's been professionally trained in delivering bad news. "Mr. Atwood attempted to take his own life last night."

"*What?*" I say. There's an inflection to my voice that must come across as shock but in truth is something closer to surprise or curiosity. "Can you tell me what happened?"

"I'm sorry," she says quickly, as if she is expecting this question. "But I can't disclose any details at this time. I can tell you that he has been transported to the medical unit."

"Is he OK?" I ask. And as I ask, I realize that this time it isn't merely a reflexive question. *This is my fault*, I think, as I have thought for eight years now. *This man's life will always be my fault.*

"He'll be fine," the woman says, her voice even, palliative. "I do know that much."

"We're leaving!" I hear Sarah call from the living room above the sound of the girl's bawling. I cover the phone to say goodbye, but already the front door is closing; a few seconds later I hear the sound of a car door slamming, an engine starting.

"He's lucky," the woman continues. "I was told that if the guard hadn't found him, Mr. Atwood would have likely succeeded."

"OK," I say. In the last months the papers have reported that Michael has suddenly dropped his appeals, paving the way for his execution. The irony of the State saving Michael from suicide only to kill him themselves seems to be lost entirely on the social worker. "So what happens next?"

"They're expecting to release him back to his unit later today."

I think guiltily about the letter from Michael that I received last week, about the visit to the prison that I've postponed a half dozen times already.

"Do you know when he'll be available for a professional visit?" I ask.

"One moment, please," she says, and I can almost see her at her computer screen, clicking through windows of state prison classification pages and notes.

"If you come this afternoon, you should be fine," she says.

"Thanks."

"I'm sorry again to call so early with this news," the social worker says. "Is there anything else I can help you with?"

Outside the front window Steven's car is backing down the driveway next door, pulling out onto the street.

"I just have a question," I say.

"Sure."

I pause for a moment, trying to capture the thought that has been hovering at the edge of my consciousness since the beginning of our conversation.

"Why me?" I ask.

"I'm sorry?"

"I'm not his attorney anymore. Why are you calling *me* with this information?"

There is a pause, as if I've found the one crack in her bureaucratic sympathy training, and then she gathers herself.

"You don't know?" she says. "You're the emergency contact in his paperwork."

PART IV

THE CASE FOR THE DEFENSE

THE PROSECUTOR HAS called her last witness. A fulcrum seems to have pivoted; we are in the downhill sprint toward a verdict. But it's the defense's turn now, my opportunity to speak to you through *my* witnesses and *my* evidence.

Often, I don't overtly, explicitly challenge the testimony presented by the State—the evidence already admitted. I rarely say, "That was not the defendant's DNA" or "All of the prosecution's six independent witnesses are lying." To do so would be to ask the jury to disregard the reality that the State has already created for them. And once a reality has been created—no matter how unlikely or untruthful or incomplete—it is difficult to destroy.

So instead, my presentations often center on the element of *mens rea*—the defendant's subjective state of mind that the prosecutor must prove to secure his conviction. In a murder case, for example, a prosecutor must prove that the defendant not only caused the death of another human being but did so "with malice aforethought" or "with a wanton and malignant heart."

The defendant's subjective truth, then, becomes the center of our case. I argue that when the defendant acted, it was for reasons that justify the unfortunate results: self-defense, or mistake, or without time to deliberate before they acted.

With each witness, with each reexamination of evidence, this is what I am telling you: The prosecutor may know many things, but he does not know my client's heart.

Here, I tell you. *Listen. This. This is the defendant's heart.*

THIRTY

WE ANTICIPATED THINGS would move quickly after Anna Weston had been found. There was a body, and bodies told stories.

They'd recovered physical evidence, DNA. An arrest was imminent. We inched closer to our televisions, our computer screens, and waited. Soon it was reported that she had been sexually assaulted—but we had already known that, hadn't we? Just as we'd known all along that she would not be found alive, that we had been waiting only to learn the cause of death: strangulation.

The courthouse vibrated with the anticipation of an arrest. News vans from the major networks stationed themselves outside the DA's office, antennas beaming live feeds to Las Vegas and Sacramento.

The Weston case had become an unspoken current in the public defender's office; there was an understanding that, in all probability, one of us would soon find the name Anna Weston on the first page of a criminal complaint in a new case file. Even our chief public defender, Pat, seemed to be anticipating the arrival of the Weston case, the microscope that the office would soon be under. At the conclusion of our staff meeting that month, he held the attorneys back, closing the conference room door after the support staff had returned to their cubicles.

"So," Pat said, his head sinking into the shoulders of his suit jacket as he leaned in over the conference table. "What are people hearing about the Weston case?"

These meetings were mostly formalities—a chance to commiserate over lost trials or obnoxious clients, to plan office parties and vacation coverage. But the mere mention of Anna Weston's name made tangible what every attorney had been thinking. A quiet fell over the twenty-five attorneys gathered around the conference table.

"I'm hearing something about a person of interest," said Sandra, an attorney assigned to Judge Greenbaum's courtroom in Department Two. The heads of twenty-four public defenders collectively turned in her direction. "Some of the guys on the SET team are talking about an arrest."

Pat nodded. SET was the Street Enforcement Team, a half dozen bearded Reno police detectives who ran their shifts in plain clothes, working downtown and the surrounding motels. They were the city equivalent of special ops, given long leashes, surfacing only occasionally to testify after major arrests. When I caught C.J.'s eye across the room, she shrugged in a vague, equivocal way.

"Is that it?" Pat said. "Someone we know? Previous client? Frequent flier?"

Sandra held up her hands, empty.

"Anyone else?" Pat scanned the room. When no one said anything, he leaned back in his chair. "Well, I think we all know there's a good chance this thing will be coming to our office."

I wondered what he meant by "thing." Whether he meant the case itself, the manila file and all it entailed, or the killer himself. People shifted in their seats, scribbled uneasily in the corners of their legal pads.

"And we all know this is a death penalty case," Pat continued. "They'll have the aggravators."

People began to look reflexively to Dan Osterman, who was sitting in a corner of the conference room. Dan was a career public defender, one of the attorneys in the office whom C.J. derisively called the "true believers." He was even-tempered and methodical, known for taking cases that other senior attorneys shied away from. Child murderers, rapists, serial killers. He'd handled every death penalty case to come through the office in the last two decades, and lost all of them. Three of his clients had been put to death, and behind his back, prosecutors and clients—and even some of the public defenders—had given him the nickname the Angel of Death.

"*If* the case comes to us, we'll deal with the defense team then," Pat said, as if reading our minds. "In the meantime, you tell me if you hear anything. Anything at all."

THIRTY-ONE

ANOTHER WEEK PASSED, and still no arrest was made. A month. The journalists stopped reporting from the ravine where Anna Weston's body had been found. The news vans thinned from the parking lot in front of the courthouse. Anna's mother began appearing again on the television, now imploring us to help find her daughter's killer. The energy was gone from her voice, her hair limp and grey.

"Good afternoon," Detective Turner said to us through the camera at one of his press conferences. "We'd like to announce some significant developments in the case of Anna Weston."

I hardly recognized him in the formal blues of the RPD dress uniform, with his brass name tag and badge.

"Our investigation continues to progress. DNA samples collected at the scene, as well as eyewitness and video evidence, have refined our profile of the suspect. We believe the attacker to be a Caucasian man between the ages of twenty and forty-five," he told the news cameras.

"I could have told you that a year ago," C.J. said. "Great detective work."

THE CITY ITSELF seemed to boil over with frustration. At bars and around dinner tables we expressed our exasperation, unable to believe that after this long—after the discovery of a body, of DNA, the wonder drug of criminal justice—the police seemed no closer to making an arrest. Rumors circulated about other assaults in the last year, speculation that Anna Weston's murderer was still loose in the community. That it was only a matter of time before the next woman disappeared. The city felt small and vulnerable, the vast desert surrounding it an endless expanse that might swallow women whole.

The appeals from the police became more forceful. People were encouraged to call an anonymous hotline at the slightest hint of suspicion.

"Think about any changes in behavior," Turner said into our screens. "Any increases in drug or alcohol use, any erratic behavior. Give us the name, and let us do the work."

We watched the people we loved—whom we thought we knew—more carefully. Could he still be here, among us?

And because little is kept secret in the courthouse, every attorney in Reno knew when Lance Davis, a deputy prosecutor, was called in for questioning. He was quickly cleared by the police—a simple buccal swab and DNA test eliminated him as a suspect—but still, suspicion clung to him like a stench. The fact that someone *thought* he might have been capable of killing Anna Weston, the possibility alone, made us wonder.

We arrived, finally, at the end of summer. A series of brush fires set off, the mountain peaks and downtown casinos alike choked in a haze of wood smoke. Still, he walked among us, shopping in our grocery stores, driving in our streets. He lived in our houses, breathed our air, tucked our children in to sleep at night.

THIRTY-TWO

"YOU DOING ALL right these days?" Jasper said one afternoon. A Miles Davis album warbled from the old record player in his living room, the trumpet slow and dramatic like the soundtracks of the Westerns my father used to watch. I watched him pinch a nub of weed into a ceramic pipe. From the next room came the scraping of a pan over a burner as Natalie cooked dinner while she chatted with Caroline. "Everything OK with the law stuff?"

My second year in the public defender's office ended in the shadow of the discovery of Anna Weston's body, and still the new cases came. For every file closed, another two seemed to open. Embezzlement. Burglary. Assault with a Deadly Weapon. Burglary. Possession of a Stolen Motor Vehicle. Possession of a Hypodermic Device. Possession of a Controlled Substance for the Purpose of Sale. Burglary. Burglary. Always, burglaries. Everything was a burglary.

"Yeah, sure," I said uncomfortably. It was unlike him to check in on me like that. "Why?"

"Well," he said. "For one, you're doing the face-touching thing again."

I suddenly noticed my thumb digging into my jawline. It was an old compulsion that first surfaced in middle school, one that had fascinated Jasper as much as it had embarrassed me. I looked at my fingers as if they had somehow betrayed me, worked without my volition.

"And you look like shit," he added.

"Thanks," I said.

I could count the number of weekends completely uninterrupted by work on two hands. I ate erratically and survived on coffee. My skin was sallow and my face had thinned from the stress, my shoulders cramped from the hours memo'ing files or waiting for court or researching and writing pretrial motions. The stream of cases had become a constant, low buzz in the back of my consciousness. Even now—on my third beer and after a second hit from the pipe Jasper had packed—I was thinking about the next week's calendar, about a motion due Monday.

"Listen," he said. He paused, as if deliberating whether to ask the question that was about to follow. "What are you doing tomorrow?"

"One guess," I said.

"Natalie and I are going to California for a few days. You two should come."

"Too much work this weekend," I said, shaking my head.

He thought about this for a moment, with that faraway look that he'd get when we were kids in our sleeping bags on Peavine Peak. He smoothed his white T-shirt, then reached for his beer.

"No," he said with finality. "You're coming. Just for the afternoon, and then Nat and I will keep going. You and Caroline can drive back together."

It was an impossibility, I tried to explain. There simply wasn't enough time. But Jasper had always possessed an immovability, a momentum like the pull of a rip current, and at eight the next morning I found myself in my car following his old pickup onto Interstate 80, Caroline asleep in the passenger seat next to me.

In our last summer of high school Jasper and I used to make this trip nearly every weekend—sixty miles west and three thousand feet above Reno. We drove over the Floriston bridge, through the tourist town of Truckee just past the California border. Past the deep green of Donner Lake and the granite walls of Emigrant Gap, out of the smoky haze of the Great Basin and down the western slope of the Sierras.

As I drove, I thought of the cases that I had scheduled for the next week, all the things I should be doing instead, all the years hanging in the balance. I thought of Anna Weston—of what had happened to her that night, of how she might have died. I thought of C.J., and tried again to make sense of her—I still couldn't decide if she was a good attorney or a terrible one. Whether she was a good person or a terrible one. And then I returned to Jasper, his silhouette visible in the window of the old Ford in front of me, his girlfriend's dark, curly hair next to him, and of the last time we'd made this trip, the week before I left for college. Finally, I thought of nothing. I rolled the window down, let the cool mountain air wind its way through my clothes, my hair. As we left the meditative hum of the highway, Caroline stirred, then sat up sleepily in the seat next to me.

"Sorry," she said. She smiled wearily. "Yesterday was my fourth straight shift."

"Don't worry about it," I said. I handed her a thermos of coffee I'd filled at the gas station that morning. I had enjoyed the simple company of her asleep in the car next to me, the chance to be with someone without having to explain anything. We drove through a small campground, the smell of pine sap and cold water old and familiar, until Jasper's truck pulled into a small turnout under a stand of ponderosa pines. Natalie dropped down from the passenger seat and reached into the bed of the truck to open a cooler. She was wearing cut-off jeans, an old pair of Converse, and a plaid button-up that used to be Jasper's father's.

"You're glad you came, right?" Natalie said. I stretched my arms over my head, breathed in the mountain air.

"Yeah," I said. "I'm glad I came."

I liked Natalie; she was witty, outspoken, crass in a way that made Jasper cringe. They'd been dating for two years and it was obvious that she was in love with Jasper, and it was this I liked most about her.

"Hey Nat," Jasper said. "Hand me the bag."

Natalie reached into the cab to retrieve a small blue backpack for Jasper, who slung it over his shoulder.

"What's in the bag?" I asked before I could catch myself. I had already guessed at the unspoken reason for the trip: that after we swam at the pools, Caroline and I would drive back to Reno, while Jasper and Natalie would continue west another five hours to the grow operations of Mendocino, where they would buy cannabis or magic mushrooms to sell back in Nevada. But until that morning I never asked what he did for money, and he never volunteered. Now, I was asking. I felt Natalie stop what she was doing, look first at me and then to Jasper.

Jasper stood there for a moment, considering the bag.

"It's forty-two thousand dollars," he said matter-of-factly. "So, you know, I don't think we should leave it in the car."

With that kind of money he'd be looking at a trafficking charge if he was pulled over, I thought involuntarily, even if it was just marijuana. Crossing state lines between Nevada and California would make it a federal charge. If there was a gun in the bag, which I knew there was, another felony on top of that.

Caroline shifted uncomfortably next to me, the moment heavy with all the questions that weren't being asked.

"You good?" Jasper said.

"Sure," I said. "I'm good."

WE SHOULDERED BACKPACKS filled with the beer and sandwiches and set off on a faint path that wound its way through a mile of granite shelves and poison oak and thick tangles of manzanita. Finally, sweaty and dusty, we arrived at the edge of a four-story precipice, the sound of yells and laughter echoing off the canyon walls. The Yuba River curled below, green and swirling, dropping from a small waterfall into a glacial tarn thirty yards wide. Through the refracting water we could see the grey outlines of stones worn smooth by eons of water, the racing silver flashes of rainbow trout along the gravel bottom.

The first pool was lined with a half dozen small groups of people in their teens and twenties, towels spread on slabs of flat rock, cans propped against backpacks. The air smelled of cigarette smoke, of spilled beer. Natalie scrunched her nose and nodded for us to follow her downriver. We picked our way over ledges and boulders for another ten minutes, arriving at a smaller pool cupped in a head-high granite wall. The rush of water drowned out the sounds of the first pool, and the canyon walls reached up around us, so that the feeling of isolation was complete and intense.

Caroline sat down against the trunk of a pine, shielding her eyes against the iridium glare of the pool's surface. Jasper dropped the bag against the trunk next to her, then reached into a zipper to fish out a Tupperware container filled with dried mushrooms.

"Counselor?" Jasper said. "Nothing crazy, just enough to feel the magic."

I glanced over to Caroline, who smiled and shrugged.

"No objections."

"I told you," Natalie said to Jasper, stretching her arms up over her head in the midday sun. "Perfect little day trip."

A half hour later, the sounds of the canyon were just starting to heighten, the pool shimmering vibrantly. Jasper stood and stripped off his white T-shirt; his torso was pale and lean, the way it had always been, the jagged line of a failed tattoo experiment our freshman year of high school still visible on his left forearm, next to a larger new design that stretched back onto his shoulder blades.

Beside him, Natalie was also pulling her clothes off, Jasper's father's shirt thrown into a heap on top of the bag. She reached back to unclip her bra as Jasper unbuckled the belt of his pants. Then they were both nude, Jasper as white as the granite he stood on, Natalie dark and beautiful against the cobalt sky, as they disappeared over the granite ledge. There was a long, perfect silence before it exploded from the sound of their feet crashing through the water's silver surface.

THIRTY-THREE

ON NIGHTS THAT I didn't work, I ran.

I'd started running in law school, the fastest and easiest way to flush the nerves, a mile or two flat out, heart rate spiking, the feeling of movement, of motion, of escape. Now, I would cram in a quick mile or two at lunch or after work, the bare minimum to shake out the cobwebs of the days.

Caroline would sometimes join me on these runs, our pace slower as we chatted easily. We had been dating for a year now, and more often than not she would stay at my apartment downtown after her shifts in the ER. We were just another of those couples who do these sorts of things, we told ourselves. People who run together after work and cook low-carbohydrate meals, who sleep through the night and say we love each other and plan for the future. We pretended we didn't spend our days in hospitals and courthouses with blunt force trauma victims and pedophiles and drug overdoses. *How normal we must look*, I would think on these runs, and when I looked to Caroline, she would be smiling and I knew she was thinking the same thing.

One afternoon in early September I knotted the laces of my running shoes and set out alone from the front steps of my apartment. It was nearly six, and a searing headwind was blowing as I set off. I tried to settle into the slap of shoes against pavement, the mindless repetition, as I made my way out of the shadows of the downtown casinos. I ran past a string of two-story motels—the Saint Francis and the Colonial and the Castaway Inn and the Reno Royal— names that showed up over and over in police reports and in declarations of residency and probation paperwork, where clients paid by the week and lived for years on end.

Soon I reached the river, a green strip of parks and trees bisecting the town. As I ran past, a girl held a handstand at the edge of the water, her legs kicking in the air as if she were running across the sky. Teenagers waded in the eddies of the Truckee and milled in small groups, drank beer from paper cups and shared single sets of headphones.

I followed the river west through Idlewild Park, past the Mexican families grilling next to the softball fields, past the old rope swing where Jasper and I had long ago tried to impress a group of girls by attempting suicidal gainers. I was two miles in now and could hear my heart thumping in my ears, could feel the sweat beginning to soak through my shirt, running in cricks down my back. I pushed farther, no plan in mind, no destination I was running toward, only away. Away from downtown, from the courts, from C.J. and from Anna Weston.

I ran through the neighborhoods of old Reno, through Crissie Caughlin Park, where the old gay men met and were sometimes raided by the Reno police. I stopped only when I'd reached the shade of the McCarran Boulevard overpass, the rolling sound of car tires drifting down to where I stood, my hands on my knees.

I stripped off my shirt, the late-summer breeze drying the sweat on my back instantaneously. A faint trail ran through a stand of wild rye, and I followed it to the river's edge twenty yards away. There, I squatted to scoop the cold water of the Truckee over the top of my head, onto my chest and shoulders. I stayed for a few minutes like that, cupping the water in my hands, listening to the wind blowing through the leaves of the cottonwoods.

It wasn't until I stood to leave that I saw it, there among the small tunnels carved through the willow stands—a pair of women's shorts, once pink but now sun bleached and mud stained. The purse nearby, its contents scattered across the grey river stones. A hairbrush, broken sunglasses. The shirt, ripped at the shoulder, discarded in a tuft of grass a few feet away.

An old story forced itself from the evidence: the girl pulled from the walking path nearby, or driven there, or simply asked. It might have been a photograph from one of the manila files that crowded the filing cabinet back in my office, an evidentiary photo clipped to a sexual assault charge. Or it was nothing at all—a teenage afternoon, the clothes falling from an unzipped backpack, the cheap glasses accidentally stepped on and abandoned.

I had been trying to forget a case I had received that week—Nolan Tenley, charged with Sexual Assault of a Minor. Now, at the edge of the river, Tenley crawled his way into my conscience, crept over me with the water dripping from my hair.

"*If* I did it," he'd said in the interrogation video. "And I'm not saying that I *did*. But if it happened, what you say happened."

The "it" he was talking about was the repeated violation of his own eight-year-old son. The detective had only nodded.

"I sleepwalk, right?" Tenley had said. "Maybe it could have happened then, right? Like I was sleepwalking?"

The rush of a passing truck shook down from the bridge overhead, and a chill passed over me as the sweat dried in the evening breeze.

I had hated Tenley when I first heard him say it, had spent an afternoon scouring the file for a conflict of interest that would allow the public defender's office to pass the case on to another court-appointed attorney. Was it really possible that someone could do these things—the worst things imaginable—and not even realize it?

But by then I knew that the inverse was demonstrably true: that one could convince themselves of having done a terrible thing, even if they hadn't. I knew about Ada JoAnn Taylor, who had falsely confessed to sexually assaulting and strangling an elderly woman in the 1980s. Taylor served nineteen years in prison before her innocence was proved by DNA evidence, but even after she was exonerated, she was racked by the delusional guilt of a crime she never committed. Her mind had betrayed her in the same way the criminal justice system had.

There at the edge of the Truckee River I understood now what Ada JoAnn Taylor must have experienced, the way reality could become unmoored by all the worst possible versions of ourselves. I sat down in the river grass next to the ripped shirt and the broken sunglasses. They were evidence, or they were nothing. I could feel time slipping, my own memory listing beneath me. Hands still cold with river water, I found myself transported to the desert hillside where Anna Weston's body had been found, the stands of black bitterbrush that had loomed behind the reporters' lights. The place felt uncannily recognizable, didn't it? Her face had become so familiar that I could almost recollect being there myself. I could see Anna Weston draw her last breaths in front of me, could feel the fabric of her shirt in my fist.

I stumbled away from the water through the river grasses, and when I reached the running trail, I started back toward my apartment in a sprint. When I arrived at my front steps twenty minutes later, a jittery exhaustion was coursing through the circuits of my body. A woman who lived down the hall—a second-grade teacher in the midst of a divorce—waved in my direction. I waved back, and when she'd rounded the corner, I folded over and vomited.

THIRTY-FOUR

I HAD LEARNED early on that to a criminal defense attorney, demographics are as important as facts. And here are the demographics we worked with every day: There are five hundred thousand people in Washoe County, which starts at the northern corner of Lake Tahoe and stretches 220 miles up Nevada's western border to Oregon. Of those half million, 62 percent identify as Caucasian, while 25 percent are Hispanic, 5 percent are Asian, and 3 percent are African American, with Native Americans constituting about 2 percent of the population (a 98 percent decline in the last two hundred years, C.J. liked to point out). With these realities in mind, as a public defender the last thing you wanted to see come across your desk was a case like Paul Harris'.

When I was assigned Paul Harris' case that fall, its facts had already become routine—a Possession of Controlled Substance charge paired up with a Battery Against an Officer. We met for the first time in the courtroom lobby, where I spotted him next to the clerks' desk. He was a tall, lanky Black guy in his early twenties, wearing glasses and an Incredible Hulk T-shirt. From his file, I already knew that he was a junior at the university and this was the first time he'd ever been arrested.

"I tried calling you a couple times," he said, after I had introduced myself.

"I have a lot of clients, Mr. Harris," I said. "And besides, there wasn't much to discuss. I just got your discovery today."

I waved his file, like it was proof I wasn't a bad lawyer.

"Yeah, I get it," he said. We sat down next to each other on the bench where he'd been waiting. Next to us, an old woman jogged a toddler on her knee. "I do. It's just, I've never been in trouble before. I don't know what to expect, you know?"

I flipped through his file, skimming the Probable Cause sheet.

"Did you get a copy of the police report yet?" I asked. He shook his head. He had a small notebook in his lap, and I saw him write down the words *police report*. I felt him reading over my shoulder, following my finger as I scanned the arresting officer's statement.

"They're saying they stopped you for jaywalking outside the Eldorado Casino," I said. "And that when they searched your bag, they found a baggie that tested positive for methamphetamine."

"Man, I'm a computer science major. Do I look like I do *meth*?" he said, waving his hands briefly over himself. He looked like he was more likely to stay up all night playing *World of Warcraft* than snorting methamphetamine.

"OK," I said. "So, what happened?"

I took notes as he told me about the night he was arrested.

"I *did* jaywalk," he said. "That much I'll admit to. Jaywalking. For sure."

"OK, got it." I smiled. "Tell me about what you were doing when they stopped you."

He'd been with a girl he'd met that night outside the movie theater, just a young white girl who had been smoking a cigarette on the steps outside a bar.

"So we hung out," Paul said. "You know, just walked around a little. She had a grocery bag with some random stuff in it. Couple beers and whatnot. I was carrying it for her when they stopped me."

"Let me guess," I said. "When they stopped you, she took off."

"Exactly," he said. "Exactly."

I continued reading the report, my finger pausing at the last paragraph.

"Did you tell them the drugs were yours?" I asked.

"What?" he said.

I pointed to a line in the police report.

"It says here that 'Mr. Harris then admitted to Officer Park that the contents of the bag were his.'"

"*Hell* no," he said, his voice wavering. "Why would I tell a cop that I owned a bag of meth?"

As I reread the last paragraph of the report out loud to him, he just sat there, shaking his head back and forth as if trying to wake from a dream.

"What about the resisting?" I said.

"I didn't resist anyone," he said quietly. "I never resisted anyone in my life."

I could see he was telling the truth, but after two years I knew it wasn't my job to believe him. It was my job to tell him the strengths of his case, about his legal defenses and his chances if we went to trial. Our only legal defense was the truth: that the drugs weren't his. But there it was, right there in the last paragraph of the police report. *Mr. Harris then admitted to Officer Park that the contents of the bag were his.*

"I didn't say that," he said.

"I know you didn't," I said. "But that cop is going to show up in court and he's going to say you did."

I could see him internalizing what I was trying to tell him. That it didn't matter what had actually happened, it only mattered who would be believed.

"This isn't right," he said. "Can't we get the tapes or something?"

"Probably not," I said. "But we can try."

I'd had other arrests occur outside the same casino, and I knew that they recorded over old surveillance footage after eight days. The tapes would have been erased a week earlier.

"This is bullshit," Paul said. The pencil trembled in his hand as it hovered over his notepad that still had only the two words, *police report*, written on it. "You know what this means for me? I'll lose my financial aid. And what grad school is going to take me with a felony on my record?"

"I know it's bullshit," I said. "But the good news is, this is clearly a probation case."

"Probation?" he said incredulously. "We've got to fight this, man."

I found myself repeating a line I'd often heard C.J. use. *You can be right and go to prison. Or you can accept the facts and get the best deal for yourself.*

Paul just sat there shaking his head. I didn't want to say what I was thinking: that if we went to a jury trial, we'd be lucky to get one Black juror in the jury pool, and that Neil would find a reason to kick them off during jury selection. That a jury wasn't going to believe Paul Harris over Officer Adam Park.

And I also knew that if he pleaded guilty to the possession charge, Neil would drop the resisting and might even agree to drug court, which would mean Paul could avoid the felony entirely if he completed treatment for the drug problem he didn't have.

But there was something in me that felt sick, a sensation that I could trace back to that first morning in court when I'd forced Ruth Walton to sign a guilty plea that she hadn't read. I'd thought that being a public defender would mean fixing the broken cogs in the system, but instead I had just become another broken cog.

"Let me get an investigator assigned to the case," I said. "You're out of custody. We'll postpone the preliminary hearing today for a couple months. I'll see if we can track the girl down, or if there's anything on the officer's body camera."

He nodded slowly.

"OK," he said quietly. "What can I do until then?"

"Just keep doing what you're doing," I said. "Keep going to your classes. Don't get into any more trouble."

"Didn't you hear me earlier?" he said. There was an exhaustion in his voice, as if this was a conversation he'd had a hundred times before. "I didn't do this. I've never *been* in trouble."

THIRTY-FIVE

IT WAS A FALL afternoon in that year of wildfires, the year of Anna Weston's discovery, the year of Paul Harris' case, when I left the office to meet Jasper for a drink. But I was caught by a client in the lobby on the way out, and the sun was already low in the hazy sky when I finally made it to my car in the office parking lot an hour later.

My phone buzzed in my jacket pocket, and I knew it would be Jasper. The morning calendar had gone poorly, a pair of clients maxed out by an ill-tempered Bartos, and now I was late for drinks. Caroline was working the graveyard shift, and I already knew how the night would play out: hopping from one bar to the next, until Jasper left to go home with Natalie and I passed out alone in my studio apartment next to a half-eaten bowl of cereal.

Gonna skip out tonight, I texted Jasper. *Too tired, fishing in the morning.*

I began driving aimlessly. At a stoplight on Virginia Street I tapped a cigarette from a pack in the glove box. The car crept slowly north until I eventually hit the interstate, smoke trickling out the window. My phone vibrated in the center console.

Sure, Jasper texted back. *Let me know if you change your mind.*

The city jostled and disappeared in my rearview mirror as I accelerated down the on-ramp, the highway following the river through Lockwood and Mustang, past the brothels at the county line, past an oxbow where I had once watched Jasper's father jump-shoot a Canada goose. I passed the exit to the Pyramid Lake Paiute Tribe Reservation at Wadsworth, where C.J. and I planned to fish for Lahontan cutthroat trout the next morning. Behind me, the horizon flashed red before being abruptly snuffed out by the mountains.

I kept driving east, no destination in mind, only the bracing sensation of movement. I was thinking about Paul Harris, who had entered a not-guilty plea to a Possession of Controlled Substance charge earlier in the week. We'd gotten lucky—our investigator had found a surveillance video from a nearby ATM that showed Paul walking along the river walk with the girl he'd met, just as he'd told the police. We had an idea of who the girl was, and the investigator was confident we could find her before the trial began. If we did, Neil would have to dismiss the case.

Finally, I pulled off in the town of Fernley, the last exit before the desert started in earnest. I gassed the car, then parked in front of a small roadside casino to buy another pack of cigarettes—something that had graduated from an affectation while drinking to a full-on habit. The casino door opened to a cloud of tobacco smoke and air freshener, country music and the electronic bells of slot machines. My phone buzzed again in my pocket, the screen flashing with another text message. This time it was Caroline, writing to let me know that she'd been asked to work a double shift that night, and not to expect her in the morning.

I held the power button down until the screen went dark, then scanned the casino floor. It was the usual weekday afternoon crowd, retirees and bikers and cocktail waitresses. I made my way to a bar along the perimeter of the casino and fed a twenty into a video poker machine. *If I hit the jackpot*, I thought, *I can have my resignation letter drafted by tomorrow morning.*

An older couple sipped Budweisers in a corner booth while a trio of truckers watched the baseball game playing on a television behind the bar. The bartender, a bearded Kenny Loggins lookalike, was talking with great excitement to one of the truckers.

"But what do *I* know?" he said as he poured my order. "I'm only the guy who's worked here every day for ten years."

I smiled sympathetically, then slid across a credit card to pay for the vodka soda.

"Keep it," he said, pushing the card back. "Free drinks as long as you're gambling."

People filtered in and out of the bar, cocktail waitresses making laps from the tables with drink orders and empty serving trays, pit bosses for an after-shifter. I glanced at my watch; even if I wanted to change my mind, it was too late to meet Jasper now, so I put another bill into the video poker machine and ordered another cocktail. After my second drink I left for the bathroom, and when I returned, the older couple had left their booth in the corner. A few minutes later the baseball game finished, and the truckers asked for their tab as well.

"Where'd everybody go?" I asked. The bartender shrugged.

"Another?" he said, pointing at the ice in my glass.

"Sure."

I was pushing another bill into my poker machine a few minutes later when a woman entered from the casino floor.

"Hey Matty," she said, taking a seat at the end of the bar. She looked out of place—too young, too pretty. She wore a dark cocktail dress and had her black hair pulled up into a tight bun. I watched her fish a bill out of her purse and feed it into a video poker machine.

"How you doing, girl?" the bartender said in that easy, natural way that reminded me of Jasper. She brushed her hair from her eyes, her face lit by the glow of the television screen behind the bar.

I hardly recognized her there, her lashes smoky with mascara, her cheeks bright with blush. The last time I'd seen Ruth Walton, she had been wearing a set of oversized jail scrubs, my first week at the public defender's office. I remembered how outsized the steel shackles had been around her waist, how young and out of place she was in the jury box next to Greg Lake and the other defendants in Bartos' courtroom. She looked older here, more dangerous.

Ruth seemed to notice me at the same time, her face going flat before suddenly breaking into a smile, as if we were both in on a secret. I looked quickly away, back at the empty glass in front of me on the bar. I was embarrassed to see her there. Embarrassed to be getting drunk alone, still in my suit from court that morning. I watched her stand from her seat at the end of the bar and prayed that she would just leave, that we could both pretend we hadn't seen each other. She stood there for a moment, as if considering this option as well, and then she walked over and slumped into the bar stool next to mine.

"Remember me?" she said brightly.

I nodded, suddenly and acutely aware of how many drinks I'd had.

"Ruth, right?"

The bartender poured Ruth a rum and Coke without her having to ask, and then filled my empty glass with soda water.

"I got your messages," I said sheepishly. "I meant to call you back. I was going to—"

"It's OK," she said. She lifted her glass and took a sip. "That's not your job, you know? You're not my babysitter."

"I know," I said. "But I wanted to. It sounded like you were doing so well."

What I didn't have to say was that she had never shown up for her sentencing hearing. We both looked at the glass sweating in her hand, the blue light of the television glinting off the ice, as if we both knew what this scene here in this sad little roadside casino in Fernley really meant.

"I was doing well," she said. "I did that program. The thing you set up for me. Then I went back to my parents' house on the reservation. Helping with the farm, and all that. I was doing good for a long time, but . . . I was only nineteen, you know?"

Her voice trailed off. I nodded.

"Anyway, I'm doing fine. Working here," she said, winking at the bartender playfully. "Just cocktailing, but the tips are decent."

The ten o'clock news was just starting on the television, the anchor's muted voice next to the familiar photograph of Anna Weston. I hadn't realized how late it was.

"I guess you know you have a warrant," I said.

"Yeah, I know," she sighed. I felt the bartender watching us, trying to figure out what our connection might be. "Either I'll get picked up for something, or—who knows?—maybe I'll turn myself in."

"That'd be the smart thing to do," I said hollowly.

"Oh, I know," she said. She stirred her drink with the red cocktail straw. "I guess I'm just not ready yet."

I suddenly remembered something, another of the million details that I'd failed to follow up on in the past two years.

"Your father called my office a couple times," I told her. I remembered the man from the back of the courtroom, the brief phone conversation I'd had with him the day after Ruth had no-showed for her sentencing hearing. The messages that he had left on my office voicemail. "He's been looking for you."

Ruth sat up, glancing around the room as if waiting for someone she was expecting. I motioned to the bartender for my check.

"You should call him, at least," I said.

Our eyes met for a moment, and something like a look of recognition passed between us. I felt that I knew her, that I could have easily *been* her, had one or two things worked out differently.

I took my keys from the bar.

"You OK to get home?" she asked.

"Sure," I said. I stood unsteadily, the unspoken irony of the situation hanging between us. I pulled my tie tight to my neck, as if this would shield me against everything waiting outside the casino doors, all that empty desert between me and home.

THIRTY-SIX

I FIND MYSELF thinking often about how much C.J. knew, and when she knew it.

A few weeks after my encounter with Ruth Walton, I was waiting with my fishing gear on the front step of my apartment when C.J. pulled up in the dark hours of a Saturday morning.

"Morning," I said groggily, climbing into the back seat behind Ray, a prosecutor who sometimes fished with us.

"Jesus, Gato," C.J. said, eyeing me in the rearview. "What did you get into last night?"

"Nothing," I said, the taste of cigarettes still in my mouth after another late night with Jasper. She handed back a thermos of coffee, but when I poured a cup, my stomach rolled with the smell of bourbon.

"Too early for you?" she said, sipping from her own mug.

As we started back out toward Pyramid Lake, I dozed in the back seat while Ray complained about his oldest son, who was always a source of great consternation for Ray and amusement for the rest of us.

"I have Benevidas calling me at three a.m. from the side of the road," Ray was saying. "When I get there, James is passed out in the back seat of his patrol car. So now I have to kiss Benevidas' ass for the rest of my life."

"Well, at least it wasn't Leadbetter," C.J. said, picking something from the corner of her nose.

Ray guffawed. Leadbetter had been the arresting officer on a case that C.J. and Ray had handled the week before. He'd fucked up just about every procedural issue you could think of: the probable cause for the traffic stop, the consent to search the defendant's car, the *Miranda* admonition. Ray had been forced to dismiss the case halfway through C.J.'s cross-examination at the preliminary hearing, and we'd all heard Ray chewing Leadbetter out in the lobby after the hearing.

"He would have loved the chance to fuck my world up for a change, I can tell you that," Ray said.

I was dying to ask about a case that Ray and I had set for trial in December, but there was a tacit understanding that pending cases weren't discussed on these outings. I leaned my forehead against the window in the back seat, watching the sun rise over the desert, the white flashes of selenite sparkling against the blue hills.

As we left the last of the city, we passed a final billboard, and for a moment the old familiar photograph of Anna Weston was smiling down at us, its corners peeling, the dark luster of her hair fading in the morning sun. An unspoken current passed through the cab, as if we were all sharing the same thought.

The investigation seemed to have gone cold. It was as if we had all been holding our collective breaths waiting for an arrest, but finally our breaths had run out. Some speculated hopefully that the killer had merely been passing through town—a trucker, perhaps. Someone on vacation. Old, more conspiratorial rumors had resurfaced at barbecues and barbershops, in late-night bars and grocery store checkout lines: that the killer had been Anna's husband, or an unidentified lover, or a police officer now being protected by the authorities. This disembodied anxiety hung over the city like the last haze of the summer wildfires.

"They'll find him," C.J. said, as if reading my mind. The way she said it sounded odd—as if she were stating a fact, not a hope or a guess.

"What makes you so sure?" I asked from the back seat.

I saw Ray turn to regard C.J., as if he, too, were surprised by her certainty, before staring back out at the long white line of the highway.

"You hear something?" Ray asked C.J.

"You're the DA," C.J. said. "If anything happens, you'll hear it before I will."

All three of us knew this wasn't true; C.J. was friends with every sheriff's deputy in the courthouse, and with most of the Reno Police Department. She knew every court clerk and was on a first-name basis with every administrative assistant at the Washoe County Jail. C.J. caught my eye in the rearview mirror, and I tried to decipher whatever message she might be trying to send. The cab was silent for a long moment as C.J. steered the car along the broad curves of the highway.

"You hear something," Ray said, "you better fucking tell me."

"Hey," C.J. said. "No office talk."

PYRAMID LAKE IS an aberration, a silvery-green mirage thirty miles long and nine miles wide surrounded on all sides by basin and range, its water green against the chalk white of the desert floor. Thirty yards from the shoreline the lake's silty bottom falls off quickly, so that fishermen cast from on top of aluminum painters' ladders they place out into chest-deep water.

It was a cold morning, wind whipping sand off the beach near the little reservation town of Sutcliffe on the west side of the lake. I spent two hours perched on my ladder, casting for the two-foot-long Lahontan cutthroat circling in the water below, the rusty red of their flanks flashing as the fish ruddered through the shallows. I fished an olive Woolly Bugger for forty-five minutes without a bite, then spent another hour switching through a half dozen different lures—Midges and Water Boatmen and Sheep's Creek Specials and Copper Johns. Finally, I retreated to the warmth of C.J.'s truck, my hands so cold that I dropped my reel in the sand before slamming the door on my rod, snapping off the top eight inches.

Ray was huddled in the front seat, warming his hands against the heater. He nodded at me as I climbed into the passenger seat, then reached over to turn the heat up.

"Jesus Christ," Ray said. We both watched from the warmth of the car as C.J. bent over to net a ten-pound trout. She held the fish in her bare hands in the frigid wind, then leaned in to pull the lure from the fish's lip with a pair of forceps. When she'd returned the fish to the lake, she pulled a small notebook from the pocket of her waders and scribbled a quick note. "That's one weird fucking chick."

An hour later I was dozing in the back seat of C.J.'s truck, Tom T. Hall singing "That's How I Got to Memphis" on the radio, when Ray suddenly sat bolt upright.

"Jesus," he said, glaring at his phone. His fat fingers swiped over the screen, the phone so close that it nearly touched his nose.

"What?" I asked.

"Fucking C.J.," he said. We both looked down the grey beach to where she was fishing, the silent cadence of her cast whipping through the wind.

"What is it?" I said again.

"Weston," Ray said. "They fucking caught the guy, that's what."

THIRTY-SEVEN

BY THE TIME C.J. dropped me back at my apartment an hour later, an autumn storm had settled in over the Sierras, the dimming sky breaking open with rain. Inside, I cranked open the cast-iron radiator and turned on the television. The screen was filled with a booking photo from the Washoe County Jail, the format of the image now so familiar: the grey lighting cast by the fluorescent lamps, the orange collar of the jail-issue jumpsuit, the squareness of the subjects as they stared, deadpan, into the camera's lens.

A white man in his midtwenties peered back from the screen, his face long, eyes set wide apart. A light mustache sat above his small mouth, a bit of grainy stubble barely visible on his chin. His sandy-blond hair was cut short at the sides and parted a little too straightly, giving him the appearance of someone younger than he probably was. He looked like no one, like an extra, like a thousand people I'd passed in airports or grocery stores or on street corners without spending a second's thought.

"Our top story tonight," the news anchor's voice began over the image. "An arrest has been made in the murder of Reno mother Anna Weston. Twenty-eight-year-old Reno resident Michael Keith Atwood was taken into custody early this afternoon after his DNA matched that of a specimen collected from Weston's body."

While the anchor continued, I hung my unused fishing net on a closet door handle, draped my waders in the shower to dry. I remembered C.J. saying once that they only use a defendant's middle name if they're *really* guilty. *John Wilkes Booth* guilty. *James Earl Ray* guilty. *John Wayne Gacy* guilty.

As I sorted through the bag of damp fishing gear, I turned over this new information, trying to make sense of the timing. Atwood had been arrested that afternoon, just as we were returning from Pyramid Lake. I'd been with C.J. the entire day and hadn't seen her check her phone once, and yet she'd all but predicted the arrest, and had seemed unsurprised when her prediction had come true. When Ray asked, she had denied knowing anything ahead of time—that a cop or a clerk or even a DA had given her a heads-up—and yet the timing seemed too unlikely to be a coincidence.

The next morning I arrived to find C.J. waiting in my office, her feet kicked up on the corner of my desk. In front of the pair of oxblood flats sat a new manila case file imprinted with a red stamp that said "Major Violator's Unit." I felt C.J. grinning at me as I picked up the file.

"What is this?" I said. "A joke?"

"Nope," C.J. said. "He's ours. Well, he's *yours*, technically."

I shook my head, partly out of disbelief and partly because I knew C.J. wasn't joking. I opened the file to the first page, and there sat the criminal complaint filed by the district attorney's office charging Michael Keith Atwood with one count of Open Murder with the Use of a Deadly Weapon.

"I talked to Pat last night," C.J. said. "It's a Department Nine case, and it just happened to be assigned to your unqualified ass."

"Dan handles all the murders," I said under my breath. I was skimming through the two-page complaint, words jumping from the paper like fish from water: *did willfully and unlawfully, with malice aforethought, for the purpose of committing sexual assault, to wit, a belt or other ligature.*

"Not this one," C.J. said. "This one is ours."

I shook my head again.

"This is a death penalty case," I said. "I'm not even qualified."

"That's why you're my second," C.J. said. Besides Dan, C.J. was one of the only other attorneys in the public defender's office to be death penalty qualified, which means that you've had enough trial experience to defend a capital case. I'd heard—not from C.J. or Dan, but instead from Joanne, our receptionist—that C.J. and Dan had co-counseled a half dozen murder cases before I'd arrived in the office. During the last trial they'd fought so bitterly over trial strategy that C.J. had abandoned the case halfway through and Dan had been forced to finish it alone. I glanced up to Washington's bust glaring down at us from the bookshelf.

"Listen. I see you're consulting with your friend up there," C.J. said, pointing over her shoulder at the plaster head. "If you don't want it, don't take it. I'll find someone else."

An hour later I had changed into my navy suit and was in C.J.'s passenger seat again, this time on our way to the jail. Several news trucks were idling in front of the jail entrance when we arrived, tripods and video cameras arranged haphazardly along the sidewalk. I followed C.J. past a half dozen reporters and into the lobby. I was carrying only the file folder and a new yellow legal pad, while C.J. had come entirely empty-handed; none of the evidence had arrived yet, so we knew only what we'd gleaned from the complaint and the news.

"We're here for—" I began, holding up the file to Omar, the desk clerk.

"Yeah, I heard," Omar said, waving us through the metal detector. He was eyeing a reporter lingering at the end of his desk. "He's in the Shoe."

The Special Housing Unit—the Shoe—is where they keep jail inmates in need of special protection, either from themselves or from other people. It's where the sick and the suicidal are sent, the actively psychotic, the snitches, the alleged pederasts. Inmates who, for one reason or another, won't make it in general population. As I followed C.J. down the white concrete hallway toward the Shoe, I wondered who would be waiting—a sociopathic killer, or some tweaked-out meth head, or perhaps someone like a Mr. Milan, undone in his own brain. I'd met killers in court before—clients with the words *murder* or *manslaughter* in their rap sheets. Most were nondescript, even ordinary. Regular people who'd drunk too much one night and made a bad decision. Others you could pick out of a football stadium, like one of C.J.'s clients who had done twenty-five years for killing his girlfriend. When he was brought into Bartos' court on a parole violation, a noiseless rage had seemed to radiate from him; even the other in-custody defendants wouldn't sit near him in the jury box as they waited for the calendar to begin. When his case was called and he walked over to stand next to C.J. at the defendant's table, I saw the words *Bitch Killer* tattooed across the back of his shaved head.

But now, as we made our way through the labyrinth of the jail, C.J. seemed indifferent to the possibilities of who we would find waiting for us. She was still going on about the trout she had landed the day before while Ray and I had been huddled in the cab of the truck.

"Big as my arm," she was saying as the cold clank of the housing unit door sounded through the hallway. An older deputy stationed behind an inch of plexiglass looked up from a newspaper as we approached.

"Number twelve," he said, pointing toward a row of blue cell doors. He pushed a button on the control panel, and the clank of an automatic lock echoed through the courtyard. Several faces appeared in the narrow windows of the other cells, peering out to where we had entered.

"Can we get the conference room?" C.J. asked. The deputy shrugged, then leaned into a microphone and pushed a button.

"Atwood, your attorneys are here," he said into the microphone. I followed C.J. into a small custodian's closet. Outside, I heard the sound of jail-issued plastic sandals shuffling across the empty common area, and a few seconds later Michael Atwood was standing in the doorway.

He looked just as he had in his mug shot—nondescript, young-faced, an oversized Adam's apple jogging at the neck of his jumpsuit. The only noticeable difference was a two-inch burgundy bruise under his left eye.

"What the hell happened here?" C.J. said, reaching a hand out toward the swollen eye, the abrasion wet-looking under the fluorescent light. Atwood flinched.

"We're from the public defender's office," C.J. began, holding out an embossed county business card. "We've been appointed to represent you in court."

I felt Atwood examining us, not exactly sizing us up, but merely taking in the information of our faces, of our forms. As C.J. continued to talk, she leaned back against the wall in a way that was casual and familiar but also gave everyone a bit of breathing space in the small room.

"It's nice to meet you, Mr. Atwood," I said, putting a hand out. "My name is Santi Elcano. I work with C.J. at the public defender's."

We shook hands, Michael not meeting my eyes as he placed a dewy, limp hand in mine. I thought about the photograph of Anna Weston that I had seen so often, the crookedness of her smile. The image ran headlong into the language of the charging document I'd received that day—sexual assault, strangulation, ligature. I considered the hand that I now held in mine, there in the harsh light of the custodian's closet. What had it touched? What was it capable of?

"Somebody got a shot in before they transferred you to the Shoe?" C.J. asked. Michael held a hand to the abrasion and nodded slowly, still not making eye contact, the way a child might answer a teacher. "If it happens again, let me know," C.J. said. "They have a duty to keep you safe in here."

"OK," he said quietly. He kicked a foot petulantly against a metal shelf lined with soaps and cleaning agents.

"All right, then," C.J. said, cracking her knuckles. "Let's get started."

We spent the next half hour explaining the basics: why we'd been assigned to represent him, what he had been charged with, what he should and shouldn't tell us, when his next hearing was set for.

C.J. was just about to wrap up when Michael mumbled something under his breath. C.J. and I shared a glance.

"What was that, Mr. Atwood?" I asked.

"I was at *home* that night," he said. "With my mom. I tried to tell the detective."

"That's great," C.J. said. "And we'll talk about that soon. Right now, though, we need to take it one step at a time. The grand jury is set to convene on Thursday. We still haven't received any discovery—that's evidence—from the DA. But they'll get their indictment, and after that we'll set a trial date."

"Which means you'll be in here for a little while," I added, just to say something.

"How much am I looking at?" he asked. "I mean, if I'm convicted—what could a sentence be?"

I had been taking stock of him, sizing up his small frame, his childish demeanor. Until that moment, it had been difficult to imagine he was capable of the things he had been accused of. But there was something about the question, as if he were tallying the bill on an unpaid check. Then again, I thought, wouldn't that be the question that I'd want answered if I were in his position, even if I were innocent?

"We're not going to talk about that yet," C.J. said. "Right now, we're focusing on your defense."

Michael shifted uneasily, but finally nodded in agreement. C.J. continued on with her first-visit pitch, as if he were just another client, just another case file. When she finished the final part of the speech—her standard admonition about the importance of shutting the fuck up—she stood off the wall, folding shut the file.

"And that means that you talk to *no one*, unless it's me or him, OK?" she said, pointing to me. "Not your cellie, not that guard out there, not your family on the phone. No one."

Michael looked up from his feet, his eyes briefly meeting mine. I searched for something in there—some tic or glint that might suggest his guilt or innocence, that might reveal the presence or absence of evil—but there was nothing. They were only two blue eyes, as plain and nondescript as the rest of him.

I opened the door of the custodian's room and we followed Michael Atwood out into the Shoe. We shook hands again, and then C.J. and I turned to leave and Michael started toward his cell door.

"Aren't you going to ask if I did it?" Michael asked suddenly across the empty common area.

The door to the housing unit clanged open. I felt the faces of the other inmates reappearing in the small windows of their cells, staring out at where the three of us stood. C.J. suddenly looked small against the cavernous room, her face drawn and tired. As she stood there considering the question, I was reminded that she, too, was human, that she was flesh and bone.

"No," she said finally. She turned to where I stood behind her. "Are you?"

I shook my head.

I'd learned never to ask that question—the question at the center of every case—unless I knew for sure that the answer would be no. There's a reason for this: A defense attorney is prohibited from presenting an argument that they know to be false, so knowing the answer to this question limits the defenses available at trial. "Don't ask questions you don't want answers to," C.J. had admonished me early on. I watched Michael Atwood try to make sense of this answer; his bony Adam's apple jumped again above the collar of his jumpsuit, and I realized that he was trying his hardest not to cry.

"Well, I didn't, OK?" he said, his voice breaking. "I didn't kill anybody."

"OK," C.J. said. "Well, that makes things easier for all of us."

THIRTY-EIGHT

I CAME HOME from the jail that evening to find Caroline, still in her work scrubs, on the front step of my apartment building. She was smoking a cigarette, something I'd noticed she had been doing more often lately.

"Hey," I said. "You'll never guess where I've been."

She stared blankly at me, the smoke curling into the cool evening air. I glanced around the apartment parking lot.

"Where's your car?"

She took another drag, then flicked her cigarette onto the sidewalk.

"Walked," she said.

"From the hospital?"

She nodded dully. I sat down on the step next to her, and she leaned the crumpled knee of her scrubs against my slacks.

"Hey," I said. She jerked a bit, as if just startling awake. "You OK?"

"Just a bad day at the hospital, you know?" she said, her voice uneven. She smiled weakly. "So what's your big news?"

I looked at the notepad with Michael Atwood's name written in the header. I knew that it wasn't the right time, that I should wait, but I couldn't hold back.

"I'm on the Atwood case," I said. It felt thrilling to say it out loud, the rush of something akin to celebrity. "Well, C.J. is, technically. But I'm second-chairing."

"Oh," Caroline said. I watched her shoulders go slack with exhaustion. "Sorry. What case is that?"

"It's *the* case," I said. "The Anna Weston murder case."

I don't know what I had expected her reaction to be, but what I saw was something between revulsion and disappointment.

"Oh, babe," she said. "I'm sorry . . ."

"Sorry?" I'd been a public defender for a little more than two years, and already I was working on the most high-profile case in a decade. "What're you sorry for?"

"It just sounds ugly, is all," Caroline said. "We get those cases, too, you know. And they're just . . . very ugly."

"Yeah, I know," I said, trying to feign somberness. Caroline occasionally mentioned patients in the emergency room that we realized overlapped with my caseload—blunt force traumas and overdoses and sexual assault examinations that made their way into my evidentiary files. "But it's also, I don't know. A good opportunity for me, you know?"

"Sorry," Caroline said emptily. She stood from her seat on the step. "I'm happy for you. Really. And I'm sure you'll be great. Just . . ."

Her voice trailed off.

"Just a bad day at the hospital," I said, completing her sentence.

She nodded.

"You coming up?" I said. "Can I get you a beer? Something to eat?"

"Nah," she said. "Think I'm just going to head home. That OK?"

Before I could answer, she leaned in, her lips dry against my neck, her arms gripping tightly against my back, then turned and started off down the dark street.

THIRTY-NINE

THE EVIDENCE ARRIVED in waves, delivered to my desk each morning by Joanne, who for once knew to forgo her usual snippiness, her complaints about clients, and her never-ending countdown to retirement. First the police reports dating back to Anna Weston's disappearance the year before, the small details that had leaked out in the press now becoming three-dimensional. A series of stuttering surveillance videos capturing the headlights of Anna's car as they entered the gas station in South Reno where she had last been seen. The ghostly form of the dead woman as she circled the back of the car.

"You need to start a trial notebook now," I heard a voice say one morning. I looked up to see Dan Osterman hovering in the doorway, staring at the Atwood file on my desk, into which I was trying to fit the latest arrival from the district attorney's office—an inventory of Atwood's truck, which had been impounded at his mother's house in Washoe Valley.

"OK," I said. "Thanks."

Dan was one of the four chief deputies—senior attorneys who oversaw a team of six PDs—so he had always maintained a certain professional distance with rank and file like C.J. and me. I knew little about him, other than what I'd heard from C.J.—that he was smart and hardworking, though according to C.J., this didn't mean he was a good attorney.

"You should be thinking about who your witnesses at prelim will be, if there even is a prelim," he continued. "They'll likely go through grand jury instead. They won't have any trouble indicting with what they already have."

He spoke quietly, almost as if he were talking to himself. Taking mental notes. Organizing the file. Preparing his lines of defense. When he left a few minutes later, I wondered—not for the first time—what it had taken for C.J. to secure the case from Pat.

THE COVERS OF the Atwood file filled quickly, spilling over into new folders and banker's boxes. Transcripts of interviews from the initial days of the investigation, when Anna Weston's husband had been the primary suspect. Hundreds of pages of call logs from the anonymous tip line. Handwritten statements given by the two men who had stumbled upon her body in the hills. Phone records. A detective's attempt to re-create the movements of Anna's last night through cell phone tower triangulation. Analysis of fiber and DNA samples. Bite mark analyses completed by the Washoe County crime lab and the FBI.

"You look at the new photos yet?" C.J. said one morning. I'd been avoiding a trio of silver DVDs that had arrived that morning.

"Not yet," I said. C.J. took a seat across my desk, gazing out my sliver of window. A blade of sun cleaved her face in two, her lips pursed in that familiar expression that flitted between concentration and amusement.

"Well, they're not good," she said. "I mean, from a jury standpoint. The body's all fucked up. But then, what do you expect after that long?"

"I'll look at them tonight," I said. I was supposed to meet Caroline for dinner, but now I realized I'd be spending the evening alone at my desk with Anna Weston.

"But other than the shock value," C.J. continued, "I don't see anything that bad. Really, the only thing they have to go on is the DNA."

The charging document had listed Anna Weston's presumptive murder weapon as a leather belt that had been recovered from under the body. The crime lab had been able to gather a sample of dried blood that contained the mixed DNA of both Anna Weston and an unidentified male, and it was this DNA sample that had eventually been matched to Michael Atwood.

But DNA was attackable, C.J. had insisted. Contaminated crime scene. Mislabeled samples. Just recently a lab tech from the Las Vegas Police

Department was found to have made massive mistakes in DNA processing that had sent an innocent man to prison.

"We're in good shape, Gato," C.J. said. She smoothed her hands over her tweed jacket, then stood to leave. "They were under a shit-ton of pressure to make an arrest. I'm telling you, they're overplaying their hand."

AS I LOADED the first disk into my office computer that night, I felt Washington staring down from his perch on my bookshelf, reading through the layers. Dread. Anticipation. A latent exhilaration. Shame.

"It's not like I enjoy looking at this shit," I told him.

I heard the disk whir in the computer, the screen lighting up with the first image: a sheriff's deputy frozen in the camera's flash, yellow police tape stretching to a dark stand of brush. A forensic investigator's white jumpsuit squatting in the dirt next to a small recess in a wash. In a corner of the photograph the faded blue of a sweatshirt emerged from a shadow of crumbled basalt, coarse and rusted.

In the next photograph a woman's hand protruded from a sleeve of the sweatshirt, the skin wilted and dark. The flash had caught on the gold band of her wedding ring, which seemed to sink into the skin beneath it. I clicked from one photo to the next, taking notes on each in a discovery review memorandum.

"Anything that might be important, you write it down," C.J. had said. "Anything that even catches your attention, that just feels a little off."

And just the act of writing, of documenting, helped tamp down the creeping sense of prurience. I stared deep into each image, scouring each pixel for the one detail that might save Michael Atwood's life. The photos clicked past, Anna Weston slowly coming alive in the light of the camera's flash. The smallness of her, even smaller in the first photographs, in which she is crumpled carelessly into the small stone shelter. The body as it is slid from its half tomb, unfolding in the gloved hands of the forensic investigators. Bits of tattered clothing, the fraying tongue of a single sneaker. The familiar brown of her hair, strewn through with gravel and foxtails.

When I looked up at Washington on the top of the bookshelf, I felt the shape of the dead man in the room with me, as I so often did that year. *That was me once*, he seemed to say. *There, on the examiner's table.*

"I'm sorry," I said apologetically to the plaster bust.

I steadied myself, then began the next disk, labeled "autopsy."

Don't apologize, the bust said. *This is how it works.*

I've been at it for too long, I told myself. I pushed my chair away from the computer, began to pack my things to go home.

Stay, the bust seemed to say. *Keep looking. I give you permission.*

KNOW THIS: SHE had suffered.

As the autopsy photographs scrolled across my computer screen, I reread the medical examiner's notes, clusters of words and phrases jumping off the page, giving life to the photographs. *Advanced levels of decomposition . . . Fractures to the radius and ulna, indicating defensive wounds . . . Fractures of first and third metatarsals . . . Blunt force trauma . . . Consumption by native fauna . . . Fracture to hyoid bone . . .* The report noted that a sheriff's deputy later discovered bits of bone fragments scattered down the ravine, that strands of Anna Weston's hair had been recovered from a scrub jay's nest in a nearby juniper.

It was nearly ten at night when I glanced up to find C.J. leaning against the frame of my office door. She was looking at the image filling the screen of my computer: the now-familiar gloved hands of the coroner stretching a tape measure across the length of the cadaver's leg.

She shook her head somberly.

"Goddamn but she still had a nice ass," C.J. said. I stared at her incredulously, a moment of silence stretching between us. She began to smile, and then suddenly I was laughing, too, because what was the alternative?

FORTY

THE NEXT MORNING I arrived to find Paul Harris waiting for me in the lobby, tracing the sentences of an open textbook on his lap with a mechanical pencil.

"I'm sorry, Paul," I said. I was exhausted from the late night before, staring at evidentiary photos until my eyes blurred. "But do we have a meeting scheduled today?"

"Sorry to stop by like this," he said. "It's just, we have the motion to confirm trial hearing set for next month, and I've been trying to get ahold of you. I've been leaving you messages, but you never call back."

A woman seated in the lobby looked up from her phone, and I smiled sheepishly.

"I have a few minutes right now," I said. "Why don't you come back to my office and we'll talk."

He closed the book, *Statistics: Principles and Methods*, and put it into his backpack before following me past our receptionist, Joanne, and the locked door of the office.

"So," I said, clearing a stack of motion work from one of the chairs across my desk. "What is it you wanted to talk about?"

He fidgeted in his chair, brushing something from the front of his T-shirt.

"Well," he said. "I guess I just want to know—are you still my attorney?"

"Of course I'm still your attorney, Paul," I said. I glanced at my watch—I had a motion to suppress evidence on Michael's case due at the end of the day, and a full court calendar to deal with on top of it.

"I mean, are you going to show up?" he said. He looked away from me as he said it. "I hear stories—especially since, you know."

"Especially since what?" I said. I was getting annoyed with being accused of not doing my job.

"Do I need to say it?" he said, running a hand from his head down to his feet. "OK, fine. My family's telling me about how I need to hire a real attorney."

"You don't think I'm a real attorney?" I snapped.

"It's not that," Paul said. "I just thought this would have gone away by now."

And the truth was that it should have gone away by now—ordinarily Neil would have offered a defer-and-dismiss, but in the last weeks he had suddenly become reluctant to offer plea deals.

"I hear you," I said. "But I can't control what the DA offers. He agreed to allow you to do drug court—that offer is still on the table. It would mean doing classes and getting tested for a year, but after that the charge would go away."

"See, that's what I mean," Paul said. "You're asking me to plead guilty when I didn't *do* anything."

"I'm not asking you to do anything," I reminded him. "I'm legally obligated to tell you what the DA's offer is. Did I ever tell you to take it?"

"No."

"You want to get a *real attorney*, go ahead." I was done with it. I was over being the one with no power, trying to make everyone happy. "That would make my life easier, trust me. But like I said, I think we have a good chance of beating this at trial."

He started to say something, but I held up my hand.

"I can't spend all morning talking to you, Paul," I said. "I have an investigator assigned. This is a winnable case, but you're going to have to let me do my job."

FORTY-ONE

THE BROWN LEATHER belt recovered from her body was the one piece of physical evidence that would forever link Michael Atwood to Anna Weston. More specifically, it was the partial, male-dominant DNA profile recovered from a smear of blood on the belt, which had matched the DNA from a saliva sample collected by detectives from Michael Atwood during his interview. *The estimated frequency of this matching DNA profile*, the Washoe County Forensic Science analysis stated, *is approximately 1 in 64.8 sextillion.*

But it wasn't just that bit of double helix that implicated Michael Atwood. The DNA had only been the marble in the Rube Goldberg machine that was a homicide investigation, the catalyst that led to the first suspect profile: Caucasian male. From there, a cascading series of events, the accrual of investigative momentum. Detectives systematically working leads as they came in, following up on hotline tips, interview after interview, DNA sample after DNA sample.

The first mention of the name Michael Atwood appeared in a detective's note three months before his arrest—just another name, nothing to trip any alarms, cops just doing their due diligence. The tip from an anonymous caller, likely an ex-girlfriend or a coworker with a grudge. Nothing specific, documentable. Just a feeling, probably nothing.

A detective had brought him in just to check him off the list, tick their little boxes. Criminal history: none. Whereabouts at the time of the abduction: at home with his mother (verified). Demeanor: nervous but cooperative.

Employment: maintenance at the Eldorado Hotel and Casino (three years). Height, weight, hair: all nondescript, unexceptional. The only detail of note was his reluctance to provide a DNA sample, though the cop had simply side-stepped this process by taking a swab from the rim of the water bottle he'd given Michael at the start of the interview.

Just a breath of mitochondrial DNA and they were off and running, locked on to their suspect. Days of unfruitful surveillance, interviews with a half dozen acquaintances, and then even though they had nothing else to go on, they made their move, because sometimes you just have to make your move. Detectives Turner and Peck waiting in an unmarked car when Michael returns to his mother's house from a swing shift, an arrest warrant based on the DNA match and a handful of other semi-fabricated, semi-exaggerated details, just enough to give a judge the pretext of "probable cause," because who wants to be the judge that lets Anna Weston's killer go free?

"Turner is like a teenager about to fuck for the first time," C.J. said, waving the Probable Cause sheet at me across the conference table. "He's trying so hard to slow himself down, but . . . no."

By then she'd begun to convince me—the lack of evidence against him, the winnability of the case, our mandate to save an innocent man's life. For a few days, I believed her.

THE INTERROGATION VIDEO arrived later that week—Detective Peck seated at the metal table waiting for Michael to be brought in, scribbling a few notes on a notepad. I wondered why they'd chosen Peck to interview him; she was a competent detective, but had only recently begun working homicide cases. C.J. had speculated that they'd wanted a woman working along with Turner for the optics, and maybe there was something to that. A delicate unease crept through me as I watched Michael Atwood slide into the seat across from her, two cans of soda on the table between them.

When the video concluded five hours later, I sat staring at the computer screen, the interrogation room with two empty chairs across the metal table now strewn with coffee cups, a pen, wadded tissue paper. Over the course of the afternoon I had watched as Detective Peck led Michael Atwood through an amalgam of evidence and invention—Michael's DNA on the belt that had strangled Anna Weston (true), statements from coworkers that Michael had acted oddly in the days after her disappearance (true), video of Michael's pickup at the same gas station where Anna had last been seen (false), a statement from Michael's mother refuting his alibi on the night of the disappearance (also false). For *four hours* he denied everything, argued against each bit of evidence that Peck had collected or fabricated.

"I'm trying to *help* you out here, Michael," Peck told him at two in the morning. "But you have to help me, too. Maybe there's something I'm missing, something that can explain how you were with this woman the night she disappeared."

"I'm trying to help," Michael argued weakly. "But I *wasn't* with her."

"But you were," Peck maintained. "We know that already. We know what happened, Michael, but I need to hear it from you."

She continued on like this, insisting on the truth of her reality, and eventually Michael's protests began to subside. In the last hour, I watched Michael sit mute as Peck led him once again through the evidence, landing on a photo of Anna's body where it was found in the desert. When she finished her recitation, she pointed to the door of the interrogation room.

"I want to get you out that door," she said. "I want to get you home, but you have to start helping me."

He stared bitterly across at Peck, and for a moment I thought he might reach across the table to grab her. Instead, he slowly extended a hand out toward a Styrofoam coffee cup. He seemed to notice the cup trembling in his grasp and placed it back on the table without taking a drink. It was then that I realized he was crying. He was crying, and he was nodding.

I CAUGHT UP with C.J. in her office that afternoon as she was returning from court.

"You listen to the confession yet?" I asked. She was simultaneously sorting through a stack of files and snacking on a bag of M&M's.

"Atwood?" she said. "What confession?"

"*That* confession," I said, pointing to the DVD on her desk.

She was expressionless for a moment.

"Peck's interview?" she said. "That's what you're calling a confession?"

"In the sense that he *confesses* to being with Anna Weston on the night she goes missing, and that he admits that the belt that killed her belongs to him, and that he *apologizes* for killing her. Yes. That's what I'm calling a confession."

"No," C.J. said patiently. "*That* is the textbook example of coerced testimony."

I stood, stunned, for a moment.

"You're saying that's a false confession?" I asked.

"This," she said, "is exactly why you need to be on this case."

C.J. patted the seat of an office chair, the way you would beckon a child. I reluctantly sat down, and she took a seat across from me behind her desk. I had the sudden, unsettling sensation that I was Michael Atwood about to be interrogated by Detective Peck.

"OK," she said. "Tell me where you hear a confession."

I began revisiting the highlights of the interrogation, but for every argument, she had a compelling counterargument ready: that he'd been under extreme duress, that it was four in the morning and he'd been without sleep for nearly twenty-four hours, that he hadn't actually confessed, but had merely agreed with Peck because he'd wanted to go home. He hadn't *apologized* for murdering Anna Weston, but he'd said that he was sorry that she was dead.

"Watch it again," she said. "You'll see. Everything he says is coached. He doesn't provide one bit of independent information to her. How did he get her into his car? Where did he supposedly strangle her? Why isn't her DNA in his truck? Why isn't there a single photo of Michael ever wearing the fucking belt that he supposedly killed her with?"

"OK," I said. "Let's say it is a false confession. It's still not going to look good to a jury."

The serene smile that she'd been wearing for the past half hour suddenly evaporated.

"My dad used to have this expression," C.J. said. It was the first time she'd ever mentioned her family. "He used to say, 'Cecelia Jane, you can put a cat in the oven, but that don't make it a biscuit.'"

"What the hell is that supposed to mean?" I said.

Suddenly she crumpled the candy wrapper in her palm and slammed it onto the desk.

"It means that something's not true just because *they* say it is," she snapped, jabbing a finger at the file. Her pale green eyes went flat, her mouth tight. "If you haven't realized it yet, it's your *job* to show the jury that."

FORTY-TWO

THE GALLERY BEGAN filling an hour before Michael Atwood's arraignment, the seats packed with reporters and bystanders eager to get a look at the man who had murdered Anna Weston. When I arrived, Linda Ernst was sitting rigidly at the State's table, with Neil second-chair next to her. Linda was a veteran prosecutor with a reputation for excoriating defense attorneys in oral argument; she'd worked a dozen murders in her two decades as a DA and had won convictions on all of them.

As I unpacked my briefcase, I noticed Linda's knee jogging beneath the table, the first time I'd ever seen her show anything that looked like nerves. She glanced up and caught my eye, abruptly stopping her knee as if she knew she'd been caught. She offered a quick, tight smile, and for a fleeting second it felt like we were on the same team, like there was an unspoken camaraderie between us. She pointed to her watch, then raised her eyebrow, as if to say exactly what I'd been thinking for the last ten minutes. *Where the hell is C.J.?*

On the table in front of me was the Atwood file, which had already grown four inches thick with police reports and witness statements, as well as a new yellow legal pad and my copy of the Nevada Revised Statutes. I'd brought along the statute book at the last minute merely as a prop, something to suggest a deep familiarity with Nevada law, as if I might flip it open at any time to the exact statute I'd been quoting. We wouldn't be dealing with any substantive legal issues today; the arraignment was only a formal reading of the charges and an opportunity for us to enter a plea of not guilty so that a trial date might be set.

An uneasy quiet began to settle over the courtroom as the time of the hearing approached. Marcia, the court clerk, emerged from the judge's chambers and began to organize the charging documents that she would read to Michael shortly. The stenographer had finished setting up her keyboard below Bartos' bench, and I noticed that several prosecutors and defense attorneys had taken seats in the jury box to watch the hearing. I fingered the Xanax in my pocket, wondering if I could surreptitiously slip another of the white tablets into my mouth without the audience of reporters noticing.

A sheriff's deputy made his way to a small desk near the jury box, then cocked his head to say something into the walkie-talkie clipped to the shoulder of his uniform. I eyed the door to the courtroom, but C.J. still hadn't arrived. In the front row of the gallery I recognized Anna Weston's mother huddled next to a handsome man in his early thirties dressed in a well-fitted suit. I had nearly forgotten about her husband, only a name in the discovery notes as an initial interview, someone who had been eliminated as a suspect early on—his alibi corroborated by several people. I wondered where Anna Weston's young son was, who would be caring for him at that moment.

Five minutes before the hearing was set to begin, the double doors opened and C.J. strode into the courtroom, a line of reporters parting in her wake. She was dressed smartly, as she always was, her copper hair pulled back into a tight braid, the starched collar of her blouse framing her thin jaw. She made her way past Anna Weston's family without even a glance, pushing through the crowd and into the calm of the courtroom beyond the back railing. She smiled quickly in the direction of the prosecutor's table, a gesture that both Linda and Neil either didn't see or chose to ignore.

"Glad you could make it," I said under my breath. She had arrived with nothing at all—not her copy of the Atwood file, not even a legal pad. I tore off a few pages from my pad and slid them over to her, along with a pen. I took two more pages and placed them in the empty space between us where Michael Atwood would sit—a trick C.J. had shown me early on to give your defendant someplace to look besides at the witness, or the jury, or the media.

The court deputy crooked his neck to speak into his radio again, and I heard the familiar knock at the door of the jury room. As the door swung open, a cascade of camera shutters rattled through the courtroom. In the time since we first visited him at the jail, Michael's black eye had faded to a sallow yellow, but otherwise he looked the same as he had that first night in the Shoe: slump-shouldered, eyes downcast. I wondered if this was who Anna Weston's mother and husband had pictured when she was missing all those months; even as he was led across the room to the defense table, his hands shackled to his waist, his lanky torso clad in a green bulletproof vest, Michael looked more pathetic than dangerous.

There was a fresh volley from the reporters' cameras as C.J. put a hand on his shoulder and leaned in to whisper something, and I already knew it would be the picture on the front page of the newspaper the next morning. I leaned over my legal pad and wrote the date and the words *Atwood Arraignment*.

Bartos took the bench a minute later, the audience standing in unison before being instructed to sit. C.J., Michael Atwood, and I remained standing at the defense table—the only people standing in the courtroom, silence stretching around us. Bartos had recently had his hair cut, I noticed, and he seemed to even be wearing a bit of makeup to hide the age spots that ordinarily dotted his forehead.

"Ladies and gentlemen in the gallery," he began, looking judiciously at the cameras, "I'm going to ask for your cooperation with the proceedings this afternoon."

He launched in on a speech about the importance of fairness in the legal system—one that had likely been scripted by his campaign manager—before starting the hearing in earnest a few minutes later.

"Ms. Clerk, would you please recite the information in the charging documents?"

"Michael Keith Atwood," Marcia began reading mechanically. I felt Michael list slightly next to me, his shoulder leaning momentarily against mine as if it were only now that he realized the severity of his situation. "You are charged by criminal complaint with Murder, a violation of NRS 200.010, in that you did, unlawfully and with malice aforethought, kill Anna Lynn Weston, a human being, in the County of Washoe, State of Nevada."

Marcia read through the additional charges, then sat back down at her desk.

"Thank you, Ms. Clerk," Bartos said, turning to C.J. and me. "Counsel, have you spoken to your client about the nature of these proceedings, and is he prepared to enter a plea at this time?"

"Yes, Your Honor," C.J. said. I had been tasked with nothing—my job was merely to stand on the opposite side of Michael Atwood and keep my mouth shut—and yet I felt a tremor making its way past the dull fog of the Xanax. "Co-counsel and I have spoken at length with Mr. Atwood, and we are prepared to enter a plea of not guilty."

"Very well," Bartos said, making a note on a legal pad. He launched into his standard plea canvass: asking Michael directly if he understood his right to a trial within sixty days under Nevada law, his right to confront witnesses against him and to compel witnesses to testify on his behalf. It was the same script we had all followed a hundred times that year, and I knew that as long as everyone followed the script, Bartos would be happy. To each admonition, Michael answered weakly in the affirmative. Five minutes later we had entered our plea and were ready to set a trial date—the whole thing over in less than ten minutes, after which the reporters would pack up their notepads and cameras, a sheriff's van would drive Michael back to the Shoe, and Anna Weston's family would return to their silent homes.

"And I'm guessing, given the nature of the charges, that you'll be waiving your right to trial within sixty days?" Bartos concluded. "Ms. Clerk, please set a date for—"

"If I could, Your Honor," C.J. interrupted.

I felt my spine go rigid. In Nevada, clients can elect to have a jury trial within sixty days of their arraignment. But for serious, complicated charges like murder, this right is almost always waived so that the defense can complete investigation, file motions, and arrange for expert witnesses. It was considered such a given that C.J. and I hadn't even discussed it.

"Co-counsel and I have spoken with Mr. Atwood," C.J. continued, impervious to Bartos glaring down at her from the bench. "And we look forward to proving his innocence in court as soon as possible. At this time Mr. Atwood will be invoking his right to a speedy trial."

In the gallery cameras snapped and pens scratched furiously in notepads. Bartos squirmed uncomfortably for a moment, then gathered himself. I tried to catch C.J.'s eye, to ask, *What the fuck are you doing?* But she stood stone faced, facing the bench.

"All right, then," Bartos said tightly. "Ms. Clerk, can you give us a trial date by . . ." He consulted a desk calendar. "January twenty-fourth."

C.J. stood at attention, her face tight and serious, while I scribbled down the trial dates. As the hearing neared its end, Bartos tried to ease back into his usual closing routine. He glanced toward the sheriff's deputies, who stood to escort Michael Atwood back to the holding cell, then cleared his throat and leaned in to his microphone.

"I'm sorry to interrupt again, Your Honor," C.J. said before he could begin. "But before we conclude this hearing today, we would like to be heard on the matter of bail."

For a moment, Bartos simply stared, open mouthed, at C.J.

"Bail," he said finally.

I looked over at the prosecution table, where Linda and Neil were both flipping frantically through their case files and scribbling notes.

"Yes," C.J. said. "Your Honor, we understand the seriousness of the offense charged, but Mr. Atwood, as he stands here today, is presumed innocent. He has never been arrested, let alone convicted, for any felony offense prior to the charges in front of this court today. He has strong ties to the community— he lives with his mother, who is present today."

The eyes of the courtroom swung, in unison, in the direction of a thin woman in her early fifties who was now standing in the second row of the gallery, behind our defense table. She was dressed in a plain brown skirt and a denim blouse, cotton-white hair tucked back behind her ears. There was a momentary silence, as if the cameras were catching their breath, before the next onslaught of clicking began again.

"He's employed, and he's not a flight risk," C.J. continued. She placed her hand on Michael Atwood's shoulder again, the way a lion tamer might pat his alpha on the head. "With that in mind, we're asking that bail be set at fifty thousand dollars, bondable."

I thought I heard a choking sound from Neil at the prosecution table; Linda was already on her feet. Fifty thousand was a laughably low amount and one that Bartos would never grant. But it had put Linda on the defensive, forcing her into action when she'd expected only an easy afternoon as Atwood entered his not guilty plea, perhaps a feel-good press conference on the courthouse steps afterward.

"Your Honor," she began, feigning indignation. "Ms. Howard's suggestion is, to be blunt, an insult. This court, and this courtroom," she said, gesturing toward the crowded gallery, "are aware of the severity of the charges and the facts that support this case. This is a capital murder case. Mr. Atwood has every reason to abscond. The nature of the charges make clear that he poses a threat to the community. The State is asking that he be held without bail. If Your Honor would like a more comprehensive briefing on the issue of bail, we would ask that a hearing be set."

I wondered what C.J. had told Michael, if he really expected to be granted bail that afternoon. But when I looked over, he was staring sullenly at the marbled blue cover of my Nevada Revised Statutes book. Bartos waved a hand in front of his face, as if swatting away a gnat. He stared impertinently at C.J. for a moment, before turning back to Linda.

"That won't be necessary," Bartos said. "I have already reviewed the file, and I can assure you that I have no intention of altering bail in this case. Let alone at the amount that Ms. Howard has suggested today."

Linda sat back down at the prosecutor's table, clearly relieved.

"Hey!" I hissed at C.J. as the clerk announced the dates of a status conference and pretrial motions. The slightest smile flashed over her face when she met my eye. She leaned in so that only Michael and I could hear her.

"Fuck these guys, right?" she whispered.

FORTY-THREE

THE NEXT DAY I was in the back seat of a government SUV as it wound up a two-lane highway toward Virginia City, an old boomtown in the hills east of Reno. Chuck, our investigator, drove while C.J. rode in the passenger seat, gazing out over the grey mountainside as we climbed a thousand feet above the valley floor. Chuck was a retired police officer from Oakland, someone who had taken a county job because working for defense attorneys in Nevada was marginally better than sitting alone in a one-bedroom apartment waiting for an aneurysm. As he drove, he narrated a story I'd already heard a half dozen times: bodega robbery gone bad, Chuck's fortuitous timing and dexterity with his department-issued sidearm, the dispatching of one subject with a well-placed round to the torso. Much applause and recognition by the community writ large. The word *hero* not expressly stated, but certainly implied.

Virginia City had been called the "richest city in the country" during its heyday in the gold rush of 1859, the strike making the mountains east of Reno a magnet for every roughneck and wannabe placer miner who had missed the California rush a decade earlier. It had been a town on fire with the fever of money, twenty-five thousand people tearing through tunnels three thousand feet deep into the mountainside, through bars and brothels and casinos. But by the time Anna Weston's body had been found in the hills nearby, Virginia City was little more than a tourist attraction where you could get your picture taken with the Silver Queen or play a hand of blackjack at the Bucket of Blood, where mock shoot-outs were held in the middle of Main Street every day at eleven and one, cowboys killed and resurrected daily.

As we passed signs advertising old-fashioned candy and Virginia City cemetery tours, I thought about *Nevada v. Estes*, a case I'd read in law school that had always stuck with me because of its Nevada connection. Two brothers from Delaware arrived in Virginia City in 1868 to strike their fortune during the gold rush like everyone else. They came a year too late and the mines were already beginning to falter; the brothers barely survived the summer, and December found them starving and unable to secure work. Finally they were hired by a local hotel owner to saw blocks of ice from a nearby pond, menial work but at least it was money. The ice was to be bound in straw, they were told, and stored in a played-out shaft mine where it would keep until doctors and grocers and saloon keepers needed it the following summer.

A few days into the job the brothers noticed a dark shadow beneath a section of ice they had recently exposed. The pond was surrounded by tall cottonwoods, and they guessed it to be an old tree limb that had fallen into the water over summer, one that their saws and picks would make easy work of. But as their crosscut made its way through the outline of the branch, the ice turned pink, then red. When they pulled loose the saw, they noticed indigo threads caught in the steel teeth.

It was then that one of the brothers rode back to town for help. James Holt, a lawman who had been on the job for all of a week, was called to the scene. He ordered the brothers, against their protestations, to cut the remainder of the body from its place in the pond. A team of mules dragged a block the size of an ore cart to the basement of the Red Rooster, one of three brothels that serviced the town of eighteen thousand men. When the ice thawed four days later, the body was identified as that of Julie Bourcier, a beloved prostitute who had gone missing that fall.

Within a week, a suspect had been arrested—a Spanish drifter named Emiliano Estes, who had been the last person seen with Julie Bourcier. Estes spoke little English, and the feeble disavowal that he offered in his own defense at trial was an incomprehensible tangle of language.

"Estes is the devil incarnate," one newspaperman had reported from the trial, "with the eyes of a viper and a slack, gaping mouth. At no time while receiving testimony did he show a wick of emotion, let alone the flame of humanity. There isn't a man in the state who would not have strung him up themselves, if presented with the opportunity."

It wasn't until five years after Estes' execution at the end of a mob's rope that Julie Bourcier's true killer was discovered—Stephen Durbin, a known drunk who had left his confession in his hotel room before shooting himself in the chest with the same pistol that had killed Bourcier.

"Well, maybe Estes didn't kill that girl," the presiding judge was reported to have said after discovering he'd sent an innocent man to death. "But I looked into that man's eyes, and I am convinced that he has done something in his life on this earth to deserve the fate he received."

I first read about the *Estes* case during my second year of law school, in a law review article about the right to an in-court interpreter in criminal trials. But the case seemed to capture something greater than that. The judge had merely repeated something that pervaded all accounts of Emiliano Estes—not just the issue of language, but of something more basic. He'd *looked* guilty.

I'd forgotten about the *Estes* case until the night before our trip to the Virginia City highlands, when I'd found Caroline reading an article about the Atwood case on her laptop.

"Don't take this the wrong way," Caroline said. On her screen was a photograph from Bartos' courtroom that afternoon, and I had the passing thought that the man in the suit at the defense table looked vaguely familiar, before realizing that I was looking at a picture of myself standing next to Michael. "But Atwood looks . . . I don't know. Scary."

Could it still be that something as simple as whether a person *looked* guilty might determine their fate? After two years in the public defender's office, it wasn't even an open question. A defendant's appearance—whether it was their race, or their gender, or whether they had tattoos, or whether they just *looked* like they might have committed the crime they were accused of doing—was as immutable and fundamental a trial issue as the existence of DNA evidence or eyewitness testimony. I had heard it said about defendants from cops and DAs and public defenders alike: He *looks* like a pervert, she *looks* like an addict, he *looks* like a wife beater. And it was for this reason that a defense attorney's opening statements at trial so often began with "My client may not look like you . . ."

The SUV plateaued on an open plain of sage bordered by a sparse juniper forest, and Chuck steered off the highway onto a rutted dirt trail, one of the thousands of old mining roads and wildcat shafts that swiss-cheesed the range. I felt an uncomfortable excitement growing as we neared the place where Anna Weston's body had been discovered. C.J. leaned her head against the passenger window, her eyes closed, as Chuck launched into another well-worn story. I jostled in the back seat, staring off into the labyrinth of canyons.

We picked our way over boulders and through knee-deep washouts, stopping periodically for Chuck to consult a GPS map. I tried to imagine Michael driving this road in his rickety pickup as the State was alleging, Anna Weston somehow with him, but it seemed too far-fetched, too incongruous. A half hour later the SUV slowed to a stop at the mouth of a ravine identical to a dozen others we'd passed. Chuck leaned over to study the GPS screen, which C.J. regarded without interest.

"This is her," Chuck said, killing the motor. It was a clear day in early December, and a crisp afternoon wind blew through the cab of the SUV, thick with the scent of rabbitbrush and sage. The three of us opened our doors and stepped down onto the rusted yellow road, Chuck continuing to point at the screen of the GPS, saying something about triangulation and satellite accuracy. C.J. peered up the ravine to a small cleft in the rock where Anna Weston's body had been found.

"That's it," I said, recognizing the contours of the hillside from the evidentiary photos. I began sifting through a stack of pictures I'd brought along, looking for the photo a forensic investigator had taken from the place where we now stood.

"I'm about her size, you know that?" C.J. said, jotting something down in one of the small notebooks she always carried with her. "She's got an inch and five pounds on me, but that's it."

"Yeah, well, that is a coincidence, isn't it?" Chuck said. He was unloading a digital camera from a black plastic case. "You want me to start at the site, or should I get some photos from down below? I figured I'll start at the place where the body was found, and then we can work our way back—"

C.J. rolled down the sleeves of her thick cotton button-up, then abruptly sat down in the middle of the dirt road where Chuck had parked the SUV. She turned over to lie facedown, her shoulders going slack as she settled into the gravel. For the first time all afternoon Chuck stopped talking, and for a moment we both stared down at her.

"The fuck are you doing, C.J.?" Chuck said.

"The fuck do you *think* I'm doing?" C.J. said, her face still in the dirt. "Crime scene reenactment, is what. Didn't they teach you that at— What exactly do you have to do to become an investigator, anyway?"

Chuck squatted down next to her, ignoring the barb. He observed her the way you might look at a feral cat—unthreatening, and yet somehow still wild, something to be handled with caution.

"All right, then," he said. He reached back into the cab of the SUV and handed me the camera and a tape measure. "You want to do this? Let's goddamn do it, then."

He hooked his hands abruptly under her arms and hoisted her into a sitting position.

"No," C.J. said, looking at me. "You do it, Gato."

"Why should *I* do it?" I asked. But I knew already that it was a stupid question, that C.J. always had a reason.

"Well, because you're closer to his size, for one," she said. She pointed up into the ravine. I followed her finger to the recess where Anna Weston's body had been discovered. "I want to know how that skinny fucker would get a body up off this road and into that cave."

Chuck chortled.

"And second, because I don't want old Chuck's dick to fall off from overexertion. Not that he's got much use for it, but I'm guessing he's become attached to it as decoration."

"Can you believe this girl?" Chuck said, as if she wasn't there. But I was too busy worrying over the prospect of dragging C.J. up the hill, already uncomfortable at the thought of my hands on her.

"All right, then," C.J. said, lying back down. "Saddle up, little cowboy."

Chuck held the video camera to his face and began to record. I kneeled down next to where C.J. was lying again, took a breath, and reached under her shoulders. It was the closest I'd ever been to her, and I inhaled the smell of cigarettes and coffee and the floral scent of her face cream.

When I hefted her up, her head fell against mine, the copper of her hair in my face. I could see the pores on her nose, the streak of sun spots across her brow. Her arms hung limply at her sides, and I was surprised at the ungainly weight of her small frame, the clumsiness of her arms and legs as they sagged under her. I lumbered awkwardly toward the edge of the road, C.J.'s heels dragging small grooves in the rust-colored gravel.

A tense quiet spread between the three of us as I began up the hillside with C.J., a ghostly sense that this re-creation was somehow aberrant, shameful.

"You getting this?" C.J. said.

"Yeah," Chuck said over the top of the camera. "I'm getting it."

C.J.'s body became molten silver beneath me, heavy and liquid. I could feel the presence of Anna Weston in my arms, the kinetic energy of her life towing me down to the desert floor.

"That's it," I said, collapsing onto a flat chunk of rim rock. "That's all I've got."

C.J. squatted in the dust next to where I sat, breathing heavily. I had made it less than a hundred feet up the ravine, still two hundred feet short of the outcropping where Michael Atwood was supposed to have dragged Anna Weston's body.

"Grab us a couple cans, would you, Chuck?" C.J. called down. "And on your way up, be sure to get pictures of those drag marks."

Chuck turned off the camera, then headed back toward the county vehicle on the road below. We watched him root around the cab, then pick his way up the hillside to where we sat. He handed us each a beer and we sat for a moment in silence, gazing up at the two hundred feet of steep, broken talus that separated us from the place where Anna Weston's body had been discovered.

"There's no way," I said, still out of breath. "No fucking way."

We sat nursing our beers. A cool wind rose up from the valley, and the black shadows of two ravens spun in the afternoon thermals. When we had finished, we hiked up to the spot in the rocks where the two off-roaders had found the body. In the sand I saw the faint trail where a legion of detectives and forensic investigators had been, leading the way up to a six-foot-tall outcropping of brown basalt. While Chuck continued to photograph the scene, C.J. scrambled to the top of the small mesa above, disappearing over the skyline. I squatted in the dirt across from the hollow, trying to imagine the body as I'd seen it in the photographs, struggling to visualize how it might have arrived there. The place felt strangely familiar; I'd been there so many times already, each time I reviewed the crime scene photographs. I recognized each protrusion of rock, each clump of cheatgrass.

"Nothing up there," C.J. said, returning from her exploration beyond the top of the ridge. Chuck abruptly stopped his photographing, and we both stared at her. She was sitting in the lee of the rock overhang exactly where Anna Weston's body had been found, leaning against the wall to light up a cigarette.

"What?" she said.

"Why do I get the sense you've been here before?" Chuck said, putting into words a thought that I hadn't quite articulated. C.J. dragged slowly on her cigarette, then flicked an ash onto the floor of the cave.

"Maybe once or twice," she said.

Chuck spat on the ground, then looked out over the valley floor. It was late in the afternoon, and the lights of the city were beginning to flicker on.

"OK, then," Chuck said. "So tell me how the fuck it is that you've been here already, when we didn't even have a client until last Monday."

But she was already off, making her way back down the hillside toward the SUV, the sun setting orange and violent behind her.

PART V

CLOSING ARGUMENTS

FINALLY, INEVITABLY, we arrive at the close of the performance.

The events have all been laid out now. Regardless of how the trial has played out to this point, we can still just guess wildly at what you might now be thinking. But everything you need, juror, is in your hands. You are left only to turn the pieces this way and that until they fit together, until everything you've heard makes sense.

The attorneys stand for one last time and make their final arguments. We each remind you of the promises made in our opening statements, of how we have fulfilled these promises or how our opponent has failed to deliver on theirs. We point to the evidence that has been presented; we rehash and distill the testimony that you have heard. *The evidence has shown* . . . we say. *The evidence has shown.* And when testimony disfavors us, we remind you that it is the providence of the jury alone to decide the credibility of each witness, or that it is the burden of the State to prove each element of the offense beyond a reasonable doubt.

Here is the true story, the prosecutor and I each say. If there are gaps in the story, it's my duty to fill them now, because I know that jurors—like all people—despise gaps. Because I know that a juror's mind will fill these gaps, most often, with fear, and that fear never rules in favor of a defendant.

Listen now, juror, as I tell you how the pieces fit together.

FORTY-FOUR

IN THE NEXT weeks the Atwood case gained a critical mass, its pieces and obstacles snowballing, so that it seemed to consume every moment of my waking life. Michael's case alone would have been a full-time job, but we still had the usual revolving door of clients and court hearings to deal with. Paul Harris' preliminary hearing was approaching, and while the investigation and preparation were relatively simple, it loomed in the background, just another thing to worry about later.

By now, I had become used to Caroline's presence in my life; there was something organic and unspoken about our relationship, a kind of pragmatism that we both appreciated. She worked long hours in the emergency room, often arriving at my apartment in scrubs streaked with blood or with scratches on her arms. Neither of us really understood the daily realities of the other person's work, and we rarely asked. This was what had brought us together in the first place, maybe: a shared need to compartmentalize.

But I felt cracks spreading through this wall, a growing unease with the realization that we might not really know the other person. We began to needle each other, prodding for hints of the lives hidden beyond the partitions.

In my few free hours I often found myself at the river, fly rod in hand, casting into the deep pools just outside town. I'd come to love the mindless obsessiveness of it, the endless small and inconsequential decisions: what fly to use, where to cast, whether and how much to sink your fly, how quickly to strip in the line, when to switch flies or rods or leaders. I'd learned to watch for evening hatches when diaphanous clouds of mayflies or moths rise over the water, the river suddenly pockmarking with ripples as fish strike at the surface.

Caroline would occasionally join me, even as the cold of late fall settled in. She didn't fish—had no interest in learning—but she would content herself with finding a nearby boulder where she would wrap herself in a blanket with a book or a magazine.

"Can I ask how the case is going?" Caroline said one afternoon on the banks of the Truckee just west of town. She was perched on a granite boulder near where I was casting, steam rising from a Styrofoam coffee cup.

"Which case?" I asked evasively.

"Which one do you think?" she said. "*The* case. The Anna fucking Weston case."

I stripped in the last of my line and recast upstream. A few weeks after Michael's initial arraignment we had filed a motion to move the trial date to June; even though this nullified our first request to try the case in two months, the continuance would give us more time to prepare Michael's defense, to complete our own investigation and consult with expert witnesses. C.J. had counted on this delay all along, I realized. She had invoked Michael's right to a speedy trial only because she wanted the drama of that first hearing in the courthouse, the appearance that we were eager to get to trial to prove Michael's innocence.

"All right, then," Caroline said, returning to her book. "Keep it to yourself."

"There's nothing to tell, really," I told her. "We're investigating. All I can say is that we're getting some good information."

This was true, actually. We'd found an expert witness on false confessions in Connecticut who had reviewed Michael's file and been eager to testify. He'd pointed out how Detective Peck had coached Michael's inculpating statements—suggesting the content that Michael had then later repeated, nearly verbatim. We'd had a comprehensive psychological exam completed by a psychiatrist who would testify that Michael was of "low-average" intelligence, which made him particularly susceptible to a coerced confession. We'd spoken at length to his mother, who could testify that she was with Michael the night of Anna Weston's abduction. The true stakes involved were gradually sinking in: An innocent man would be put to death if we fucked up this trial.

Caroline sipped at her coffee.

"Well, I find that hard to believe," she said, a sharpened edge to her voice.

"What's that supposed to mean, exactly?" I asked.

"All it means is that everybody's made up their mind about that guy," she said. "They said in the paper that there's DNA. I mean, he *confessed* to the cops, right?"

I watched the speck of my fly drift along the bank with the current. This was exactly why we'd filed a motion to have the trial moved to a different jurisdiction—a motion that Bartos had summarily denied. The jury pool was already poisoned. But I also knew Caroline was right—the publicity Michael's case had received was unprecedented for Reno, and all of the press had been bad for our side. I'd begun noticing the looks that C.J. and I received when we went to lunch, the way that the bartender at the Over Under had stopped buying our first rounds. Even my mother had called from North Carolina to tell me she'd been reading about the Atwood case online, that they'd seen a picture of me standing in court next to Michael on a national news site.

"I don't like this," my mother had said.

"It's his job," my father argued in the background.

"Nonsense," she said. "Some things just can't be defended."

I tried to get back into the rhythm of the cast. The line looped lazily in the cold afternoon air, the fly unfolding into a dark eddy.

"It's a lot more complicated than that," I snapped at Caroline. "And to be honest, it's people like you I'm most worried about. It's jurors with their minds already made up who send innocent people to prison."

Just then I heard the reel whir, felt the line go electric. The surprise of the strike pulled me off balance, and I staggered into the icy river. The world beneath me felt fluid and movable, my wading boots sliding over the mossy river bottom. I felt the line tug once more and then go slack as the fish spit the hook. When I looked back to where Caroline had been sitting, she was gone.

FORTY-FIVE

WE CONCEDED NOTHING. We filed motions to change venue, motions to limit the number of autopsy photographs that the prosecutor could show the jury, motions to exclude evidence because it was improperly collected, motions to keep Michael's confession out of the trial because it had been coerced. We filed motions to prevent the State's expert witnesses from testifying, to preclude mention during trial that Michael had a tattoo or that he'd been in trouble with the law as a kid. We filed motions to dismiss all charges, motions alleging prosecutorial vindictiveness. We filed a motion to prevent the prosecutor from referring to Anna Weston as a "victim." We refused to concede even this.

By spring, C.J. and I were working four days a week on the Atwood case. Other attorneys stepped in as they could, taking cases from our weekly calendars so that we could continue to prepare for trial. We spent afternoons barricaded in the conference room, the mass of indexed discovery documents spread out over the large glass table. We were with the evidence so much that it began to blur, the reports and photographs stripped of their meaning through sheer repetition. Anna Weston's dead body became merely another obstacle to overcome, a two-dimensional adversary to attack.

We began to create a battle plan, to divide up who would be tasked with what witnesses, who would get opening and closing arguments.

"You're going to take Turner," C.J. said one morning. We were at a nearby coffee shop, where we often met to discuss the case. "I'll take Jones on false confessions, and you've got the State's DNA guy. If I do it, I'll fall asleep on cross."

"I think it'd be safer if you took Turner," I said. Because he was the lead detective, Turner's cross-examination could make or break the case for us, and I didn't want that pressure. But C.J. was already shaking her head.

"You can fuck this guy up, Gato," she said. "I've seen you do it plenty of times. You lay your trap—the nice guy, the young attorney—and then you turn that fucking knife in his side."

"You sure?" I said doubtfully.

"Of course I'm sure," she said, a smile flashing. "And besides, if you fuck it up, I can always clean it up in my close."

We spent a couple of evenings a week at the jail, apprising Michael of new developments in his case—the delays that continued to mount as we filed motions and pursued witnesses—or to discuss trial strategy or an expert witness's report, or sometimes just to check in. They were conversations that we might just as easily have conducted over the phone, except that C.J. had grown increasingly paranoid that a detective might be listening in on our conversations. It was illegal and would be inadmissible in court, but it wasn't unheard of.

"I used to see it all the time," said Chuck, who had been a homicide detective for twenty years before coming to work at our office. "Hell, I probably listened to a half dozen attorney conversations myself."

Like the evidence itself, Michael began to come into focus, to become something other than another defendant. We came to know him. His demeanor became familiar, his strange facial tics and gloominess less annoying, more terror than apathy. We learned to recognize when he was feeling anxious, or frustrated, or afraid. We knew when the guards had rough-handled him, or when his mother had been unable to put money on his books, or when the jail had been serving nutraloaf for a week straight.

And Michael began, slowly, to warm to us. We would find him waiting in the custodian's closet for our meetings rather than having to be called out from his cell by the deputy. He'd shake our hands, ask how we were doing. He and C.J. would often chat carelessly about fishing, about camping trips he'd taken with his father as a kid, about the places he planned to visit when he was out of jail.

The more time I spent with Michael, the more layers seemed to peel away from him. I learned that he worked maintenance for the Eldorado Hotel and Casino downtown, graveyard and swing, where he fixed leaky sinks, repaired broken bed frames, replaced burned-out light bulbs. He liked hockey and video games, and especially video games about hockey. I learned that he'd enlisted in the Air Force out of high school but had washed out in basic training. I learned that he liked to sleep late and that he was left-handed, that he'd been afraid of the dark until he was in his twenties and that his favorite food was an ice cream sundae.

I learned that he'd shared an apartment with a friend until the previous summer, when he'd moved back in with his mother to save money. I learned that in his entire life Michael Atwood had had only two girlfriends, both of whom had little to say one way or another about him. In both women's accounts Michael was a short fling that they'd nearly forgotten until they'd seen his face on the news. It was as if he were a man without qualities: quiet and kind and polite, but entirely unremarkable.

"I sure hope you're not losing sleep over all this," he said to me one afternoon. On the table between us were several volumes of discovery binders that I'd brought to the jail to review. I'd been up until three the night before researching case law, and I wondered if I looked so worn through that even Michael Atwood noticed. "I hear about you guys in here, and I know you've got other cases and all."

It was perhaps the longest string of uninterrupted words I'd ever heard come from Michael's mouth.

"Never mind all that," I said. I nodded toward the courtyard of the housing unit. "We just want to get to trial so we can tell your side of the story and get you out of here."

But telling Michael's story was proving tricky. I'd learned early on that a defendant's testimony could be one of the strongest weapons a defense team had; a jury wants to hear the defendant say they're innocent in their own words. But the risks of testifying are huge, and any decent prosecutor can make an innocent person sound guilty on cross-examination. For this reason, when a defendant testifies, it is most often against their attorneys' advice and results in a quick conviction.

We knew already that Michael would present horribly to a jury. He seemed unable to shed the reflexive sullenness that appeared whenever he was under stress, something that would scream "sociopath" to any juror. And the flashes of humor and sensitivity that C.J. and I saw in the jail evaporated each time we rehearsed his cross-examination. As Caroline had said, he looked guilty.

"So how do you explain the DNA, Mr. Atwood?" I asked him during one of these rehearsals, in the familiar confines of our custodian's closet with C.J. and Chuck. I'd adopted the DA's familiar tone of righteous indignation, pointing a finger at him as I spat the words. "Your DNA was found on the belt used to kill Anna Weston. How do you explain that?"

Michael slouched lower in his chair, breaking eye contact even before I had finished asking the question. This, we knew, would be the central question in the trial. The rest—Michael's whereabouts on the night of Anna Weston's disappearance, the ambiguous statements he made in his videotaped interrogation—we could explain away with his mother's alibi and with our expert on coerced confessions. But the DNA was the one tangible thing that linked him directly to the dead body.

"Don't overthink it," C.J. told him. "Just tell the truth—you don't know how your DNA got onto that belt."

"I'm sorry," Michael said. "I'm just nervous, is all."

Chuck shook his head. We had rehearsed his answer a dozen times, and still he went blank. It was the simplest answer, unsatisfying but still the best one we had.

After a few more rounds of practice it was obvious that we'd never be able to put Michael on the stand. So instead we switched our focus. We began to work on the little things, the ways in which Michael could testify without ever taking the stand: maintaining eye contact with the jury, staying silent even when a witness was lying, what to do during recesses, how to avoid looking toward the front row of the gallery where Anna Weston's family would be seated.

At C.J.'s direction Chuck had begun to dig further into Michael's background. We discovered that he had a history as a CHINS—a child in need of supervision—both in Reno and in Northern California, where he had spent summers with his father. He'd been arrested for misdemeanor Assault for a fight at school, a misdemeanor DUI, a minor Drug Possession charge when he was twenty. This was a criminal history that would have caught my attention before starting at the PD's office but by now barely registered a blip.

"Can you imagine the life this kid had?" I said to C.J. one afternoon in the conference room. I'd just read a series of Child Protective Services records from Michael's years in elementary school—unsubstantiated reports of bruising along the back of the legs that we later learned were from beatings he'd taken from his biological father before his parents divorced.

C.J. pushed her reading glasses onto her forehead and squinted at the file.

"Yeah," she said, returning to her work editing a set of jury instructions that I had drafted. "I think I can."

WE EXPECTED TO be fighting with the DAs, but we didn't expect to fight our own side.

"Why do I feel like I'm throwing good money after bad here, C.J.?" Pat said when we asked him to sign off on flights and a hotel room for our expert witness on coerced confessions.

"This is bullshit, Pat," C.J. said indignantly. "We *need* this guy. Without him, we're done. They're trying to kill our client, and you're trying to hamstring us from our own sideline?"

Pat looked sharply at C.J., his lips pursed. His pen hovered over the authorization for funds that I had prepared.

"C.J.," Pat said evenly. "You need to calm it the fuck down."

C.J. fumed in the doorway of Pat's office, but didn't respond. Pat paused, as if considering whether to say something else, then leaned over and signed the authorization.

"Be careful what you're learning here," Pat said to me tersely, before sliding the form across the desk.

As the trial approached, we saw a change in Bartos himself, a new edginess to his in-court demeanor. He and C.J. were both die-hard baseball fans, and for eight months each year they would linger after court to banter about trades and prospects, chatting happily about playoff runs and commiserating over postseason losses. But since the Atwood arraignment I noticed that Bartos no longer stayed at his bench after the court calendar. Sentencing hearings had become unpredictable, the punishments for our clients suddenly harsher and more arbitrary. First-time drug offenders began to be sent to jail instead of to drug treatment programs, shoplifters sentenced to prison on inflated burglary charges.

I heard rumors that the district attorney had imposed an office-wide policy that C.J. and I were not to be negotiated with. Our workload exploded, and it was all I could do to keep up with my regular calendar, let alone work on the Atwood case. Cases that were rife with evidentiary issues or sympathetic defendants or squirrelly prosecution witnesses—cases that would ordinarily have been resolved quickly with a plea to a misdemeanor offense or an all-out dismissal—were suddenly set for trial.

Cases like Paul Harris, the college kid who'd been caught with a few grams of someone else's meth in a bag he'd been carrying. We had conducted a preliminary hearing, in which we introduced video from an RPD dashboard camera that showed the girl with Paul taking off at the first sight of the police. And the arresting officer testified that the contents of the bag Paul had been caught with included a tampon and a tube of glittery lip balm, which supported what Paul had been saying all along: that the bag wasn't his. It was a case that Neil would ordinarily have dismissed but that I now found set for a felony trial in front of Bartos.

"This is a good sign," C.J. said one evening as we worked on lines of questioning in the conference room. She leaned back in her chair, sipping a can of Sprite. "These fuckers are pissing in their boots, thinking about losing this case."

"Yeah, except all my other clients are getting hammered at sentencing," I said. I couldn't help thinking about the two people Bartos had sent to prison that morning; it felt like I was sacrificing years of my clients' lives for Michael Atwood's case.

C.J. brushed the issue away, as if it were a question no good attorney would ever stop to ask.

"Bartos sentenced those kids to prison because he hasn't been laid in five months," she said. "Believe me. Marcia told me just this morning to be on the lookout for him this week. If you'd asked, I would have told you to continue those cases."

"Even *if* Michael's innocent," I said before I could catch myself, "is it still even the right thing to do? To let a bunch of other people have *their* lives ruined?"

"You picked the wrong career to have a conscience," C.J. said. "All this Lady Justice shit, weighing the good against the bad. They're going to *kill* our guy if we don't win. You know that, right?"

"Yeah."

She pointed across the conference table to where Michael Atwood's mug shot lay next to a photograph of Anna Weston's desiccated body.

"Those are the only two people in this whole goddamn state who matter right now."

FORTY-SIX

AS THE TRIAL approached that summer, the threats began in earnest.

Over the past three years I'd grown accustomed to the passing intimidations that were an inevitable part of the job. Defense attorneys are frequently the bearers of bad news to clients who are often psychologically unstable, or in the throes of addiction, or simply violent by temperament, and so the occasional in-court argument or hostile voice message are to be expected. I'd been receiving menacing messages from Mr. Milan, the old paranoid schizophrenic, since my first week in the office. The first time he threatened to take my life— *kill you, you pussy fuck*, the message had said—C.J. had to talk me down from calling the sheriff. But I came to ignore his threats, to even look forward to the gems they sometimes elicited.

"Just try and sleep," he would say in a five-minute rant left on my voicemail at four a.m. on a Tuesday. "You'll catch your fucking death, you pussy fuck."

Those sorts of threats didn't frighten me. What caught my attention were the calls that began to arrive in the months after Michael Atwood's arrest. Calm voices calling at three a.m. and three p.m. alike, mentioning Anna Weston by name, noting the street I lived on or the kind of car I drove.

"I saw you yesterday," said a man's voice waiting on my voicemail one morning, a month before the trial was to begin. "Walking back to that shithole apartment on California Avenue. Cute girl with you. Your girlfriend, I guess."

"Yeah," C.J. said when I played the message for her. "He's been calling me, too."

"Well?" I asked. "Shouldn't we do something about it?"

"It's all talk," she said. "I've seen this shit before, and nothing ever happens."

But I wasn't so sure. I found myself watching for people lingering in the parking lot outside the office building.

"You seem a little . . . on edge these days," Caroline said one evening as I rechecked the lock on my apartment door for the fourth time. She'd had the evening off and was reading a book in her pajamas on the couch while she sipped a glass of wine.

"It's just this trial," I said. I hadn't told her about the threats—especially the ones that mentioned her. "It'll be over soon, and things will go back to normal."

I watched her expression change, the lines of her eyes tighten. She picked quietly at the corner of her book.

"Were things ever normal?" she said. She'd been asking variations of this question lately, feeling out some new dimension to our relationship.

"Really?" I said. I saw her jaw waver, her brow crumpling, and the idea that she might cry seemed to me unforgivably selfish. "Now, of all times? You have to do this now?"

"I told you yesterday that I had three people in the ER die on me this week," she said flatly. "*Three*."

"And?" I said. She looked at me incredulously.

"And you never once asked about me. If I was OK."

I hadn't asked because I knew too well what the answer was. She wasn't OK, just like I wasn't OK anymore. But we both knew that, didn't we? Wasn't that the foundation of our relationship—the unspoken understanding that we were both not OK?

"I just need someone who will . . ." she said, her voice trailing off.

"Who will *what*?" I snapped.

She began to gather her things from my bed, stuffing a sweater into her backpack.

"Not that much," she said. "Just a little."

"Just a little."

"Yeah, a little," she said bitterly. "Maybe put a fucking arm around me once in a while. Tell me it's going to be fine."

"Sure," I said. "It's going to be fine. Feel better?"

"Fuck," she said. "All I want is for you to act a little human again. Not all the time, just every once in a while. Is that too much to ask?"

"Yeah, it is," I said. I began flipping through a stack of evidentiary photos on the table, making a note on a yellow pad of Post-its.

"Why is it always her?" Caroline asked. I thought at first that this was some admission of jealousy, that she was asking why the Anna Weston case took precedence over her. But there was no edge to her question; instead, her voice sagged with weariness. It was then that I understood what she was asking. What about this woman's death was so familiar? What made Anna Weston like all the other dead women—the prom queens gone missing, the Laura Palmers and the Black Dahlias and the Sharon Tates?

"I don't know," I said.

We shared a look, and I knew I only had to go over to her. Just extend a hand. Finally, the moment passed. She zipped her backpack, grabbed her keys from the counter.

"Do you realize that we've been doing this for more than a year now, and we've never once talked about the future?" she said. She turned to leave. "It used to be easier. More fun. You used to care about things."

"No," I said. I reached across the table for a pack of cigarettes. "No, I didn't."

I watched as her face fell flat.

"Well, at least you acted like you did," she said.

She paused for a moment in the doorway, waiting one last time for me to say something to keep her. In the hallway behind her a man shuffled past carrying a load of laundry. He smiled sheepishly at the two of us while we stared at each other across some unspoken chasm.

ANOTHER MESSAGE WAS waiting when I arrived at my office the next morning. This time the man's words were slurred, the threats more explicit. I picked up my phone to call the police but stopped, remembering C.J.'s admonition. Instead, I typed a message to Jasper.

He picked me up after my morning calendar three hours later, the oil and tobacco smell of the old pickup familiar and pleasant, a flat of generic soda cans stacked in the bed. Across the street I noticed a man lingering in front of the county library, stealing glances our way; I folded my suit jacket over the back of the passenger seat and climbed in.

"Is that guy looking at me?" I asked, rolling down the window.

"What guy?" Jasper said, scanning the street. I nodded in the direction of the man, who had taken a seat on a bench and was now reading a folded-up newspaper. "*That* guy?"

"Never mind," I said. "Let's just go."

I felt Jasper sizing me up, trying to parse out the subtext of the question. Finally, he put the truck in gear and pulled away from the curb.

"So?" Jasper asked. He turned south onto Virginia Street, past the bodegas and downtown weeklies. "What are you looking for?"

"Just something for self-protection," I said noncommittally. Even though my father had grown up on a sheep ranch, I had been raised in a gunless household, a rarity in Nevada. Jasper, on the other hand, had a strong appreciation for the Second Amendment instilled in him from an early age. His father not only owned guns—lots of them—but even went so far as to load his own rounds at his garage workbench, funneling black powder into the brass casings while classical music played over the radio.

"You know I've got to ask," Jasper said. "Why the sudden interest?"

"It's nothing," I said. "I've been getting some strange phone calls, is all. Ever since I started working on this Anna Weston trial."

He eyed me quickly, before steering the truck east onto Vassar Street.

"How's that going, anyway?" he asked.

"Fine," I said. "Why?"

"You seem—" he began, searching for the right word. "Stressed."

I caught myself rubbing my jawline again; the old tic had become more prominent over the last month. I forced my hand down into my lap.

"Well, it's going fine," I said again. I didn't mention the argument with Caroline the night before, or my growing certainty that Michael Atwood was actually innocent, or the fact that someone might be trying to kill me. "Just a little back on sleep."

We drove in silence for a few blocks.

"So anyway," I said, changing the subject. "What do you suggest? For this fucking weirdo, I mean. Maybe a nine-millimeter?"

He leaned forward and reached under his seat, then passed over a stubby black pistol that fit in the palm of my hand.

"Everyone thinks they want a fucking nine-millimeter," he said. "But you want something small. Something you can have handy without looking like some NRA jackass with a holster on your belt."

I turned the pistol over in my hand, its body dull and malignant-looking.

"That's a Smith and Wesson .380," he said. "It's tiny, but it thumps."

We pulled off onto an unsigned road north of town, the truck shuddering as it dropped onto gravel. The road traced a canyon floor into the foothills another couple of miles before Jasper pulled to a stop at a bend. The ravine flattened for a hundred yards until it ran headlong into a hillside. There, the tailings of an old mine created a twenty-foot berm of yellow gravel, its face glittering with the greens and ambers of exploded beer bottles.

Jasper took the case of soda from the bed of his truck and began shaking the cans one by one. He spread a dozen of the cans across the hillside, then handed me the pistol from his truck.

"That's yours, OK? I'm giving it to you, so just don't say anything about it," he said. I began to protest, but he was already walking behind me. "It's not loaded. Just hold it for a minute. Get the feel for it, and then we'll load it up."

He spent an hour taking me through the pistol before we ever took a shot. He showed me how to load and unload the magazine, counting and thumbing in each round. He showed me how to free the safety with the flick of a thumb, how to sight, how to breathe.

"Should we use earplugs or something?" I asked when I was ready to take my first shot.

"My dad always said you need to get used to how loud a sidearm is," he said. "This thing pops like a cannon."

"OK," I said skeptically.

"The last thing you want is to be scared when real life happens."

Jasper stood behind me as I leveled the pistol against the hillside. The afternoon light was thinning, long shadows raking the horizon. I sighted one of the cans in the notch at the end of the barrel, just as Jasper had shown me.

"Good," he said. "When you're ready, exhale and squeeze."

I waited for the feeling the pistol was supposed to bring—the cold sensation of power, of holding death itself—but it never came. Instead, I felt like I had already lost something, the very thing the gun was supposed to protect against.

The silver cans jogged in and out of my sights. I exhaled, then squeezed the trigger.

FORTY-SEVEN

IT'S THE PHYSICAL evidence itself that makes a case come alive in a courtroom; glossy photographs and witness testimony rarely evoke the emotional reaction that a piece of bloody fabric or a murder weapon will. This isn't lost on prosecutors, and we knew Neil and Linda would use any opportunity to introduce the physical evidence of Anna Weston's murder into the courtroom. They would show the jury her bloody clothes, the hanks of her hair they had recovered at the scene. They would make every effort to introduce the exhibits into evidence so that the jury would actually have the clothing there with them as they decided Michael Atwood's guilt or innocence. So that Anna Weston herself would be in the jury room while they deliberated.

FOUR WEEKS BEFORE Michael Atwood's trial was scheduled to begin, C.J. and I drove to the Reno Police Department evidence locker, where Neil was waiting for us with Detective Turner. A deputy waved us through the locked door and into a long concrete room lined with industrial shelving.

We followed Turner down the aisles of the evidence locker to a dozen cardboard banker's boxes labeled with Michael Atwood's name and case number. He slid one of the boxes off its shelf.

"Grab those for me, would you?" he said, nodding at the other boxes nonchalantly, as if we were helping him pack a moving truck. Neil and I picked up the two remaining boxes and followed Turner over to a stainless-steel table, the box unexpectedly light in my hands. As Turner opened the first box and began removing plastic bags onto the table, a momentary quiet settled over the room.

"Pass me those gloves, Rob," C.J. said abruptly, breaking the trance. "We're going to need to get in there and pull everything out."

Even now she was trying the case, I realized. Breaking through the physicality of the evidence, stripping away the emotional energy of the dead woman, and guiding a jury's attention back to the law. Back to burdens of proof and reasonable doubt. Turner aimed a sharp look in C.J.'s direction, then pushed a box of blue examination gloves across the table. C.J. took two out and handed them to me, then plucked out another pair and pulled them on. I noticed now how slender C.J. had gotten in the past few months, the gloves loose-fitting on her small fingers. She'd always been slight, but now I could see faint veins tracing their way across the back of her hands. Her green eyes seemed to have settled into her skull, her teeth grown larger in the tautness of her cheeks.

"Victim's shirt," Turner said, holding up a gallon-sized paper bag. "You want it out of the bag?"

"Yep," she said. "Everything out of the bags."

Neil sighed, realizing that he'd be spending his afternoon in the evidence locker. He waved away the box of gloves, then sat on the edge of a nearby table and began typing a message on his phone.

Turner made a note in the evidence log, then broke the first evidentiary seal and held the bag open toward C.J. Without hesitating, she reached a gloved hand in to remove an oily bundle of cloth. A cloying metallic smell made its way into the room as she spread out the shirt that Anna Weston had been killed in. I recognized it from the news reports when she had first gone missing; the shirt had once been beige but was now black with blood and dirt. The words *Thanksgiving Turkey Trot 10k* were printed across the back above the cartoon logo of a turkey in running shoes. I watched C.J. lift the shirt up, turning it over under the fluorescent light. She found a small rip at the neck and brought it in close to examine it, so that her face was nearly touching the fabric. She made a note in her small notebook, then held the shirt back up to the light.

"I want a picture of this tear," she said, holding the collar up in front of me. "And this stain, here."

She turned the shirt around, pointing out a stain on the back that I recognized from photos the prosecutor had sent over months before. I held the shirt in my hands, turned it over. The greasy texture of old blood and cotton slid sickly under the fingertips of the latex gloves. I held the shirt up into the light, trying to still the tremble in my hands while I moved the fabric back and forth as C.J. snapped photographs with a digital camera.

"Good," C.J. said. "Next item."

Turner placed the shirt back into the evidence bag and secured it with a new seal, which he signed and dated. C.J. was already removing the next bag, breaking the seal to take out the next pieces of evidence—a small envelope that contained two rings and a pair of earrings.

We moved methodically through the evidence, jotting notes and taking pictures, sipping sodas and chatting about other cases. By the time we finished, I'd held the leather belt that the State claimed had once been cinched around Anna Weston's throat. I had unbagged the dead woman's shoes, had examined her underwear and bra. In four hours we learned little that we hadn't already gleaned from the hundreds of evidentiary photos in Michael Atwood's file back in the office. There was no undiscovered evidence, no exculpatory detail that would save Michael's life. But the visit had also been about something else.

C.J. had set up the viewing for me, to expose me to the evidence itself. To force me to handle the bloody clothes, the samples of Anna Weston's hair and clippings of her fingernails. I was being inoculated against the power of the dead woman's blood.

FORTY-EIGHT

THE COURTS HAD cleared their calendars for the Friday before Memorial Day weekend, and most of the attorneys in the office had left before noon. Even Joanne—who liked to remind me that a vacation day was just another twenty-four hours she'd have to wait until retirement—had taken the day off.

Jury selection in the Michael Atwood trial was set to begin in three weeks, and we'd just filed our notice of expert witnesses and final evidentiary motions. After six months of seventy-hour workweeks we'd entered a brief period of reprieve, the final calm before the storm that would arrive when Bartos' clerk sent out a list of prospective jurors the week before trial. I was enjoying the rare quiet of the office in daylight, taking advantage of the lull in the court calendar to catch up on other case work I'd neglected, when C.J. appeared in my office doorway.

"Hey," I said. "What's up?"

She leaned against the doorframe, staring blankly at Washington's plaster bust on his perch atop my bookshelf.

"C.J.?" I asked.

She continued gazing at Washington.

"C.J."

"Sorry," she said, jerking out of her trance. She began to turn to leave. "It's nothing."

"Hey," I said. "Everything OK?"

She hovered in the doorway, as if considering whether to answer.

"I was just at the jail," she said slowly. "With Michael."

"All right," I said. "And . . . ?"

"Who *was* this guy, anyway?" she said, nodding toward Washington on my bookshelf. She stepped closer to the bust, as if suddenly interested.

"C.J.," I said. "What happened at the jail?"

She hesitated for a moment, still not looking at me.

"Nothing happened," she said finally. She turned to start back down the hallway. "My house at five thirty tomorrow. Don't be late."

IT WAS STILL dark when I pulled up to C.J.'s place the next morning. She lived in a boring new subdevelopment in what had once been farmland south of town, a square-mile grid of stucco homes with luxury SUVs in the driveways. I'd only ever seen the inside of her house once, when we'd closed down a nearby bar to celebrate a lost jury trial and I'd been too drunk to drive home. Like her office, the tract house had been unadorned to the point of abandonment, the walls nude, the bookshelves and mantel clear of anything that suggested a life beyond its walls.

When I arrived, I found her waiting in her driveway, as she always was on these mornings. For a moment she was spotlighted in my headlights, standing next to a large duffel bag, a nylon fly rod case slung over a shoulder, an American Spirit already glowing at her lips. She looked washed out in the harsh yellow light, older and smaller than she actually was.

"So?" I asked once we were on the road. The highway was humming below us, the eastern sky warming as we drove the familiar road out toward Pyramid Lake. "You get any sleep last night?"

"Slept like a baby," she said, sipping at a cup of coffee. "You?"

I hesitated, trying to gauge whether her one-word question was sincere or just another of the small tests that C.J. was constantly administering. I knew the correct answer was yes, but I couldn't bring myself to say it. We drove for a moment in silence. The yellow diamond of a road sign riddled with bullet holes flashed past.

C.J. was reaching toward the dash to turn on the radio when I finally spoke.

"Not really," I said. Her hand hovered over the dial. "I'm getting really worried about the trial."

She gathered her breath, the way I'd seen her do a hundred times as she cross-examined a witness on the stand.

"Let me ask you this," she said. "Are you worried about the trial, or are you worried about Michael?"

She was asking, I realized, if I thought that Michael Atwood was innocent. If I believed—as she had from the beginning—that he hadn't killed Anna Weston. The piles of evidence that I'd studied in the past six months unspooled in front of me, each damning piece counterbalanced by a fact that seemed to corroborate his innocence. The car crested a final hillside, and the entirety of Pyramid Lake spilled out before us, dark and lustrous in the overcast morning light.

"I'm worried about Michael," I confessed. Out of the corner of my eye I caught C.J. smile, thin lines appearing in the corners of her green eyes. She reached down to retrieve a green plastic fly box. She opened it on her lap as if it were a small book, its pages illuminated with dozens of iridescent lures. She probed a finger through the extravagant tinsel streamers and beaded copper heads that filled the box before settling on a Woolly Bugger the color of green turquoise. She plucked the fly from its place in the box and placed it on the dashboard in front of me.

"Good," she said, putting an end to the conversation. "Now I want you to start off with *this* little guy. Get him out there as far as you can, and then let your line sink awhile before you bring it in."

IT WAS A windswept morning, and we had the beach nearly to ourselves. We waded out chest high and set our ladders, then began to cast from the top step out into the choppy water. Within an hour I had landed five Lahontan cutthroat, each over ten pounds and longer than my forearm, their bodies powerful against the line, the bright red of their gills flashing in the slate-grey water. As I reeled in the sixth, I felt the line tighten, then suddenly go slack; the fish had snapped my line, taking C.J.'s lure with it.

By midmorning the sky had broken open, and the vibrant blue of the desert sky washed over the mountains across the lake. This was spring in Nevada, immoderate and changeable. In the space of a few casts the temperature rose fifteen degrees, and I found myself sweating in the jacket I wore under my waders. A few minutes later I noticed C.J. stepping down from her ladder and starting back to the car.

She rummaged in the back seat, peeling off layers in the sudden heat, then emerged in jeans and a shirt, her feet bare in the silty sand. Her copper hair flicked in the wind, her thin lips pursed. She began walking down the beach, until soon she was only a tiny silhouette against the vast basin behind her. I watched the small dot of her as she stripped off her remaining clothes and left them in a pile on the shore.

"Hey!" I shouted as she waded out into the frigid water. The wind gusted, blowing my words out across the lake. I called her name, but she was already bent at the knee, already diving under the surface. There was a sudden stillness in the grey plane of the lake, as if she had disappeared forever beneath it, and in that silence I imagined Reid Wilson, the football player who had drowned in this lake our senior year, his bloated grey fingers reaching for C.J.'s pale ankles, pulling her to the lake's bottom.

She came up ten feet later, floating calmly on her back. She pitched and keeled in the gunmetal water, her small white breasts bobbing against the surface, little whitecaps lapping at her face. Finally, after a few minutes, she wheeled around and took a few strokes back toward shore. From my ladder a hundred yards down the beach I watched her body emerge from the lake, lanky and awkward and sexless. She walked to her small heap of clothes on the beach, dried herself off with an old T-shirt, and gathered her things. When she had dressed, she stretched her arms over her head and then started slowly back to the car.

I waited a few minutes, then gathered my ladder and gear. I found her sitting in the passenger seat, blowing cigarette smoke out the open window. Her skin was pale and tight, her lip trembling almost imperceptibly with cold.

"What the fuck was that?" I said, trying to disguise an inarticulable sensation of rising anger.

She squinted at me through the stark sunlight.

"What the fuck was what?" she said.

"*That*," I said, pointing down the water's edge toward where she'd gone in.

"I was hot," she said. "What, you've never seen an old lady's ass before?"

"Goddamn it," I said before I could stop myself. "This is the type of shit people are starting to talk about."

"What's that mean, exactly?" she said. There was a sudden cut to her voice, the belligerent tone that had become more pronounced in the last few months. The venom that I'd seen Pat warn her about, that had cost her clients months or years when she turned it against Bartos.

"Nothing," I mumbled. "Forget it."

I felt the power of her coiled in the passenger seat, sizing me up, before slowly unwinding. I shucked off my jacket and tossed it into the back seat.

"Good. Now let me ask *you* something, Gato," she said, the edge fading from her voice. "What the fuck is *this*?"

When I turned around, I saw the glove box open onto C.J.'s knees. In it was the black snub of Jasper's pistol. I felt my face go red, my fingertips light up with heat.

"It's nothing." I found myself suddenly recycling the feeble lies that I read every day in police reports and interrogation transcripts. "I'm just keeping it for a friend."

I felt C.J. watching me carefully as I fidgeted outside the car, still in my fishing waders. Finally she pushed the glove box closed and leaned back in her seat.

"Bullshit," she said. She nodded to where my phone sat on the dash. "You've been ringing off the hook, by the way."

I reached in and grabbed the phone, then retreated to the back bumper. I began to extract myself from my waders, scrolling through my call log with one hand. A call from an unknown number, followed by eight missed calls from Caroline. We hadn't talked since our blowup at my apartment a few weeks before, and my mind jumped to all the usual worst-case scenarios. A pregnancy? A recently discovered communicable disease? To tell me off again? I walked a few yards from the car, then pressed "call back."

Caroline answered after the first ring.

"Where the hell have you been?" she said. "Didn't you listen to the messages I left?"

"No," I said. "I didn't have my phone on me."

"Well, have you talked to him yet?" she said.

"Talked to who?"

I pinched the bridge of my nose, still trying to make sense of the conversation. The disparate elements of the day whorled together with the internal logic of a nightmare—the looming trial, Anna Weston, C.J.'s erratic behavior.

"To Jasper," she said. "They arrested him this morning."

FORTY-NINE

I LEFT C.J. in front of the public defender's office, stopping home just long enough to put on a pair of slacks and a shirt. Ten minutes later I was in the lobby of the Washoe County Jail, giving Jasper's name to the front desk clerk.

"In on a Saturday?" asked the clerk. "Must be serious."

"Something like that," I said. I passed her a paper with Jasper's full name and date of birth on it, then checked the time; if I didn't clear security by two, I'd be waiting for an hour until they completed the afternoon count.

"Housing Unit Four," she said, waving me through the metal detector. I followed the old familiar blue line to the first Area Control, nodding quickly to a familiar-looking inmate—an old client, or a witness, or a co-defendant, I couldn't remember which.

"*¿Cómo estamos, hermano?*" he asked.

"I'm fine," I said tightly. "*¿Usted?*"

"*Aquí no más,*" he said, smiling, before turning to face the wall as I passed.

When I arrived at the housing unit, the deputy pointed to a small, windowed conference room. Inside, I saw Jasper in an orange jumpsuit, sitting at a metal desk.

"What, so you're my lawyer now?" he said, smiling.

I shook my head. Behind us, inmates in orange jumpsuits watched TV in the common area or walked laps in the small concrete courtyard. I slid a legal pad onto the table and sat down across from him.

"What happened?" I asked. I'd already pulled up his charges from the sheriff's office website and had seen the string of charges next to his name:

Trafficking of a Controlled Substance, Possession of a Controlled Substance for Purpose of Sale, Possession of a Firearm with Obliterated Serial Number. Serious felonies—the trafficking charge alone carried a mandatory ten-year sentence. He shrugged noncommittally, as if he'd just been pulled over for speeding.

"Nothing that should be surprising, I guess," he said. "You saw the charges, I'm sure."

I wondered if he realized the danger he was in. Most of my clients had no idea what sort of time they were facing on charges like these, and I hated the idea of having to tell Jasper about the worst-case scenario. Already I was thinking about the possible defenses, which were few.

I considered, for a moment, whether I might be able to simply call the DA assigned to the case and beg for a dismissal, call in every favor I might have accrued over the past three years. I wondered if I could agree to throw one of my clients under the bus, persuade them to stipulate to a maximum sentence, if the prosecutor went easy on Jasper. But this was panic talking. And besides, after six months of C.J.'s scorched-earth approach to the Atwood trial, whatever goodwill I might have once enjoyed was long gone; the fact that Jasper was a friend of mine would more likely make things worse, not better, for him.

As if reading my mind, Jasper held up a hand.

"I don't need you to step in here, OK?" he said. "I told Caroline not to call you."

I slumped down into the hard plastic chair. Outside, an old man in an orange jumpsuit shuffled to a fountain to fill a water cup.

"All right, then," I said heavily. I felt a cumulative exhaustion settling in. "Well, at least tell me what happened."

It was a story I'd read a hundred times in various permutations. Natalie had come by Jasper's house the night before with a friend, a shifty guy who had made Jasper uneasy from the outset. He'd seemed wild-eyed, too twitchy, but Natalie had vouched for him.

"He's just a little spun," she'd whispered, sensing Jasper's unease. "But he's a good guy, really."

"Should have seen it coming a mile away," Jasper said. "But I sold him something anyway. Twenty minutes later, Nat and I are both in handcuffs and they're tearing my house apart."

He told me that Joe Ramos, a detective I knew from the narcotics unit, had executed the warrant. Unfortunately, Ramos was a careful detective—I knew not to expect any procedural or evidentiary slipups that might result in a quick dismissal or a favorable plea bargain. They'd made short work of the house, a drug-sniffing dog alerting on a lockbox hidden in an air vent.

"What did they find?" I asked.

He drew a palm over his mouth as if he were considering a poker hand.

"It doesn't matter," he said. "I knew what I was doing. I knew what the risks were."

A group of three inmates passed the doorway behind us on their way to the common area. I leaned in over the table, lowering my voice.

"This is my job," I said. "I want to help."

"I know you do." He stared across the table at me, his face calm and unworried. "But I'm not asking for your help."

THE MONDAY AFTER Jasper's arrest I was waiting in the lobby at seven thirty when Joanne arrived to open the office, shuffling out of the elevator, wearing a cheap pair of headphones. She was laden with a small lunch cooler and a plastic grocery bag containing a sweater and several romance novels. It was only after she'd made it a few steps into the office that she spotted me sitting in one of the hard plastic chairs, a notepad on my lap. She looked over a shoulder as if hoping that someone might be there to save her from the privacy of the lobby; realizing we were alone, she slowly reached up to take off her headphones.

"Well?" she said, sparing any formalities.

Now I was the one who felt ambushed, even though I'd been planning this meeting for the last two days. I stood up awkwardly.

"Just getting an early start on the week," I lied. "I was hoping to get a look at the arraignment calendar for this morning. There's a file that might be coming my way—a trafficking case. Last name is Bailey. I was hoping to get a look at it."

Joanne eyed me suspiciously, weighing the possible implications of my request—my motivations, the liabilities I was asking her to undertake. Finally, she hiked the bag onto her shoulder, an unspoken understanding emerging between us in the dim light of the lobby.

"Come on, then," she said, fishing a set of keys from her purse as she moved toward the security door. "Grab that cooler for me."

I followed her into the office, the open doors and empty cubicles sagging with a stillness that made the place feel abandoned and unfamiliar. She piled her things onto her desktop, then pointed to an empty spot where I was to leave her cooler. In that moment, I was struck with the suspicion that Joanne already understood everything I was about to ask of her—that she knew even more than I did what I was asking, that she had always known more than I had.

"Follow me," she said. She started down a hallway toward the window-less filing room where new cases were processed and closed files were stored, a thirty-foot-long space filled like library stacks with manila folders. The room was heavy with time and with history, the rows of files like a sprawling burial ground. "Last name was Bailey, you said?"

"Yeah," I said. "Jasper Bailey."

She paged through a banker's box filled with stacks of paperwork bound in red rubber bands, new charging documents and police reports that hadn't yet made it into the public defender's system. I watched her glossy purple nails as they skipped through the stack, landing on a Criminal Complaint with Jasper's name on it above the name of the assigned attorney, Judith Kidder.

"Put it back when you're done," she said, and started back toward her desk.

"Joanne," I called after her. We both realized that what she was doing— passing me another attorney's file—could cost her her job. I felt the impulse to acknowledge what had just transpired between us, to express my thanks, but she just waved a hand behind her as if shooing away a fly.

I sat at my desk and pulled off the red rubber bands that bound Jasper's file.

"Goddammit," I said, paging through the paperwork. Jasper's case had been assigned to Judith, an attorney who had been in the PD's office for a decade after leaving private practice. She had a reputation as a lazy attorney who avoided trial whenever possible.

"She's gonna dump truck his ass." The whisper came from across the room, where the plaster bust squinted down from his perch. "He'd be better off with Tara. Or with C.J."

"Doesn't matter who he gets, if there's nothing in here to work with," I said. I began reading through the arresting officer's report, the grey areas of Jasper's account already becoming clear. As I read, I started my mental tally. Possession of a Controlled Substance: felony, one to four years. Possession of Drug Paraphernalia: misdemeanor, maximum six months county jail. Possession of Marijuana: misdemeanor, another six months. Possession of a Firearm with an Obliterated Serial Number: felony, one to six years. Trafficking of a Controlled Substance (methamphetamine over ten grams): ten years. Trafficking of a Controlled Substance (cocaine over twenty-seven grams): ten years to life in prison.

I heard Washington whistle, as if reading my mind.

"Fuck," the plaster head said.

"Calm down," I said, as much to myself as to the dead man. People were rarely convicted on the most serious charges, especially if they didn't have a prior criminal history.

"Sure," Washington said. "But do you even *know* if he has priors?"

A jolt traveled through me. I paged through the file until I found the NCIC report. There it was: a prior arrest four years earlier, for Possession of a Controlled Substance. He'd completed a drug treatment program and the charge had been dismissed, but it had been a felony charge and was something that could torpedo any sense of lenience that a prosecutor might have.

As I started reading the file from the beginning, my hand crept toward the desk drawer. I opened and shut it, and this little ritual satisfied something in me. I opened the drawer and shut it again, tapping out my little rhythm. *One... two... three... four.*

I read further, through police reports and witness statements and lab reports, the tapping growing faster, the rhythm quickening. I remembered my grandmother's tapping at Mass when I was a child, the four points of the sign of the cross, head, sternum, left shoulder, right shoulder. *One... two... three... four.*

I wanted C.J. to be there, to tell me how we could game the prosecutor or leverage another client's sentence to make this all OK. I read the copy of the warrant—signed by none other than Judge Bartos—which had allowed the raid of Jasper's house based on the testimony of the confidential informant who had seen and purchased methamphetamine from Jasper. I mindlessly continued to slide the drawer open and shut, repeating the sets of fours, as I read the inventory of items in Jasper's pockets: a folding knife, a wallet, a set of keys, a lighter, a receipt from a gas station, a half roll of electrical tape. I slid the desk drawer open and shut, faster now, louder now, still counting out my little patterns as I turned next to the written statement of the confidential informant. Natalie Wohl.

It all made sense now. How Natalie had been arrested for possession a week earlier—a random car stop, a small baggie of cocaine in her purse. It was on her way to the jail in the back of a patrol car that she told Detective Ramos she had personal knowledge of a large quantity of narcotics hidden in a crawl space at Jasper's house. Jasper still had no idea, I realized, that Natalie had turned him in.

"What is going *on* in here?" I heard Joanne's voice suddenly say from my doorway. I stopped abruptly, staring dumbly at the desk drawer that I had been slamming shut for the last several minutes. "Have you lost your danged mind?"

"Sorry, Joanne," I said. Out in the hallway I heard a door open, and a juvenile court attorney named Christine waved hello on the way to her office. Joanne continued to look at me suspiciously.

"You done with that yet?" she said, pointing to Jasper's file on my desk.

I nodded, then stood up from my desk and walked the stack of charging documents and police reports over to her.

"Listen," I said to her quietly as I handed her the file. "I have another favor to ask. I'm sorry."

She took the file and looked me in the eye, as if she were expecting this. Her eyes, which sat below blue eyeshadowed lids, seemed to narrow a bit. Her small lipsticked mouth tightened, but she didn't say anything.

"This case is assigned to Judith Kidder right now," I began. "But I don't think that's right. I know Judith is upside down right now, and I really think it would be better if this case went to Tara."

Tara was the other attorney assigned to Department Three, Judge Hamilton's courtroom. She was only a few years older than me, but she already had a reputation as a fighter, someone that prosecutors avoided taking to trial. If Jasper had a defense, she'd find it. And if not, the DA assigned to Jasper's case would give him the best plea bargain possible.

Joanne raised an eyebrow.

"Is that what you think?" she said.

"Please," I pleaded under my breath. Outside the door, the office was coming to life with attorneys and staff arriving for the start of the week.

She pulled gently at the file, and I let it go.

"I'll see what I can do," she said, and before I could thank her, she disappeared around the corner.

FIFTY

IT HAPPENED THE Thursday before jury selection for the Atwood trial. By then both sides had noticed our witnesses and filed our final evidentiary motions. Procedurally, this was the time when each side was forced to tip their hand—the State would see that one of our expert witnesses would be called to testify about false confessions while another would testify about potential alternative sources of DNA. They would be certain now that we weren't pursuing a lesser sentence or simply trying to avoid the death penalty. We were going all in for a not-guilty verdict.

During this lull I had fallen into a solitary existence, tending to the raft of anxious tics that had continued to emerge. Caroline's absence had left a large gap in my life; I found myself visiting Jasper at the jail a couple of times a week, where he waited for his case to make its slow progress through the courts. I couldn't quite bring myself to ask him about Natalie, though by now I was sure he'd figured out she'd been the one to set him up.

"Is Tara taking care of you?" I asked during one visit. I'd checked in with her once or twice, mentioning only that he had been a friend in high school, but she'd politely refused to discuss his case. "I know a couple good private attorneys. I could help—"

"Don't worry," he said, cutting me off. He seemed at ease in his orange county jumpsuit. As if, as with all things, he was just taking it in stride. "She's doing a great job. It's just dog-shit facts, unfortunately for me."

C.J., for her part, crackled with the electricity of the trial. She berated her secretary for the smallest irritations and continued to argue with Pat about the use of our limited office resources.

"Goddamn," I heard Cheryl, another attorney, say after a staff meeting. "If this trial doesn't kill her, Pat will."

We were halfway through Bartos' Thursday morning calendar—the usual mad scramble to get six different clients to sign guilty pleas, to strategize about sentencing arguments, and to organize letters from drug counselors, spouses, and bosses to present to the judge when we asked for lenience. I was in the jury box, explaining the plea negotiations on a Burglary charge to my client for the fourth time, when I heard Bartos raise his voice suddenly.

"Counsel!" he said sharply. The entire courtroom quieted, and even the in-custodies in the back row turned toward where C.J. stood at the defense table. "You need to be very careful how you proceed."

"What the fuck is going on?" I whispered to a private attorney sitting next to me in the jury box.

"No idea," he said. "Neil just asked Bartos to send C.J.'s client to drug court, and C.J. went apeshit."

At the defense table, C.J. was holding a plea negotiation in the air with one hand while jabbing a finger at Neil with the other.

"I'm sorry, Judge. But the district attorney is trying to screw my client in your court right now," she said.

Neil sat in stunned silence, before gathering himself and standing abruptly.

"Your Honor—" Neil said.

"Don't give me that 'Your Honor' horseshit, Neil," C.J. hissed. She waved the paper in his direction. "This plea says that the State will recommend probation for my client. That's what the plea negotiation *says*. Now you come in here—"

"C.J.!" Bartos snapped from the bench. I saw the bailiff stand at attention, unsure what was happening or what his duty might be. C.J. stood hunched at the counsel table, her small body winding up with rage. Her client, a woman in her early thirties, and Julio, the court interpreter, both stepped away from C.J.

Bartos lowered his voice.

"C.J., what the fuck is going on?"

I glanced over to Deborah, Bartos' longtime stenographer. She stared ahead mutely, her fingers hovering over her keyboard, as if she knew what Bartos would want on the record and what he'd want omitted. What it would mean for C.J. if she continued to type.

C.J. stood seething for a moment, then suddenly swept an arm across the counsel table, her stack of files spilling onto the courtroom floor. The entire courtroom was silent, all eyes fixed on C.J.

"Judge, I think we need to make a record here," Neil said from the prosecutor's table.

"Shut the fuck up, Neil," Bartos said tightly. Deborah's hands still hung over the keyboard, not moving. Bartos stared intently across the courtroom at C.J., as if trying to decipher some lost language.

"Bailiff," he said abruptly. "Please take defense counsel into custody."

"Your Honor," C.J. said. She bent over and began to pick up the files that were across the floor. "Judge, I'm sorry . . ."

Bartos held up a hand. The bailiff, unsure of himself, began to move slowly from behind his podium.

"Take her back and have her tested," Bartos said quietly to the bailiff. He shook his head, and I could see how much he hated what he was doing.

"Your Honor," C.J. said again. She glanced over at me in the jury box. She was pleading now; it was a voice I no longer recognized. "Judge, please don't do this."

The bailiff touched C.J. lightly on the shoulder, and she started. The bailiff began to move one of her hands slowly behind her before Bartos stopped him.

"Not here," he said, nodding to the door that led to the holding cell. "Take her back. You'll go, won't you, C.J.?"

She nodded weakly, and I finally realized what should have been so clear for so long.

FIFTY-ONE

THE NEXT DAY I found myself in the conference room with Dan Osterman, the mass of evidence and trial exhibits sprawling over the glass table between us. Pat had assigned Dan to first-chair the Michael Atwood case the same afternoon that C.J. had been taken into custody for being drunk in court, as if Pat had anticipated this might happen all along. Within an hour I had received an email from Dan asking to meet as soon as possible to get up to speed on the trial.

Now, spread out in front of us was the entirety of the Atwood case file. Dan flipped through our binder of motion work, hundreds of pages of evidentiary motions that we'd drafted in anticipation of trial. He moved on to a binder labeled "Experts" and traced a finger down our list of witnesses: an independent medical examiner, a DNA expert, and our star witness, the expert on coerced confessions. It'd taken C.J. three months of arguing, threatening, and pleading with Pat to secure funding for these witnesses. She'd nearly lost her job once or twice to get that list, I knew, though none of this was apparent to Dan. Instead he was looking at a stack of CVs, and at a trial strategy that wasn't his.

When he looked up from the binder, I was sure he'd at least appreciated the work we'd put into the case thus far. What it had cost us. At least that was apparent, even if our strategy might have differed from his. He tapped a finger lightly on the binder of motion work.

"This . . ." He looked at me incredulously. "This is work for an 'actual innocence' defense?"

I looked at him dumbly. Of course it had been an actual innocence defense;

C.J. and I had been certain of Michael Atwood's innocence for months now. I tried to calm the unease welling somewhere deep below. Dan was new to the case, I reminded myself. He hadn't had time to review all of the evidence. He hadn't even met Michael.

"It's a lot more complicated than we thought at first," I began. I started to root through our stacks of evidence, looking for the photographs we'd taken from the scene where Anna Weston's body had been discovered, where I'd been unable to drag C.J. up the steep ravine. "When you get a chance to review—"

"Why would you do that?" he said softly, still flipping through the binder of motions. He seemed to be talking not to me, there in the conference room with him, but to C.J., wherever she was by then.

"It's more complicated than it looks," I mumbled again. I felt Dan studying my face across the conference table, as if seeing me for the first time.

"Are you doing OK?" he asked. I caught myself rubbing at a bald spot on my beard.

"Fine," I said shortly, forcing my hand down. "It's just, we've put a lot into this defense. I think that once you review the discovery—"

"I *have* reviewed the discovery," Dan snapped. "I've read every last transcript, seen every picture, watched every damned interview. Including, I'll add, the one where our client confesses to murdering this woman."

He stabbed a finger at the pile of glossy evidentiary photographs.

"'*I hit her in the back of the head.*' That's what Atwood said. '*I got scared, and I put the belt around her neck.*' His exact words. On tape."

I shook my head.

"*Three* times he tells Peck he killed that girl."

"It's a coerced confession," I said. "Textbook case."

I reached for the binder with the expert from Connecticut's report, but he slid it just out of my reach, as if I might have been grabbing for a pistol left on the table.

"It's not," Dan said evenly. "We're on the same side here. You know that, right?"

I nodded warily.

"Coerced confessions, false confessions—they happen. I've even seen one once. *Once.* But this . . ." He slid the binder back across the conference table to me, as if disgusted by its very existence. "This isn't one. And no jury in the world is going to believe it is."

I stood to leave. The world that I had lived in for three years seemed to teeter around me. Jasper vanishing into the Washoe County Jail, C.J. disappearing into thin air from Bartos' courtroom. And now Michael Atwood's defense being torn down in front of my eyes.

"So what are you saying?" I said.

I already hated him, because I knew what he was going to say: that this wasn't a case about guilt or innocence. It was about mitigation, about attacking a single element of the offense, about trying for anything short of the death penalty. It was a strategy that C.J. had warned me about early on, as if she had anticipated this moment long before it occurred.

"We're not going for some scattershot, *lesser offense* play like most attorneys will go for around here," C.J. had said on a late-night drive back from the jail. "That kind of half-assed defense is what gets people sent to the gurney."

It was a defense strategy that Dan had, somewhat notoriously, employed in several capital cases over the past two decades—an endearing in-court demeanor and unwavering professionalism that more often than not landed his clients on death row.

Dan seemed to soften, as if sensing my line of thought. I knew what he wanted to say—that it was absurd to try an "actual innocence" defense in Michael's case. That we needed to focus on Michael's state of mind, to consider a "not guilty by reason of insanity" defense. He leaned back in his conference chair and sighed at the ceiling.

"I'm just saying that we need to rethink this thing," he said.

FIFTY-TWO

A COUPLE OF weeks later, a secretary escorted me down the halls of the DA's building to Neil's office, where I found him at his desk, talking on his cell phone.

"I have to go," he said into the phone. He motioned me into a seat across the desk. In the corner was the small basketball hoop where I'd shot for Drew Alder's sentence two years earlier. "Call when the tow truck gets there."

"Sorry," he said. He set the phone facedown on his desk and leaned back in his chair. He didn't have court on Thursdays, I knew, and he was wearing a pair of grey chinos and a light blue button-up cuffed at the elbows.

"Mallory?" I asked.

"Yeah," he said. "Taking the kids to see her family in San Jose. Got a flat in Sacramento."

"We can do this another time," I said. I didn't fully understand what I was there to do, exactly, but Neil waved the suggestion away.

"You're here on Beasley, right?"

Nia Beasley had taken a bus up from Oakland for Super Bowl weekend and gotten into a fistfight with a local young woman at a casino club. It wouldn't have been anything other than a drunken bar fight, but the woman had fallen against a table and fractured her orbital bone. It was a defensible case—a witness was willing to testify that the victim had thrown the first punch—but because Beasley couldn't make bail, she'd been sitting in the county jail for two months waiting for trial.

"Actually, no," I said carefully, testing the waters. "I'm here on another case."

"OK . . ." Neil said, leaning forward in his chair. Though we were both second chairs on the Atwood trial, we had nothing to discuss on the case—there wasn't anything Neil could offer me, and there was nothing I could offer him. I could feel him studying me, looking for my angle.

"You have a case with Tara," I continued. "Bailey. Jasper Bailey."

He looked at me blankly, and it was clear he didn't remember Jasper's case.

"Level One Trafficking. Cocaine. Meth. A few pills. Some other shit tacked on."

"You're here to talk to me about one of Tara's cases?" he said. I could feel him running through my possible reasons for being here. For making this sort of transgression. "I don't think Tara would appreciate that too much."

I smiled weakly, like this was just something between friends.

"Listen," I said. "Bailey's a . . . he's a family friend. He's a good guy, and I just wanted to talk to you directly. You know."

My cards were on the table now. We both knew I was here to beg.

I sat in an uncomfortable silence as Neil seemed to think things over, to evaluate his position. Finally he swiveled around in his chair and slid open a drawer of his filing cabinet. He fingered through the column before pulling a file. As he skimmed, I stared out the window at the desert hills east of town. They were lit up an opaque orange, the dips and valleys shadowed a darker violet.

"What are you asking for, exactly?" he said, closing the file. "This isn't just a little weed and a bag of pills. And he's got some history, too, you know."

"I know," I said. I hadn't really known what I was there to ask for; I hadn't even expected Neil to consider my plea, really. But now I was crunching numbers, running all the possible plea bargains that would prevent Jasper from spending decades in prison but wouldn't scare Neil off the idea entirely. "Plead to a lesser. Take the big stuff off the table. He does some time but has a chance to get out."

He tapped a finger on the manila cover, considering this offer that we both knew I had no authority to make.

"He willing to work?"

I shook my head. If I was certain of one thing, it was that Jasper would never agree to be a confidential informant.

"Tell you what," he said, a small smile appearing at the corner of his mouth. "I'll let you shoot for it again."

"I'm not going to shoot for it," I said.

The room filled with silence again. Out in the hallway I heard a man laughing.

"We're set for trial on Paul Harris in a month," he said finally. "My kid's got a baseball tournament in Vegas that week, and I sure as hell don't want to be in trial."

I felt him watching me as a look of recognition came over my face.

"That's a defensible case," I said.

"Maybe."

I felt a wave of nausea come over me as I considered Neil's unspoken proposal.

"Get him to plead to the felony," he said. "I won't object to probation. Hell, you can even argue for drug court."

I wish I could say that my first reaction was shock. But I'd done this too many times by now, or at least too many other versions of it. Balancing scales, doing the quick math. How much one person's life mattered over another's. Where I wanted to spend my capital.

"OK," I said.

I must have known even then, even before I set foot in his office, that I was capable of this. That I would get Paul to plead guilty to a felony—a charge that would follow him like a ghost for the rest of his life.

"See . . . that was easy enough, wasn't it?"

AND IT WAS that easy, wasn't it? It was easy to pick up the phone and call Paul Harris that afternoon, and to tell him that we'd lost track of the girl with the bag. It was easy to warn him of the threat of trial—of his word against an officer's. It was easy because, in the grand scheme of things, this was a net-positive. Jasper would have the chance to get his life back, and it would cost Paul only a year of drug court.

"You're really telling me I should plead guilty to this?" Paul said. "I'm supposed to graduate next year. How am I going to go to drug court if I don't *do* drugs?"

"Just do the classes, show up on time to your check-ins, and test clean. In a year it all goes away—like it never happened."

"Yeah," Paul said bitterly. "But it *did* happen."

And it was easy, or almost easy, to stand next to Paul a week later as he entered a guilty plea and—as I told him would happen—Bartos sentenced him to drug court.

FIFTY-THREE

AFTER C.J. WAS fired, the first thing Dan did was obtain a four-month continuance of Michael's trial. Next, he called off our expert witness on false confessions. It was a lost argument, he had already decided.

For the first week or so after C.J. disappeared, I refused to throw away all of the work we had done. I might have been terrified at the prospect of an innocent man being sent to death because C.J. and I had lost the trial, but to give up the idea of an acquittal entirely felt like an even bigger betrayal.

But Dan was calling the shots now, and I had no choice but to accompany him to the jail to help convince Michael that our best course of action was to beg for his life to be spared.

"So now you're saying you think I did it, then?" Michael said, when he finally understood what Dan was asking. He looked to me incredulously.

"We *know* you didn't do this," I said. I could hardly bring myself to look him in the eye. For the past several months he'd been preparing with C.J. and me to stand up in court and declare his innocence, and now this stranger was telling him the most we could hope for was that he'd spend the rest of his life in prison. "But Dan has handled a lot of cases like this before."

"No one is saying you did it," Dan said calmly. "All we're saying is that the amount of evidence the prosecutor has is overwhelming. The DNA evidence alone is a massive obstacle."

I thought there was no way that Michael would agree to this change in strategy, but each time we visited him at the jail, Dan returned patiently with his argument. I could see Michael tiring with each visit, and with the cumulative stress of jail and the approaching start of trial.

And the more I listened to Dan's reasoning, the more I began to buckle to it myself. The amount of evidence against us. The unthinkable consequences of miscalculating, the finality of being sentenced to death. Finally we arrived at a point at which he didn't even have to say it out loud—Michael would let Dan plead his case. Which meant Dan and I would spend the trial pleading for Michael's life.

"There's no jury in the world that would have believed he didn't do it," Dan told me one afternoon as we prepared our final notice of witnesses. Now, we listed a local psychiatrist who would testify that Michael was borderline low-functioning, and a social worker to testify about his turbulent childhood, a coworker who had always known Michael to be kind. "From the first day of trial, we have to be humanizing him."

It was a strange thing to say, so close to trial. What he was asking, I realized, was whether I had fully come around to his strategy. Whether he could count on me in the courtroom.

"I know," I said, the unspoken truth of Michael's innocence hanging between us.

"This trial is about mitigation. The only thing we're doing is trying to save his life."

WHEN THE TRIAL began late that year, it was scheduled for three weeks in Bartos' courtroom, but in the end it took all of nine days, including jury selection. The State made its predictable presentation, the photographs of Anna Weston's body projected over and over onto the courtroom screen. Her clothes, still blackened with blood, paraded through the courtroom, passed in front of the jury box. We heard the testimony of her mother and her husband, which established what Anna Weston had been doing in the hours before her disappearance, but more importantly established for the jury that she had a family, that this death would have consequences forever.

During his direct examinations of the arresting officers, Neil played all five hours of Michael's interrogation two times through, lingering on the moments that Michael seemed to admit having seen Anna at a gas station on the night of her disappearance, to having struck her in the head before strangling her with his belt. Next the State's DNA expert testified for an entire day, beginning with a rudimentary explanation of DNA pulled straight from *Jurassic Park* and concluding five hours later that the odds of someone other than Michael being the source of the DNA recovered from the belt that had killed Anna Weston were one in sixty-five sextillion.

"And just for reference," Linda Ernst said, "how many people are alive on the planet today?"

"Seven point five billion," the expert said with a look of deep self-satisfaction. I saw several jurors taking note of this fact, as if it suggested that another suspect would have to be extraterrestrial.

For the nine days of trial we hammered at the State's burden to prove each element of every offense beyond a reasonable doubt. We attacked forensic methodology and crime scene contamination. On the third day, Anna Weston's husband, Grant, testified about the night of her disappearance—the sickening hours of that first night when Anna's phone first went directly to voicemail.

"I picked up our son, Tyler, at day care that afternoon," he testified. There in the courtroom he seemed less perfect than he had been once, when I'd seen him standing next to Turner during those early press conferences, back when Anna Weston had been only missing. There was a red streak of razor burn at his neck, and an exhaustion seemed to hang over him. "She went to the gym after her shift, then met her friend Brooke for dinner."

"What was the last communication you had from your wife, Mr. Weston?" Linda asked from her podium.

"She sent a text message from the restaurant," he said heavily.

"And what did that text message say?" Linda said, already flipping through her trial notebook to find the copy of the message she would now introduce into evidence. Anna Weston's husband seemed to waver for a moment there on the stand, listing a little to one side.

"Do we need milk?" He seemed surprised by his own answer. "It's so stupid, but she just wanted to know if we were out of milk."

When Linda completed her direct examination, I stood at the podium and asked Grant Weston about the arguments they'd had after a brief affair he'd had the year before, the marriage counselor they'd been seeing, the fact that the police had first considered him a suspect. Anything a jury might hang their hat on to find that undefinable thing: reasonable doubt.

We homed in on *mens rea*, the specific element of a murder charge that required the prosecution to prove Michael had explicitly intended to kill Anna, hoping that the jury might convict on a lesser second-degree murder. We called Michael's mother, who testified not about his alibi but about a head injury Michael had suffered at the hands of his alcoholic father.

"His dad would beat us until his fists hurt too much," she said. "It got so bad that we up and left in the middle of the night. Nowhere to go, just away from him."

It was a detail from Michael's childhood that I'd never heard before, even when C.J. and I had prepped her to testify. I searched Michael for any sort of reaction, but all I found was that familiar blank stare. This testimony, I knew, had little to do with the jury's finding of guilt or innocence, with the issue of whether Michael had *actually killed* Anna Weston, which Dan seemed to be conceding without ever explicitly saying so. Instead, he was hoping just to humanize Michael enough to avoid the death penalty when it came to sentencing.

When we had called our last witness, Bartos leaned forward on his bench.

"Counsel," he said. "Have you advised Mr. Atwood of his right to testify on his own behalf at trial?"

Dan nodded to me, and I stood to address the court.

"Stand up," I whispered to Michael. He remained slumped in the chair between us, unmoving. "Michael, goddamn it, stand up," I hissed.

Michael stood, his Adam's apple bobbing at the neck of the secondhand suit he'd been wearing all week. His eyes were rimmed in red, and his chest was heaving as if he were having trouble breathing.

"Yes, Your Honor," I began. I felt like I was walking Michael the final steps to a hangman's noose, and I despised Dan for every second of it. "We have advised Mr. Atwood of his right to testify on his own behalf, and at this time Mr. Atwood will be waiving those rights."

"Mr. Atwood, is that correct?" Bartos said.

Fuck you, Dan, I thought.

I thought briefly about the unmade bed in my studio, and the small square of light that landed on it on afternoons like this one. I thought of Caroline's wet hair after she got out of the shower, and how she used to wrap it in one of my clean T-shirts and walk around the little apartment with nothing else on, reading from one of the science fiction paperbacks she liked.

Michael nodded, rubbing a palm over the back of his neck.

"Mr. Atwood," Bartos said, pointing down at the stenographer typing next to his bench. "You're going to need to answer audibly—out loud—so that the court reporter can make a record of your answer. Now, is it your intention to forgo your right to testify at trial, as you discussed with your attorney?"

Fuck you, Bartos. Fuck you, C.J. Fuck you, Caroline. Fuck you, Jasper.

"Yes," Michael said quietly. "I understand."

AFTER CLOSING ARGUMENTS Bartos spent an hour reading out instructions to the jury, and then it was over. The twelve jurors stood in unison, took a last look at Michael, and then followed the bailiff into the jury room to deliberate.

"So now what?" Michael asked. Like me, he seemed caught up in a riptide of events, time sucking us into a black future. "What happens to me now?"

"Now?" Dan said, packing up the notes and exhibits from his closing argument. "Now we wait."

When the jurors had cleared the room, a team of deputies manacled Michael's wrists and ankles and led him—still in his suit—off to the holding cell. Dan and I made our way out of the courthouse, past the battalion of reporters and photographers lining the front steps. When we reached the calm of the street corner, Dan turned in the direction of the public defender's office.

"You're going back?" I asked.

"I have some calls to return," he said, as if it were just another day of court. "I have a prelim set for Monday. You coming?"

I shook my head.

"Well, make sure your phone is on," he said, smiling weakly before turning to leave.

I stood on the corner of Sierra and Court Streets, watching the spectacle outside the courthouse a block away. After a minute I fished my phone from my pocket and dialed C.J.'s number. The phone rang, and rang, and rang.

WE DIDN'T EXPECT a verdict that day, but when two full days of deliberation had passed and we still hadn't received a decision, I allowed myself a bit of optimism. They were thinking about it, I knew. There was something to deliberate. That was all we could hope for.

On the afternoon of the third day I received a call from Bartos' court clerk. "We've got a verdict," she said. "Judge wants you here at two."

When I arrived at the courthouse that afternoon, Dan was already standing at the defense table next to Michael.

"This isn't good," Michael whispered to me as I took my place, his breath warm and acrid. His rangy muscles tensed and flexed under his suit, his eyes squinting and relaxing. Next to him, Dan was jotting down a note in his file.

"We don't know yet," I said, fighting the compulsion to rub my face, to count out the number of times I touched the marbled blue cover of my statute book. "They've been thinking about it for two days."

"This isn't good," he repeated as Bartos took the bench.

"Ladies and gentlemen," Bartos began, addressing the packed gallery. In the front row I saw Anna Weston's mother, her hands clasped as if she were praying the rosary. She was praying, I knew, for Michael's death. "We'll be reading the verdict in a moment, here. I'm going to ask you to remain quiet as the verdict is read, regardless of the outcome. Bailiff, you may now bring in the jury."

I felt Michael reach a hand over, and I took it, his fingers thin in mine.

"I don't want to do this," he pleaded in a whisper. "I don't want to do this."

But we both knew there was no stopping the momentum that had already amassed.

"Stand up straight," I whispered back. "It's going to be OK. Just look them in the eyes."

The gallery hushed as the twelve jurors filed slowly back into the courtroom, none of them looking in our direction as they took their seats. A long quiet stretched across the courtroom. I heard a photographer's shutter click, Michael Atwood's breath quick and gasping next to me.

"Mr. Foreman," Bartos said. "Have you reached a verdict?"

An old white man in faded jeans and a flannel shirt stood up. Juror Number Six, I thought. Retired contractor. Three kids, four grandchildren. Someone we had hoped to preclude from the jury during voir dire.

"We have, Your Honor," he said.

PART VI

VERDICT

BY THE CLOSE of a trial, each side will have spent endless hours preparing for their presentations in the courtroom. We'll have honed our lines of questioning for each witness, debated when and how each trial exhibit will be introduced (or how we could exclude it from the courtroom entirely). But the part of a trial that remains a mystery—out of the control of the lawyers on both sides—is also its most critical.

When the judge finishes reading his instructions, a sheriff's deputy leads you, single file, out of the jury box and into the deliberation room. And now, juror, you are behind a closed door, beyond our grasp. Here, in this windowless room, you are left alone with only the evidence, and the judge's instructions, and each other.

We have chosen you carefully. We think we know how you will interact with each other—which of you will speak up, which of you will stand by your convictions, which of you will allow yourselves to be swayed.

You disappear behind the door for a minute, an hour, a day. *What could you be talking about?* we wonder. We had been so certain, so forceful, during the trial, in our closing arguments. But it's here, during deliberations, that our certainty wavers. *What is happening in there?*

Finally, our phones light up with a call from a county line—the judge's clerk.

When you are led back into the courtroom, we rise the same way that we would rise for the judge. There's an unsettling tidiness to the room now; for the past several days or weeks the counsel tables have been strewn with binders and laptops, legal pads and photographs. But now each desk is clean, as if a dinner table has been cleared and it's time for the guests to all go home.

No matter how the trial has gone—even if each witness has testified exactly as we'd hoped, each objection we've made has been sustained by the judge, each piece of evidence has been admitted or excluded—the room fills with uncertainty. We try to catch your eye, to find some small tell in your body language.

Mr. Foreman, the judge says. *Have you reached a verdict?*

FIFTY-FOUR

IT TAKES A FEW moments to process the information that the Nevada State Prison's social worker has just given me—that Michael Atwood has barely survived his suicide attempt. I hang up the phone and stand, stunned, in our living room, considering where to go, what to do.

I spend the first hour at my desk scrambling to reshuffle the day's court calendar so that I can be there when he is released from the medical unit at the Nevada State Prison this afternoon. Three hours later I am alone in a white county-issued sedan making the forty-five-minute drive from the public defender's office to the prison in Carson City, Michael's letter in a folder on the passenger seat next to me.

He's trying *to die,* I think. *First by abandoning his appeals, and now by his own hand. But what does he want from me? Why did he ask me to visit, if he's already given up?*

"Listen," I tell Sarah when I finally catch her between classes. "Something came up. Can you pick up Rosa today?"

I hear her exhale heavily on the other end of the line. There's an unspoken frustration in the pause before she answers.

"I'm going to have to move a bunch of things around," she says. "There's no way you can do it?"

I know that by the time I drive to the prison in Carson City and clear security, it'll be midafternoon, and if there's a lockdown or any other delay, there's no telling how long I could be stuck.

"Sorry," I say. "There's just something I have to deal with."

I don't tell her that I am on my way not just to the prison where Michael Atwood has been caged for eight years, but to the place where he will also die, tomorrow or twenty or forty years from now. I don't explain that I am visiting a murder scene before the murder happens, but because it is the state of Nevada that will carry out the killing, it will not be considered a murder. And because I am a defense attorney who works for the same state of Nevada, I won't be considered an accomplice.

"Wow," she says. "Thanks a lot for the explanation, Santi."

TODAY HAPPENS TO be one of the rare, unseasonably warm days that occasionally arrive in spring. As I leave the highway, I roll the window down, fresh air blowing through the car, the cool air twisting sharply through the roots of my hair. Soon, the sandstone towers of the prison rise from the desert floor, concertina wire stretched like Christmas tinsel along the perimeter.

NSP fulfills every *Shawshank* expectation one could have. It is one of the oldest prisons in operation in the country, complete with clanging metal doors, Gothic stone porticos, masonry chipped away and scratched into by one hundred and fifty years of Nevada's hardest criminals. Somewhere among them, I know, is Jasper.

When I arrive at the stone walls of the old prison itself, I am met by a uniformed guard who looks to be barely out of high school.

"Sir," he says, nodding mechanically. He leads me past a sign informing me that the state of Nevada has a policy of not negotiating for prisoners in the event of a hostage situation.

"Something to keep in mind," he says, tapping the sign with his clipboard and smiling.

"I don't think defense attorneys would be worth much to you guys," I say, and the guard laughs.

"Yeah," he says. "You're probably right."

I follow the young guard through prison industries, where trusties are at work making box springs for a mattress company the state has contracted with.

The last time I visited Jasper a few months earlier, he'd been assigned here, working with another inmate to staple mattress frames together. I look for him now, and when I don't find him, I feel a moment of worry. He has just a few months left until he is eligible for parole, and he has only recently begun to talk about a life beyond the walls of NSP.

"You know you can stay with us," I'd told him. "We have an extra room."

He'd rolled his eyes, as if I'd suggested the stupidest thing in the world.

"I appreciate it," he said. "I do. But I don't think Sarah would be exactly thrilled about having a felon in the house."

When I started to protest, he held a hand up.

"Just stop," he'd said abruptly, before relaxing back into his chair. I'd followed his eyes as he looked around the visitors' room. A half dozen men in prison jumpsuits sat at tables talking with visitors, mostly women. A few kids lingered awkwardly, coloring pages provided by the prison or sipping sodas from the vending machine in the corner. "Besides, I'm looking forward to not having roommates for a while."

THE GUARD AND I continue through the general population yard, inmates loitering in old-school black and white stripes, sizing up the civilian as I walk through the yard. We pass the segregated gang housing units with their neat rows of winter vegetable gardens, and then go up the hill toward a squat white concrete block.

"So, you been out to the row before?" the deputy asks.

"Yeah," I say, and I feel the unspoken sense of camaraderie that all people working in the system feel, regardless of what side you're on.

"We had one last month," he says. "Don't know if you saw it."

I nod. I had read about the execution. The prisoner had been one of Dan's clients, a man with schizophrenia who beat his landlord to death with an empty vodka bottle two decades earlier. The inmate wanted to die and had quit his appeals early on, but it had taken the State that long to get their ducks in a row.

As we near the building, the young guard seems to hesitate. His steps become slower, as if matching the machinations of his mind.

"They let me watch," he says as we are arriving at the tall steel door. "I've only been here less than a year, but my CO put me in there. Don't know if I wanted to, but I saw it."

There is a loud buzz, and the steel door begins to slide open.

"I'm sorry," I say.

He nods, staring into a corridor of closed prison cells. Another deputy stands from his desk to meet me.

"Anyway," he says, turning abruptly to leave. "Enjoy your visit, I guess."

FIFTY-FIVE

ONE OF THE death row guards escorts me down a blank concrete hallway to the professional visiting room where I find Michael sitting at a white metal table that has—like all fixtures in the unit—been bolted to the floor. His arms are at his sides, his wrists thin and slack in the steel handcuffs, which are also chained to an eyebolt at his feet.

I haven't seen him since his last post-conviction hearing eight years earlier, and the change is shocking. His hair is shaved down to a wicked bristle, and large bays circle either side of his hairline where he's begun to bald; his skin is sallow as sour milk. As I enter the room, I can tell he's taking stock of me, too—my own hair beginning to grey, a fullness to my face and body that I didn't have the last time I saw him. *We're entering middle age together*, I think. As if visited by the same realization, Michael flashes a defeated smile. There is a black gap where his right incisor ought to be.

"It's nice to see you," he says.

"You too," I say, surprised to find that I mean it. I realized a long time ago that I'd come to care for him, which had only made the disappointment of his verdict more cruel. We sit for a moment, looking at each other, as if we are old friends who happened to cross paths.

"I guess I'm supposed to ask how you're holding up," I say. He shrugs his thin shoulders in a way that suggests he isn't holding up at all. He looks up to a corner of the room.

"Sorry to bring you out all this way," he says. "It's just, I don't know another way to ask you what I got to ask you."

"It's not a problem," I say. "Really."

He turns his hands out on the table between us, palms up. I see a large bandage next to a series of ugly scars thatching his forearm, jagged ridges where the skin has been sewn together by a prison doctor. He catches me staring.

"I've tried three times," he says. "Did they tell you that?"

I shake my head.

"Never been good at finishing what I started," he says. He laughs emptily. "That's what my dad used to say, anyway."

"Is that why you're giving up your appeals?" I ask.

He rocks in his chair, his eyes gazing off a mile beyond me.

"I'm *going* to die in here," he says. "It's going to happen. You know that. And there's no way I'm spending another fifty years in this."

He looks over his shoulder; through the window we both see the empty row of cell doors, all closed and solid but for the small slots where food is delivered three times a day.

"There's always a chance," I say. "New evidence. Or maybe they find someone else who cops to it."

There's a loud metal clang from somewhere outside and I see Michael go rigid, his head swiveling like a prey animal. I think of all the ways that I have changed, and about how he, too, must have been changed.

"So," I say carefully. "What can I do for you?"

He's quiet for a moment. His eyes drop to the floor, and there's a bashful nervousness about him.

"I wanted to ask you something," he says tentatively.

"Sure," I say. "What is it?"

"I wanted," he starts, then falters.

"It's OK," I say. "Go ahead."

He looks up.

"I wanted to know if you'll come," he says. "When they do it, I mean."

He must notice the shock that registers on my face before I can recover.

"I know you're busy," he says. "It's just, my mom died a few years back. And I don't want to be alone when they do it."

I reach across the table and take his hand in mine. It is trembling, and I remember the last time I held this hand, as his verdict was being read. I want to talk him down—to tell him not to give up, to refile his appeals. But this isn't what he's asked me here for.

"Of course," I say instead.

A guard raps at the plexiglass window.

"No touching!" the guard barks.

Michael clasps my hand briefly, then releases it.

"Thank you," he tells me. "It means a lot to me."

I try to smile, but already I am dreading what I have agreed to. I don't want to see Michael strapped to a gurney while a prison doctor ends his life.

"The other thing," Michael says, beginning to relax again. "I just wanted you to come here so I could say I'm sorry. About the trial and everything."

After his guilty verdict, Michael had been appointed an appellate attorney. One of the grounds of the appeal—as it always is—was a claim of ineffective assistance of counsel at trial. That Dan and I hadn't done our jobs. I remember the afternoon on the witness stand being interrogated by Michael's new attorney, whose line of questioning suggested that we hadn't done enough to prepare for trial, that we hadn't fully informed Michael of his right to testify, that we hadn't consulted with the right expert witnesses. No one likes being Monday-morning quarterbacked by an appellate attorney like this, but it's a part of the job.

"You don't have to apologize about that," I said. "You did what you needed to do. I only wish you'd had a better result."

"What I needed to do . . ." he says.

"The ineffective assistance of counsel claim," I say. "The post-conviction hearing."

He stares blankly at me, that same dumb look he had the first time we met at the Washoe County Jail. Finally, he shakes his head.

"I didn't call you all the way out here about that," he says. "I just want to apologize for, you know, the whole *situation*. You and C.J. were the only people that ever cared about my case, and I heard about what happened to her. I thought maybe that had something to do with me."

My finger begins to tap at the edge of the yellow legal pad that I've brought along. The little mental parasite has reemerged, as if sensing danger. *What am I doing out here?* I think. I silently begin to count out numbers. Sets. Multiples. *What's his angle?*

"You still doing that?" Michael says. He smiles sympathetically. "The tapping thing?"

"So what did you really bring me out here for?" I say, ignoring the question. "I should be apologizing to you, not the other way around."

He stares at me again, that same vacuous look that appeared every time we met in the early months of his case. I find myself growing irritated; I've come here for catharsis, I realize. I want him angry, straining against his restraints, berating me for having failed him.

"She never told you, did she?" he says, as if putting together the last piece of a puzzle.

"Who never told me what?"

He leans back in the hard metal chair, exhaling loudly through pursed lips. Outside the safety glass windows of our conference room the guard sits in his control room with his feet up, sipping at a cup of coffee.

"C.J.," Michael says. I see him slowing himself down, trying to gauge how to proceed. How much to say.

"What the fuck was C.J. supposed to tell me?" I snap.

"Memorial Day," he says. He pinches his bottom lip, still stalling for time. "Did she ever tell you about Memorial Day?"

"What about *Memorial Day*?" I say. He looks over his shoulder, as if someone might be eavesdropping in the empty room, then hunches close over the table.

"We're still privileged, right?" he asks. "This is all confidential?"

I nod, a sickly ball accruing in the pit of my stomach.

"All right," he says. He lets out a long exhalation, leans down to a chained hand to wipe a palm over his head. "C.J. came to visit me that year, around Memorial Day weekend. Right before we were first set to go to trial. She never told you that?"

"No."

"So she never told you about her," he says. His face seems to blanch; his hand begins to tremble again on the tabletop. "The other girl."

The three words curdle sickly as he says them. It feels like he's telling me something so obvious, but I still can't grasp its meaning.

"What other girl?"

"I'm sorry," he whispers. "Jesus, I'm sorry."

"I'm getting tired of this conversation, Michael," I say. "*What* other girl?"

The guard outside looks up from his newspaper, watches us for a moment through the multiple layers of safety glass. I nod, and he begins reading again.

"The other girl," Michael says, almost in a whimper. "The other fucking girl."

FIFTY-SIX

AN HOUR LATER I crest a last ridge and Reno stretches out before me, cold and airless in the last of the afternoon sun. I keep the pedal floored, the county car streaking through town toward the looming shadow of Peavine Peak. Time bifurcates; part of me is still inside the prison, still listening to Michael as he says the words: *the other girl*.

"What other girl?" I'd said, even as a part of me seemed to know already, seemed to have always known. His hands continued to shake with the force of a tremor.

"I told her," he'd whispered. "I told C.J. You were supposed to know."

"*What* did you tell her?" I'd said, not wanting the answer.

HE'D MET THE woman at a sports bar in North Reno, six months after Anna Weston had disappeared.

"She was looking to party," he'd said miserably. "We got in my truck and took a case of beer out to the hills on the other side of Peavine."

His voice had wavered and failed as he spoke. Once or twice, we sat in silence as he stopped to gather himself. I said nothing, tried to feel nothing. Tried to keep down the thing I felt unfolding inside me. I wanted him dragged through the desert, left in some anonymous ravine to be picked apart by coyotes and birds, not just for what he'd done to this other girl but also for what he'd done to me.

"Who *was* she?" I asked.

"Back then, it was bad—" he said, almost to himself. He picked at an invisible spot on the table. "I'd be on a runner for eight, ten days. I'd come into a bag of crystal, say, on a Tuesday. Wouldn't be back in the world till the next Thursday."

I stared through him.

"You know, I've been sober since the day they arrested me," he said.

"Good for you," I said bitterly.

"You think that's easy in here, but it's not," he said. "It's the longest I've been sober since I was thirteen years old."

"Who *was* she, goddamn it?" I slammed a hand down against the table's metal plane. The guard stood at his desk, starting for the visiting room before I waved him off. Michael shifted uncomfortably across the table.

"I don't know," he said quietly. "Just some girl. I don't know."

"Describe her."

"I don't want to do this," he said. "That wasn't me back then."

"Tell me what she looked like."

He wiped his hands heavily over his face, his fingertips tracing red furrows across his pale cheekbones.

"Young—" he said. "Like, my age. Skinny. Straight black hair. Dark skin. Could have been Mexican, maybe."

Something uncoiled inside me, some sense of inevitability coming to fruition, the past becoming the future.

"Native American?" I heard myself say. "Maybe Indian?"

"I don't know," he said, shaking his head. "Maybe."

THE SUN IS down by the time I take the exit for Lemmon Valley on the north side of Peavine Peak. On the way back through Reno I call Sarah, tell her I won't be home for dinner.

"What is going *on*?" she asks. This time there's worry in her voice. "Is everything OK?"

"It's fine," I tell her. "I'll catch you up when I get home, but it's going to be fine."

I hear Rosa's tiny voice in the background, above the sound of a cartoon on the television.

"Can you put her on?" I say. "I might not be back before she goes to bed."

The phone knocks around, clumsy in her small hands as Rosa takes it from Sarah.

"Pokey?" I say.

"Hi, Dad," she says. "We read the mummy book again today. Mom and me."

"That's great, baby," I say. "Listen, I have to go, but I just wanted to say good night, OK?"

"Did you know mummies don't even scare me anymore?" she says.

"That's great, Pokey," I say. "That's great."

MY HEADLIGHTS BOUNCE over the rutted dirt road as it winds through the bones of a ghost town, past yellow towers of mine tailings, through crumbling foundations and brittle tangles of lumber. After forty-five minutes I arrive at the place that Michael had described—a two-headed bristlecone pine at the foot of a steep hillside.

I pull the emergency brake and kill the engine, the black of a starless night flooding into the cab. I grab the flashlight I bought at a gas station on the way, then step out of the car. The old familiar smells of the desert come, and I remember a night in high school when Jasper and I camped not far from where I am now, one of a hundred nights where we fell asleep staring up at this same blackness.

I aim the light across the hillside until I find what I am looking for: a pile of tailings streaked red with copper ore and silica, and above it the small frame of an old wildcat mine, its black mouth gaping and awful.

My breath gathers in pale clouds in the darkness as I push my way through brush and lifeless grass. When I reach the mouth of the mine, I sit down on the flat area in front of the entrance. The earth is jagged in my fingers, sharp pebbles jabbing through the thin fabric of my suit pants.

You can still go back, I tell myself. *There is nothing different between today and yesterday. You can just go home.*

My fingers land on something small, too regular in shape and too pliable to be natural. When I aim the flashlight down, I see that I am holding a faded cigarette butt. I let the light wander over the bald patch of tailings and see that the ground is littered with cigarette butts of varying ages, some faded and frayed by weather, others that might have been stubbed out this same afternoon. I bring the butt in my hand close, and read the small logo printed into the bottom of the cigarette paper. *How many times has she come here?* I wonder. *How many hours has C.J. sat in this very spot, consumed just as I am now with the knowledge of what lies buried in the mountain behind me?*

I stand abruptly and flick the cigarette out into the darkness. Then, before I can reconsider, I crouch down and make my way through the mouth of the mine.

Inside, the air is cold and stale. The heavy smell of putrefaction hangs in the air, seeping into my clothes and hair as I crawl farther back.

After fifty feet the walls of the mine grow tighter, the earth crumbling and rounded in my spotlight. I can feel the cold weight of the mountain atop me. The few timbers bracing the ceiling are cracked and decayed, rimed silver with ice. Twenty feet farther, the light lands on a wall of rock and timber where the mine collapsed decades ago.

I edge forward and begin pulling at the tangle of rotted timber, the wood crumbling in my hands. I push the debris aside, my fingers clawing at the pile, the flashlight casting erratically on the walls of the mine.

A board breaks loose, and then I see it.

A woman's shoe protruding from a small depression on the floor of the mine, as if it might have simply been left behind by some earlier visitor. It is a cheap canvas sneaker, the fabric dingy with dirt, the brown rubber heel worn to an angle. I sit down next to the shoe, the sharp angles of rock digging into my shoulders.

It isn't her, I tell myself. I try to piece together when exactly it was that I ran into Ruth Walton at the casino, all those years ago. I know that two hundred people go missing each year in Nevada, that it would likely take investigators days or weeks to identify the woman hidden here in this mountain. But at the same time I am replaying the messages Ruth Walton's father has left on my voicemail over the years, the dread of his voice caroming off the earthen walls of the mine. *It doesn't have to be Ruth. It could be any of them.*

I should be afraid, but I have arrived at a place past fear. As I reach out and take the shoe in my hand, I have the absurd thought that I am not alone in this mine, that C.J. is here with me. Inside, beneath the thin grey canvas, I feel the hollow shape of the woman's foot, the ridges of bone thin and identifiable.

FIFTY-SEVEN

IN THE YEARS just before she died, my grandmother became lost in time. She would be there, with us at the dining room table in my parents' house as I studied for an algebra exam, and then suddenly she would be back in Spain, cleaning the apartment where she had worked as a domestic servant fifty-five years earlier. She would begin spit-shining the scratched oak tabletop, or using my toothbrush to scrub the kitchen sink, calling my father *Don* and my mother *Señora*. Or she would travel back in time to the sheep ranch where she had been employed as a cook when she first arrived in this country. Our house would fill with smoke, the alarms shrieking, and we would rush into the kitchen to find a stockpot left on a hot burner, the inside scorched with burnt salt and perfectly chopped garlic.

¿Dónde estamos, Amá? my father asked her once, when we found her kneeling in the middle of our empty living room.

En la iglesia, por supuesto, she said, making the sign of the cross. *Ponte de rodillas, Enrique.*

I watched my father kneel on the carpet next to her, in the living room that had suddenly become a cathedral. They began to pray together even though my father hadn't been to church since my first Communion, the ancient lilt of Latin filling our secular home.

The last time I saw my grandmother was on a visit back home for the holidays during my first year of law school. By then, she hadn't spoken a word in years; she seemed to have receded into herself, into the memory loop of her life. A nurse came to the house three times a day, to move her from her bed to a chair in front of a television that played Spanish-language telenovelas and then back to her bed, where she would stare at the ceiling, her lips still moving.

On the last day of my visit I came home to find my father searching frantically around the house, the nurse crying in a chair in the living room. My mother was on the telephone in the kitchen, and when she noticed me, she held a hand over the receiver.

"She's wandered off," she said. "She's been gone for an hour already—I'm on the phone with the police."

I watched my father opening closet doors, calling his mother's name down into the basement.

"Outside," he said, catching my eye. "Start searching the neighborhood."

It was getting dark outside, a light snow beginning to fall, the city suddenly silent. I began jogging the alleyways behind my parents' house, looking behind tipped-over garbage cans and under cars as if I were searching for a lost cat. At the end of the road I stopped dead in my tracks; there, in the newly fallen snow, were the black outlines of two small feet.

"*¡Amá!*" I yelled. I started off into the quiet of the snowstorm. The small tracks leading out into the desert had already begun filling in, disappearing into the night.

When I found her, she was crouched in the lee of a stand of bitterbrush, her feet bare and bloody, her hands worried in the folds of her blue wool skirt.

"*Amá,*" I said again.

"*¿Hijo?*" she said. She peered into the snow, not seeing, her eyes milky and red-rimmed.

"*Sí,*" I said to her in my clumsy Spanish. I thought maybe it would put her at ease, to think that I was my father. "*Aquí estoy, Amá. ¿Estás bien?*"

"*Sí,*" she said. She began crying softly. "*Estoy muy bien, hijo.*"

In the distance I heard my father calling through the falling snow.

"Over here!" I yelled back.

I took off my jacket and put it around her shoulders, and then I sat down next to her. I wondered if she had any idea who I was or where we were, or more accurately, *when* we were.

"*¿Y dónde estamos, Amá?*" I asked her. Where are we?

She looked at me as if I was insane, and then she smiled, as if she'd caught me playing a joke on her.

"On the ranch, of course," she said in Spanish. "In Nevada. I know you've had problems with the other boys at school, Enrique. But you have to keep your faith. Do you understand?"

"Yes," I said. The snow around her feet was streaked with blood; I reached down and took her feet in my hands and began to rub heat into them. My father's figure slowly emerged from the whiteout, following our voices. "I understand."

I THINK ABOUT her now as I sit on the rough bulge of the mine tailings, staring out at the glittering casino lights downtown. About how time moors itself to these little islands of joy, or mundanity, or anguish. *Is this just another of those islands that my memory has tied itself to?* I wonder. *Has all this happened already, in a life far behind me? Is this the moment that I am bound to relive forever?*

FIFTY-EIGHT

I ARRIVE AT C.J.'s house in South Reno just before midnight, the white county car dusty and brush-scraped, my slacks and shirt filthy with dirt. Lit by the streetlamp, the place looks just like I remember it from the last time I was here: her lawn a plane of slate grey in the dim light, shadows gathering in the windows of the house. I park across the street and sit in the dark car. Outside, a man passes, walking a small dog—a swing shifter, maybe a casino dealer or restaurant manager. I wait until he turns the corner at the end of the block, then dial C.J.'s number again.

After her implosion in Bartos' courtroom the deputy had taken her into a holding cell, where she'd been forced to take a piss test. Pat had offered to keep her job while she completed an inpatient program, he told me later, but she'd turned in a letter of resignation the same day. She had left every phone call unanswered, had refused to come to the door when I stopped by unannounced.

One afternoon nearly a year later I came into the lobby of the justice court and found her like an apparition, leaning against the counter of the check-in window to show the deputy a picture of a fish she'd caught that weekend. I saw her catch my eye, then quickly turn away to talk to a DA.

I finally cornered her next to the elevator on her way out of the courthouse. "You back?" I said.

"Oh, I've been here, Gato," she said. The elevator dinged, and she darted in, standing close enough to block me from getting on with her.

"Maybe we could get a coffee sometime," I said. "Talk about things."

She had on her courtroom mask, austere and impenetrable. She hiked her shoulder bag up, then reached over to push the button for the ground floor.

"Sure," she said. "Anytime. I'll call you."

But she never called, and she never returned my messages. I heard from other attorneys that she was working misdemeanor cases in the cow counties, driving two or three hours to churn out DUI pleas and Domestic Battery trials in the justice courts. Once or twice a year, we'd cross paths in the courthouse or at the jail, but each time she slipped away, shaking me like I was a bad memory. Now, shivering in the car outside her house, I realize how true that must have been—how every time she saw me, she must have also seen Ruth Walton's body entombed in some abandoned mine.

The phone rings and rings, until it is finally interrupted by her voicemail message. I push the green button again, hear the digital whir of the ringtone. In the house, the dark socket of a window on the second floor is suddenly illuminated in a pale yellow light. A shadow passes across the blinds, shapeless and ghostlike, as the phone continues to ring. Abruptly, I hear the robotic voice of the automated messaging system again, and a few seconds later the light from the window goes black.

For the hundredth time that afternoon I replay my conversation with Michael. He'd dictated a map to me, told me how to find her. Even with all this, I still hadn't been able to connect it to the Weston case. How could he have been falsely accused of murdering Anna, and yet be guilty of killing another woman? Was this some strange, sick coincidence?

"So what about Anna Weston?" I'd managed to ask after he finished. He'd stared vacantly at me for a second, then leaned in over the metal table.

"What *about* Anna Weston?" he said. It was, I realized, the first time I'd ever heard him speak her name.

"How?" I demanded. "How did she die? How did it happen?"

"What do you mean?" he said. When he realized that the question was in earnest, he looked at me with pure bewilderment. Something like thunder traveled across the surface of my skin, through the tips of my fingers.

"You know how it happened," he said. "I told them. I told the detective."

***

OUTSIDE HER HOUSE, I realize now that C.J. is the only other person in the world who knows what I have just learned. I can almost see her there in the dark windows of the house, just on the other side of the glass. And at the same time I realize that I am the last person to know what so many people knew all along—Michael, and Neil, and Detective Turner. Caroline, and Pat and Dan, and the twelve people of the jury who sentenced him to death—that Michael killed Anna Weston.

The wallpaper on my phone beams a photograph of Sarah and Rosa through the darkness of the car. The picture was taken last summer, at the Washoe County Fair. In it, Sarah is kneeling next to our daughter, her hair plaited back. Rosa has just had her face painted at a booth, and she has the enormous, exaggerated eyes and bulbous, whiskered mouth of a cartoon cat. In her hand is a clear plastic bag, and inside this bag levitates the orange flash of a goldfish, as sharp and pointed as an arrowhead.

I remember back to my first day in Bartos' courtroom, Ruth's parents there in the back of the gallery. I can hear her father's voice as he left message after message on my office voicemail all those years ago, looking for his daughter. Seeking. I know now the sickening uncertainty that must hold them as captive as a prison cell, how they must look at old photographs of Ruth the same way that I look at this picture of Rosa now. How close Ruth must feel, how very, very close.

I open the car door and stand out in the empty street, shivering under my filthy dress shirt in the clear winter air. I lean against the fender of the car and light a cigarette, watching the house. When I finish the cigarette and can't stand the cold any longer, I dial the number again. This time there is no ring at all, just the sound of the voicemail robot. I cross the street and knock loudly at the door, and when still there is no answer, I pick up a rock from a planter box along C.J.'s sidewalk.

The sound of breaking glass clatters down the empty road, a black hole gaping in the middle of her living room window. I stand on her front lawn, tensed, every neuron in my brain tuned toward the dark window on the second floor. I wait for chaos to break out—the lights from a neighbor's porch, the sound of sirens approaching—but there is nothing. The hiss of a breeze blowing ahead of an early spring storm. Somewhere, a dog's muted bark.

I can sense her there, just on the other side of the wall, the two of us separated by only a few inches of lumber and drywall. A minute passes, the house in darkness. I am about to leave when the front door opens. Framed in the doorway is the small shape of an old woman wrapped in a grey bathrobe, and it is only after a moment that I recognize her.

"So you know," C.J. says. There is something I've never heard in her voice before—a wretched sadness. "The other girl."

My legs feel weak beneath me, and I sit down on the sidewalk. C.J. watches me from the doorway for a moment, then sits down on the threshold, holding her knees to her chest.

"I was just there," I say. I hold up my filthy hands as if they are evidence, my fingers jerking and trembling in the cold. "I saw her."

She inhales sharply, exhales. A plume of her breath hovers in the air in front of her, illuminated in the streetlight.

"I'm sorry," she says. There is a crack in her voice, the last word swallowed. I wonder what she is apologizing for—for not telling me about the dead woman earlier? Or that I now know, that I have been sentenced to the same miserable knowledge that she has been living with?

"I know," I say.

We sit there, both of us alone in the empty streetlight.

"OK," she says. "So now what?"

"Now?" I say. The word itself feels alien. I already feel myself unsticking from time, slipping back into the mine shaft.

"Yes, now," says C.J. I can feel her gathering herself, the way she would when a witness went sideways on the stand. Readjusting her sights, recalculating her line of attack.

"He was guilty the whole time, C.J.," I say. "He killed that woman. He *admitted* to it."

"That's not the point," she snaps. "Do you not understand that yet?"

"How?" I say tightly. Rage roils inside me like a viper in a sack; the hand that held Ruth's shoe curls into a fist. "How is it not the point?"

"The point is, what if he hadn't been guilty?" she says, her voice breaking.

I stare at her blankly.

"That girl up in that mountain," I say. "She's someone's daughter. They have a right to know."

"But that's not your *job*," she says. She stands up in the doorway. "Don't you understand that yet? Finding that girl is someone else's job. Yours is to be his fucking lawyer. And if you're not going to do that, you need to quit."

She turns, starting back into the house.

"Is that what you did?" I say. "Quit?"

She freezes, her back to me, staring into the black maw of the house. I wait for her to wheel around, for the onslaught that is about to come, but it's as if we both understand that we have already had this argument, have been having it all along. Her shoulders go slack, her movement suddenly exhausted. Without looking back, she closes the door behind her.

FIFTY-NINE

I WAKE ON the couch the next morning to the sensation of something cold and wet crawling through the canal of my ear, reality still muddled with the dream world, so that I have the sudden sensation of drowning, of being buried alive. My eyes start open, and I am staring directly into Rosa's large dark eyes.

"Wet Willie," she whispers, a glistening finger held aloft, before running down the hall toward the bathroom. She forgets to close the door behind her, and I hear the sound of her urinating into the bowl of the toilet.

"Wash your hands, Pokey," I hear myself tell her.

"O-*kay*," she says with melodramatic exasperation. I listen to water rushing from the faucet, and then the sound of Sarah pulling back the sheets from the bed, the box spring creaking as she sits up. The winter morning is still dark, and when she clicks on the reading light, a yellow beam casts into the hallway from our bedroom.

When Sarah emerges, I am in the kitchen, readying the coffee machine. She looks at me with a strange expression, and I realize then that I am still wearing my clothes from the night before; the elbows of my white oxford shirt are brown with dirt from the floor of the mine, the knees of my slacks frayed.

"Good morning," I say. I feel her studying me, trying to formulate the right question to ask. I should be attending to her, should be telling her that there is nothing to worry about. I could say something as simple and as vague as "crime scene investigation," and it would be enough. But instead, as I begin to grind the coffee, I can feel only the dead woman's shoe in my hand.

"Oh no," she says gently, and I realize that I have begun, involuntarily, to sob. The bag of coffee slips from my hands, the dark beans skittering across the kitchen floor.

"Dad?" I hear Rosa say.

"He's fine," Sarah tells her. "Just stay where you are, baby."

The coffee snaps and crunches under Sarah's feet as she crosses the kitchen to where I am kneeling, trying to scoop up the mess. She sits down next to me, leaning back against a cabinet. I feel her hand rubbing circles over my back, smell the sleep still on her.

"I'm fine," I tell her when I am finally able to catch my breath. "Just caught a bad case, is all."

She retrieves a broom and dustpan from the laundry room, and together we sweep up the mess. She helps me into the bathroom, unbuttons the filthy shirt. The faucet runs in the shower, the room filling with steam. Water spills over me, and a thousand tiny cuts on my hands and elbows and knees light up momentarily with pain before being washed down the drain.

"Can you take the day off?" Sarah asks when I emerge from the shower. She teaches today, a seminar on the economics of western expansion, so she is dressed in a topaz-colored wool skirt and a white ironed blouse, her hair pulled back. Rosa is sitting next to the front door, trying to wedge her foot into a purple Velcro shoe.

"No," I say, thinking of the Greg Lake case, and the twenty others set for hearing this week. "But I'm going to anyway."

She smiles, then leans in to kiss me goodbye.

"Let's go, Mom," Rosa says, tugging at the door. I gather her into my arms, pull her squirming body to me.

"Ugh," she protests. "Too tight!"

As I watch Sarah's station wagon pull out of the driveway, I call the office. I tell the new receptionist that I won't be in, that I'm not feeling well. I send an email to Danielle, the new attorney assigned to work Bartos' courtroom with me, instructing her to continue all of my hearings set for today, and then I unearth an old pair of running shoes from the closet.

I am not required to do anything, I tell myself. In fact, as C.J. told me—what every legal ethics book would tell me—I am required *not* to do anything. Michael Atwood is still my client, and I am ethically compelled to inaction.

I consider the hole in the mountain where the dead woman lies hidden, and the slow creep of the suburbs out into the desert. How much longer before she is discovered, before some backhoe or curious kid unearths her grave? A year? Five? And by then Michael will already be gone, the ghost already vanquished.

The morning is still cold, the lawn glittering with frost in the early light. The first mile is a fight, my footsteps heavy against the pavement, but then I hit the yellow gravel of the foothill trails. I snake along the singletrack, my body finding the rhythm of the land. I wind through stands of sage, under the brown canopy of the occasional poplar, the mountain that possesses the girl looming above me. A mile passes, and then another, and by the time I arrive back at our house an hour later, exhausted, my T-shirt stained with dust and sweat, I know what I will do.

SIXTY

THE WALTON HOUSE sits just outside the town of Nixon on the Pyramid Lake Paiute Tribe Reservation. The homestead is maybe ten acres in size, an island of cottonwoods and tidy alfalfa fields surrounded on all sides by the muted grey of the desert in winter.

Out in the field I spot a woman driving a pickup truck, her limbs thin and lanky, jostling with the rutty road. Even from this distance I can see Ruth in her—the young woman who had been there, in chains and the jail's orange jumpsuit, on the first day I set foot in a courtroom. Dust rises from the truck's wheels as Ruth's mother drives across the fallow field toward the ranch house. I scan the rest of the property, stare into the empty hollows of the house, hoping that I might see Ruth's slim silhouette there, that I am wrong and that the body in the mountain might belong to another life, another history.

The fact that I haven't found Ruth waiting for me here means nothing, of course. She could be at work, or perhaps she's moved away long ago—maybe she is simply living her life elsewhere, Nevada a fading reflection in the rearview mirror.

I watch the truck park in front of the house, Ruth's mother stepping down out of the cab. She turns suddenly toward where my car sits idling on the side of the road two hundred yards away, as if she can feel my eyes on her.

I see her peer in my direction, a small speck the shape of a human, and then wave a hand—the universal greeting of all people who live outside the city, the simple acknowledgment of another human likewise surviving in this inhospitable place. I wonder if she somehow knows what I have just done, if she can see the set of GPS coordinates included in a typed, unsigned letter sitting on the dash of Rob Turner's car. I think of the mountain, and the desert, and the things that they might come to represent for her and for her husband today, as they have for me. And if the woman in the mountain is not their daughter, I wonder what this may also mean for them, what sorrows and phantoms this, too, might revive in them.

I wave back, then put the car into gear. I drive west out of Nixon, past the high school, over the thrum of cattle guards and onto the highway. The road breaks away from the green strip of cottonwoods and salt cedar along the river, and quickly I'm in lowlands burnt orange with rabbitbrush. I drive past the familiar beaches of Pyramid Lake's west shore: Popcorn Rock and Blockhouse and Rawhide, Wino Beach and Tamaracks, then the Nets and Pelican Point and Windless Bay, Spider Point and Shot Dog Beach.

I slow at the turnoff for Warrior Point, turn onto the silty sand of the old ocean floor. I back the car up so that it is nearly at the water's edge, the beach empty. Wind whips the surface of the lake, white peaks flaring on the grey-green water. I can almost see C.J. here, the thin copper of her body atop her fishing ladder, the silent metronome of her backcast as the line curls and flares.

In the trunk of the car is a bag with my fishing gear, the pole dusty in its case, the reel slow with rust, the waders mildewed with disuse. I must have known that I would come here, or it would not be there in the trunk of the car. But when I search my memory, I have no recollection of placing the gear there, of retrieving it from its home in the crawl space of our attic behind a bin of Christmas ornaments and Sarah's boxes of doctoral research.

In the chest pocket of the waders I find an old pack of cigarettes; when I tap one out, it is stale but still dry, the tip flaring when I hold a match to it. I sit on the back bumper and smoke and watch the lake. Behind me, I can sense the weight of Greg Lake's file from where it sits on the passenger seat.

I take a look down the beach, and when I'm sure I am alone, I shrug off my jacket and place it, folded, onto the floor of the trunk. In a minute I'm naked, the cold desert wind weaving patterns across my skin. I am up to my knees, then to my waist, the cold racing up my veins, and then I am underwater, the wind abruptly silenced, my fingers gripping involuntarily against the cold.

After the initial shock a certain heat begins to take over, a calm rising through the panic. Warmth is being diverted from my extremities, the body drawing into itself, preserving the vital organs. I think back to a case I had several years ago, a drug deal gone bad. My client and two other defendants had driven a man out into the mountains in the middle of January, had beaten him with a pipe until they were sure he was dead. It took the man two days to crawl a half mile through snow to the highway; he lost a foot and six fingers to frostbite, but he lived.

"If it had been summer, he would have exsanguinated in an hour," a doctor had testified. "The cold saved his life."

I feel the cold doing this work now, thickening the blood in my veins, slowing down time. I stay there, underwater, until I can no longer stand it, my lungs heaving for air. When I come to the surface, I see the enormous arc of the Nevada sky above me. The desert basin seems to overflow with ghosts, the ghost of Numaga, the Paiute war chief who led his people into battle here, and the ghost of Reid Wilson, who would drown in the lake a century and a half later during a stupid high school bonfire. The ghosts of Ruth Walton, and Anna Weston, and C.J. and Jasper, piled one on top of another like layers of geological time. I set off toward shore, the water like black sand in my fingers.

SIXTY-ONE

MY HAIR IS still damp with the silty lake water when I pick Rosa up at school, the afternoon already going black. She is unusually quiet as she walks with me to the car, as if she can sense something ominous hanging in the air.

"Why are we going this way?" she asks from her car seat as I turn left out of the parking lot. "This isn't the way we usually go."

"I just want to see something," I tell her.

She nods in the rearview mirror, taking this information under consideration.

We take the long way home, following a four-lane road that traces the foot of Peavine Peak. After a few minutes I pull into the lot of a county park complex at the base of the mountain. Four softball fields are lit up with stadium lights, and the parking lot is filled with players from an adult league, their arms sagging with coolers and bat bags, their faces smeared with eye black.

I take Rosa out of her car seat and we walk together to the concession stand.

"What do you want?" I ask. The stand is filled with colorful boxes and knots of golden pretzels, pink cotton candy and metallic bags of potato chips.

"Mom says we're not supposed to eat candy before dinner," she says, eyeing me suspiciously.

"I know," I say. "But today is a special day. Just today, we get to do whatever we want, OK? Just for today, and then tomorrow everything goes back to normal."

She hesitates, as if taking in the possibilities of this sudden, temporary moral relativity.

"Don't think," I tell her. "Just pick something."

She gets three ropes of red licorice and a lemonade, and I order a beer. We sit in the empty stands to watch a couple of innings, Rosa transfixed by a game she doesn't understand. She follows the ball as it lobs through the air, is captured by the momentary excitement created by the batter's swing and the ensuing idleness as the process repeats itself.

As she watches, I peer past the field lights, out into the dark. From where I sit I can see the yellow beams of the search vehicles climbing the shoulders of the mountain through the twilight, the jerking spotlight of the sheriff's helicopter as it circles the peak. I know that within a matter of hours they will arrive at the tailings of the mine where I was the night before, and they will discover her there. The forensic investigators will begin taking their photographs, will collect the dead woman's shoes and clothes and place them into bags to be shipped off to the evidence locker. That they will take samples and swabs, which will or will not bring them back to Michael Atwood, which will or will not bring them to Ruth Walton, which will or will not fill a new file in the public defender's office.

I think of the plastic bag that sits now in the trunk of my car, filled with the years' worth of C.J.'s cigarette butts that I collected the night before. I consider all the other evidence—the letter now sitting in Detective Turner's office that might somehow be traced to me, or a missed cigarette that might bring them back to C.J. I know that even now, they will be pulling camera footage from the highways, from gas stations. That they will be scouring the mine where the body was discovered, searching for a hair, or a clothing fiber, or a tire print. Any one of a hundred things that might bring them to me.

I am visited by a sudden vision, time slippery beneath me, my life unfolding with a startling clarity. In the vision, Rosa, Sarah, and I are having dinner together at the kitchen table, as we rarely do. I ladle stew into each of our soup bowls, being sure to add an ice cube to Rosa's, the shape of the ceramic bowl warm in my hand. At the table, Rosa is blowing bubbles through a straw into her milk cup, her eyes wide in surprise and delight, and from her chair next to the back door Sarah is laughing. When we are done with dinner, Sarah bathes

Rosa as I clear the table, the house filling with the sounds of dishes clattering and water lapping.

I see Rosa emerge from the bath, her hands and feet and buttocks red with heat, and after she dresses in her blue pajamas, I lie next to her in her too-small bed. I watch as I read a book to her, the one about the pharaohs who became mummies, about their trip across the Nile into the afterlife.

I can see it there, as clearly as I now see the azurite blue of the desert sky above the baseball field. An entire moment waiting to happen. How Rosa will point a finger to the hieroglyphic of a pharaoh atop a golden boat, a two-dimensional man at the stern, steering the ferry across the river.

"Who *is* that guy?" she will ask, pointing not at the blue-skinned deity bound for the afterlife but at the man behind him, steering the ship.

"That?" I will say, looking at the man. He is dark skinned, wrapped in a white cotton tunic, one hand gripping the tail of an asp while the other guides the till. "He's just the boatman."

I can feel the pages of the book in my fingers, smell Rosa's damp hair in my nostrils, even as we are here now, in the stands of the baseball field, the stadium lights bright in the vacuum of night. I think of the stacks of files strewn across the desk that I will not be returning to, of Jasper walking out of the Nevada State Prison on a bright fall day a few months from now, of Greg Lake and all the other clients who have already begun to recede into memories of a life that I have left behind with the letter on Turner's windshield.

And then I am visited by a final vision. In it, I am watching you, juror. You rise in your seat, filing out of the courtroom into the jury room where you will sort through the evidence, where you will weigh the testimony against me.

Have you already made up your mind, juror? I wonder. *Is there anything left for you to deliberate, or have you decided my fate long ago?*

Suddenly I feel the tiny power of the girl's hand in mine, her small body tethering me to this world. On the field below us a batter swings. A metallic ping ricochets into the night, the ball suspended in midair across the black backdrop of the mountain.

ACKNOWLEDGMENTS

THIS BOOK HAS been a marathon, and I am grateful to have had so many people running the race with me.

This is a book about the power of advocacy, and so it's only fitting that I start with the best advocate a writer could hope for in Duvall Osteen—I think you've dragged me and this book across the finish line about five times already! Thank you for always believing in the book and fighting for it. Huge thanks as well to Kristina Moore, Geritza Carrasco, and the rest of the remarkable team at UTA.

I am incredibly grateful to have this book land in the hands of the folks at Algonquin and Little, Brown—Nadxieli Nieto and Betsy Gleick, I couldn't ask for two better editors to shape this book and bring it out into the world. Thanks to Chloe Texier-Rose and Kara Brammer for your work in introducing *The Silver State* and connecting it with readers—your work is a truly mystical art form, and I greatly admire your creativity. A special thank-you to Jovanna Brinck for your tireless work and always insightful opinion!

This book has changed so much since I first started it almost a decade ago. I'm hugely grateful to early readers Adam Carter, Derek Palacio, Ben Rogers, Sierra Crane-Murdock, Leni Zumas, and Christopher Coake. Thanks as well to Sally Denton and John L. Smith, CVW, Luca Dipierro, Matt and Laurel Boyd, Han Lu and Imogene Mankin, Haakon Ogbeide, junior elk Kevin Hanson, Shawn Hart, Manuel and Mikka Irusta, and to my friends and colleagues at Portland State University, especially Paul Collins, Janice Lee, John Beer, Justin Hocking, Consuelo Wise, and Michele Glazer. Thanks to friend and website designer extraordinaire Ilsa Brink. To my parents, to Ali, Ryan, and Kepa, and to Peter Bushnell and Elise Gettleman. To Cheryl Watson and Steve Koesterer, for helping us build a house (twice). To Silas Wright, for teaching me how to think about this book and this life. To Andrew Bushnell, for giving me a place to work (twice). And especially to my copilots Raija, Scout, and Sula—thanks for your love, baby bear.

Special thanks for support from the University of Nevada Las Vegas and the Black Mountain Institute, especially Beverly Rogers and the Hon. Miriam Shearing, and Literary Arts in Portland. These are remarkable institutions that give writers the things they need most to exist and to work—time, space, encouragement, and community.

This book and its characters are fiction, but they are informed by many books, articles, and texts. A few that were particularly influential are Alex Karakatsanis's *Usual Cruelty: The Complicity of Lawyers in the Criminal Justice System*, Ernest J. Gaines's *A Lesson Before Dying*, and Vanessa Place's *The Guilt Project*. Attentive former law students will notice elements of the Buried Bodies Case, a classic ethics case that was given a deserved revisit in a 2016 episode of *Radiolab* produced by Matt Kielty and reported by Brenna Farrell.

And most importantly, my thanks to and admiration for everyone I've worked with in the courts system. There are too many to name, but for starters: Joe Goodnight, Theresa Ristenpart and the team at Ristenpart Law, Tobin Fuss, Sean Sullivan (who taught me how to be a lawyer *and* a terrible fisherman), Jay Slocum, John Malone, Eric Nickel, Emilie Meyer, Linda Nordvig, Patrick McGinnis, Maizie Pusich, the late Michael Specchio, Biray Dogan, Tom Bolan, Laura Rivera, the Hon. Cynthia Lu, the Hon. Justin Champagne, the Hon. David Hardy, Kim Oates, and Maureen Conway. A life in the law is a difficult and often thankless one; for all of the criminal justice system's faults, the best, smartest, strongest, most compassionate people are often found here.